DOWN
AT THE
DEVLIN BAKERY

Deborah Goodacre

Down At The Devlin Bakery

A Novel

2024

To schedule an interview or book an event with the author, contact Ms. Goodacre via her website at:
website: deborahgoodacre.com
or by email: deborahgoodacre2001@gmail.com

PALMETTO
PUBLISHING
Charleston, SC
www.PalmettoPublishing.com

Published by:
Palmetto Publishing
2837 Rivers Ave, North Charleston, SC 29405, USA

Disclaimer: This book is a work of fiction. Names, characters, businesses, events, and incidents are the product of the author's imagination. Any resemblance to actual persons, living or dead, is purely coincidental. The opinions expressed are those of the characters and should not be assumed to be those of the author. The role played by John Wayne is entirely fiction.

The following quotes are from masters who believe their creativity and inspiration came from the universe.

"When I am completely myself, entirely alone…or during the night when I cannot sleep, it is on such occasions that my ideas flow best and most abundantly. Whence and how these ideas come I know not, nor can I force them."

Wolfgang Amadeus Mozart

"Straight away the ideas flow in upon me, directly from God and not only do I see distinct themes in my mind's eye but they are clothed in the right forms, harmonies, and orchestration."

Johannes Brahms

Over the years, I have occasionally said, "I think I have a book inside me." I guess I was right. I feel incredibly accomplished having written *Down At The Devlin Bakery*. It was often hard work, but it brought me great joy. Here is how it began.

As a genealogy research group member, I was interested in Janice Wells Hood's stories about her family's multi-generational business, the Devlin Bakery, in Martinsville, Illinois. She and her siblings spent the summers visiting their grandparents, the proprietors, who lived above the bakery. Her childhood memories gave me ideas for a storyline; however, I soon set those ideas aside to write a story for the Daughters of the American Revolution 2020 annual contest, the theme of which was the 19th Amendment. Over the next few months, I wrote and submitted my story. With 172 entries nationwide, my story won 3rd place. Wow!

Soon, my thoughts returned to the Devlin Bakery, and the storyline picked up where I had left off. I had not yet put pencil to paper or touched a keyboard; it was all in my head. Then the Covid Pandemic hit. To say we were uneasy is an understatement, as my husband was due for a serious operation. So we packed up much of the household, and with the dogs, we secluded ourselves in our house in Show Low, Arizona, for a month.

Every morning, as I headed toward the kitchen in my slippers and robe, the main character, Ella Watson, began to tell me her life story nonstop. The timing was right; she knew I had nothing else to do and that she could command my full attention. To put it bluntly, Ella would not shut up. I had no choice but to start typing. I sat at my desk and typed for five days straight. At the end of each day, my eyes were so dry and tired that I could no longer see the computer screen; I had double vision. I spent the rest of each evening in front of the television, with my sore eyes shut until it was time to retire.

Those five days began the long process of writing the entire book. I attribute the phenomenon of gifting me the book to the work of the universe. That's right; the universe had Ella relay her life story to me, and I delivered.

Before writing *Down At The Devlin Bakery*, my experience with writing was limited to family short stories. I have never taken a writing course, created a story outline, or developed character sketches. I did pick up a few books about writing techniques and instructions, hoping they would aid me in my journey, but they quickly made their way into the recycle bin. They didn't give me what I wanted and needed in a manner that made sense to me.

Then I found the book I learned the most from, *On Writing*, by Stephen King. It gets to the meat of writing fast. I carry the book almost everywhere, anticipating a free moment to reread his excellent, plain-spoken, and often amusing advice and examples. Stephen King's opening comment that stays with me is, "What writing is. Telepathy, of course." *Down At The Devlin Bakery* is a testament to that statement.

Deborah Goodacre
Chandler, Arizona
2024

INTRODUCTION

*"Isn't it funny how a little place like the
bakery brought so many people together?"*

Marion Devlin's world is about to change. Widowed and in poor health, Marion no longer has the strength or energy to operate her multi-generational family bakery. Her only option is to close the bakery's doors, as her two daughters have no interest in becoming the next generation to run the operation. Alone and without her life's passion, Marion gives in to her daughters' pressure to leave Martinsville, Illinois, and live with one of them in Reedsburg, Wisconsin, for what she assumes will be the rest of her life. She has misgivings about this decision; however, there seemed to be no other choice.

With the bakery shuttered, the little mid-western town of Martinsville no longer has its anchor, where folks had gathered to connect and converse with their neighbors. With the bakery shuttered, people no longer wake to the heavenly aroma of freshly baked goods gently wafting in the early morning air, which comforted them by reminding them they are not alone.

Three years later, Ella and Tom Watson, soon-to-be-retired farmers from Naperville, consider spending their retirement years as the next owners of the bakery. They travel to Martinsville to investigate, and in short order, they find themselves doing just that. With the bakery reopened, the town's spirit is renewed, providing a much-needed place for personal camaraderie and connection.

Friends reconnect, long-lost family members appear, mysteries are solved, and love knocks on the door of two unsuspecting people for the first time. And, what secret is the mayor trying to keep from the townsfolk? Experience the ebb and flow of energy that transforms Martinsville, Illinois, once the bakery doors open again after three long years.

CHAPTER I

The Family, The Farm

Marion

Martinsville, Illinois, 1945. It is one o'clock in the afternoon, and I am in town, standing on the walkway at the bakery where I spent so much time working and living. My heart weighs heavy as I hear the familiar thud and click of the door as it closes and locks behind me. Some say when one door closes, another opens, but optimistic schools of thought do not console me. I pocket the key, knowing it will be the last time I use it.

I look through the glass for the last time, its shelves empty of the fresh-daily loaves of bread and biscuits that once beckoned to passersby, and step away from the storefront that bears my name. The reality of how life has changed sets in and overwhelms me. I swallow yet another sob. I want no witnesses to my grief.

In my youth, I thrived on change, sought it, and found it compelling. Then work and life's responsibilities set in, and over the years, my husband and I embraced the predictable pace of operating our bakery and raising our family. Change no longer had a place in our lives.

Now, I find that change is thrust upon me as I shift from a widowed bakery owner to who knows what. Even though I no longer have the enthusiasm and energy required to operate the bakery, I cannot envision a sedentary life with no purpose. I must figure this out and live fully without my husband and the bakery.

Perhaps a change of scenery will open new doors and inspire my new life's purpose, which is why I have given in to my daughters' insistence that I move to Reedsburg, Wisconsin, and live with one of them.

And here they are, pulling up in Natalie's new Coupe to whisk me away. I cannot let them see the signs of my distress and uncertainty. They will view them as an indication of weakness or helplessness and use them to confirm their right to control my affairs. Shaking off my emotions, I put on a smile and force myself into a lively, brisk pace toward their car, telling myself they have good intentions in spite of my apprehension.

Ella

It has been three years since the war ended; the year is 1948, and the Walton family farm, located some five miles outside Naperville, Illinois, is thriving.

At the Walton farm, we have a regular crew of farmhands that live and work here throughout the year. Ever since the war's end, the team of farmhands has been mainly older men. Many of the younger men who worked on the farm went off to the war, and only a few returned to us when it ended. We also hire part-time hands and workers during planting season or when it's time to harvest the crops. We have no problem getting workers to commit to the schedule, as the Walton farm is known for having the best-built bunkhouse and the most delicious food for miles around.

Several years ago, we tore down the old bunkhouse and constructed a new, larger structure next to the barn. We supply the workers with comfortable, clean, warm beds and plenty of good food to fill their bellies. The bunkhouse has large windows to let in fresh air, which helps to keep the men healthy. We also built a fancy composting toilet, a two-holer with doors from the bunkhouse, and another that leads outdoors. We keep the outside door locked during the off-season to keep folks wandering the countryside from making themselves at home.

Another reason we have no trouble attracting and keeping our workers is that Daddy treats the men respectfully and kindly; however, he has rules the men must abide by. He doesn't put up with any shenanigans, no gambling or drinking unless there is a good reason to celebrate, such as a plentiful harvest. Nobody takes a nip unless sanctioned by Daddy.

While traditional farm life dictates that the family property is passed down to the eldest son, one generation to the next, Momma and Daddy had no sons. Therefore, being an only child, I knew I would inherit the farm someday. My name is Ella Marie Walton.

I was born on the farm and fully intended to spend my life there unless age or desire led me down a different path; nevertheless, after years of working the farm and raising our children, now grown, my husband Tom and I are contemplating what our future will hold.

We aren't getting any younger, and as much as we have benefited from farming life, it is not easy. Work never stops. From sunrise to sundown, there is something to do, something to take care of, whether feeding the animals, planting crops, harvesting, baling hay, shoeing horses, or repairing fences.

We have seriously considered selling the farm to our children, we have a boy and a girl, or to Tom's family. Tom has several brothers who are interested in owning and working the land. Perhaps we could combine the ownership among our families, which would spread out the responsibilities and provide for all of them. The farm is extensive, approximately 433 acres, and profitable, so selling it to them would ensure their future and provide us with a small yet steady income stream.

Before I get too far into my story about the current day, I want to go back in time and tell you about growing up on the farm and how Tom and I met.

Momma had two more babies after I was born; however, both died early in life, leaving her with a broken heart. She grieved her losses for months and months, secluded in a small room under the stairs that Grandma and I called the grieving room.

While she suffered alone, the daily chores, household responsibilities, and preparation of the ranch hand's meals fell squarely on Grandma's shoulders. It wasn't long before Momma removed herself from the everyday life, duties, and obligations one would expect a wife and mother to carry out. To make matters worse, she kept her distance from her family, especially me.

I vividly remember the morning we heard the creaking sound of the grieving room door opening. Grandma and I looked up to see Momma walk into the kitchen dressed in her Sunday apparel. We were amazed; today wasn't Sunday. Then, without even the slightest glance in our direction, she strode by us and headed out the door and down the porch steps. The sound of the old car's engine coming to life and the tires crunching on the gravel drive told us Momma was headed to the main highway.

Grandma and I looked at each other, shrugged our shoulders, and returned to our morning tasks. Nothing Momma did could surprise us anymore; this was one more example of her indifference, her lack of consideration for the people living under the same roof.

From that day forward, Momma spent most of her time in town with the Ladies Auxiliary League, a select group of townswomen who became involved in local politics, stumping for civic and city improvements. When not with the Auxiliary League, Momma maintained her seclusion in the parlor, reading her books and writing letters to whom I had no way of knowing.

Years later, Tom and I were married and living on the farm with Mother, Daddy, and Grandmother when Congress passed the 19th Amendment on June 4, 1919, and ratified it on August 18, 1920. The battle to win women's right to vote had raged for over 100 years across the United States and England, weighted down by heavy opposition from men, including then-President Woodrow Wilson and even some women. President Wilson had avoided the issue for as long as possible, downplaying its importance, and finally backed the war for women's right to vote before the end of his second term.

Later the next week, Naperville held a rousing celebration in the town square on the steps of the courthouse. Mother went into town early that morning; Daddy, Grandmother, Tom, and I went a few hours later. Upon reaching the edge of town, we began to search for a place to park the truck.

People were everywhere, in cars and trucks, on bicycles, and even on foot. A small orchestra, complete with violins and brass instruments, seated in the gazebo on the corner of the town square lawn, played lively music for the large crowd. Adults and children of all ages danced and clapped to the rhythm; the atmosphere was gay and boisterous. The four of us inched our way through the crowd toward the courthouse steps to get a better view of the festivities.

I will never forget that historic day and remember the events clearly. The women of the Ladies Auxiliary League milled about on the courthouse porch in a state of high spirits. In front of the courthouse stood a tall wood platform. A man dressed in a black tailcoat and a top hat, his camera on a tripod, was setting up to take an official photograph of the women of the auxiliary league.

On his cue, the women composed themselves and lined up in neat rows on the courthouse steps, ready to be photographed, when everyone heard a loud whoosh, then a sharp snap, coming from overhead. The crowd looked up in time to see a banner unfurl from the edge of the courthouse roof announcing the enactment of the 19th Amendment. People gasped at the sight.

The man in the top hat and tails had also looked up. Once the crowd settled, he bent over to look through the camera lens again and rechecked the focus. Now ready, he clicked his fingers and called to the women to look his way, pose, and smile. Momma stood in the middle of the front row, center stage. I saw a huge smile on her face as he snapped the picture. It was the only time I can recall seeing Momma exhibit such joy.

After the photo session, we made our way through the milling crowd to the old truck and headed home. We did not see Mother again for the rest of the day. When I rose the next morning and descended the staircase, I passed by the parlor as I headed toward the kitchen. Once again, the parlor doors were shut; Mother had sequestered herself in the parlor yet again, oblivious to her family's needs or want of interaction. Nothing had changed, yet everything had changed.

Years later, after Mother had passed, I found stacks of her correspondence in her desk drawers, and others tied with narrow ribbons tucked behind books on the parlor bookcase. It took weeks to read through them; however, I now know what she was writing about and to whom, all those years behind the closed doors of the parlor.

I learned to appreciate her contribution to the struggle for women to win the right to vote and understood her passion for the cause. I believe it gave her a place to put her energy, heart, and soul, a reason to live. Perhaps more importantly, her dedication to the suffrage movement provided a distraction from the realities of her life. Unfortunately, she never considered how her physical and emotional separation from the family affected Daddy, Grandmother, and me. She discarded me, and for that, I have a hard time forgiving her.

You might think that having a negligent mother would tarnish my attitude toward life, and it did at first. I was so young. I didn't understand my feelings; confusion turned to anger, and I couldn't make sense of it. I had no idea why my mother ignored me. Had I done something wrong? Fortunately, my sweet grandma lived in our house before I was born. Grandma saw my struggle and came to my rescue. She stepped in and took full charge of my care. She ensured I had clean clothes and healthy food to nourish my growing bones.

She sat cross-legged on the floor and played with me and my dolls. She bandaged my scrapes and iced my bumps. Grandma paid attention to me, hugged me, and told me she loved me. She held me, rocked me, and caressed my face when my emotions got the best of me. Grandmother distracted me from the painful realization that my mother wanted nothing to do with motherhood.

Even with my grandmother's care, it took many childhood years for me to understand and accept that my life would never be a part of my mother's. As painful as her estrangement was for me, once I quit vying for her attention, stopped looking backward, crying over this loss, and came to terms with the fact that she would never be the mother I needed and wanted, my life became more pleasant, calm, and manageable.

I once heard a wise woman say you have two chances at motherhood; if you don't have the good fortune to experience having a good mother, your second chance is to be a good mother. I have two adorable and rambunctious children; I have given them the mother I did not have.

Eventually, as I grew taller and could reach the stove, I worked alongside Grandma, preparing the farmhand's midday and evening meals. Watching and listening to Grandma, I learned how to cook delicious food and bake biscuits, pies, and cookies. I am proud to say I look very much like her. I am tall and slim and have the same hair; dark, thick, and shiny.

Farm work started at the crack of dawn, regardless of the weather. There was always work to be done in the barn or the yard. Grandma and I served the farmhands' midday meal around 11:00; the men were plenty hungry by then. After that, Grandma and I began my school lessons. There was a schoolhouse nearby, but the schoolmarm had married and moved away long ago, shutting down the only place of learning for miles around; therefore, the responsibility of teaching me my lessons fell to Grandma. She was an excellent teacher.

Sitting together in an oversized rocking chair, she taught me my letters and numbers on a chalkboard. When I was old enough to hold a needle, she taught me how to sew, first making basic stitches, then French knots, and eventually the art of embroidery.

I am a better wife and mother for having lived every day of my life with this remarkable woman who taught me so much about being kind and considerate. She taught me to think logically and rationally, to look at both sides of an issue, and to make decisions based on clear thinking. She taught me the true meaning of love and affection. I am a better human for all her wisdom and fair treatment of man and beast.

Daddy, too, was a kind and principled man. He set the standard for running a farm; the farmhands admired and respected him. You would never see him whip an animal to make it obey. He knew how to communicate with love and understanding. I often saw him stroking an animal's main, speaking softly and in a low tone as he looked into their eyes.

People often said we had the best herd of cattle for miles around. When Daddy and I entered the barn, the cows raised their heads and mooed loudly at the sight of him. Funny, they made so much noise that Daddy and I couldn't hear each other talk until they settled down.

Daddy knew I would inherit the farm someday, so schooling me in the daily workings and responsibilities of the farm began at an early age. I often joined Daddy in the barn or the fields. Every afternoon after serving the midday meal, you'd find Daddy and me riding into the fields on a mission.

Whatever chore Daddy was tending, he would say, "Now Ella, watch what I'm doing. You'll need to know how to handle this when you are in charge of the farm." Daddy taught me how to mend a fence and gather dogies - motherless calves - who had strayed into the adjoining areas through breaks in the fence line. I learned to bind a sprained leg, dress a wound, and mend a tear in an animal's ear.

I will never forget the day Daddy led a horse out of the barn, all saddled up and ready to ride. To my surprise, he picked me up, placed me on the horse, showed me how to hold the reins in my fingers, and told me to hang on. Being so far from the ground scared me, but I knew Daddy would never put me in harm's way. I knew I could trust him with my life. He led the horse around the corral twice, then lifted me to the ground. Eventually, I became an accomplished horsewoman.

In my teen years, he taught me the record-keeping system for the farm. He explained the art of finance. Late in the evening, we would sit at the old oak desk in the corner of the kitchen and review the journals and statements by the light of a kerosene lamp. He wanted to prepare me to handle the business side of farming when he would be gone from this earth one day.

Early on a sunny Friday morning in June, I don't recall which year, Daddy asked me to ride into Naperville with him to the feed store to pick up supplies; that is where I caught the eye of Tom Watson, the eldest son from a farm not far from ours.

There must have been a spark in the air that morning, as it didn't take long before Tom began frequenting our farm. He spent every free moment he could spare, beg, or borrow from his family farm duties to come to ours and work with Daddy. Soon, it became apparent that something else was on Tom's mind. Little did I know this tall, handsome man would someday become my husband. Daddy never ceased to tease me since I didn't have to change the initials on my pillowcases.

My name is Thomas Edward Watson. I am the oldest of four boys raised on 528 acres of prosperous land on the outskirts of Naperville, Illinois. After school, my three brothers and I work the farm alongside our father, leaving little to no time to get under each other's skin. While we grow wheat and corn, our mainstay is the cattle we raise and sell to nearby cities and town slaughterhouses.

One of my responsibilities is purchasing supplies from downtown Naperville's local grain and feed store. One day, a neighboring rancher, Mr. Walton, walked into the feed store with his daughter while I was making the monthly purchase. I hadn't seen her since we were kids; now, she had grown into a lovely young woman.

Entranced by her grown-up beauty, I kept out-a-sight behind a stack of hay bales, not wanting her to notice my stare. I couldn't take my eyes off her slim figure and her long mane of dark hair. I kept quiet as a mouse behind the tall stack. I watched as they chose their supplies, grains, and seeds and then paid the bill. After she and her father left the store, I went to the window to watch them load their sacks and crates into their truck, hoping to make the sighting of this young woman last as long as possible.

I'm not sure what happened that day, but I seemed to have contracted some strange ailment. For several nights, I lay in bed in the dark, sleepless, restless, and dreaming about the tall, slim girl with the lustrous mane of dark hair. Unable to quiet my spirit, I turned over in my bed and stared at the moon outside my window. Then it came to me; seeing this charming young lady again was the best way to cure my ills. Then and there, I decided to make my way to the Walton farm. I figured it was my only hope of catching a second sighting of her.

The next afternoon, instead of heading home after a trip into town, I made my way to the Walton farm. Upon entering the property, I drove past the farmhouse and parked my truck. The air was silent and still. No one seemed to be around. Thinking I might find Mr. Walton in the barn, I headed toward it, and there I came face to face with Mr. Walton, tools in his hands. I had not prepared myself with words to say to him, so I looked down at his implements, introduced myself, and asked if he needed any help. Mr. Walton replied, "Sure thing Tom, follow me." He led me to the back of the barn and put me to work on the old tractor's engine.

From that day forward, I used every free minute I could carve out of my day, every excuse I could muster, to make my way to the Walton farm. Try as I might, I could never catch another glimpse of his daughter, but I continued to help Mr. Walton with projects and repairs. It wasn't long before we became good friends. I believe he began to think of me as a son, as he had no sons, and I know he liked me plenty.

After weeks of trips to the Walton farm, still hoping to get to know his daughter, good fortune came my way. As I drove the long driveway, I saw her, Mr. Walton's beautiful daughter, coming out of the barn, holding a newborn calf in her arms. I parked my truck, walked up to her, tipped my hat, and said the only thing that came to mind. "Ma'am."

"If you're lookin' for my father, he's in the barn. Here, take this calf. It was just born, and it needs bathing."

I plopped the calf into Tom's arms against his freshly washed shirt, turned, and sprinted down the gravel path and across the yard toward the house. Taking the porch steps in one giant leap, I ran into the house and bounded up the stairs, two at a time, to my bedroom. I remember peeling the wet clothes off my body and giggling, recalling the surprised expression on Tom Watson's face when I landed the wet, slippery calf in his arms.

My thoughts were interrupted by Daddy's laughter, again and again, coming through the open bedroom window. I wondered what was tickling him, but it had to be the sight of Tom holding the calf. Later, Daddy told me Tom had walked up to him, the calf in his arms, and said, "Mr. Walton, with your permission, I'd like to court your daughter."

Weeks later, while upstairs putting clean sheets on the beds, I heard the familiar rumble sound of Tom's truck entering our driveway, but instead of passing by the farmhouse on its way to the barn, the rumble stopped near our porch. I stood stock-still, waiting for what was to come. I heard the truck door slam and slow, heavy footfalls coming up the steps and across the porch, followed by a knock on our screen door. Then silence.

Moments later, Grandma hollered from the bottom of the stairs, "Ella. You have a gentleman caller. Ella, you hear me? A young man is here to see you."

Looking over the railing from the top of the stairs, I answered, "I'll be right down, Grandma."

And there he was. The most handsome man I had ever seen was standing on our porch. And I have seen a few, but something was different about this one, this man named Tom Watson. I walked up to the old screen door, and we stood, eyes fixed, our noses inches apart, and then I whispered, "Care to sit a spell on the porch?"

"Why, yes, Miss Walton, I'd like that very much."

Two weeks and three visits later, while sitting on the porch swing sipping lemonade, I told Tom Watson he could call me Miss Ella. I admit I was smitten, but I was in no rush to get involved with a man. This business of sitting on the porch swing could only go so far, or else it would be a waste of my time. I did not need or want more interests or distractions of any kind.

First and foremost, the farm required my attention. Daddy needed me to help work the fields, herd cattle, and tend the fence line. Yes, we had ranch hands to handle these duties, but this was part of my training, learning the duties and responsibilities of running a farm. Plus, Grandma needed me to help cook the midday and evening meals for our farmhands, maintain the house, and do the washing and cleaning.

Grandma and I relished spending early mornings together. Shortly after sunrise, she and I would feed the chickens, then head to the garden to pick fresh vegetables and pull weeds. All this work I did with a willing heart; I never regretted a moment of my day as hard and tiring as many of them were. I liked my life. It was whole and satisfying.

Tom Watson continued his trips to the farm several times a week, but I often made myself unavailable. I figured if Tom was genuinely interested in me, if we were to have a future together, he needed to prove his intentions by the tenacity of his pursuit. Fortunately, my unavailability did not dissuade Tom from helping Daddy with whatever work or projects required tending.

Then, one afternoon, Daddy came into the house as the sun began to set and sat at the kitchen table. Looking tired and worn out, he told me he had hired Tom Watson to work on the farm full-time. I was taken aback at first, but I knew how much Daddy liked Tom and how vital Tom's help was to him. I had to face reality;

Daddy was getting older and managing the farmhands, and a large farm's expanding daily duties was more than any human being could oversee singlehandedly.

The decision to hire Tom turned out to be more than a good idea, for it didn't take long for Tom's knowledge of farming and leadership skills to improve and streamline the farm operation. In a short time, he proved himself to be an intelligent and popular leader, earning the respect of the squadron of mostly older men who worked on the farm, many of whom have been with us for years.

Three weeks later, Tom moved into the bunkhouse with the farmhands. From that day forward, Daddy relied totally on Tom for his abilities to organize the farm's daily routine and manage the team of farmhands. After a long hot morning's work, Tom would join the men at the midday meal. Later in the day, at four o'clock, he joined them for the evening meal, sitting on the long benches at the harvest table, where the men would often remain and talk about the farm or share stories from their past. Sometimes, they played card games, but no money was ever involved. Lights out was at nine o'clock.

Our porch dates continued when Tom could see his way clear to call on me, and I knew I needed to make a decision soon. I couldn't let Tom believe I was interested in a future with him if I wasn't. I couldn't hold a man back from his destiny, a life with a wife and perhaps children. I gave our relationship a lot of thought, and finally, I decided.

The following Friday afternoon, I saw Tom get in his truck and start the engine. I ran out the screen door, down the porch steps, and across the lawn in time to stop him from driving away in his vehicle. Out of breath and hanging on to the door handle of his truck, I said, "Tom, there's a dance in town Saturday night. Do you think we could go to it together?"

"Why yes, Miss Ella, we certainly can."

Now I've gone and done it. I fell in love that night, dancing, encircled by this handsome man's strong yet gentle arms. I opened my heart to a world that could include this loving, kind, and attractive man, Tom Watson, but still, I knew our future together would be in the offing, should be in the offing. Nevertheless, managing all aspects of running the farm left little time for Tom and me to pursue each other. Fortunately, we managed to find time to build a relationship over the hot summer months.

The following winter was freezing, with heavy, wet snow falling. The animals were distressed by the cold and dampness and let us know their displeasure with their constant mooing. To make them more comfortable, Tom and the farmhands designed and built a large shelter on the leeward side of the barn to help protect them, filled with piles of clean hay for a warm place to lie down.

During those cold months, I saw a marked change in Daddy. I'm not sure what caused the change; was it the cold weather that slowed him down both physically and mentally? Or was it something else?

The following spring, the weather was glorious, and the snow melted quickly. Tom and I were immeasurably in love. I told Grandma it was time to sew a new white dress for me. We were married in the Naperville Presbyterian Church on June 1 of that year. Daddy walked me down the aisle.

That was many years ago. Tom and I are in our early fifties and contemplating retirement; what will the future hold for us?

It has been two weeks since the mail brought a letter from my cousin Sharon, who lives in the tiny town of Cooper, Illinois. Many months have passed since last we were together. She wrote of her plans to come for a visit soon; her letter included a postscript stating that she had something important she wanted to discuss with us. She has my curiosity piqued.

Sharon's mother and my mother were sisters, making us first cousins. Though they were sisters, our mothers were complete opposites. Sharon had the textbook mother, the cookie baker, who never missed tucking her daughter in at night after a story read with a hug and a kiss goodnight on the forehead.

Mine was the flip side of the coin; self-serving, cold, and distant. Sharon summed up my mother best with this one-line comment. "Cousin Ella, your mother's face will never end up on a box of cookies." Her comment made me laugh, but sadly, I knew she had hit the nail squarely on the head.

Sharon and I are more than cousins; we are good friends; however, my life has followed society's traditional norm; marry young and raise a family. Sharon never heeded the dictates of society or cared to be confined by them. You might say she marches to a different drummer.

Sharon has worn cowboy boots and men's blue jeans most of her life. Try to get a brassiere on her; it will never happen. That is not to say she is not feminine; she is, in her unique, uncomplicated way. Sharon's creamy complexion is flawless. Her naturally blushed cheeks are sun-kissed. Her untamed curly brown hair can blow in the wind; she doesn't mind. She has rarely had a beau and hasn't cared one way or another. Men are attracted to her distinctive traits and mannerisms; her demeanor and personality have never failed to turn a man's head.

At noon on Friday, Sharon arrives at the train depot. We throw our arms around each other for a big hug, then toss her suitcase into the back of the truck and head off to the farm. After Sharon gets settled in the guest bedroom, we gather in the kitchen to catch up on the latest happenings in our lives while preparing the evening meal.

I set the table with Grandma's good china and linens for this family occasion, and after dinner, Tom, Sharon, and I make ourselves comfortable in the parlor, where I serve dessert and coffee. Full of excitement, Sharon is ready to tell us her reason for coming here other than for a family get-together.

"Listen, you two; I know you have worked hard all your lives and will probably sell the farm to your families. But what will you do then? Surely, you'll need something to occupy your time. That is one reason I wanted to come now; to tell you about a business opportunity that could be of interest to you."

"What kind of opportunity?"

"In Martinsville is a bakery that belonged to a local family. Over the years, the family handed the bakery down from one generation to another. The most recent owners had two daughters who were never interested in owning and running the bakery. Eventually, both girls married and moved to Wisconsin.

"Six years ago, their father died, leaving their mother to run the bakery with the help of several employees. Growing older and no longer in good health, the mother closed the bakery late in 1945. The bakery has sat empty ever since.

"You are so talented, Ella. The loaves of bread, biscuits, and pastries you bake are so delicious. It might be a good opportunity for you to own and run the bakery."

Tom and I look at each other quizzically.

"I know you are passionate about baking, and you're famous for your pies, cakes, bread, and biscuits, so naturally, you came to mind. Of course, you will have to rise early in the morning to bake biscuits and loaves of bread, but you're used to being up early, and you can set your hours. You don't have to be open late in the afternoons or on Sundays. And I bet you can easily find good help once you get it up and running."

"I guess it is something we could give some thought to. What do you think, Tom?" It appears my question has fallen on deaf ears; he sits staring into space. I wonder what he is thinking.

Sharon reaches over and takes my hand.

"Ella, you would be great at running a bakery, and the townsfolk would give their right arm to have the bakery open again. The people of Martinsville looked forward to eating Mrs. Devlin's baked goods, and the Devlin family was so dear to the townsfolk. Seeing Marion, chatting with her, and eating her delicious baked goods comforted them. People have told me they miss waking up in the morning to the rich aroma of biscuits and bread baking floating in the air.

"Years ago, I was in the bakery and heard an older widowed woman say, "You know you are not alone in this world when you wake to the aroma of fresh baked goods."

"Goodness, that's a lot to digest. Tom and I will need to mull it over for a bit."

Tom and I have not spoken about the bakery or anything else, for that matter, as we prepare for bed. Now tucked under the covers, I lie in the dark, staring at the ceiling, wondering what our future will hold. I am about to fall asleep when I hear Tom murmur, "I think we should give it a try." I didn't sleep a wink all night.

Sharon and I spend the rest of our time together reminiscing about family times, laughing about some, and crying about others. All the while, neither of us mentions the bakery until the day I drive her to the train depot. I help her lift her suitcase from the back of the truck, hug her, and tell her I love her. Sharon turns to face me, places both hands squarely on my shoulders, and utters her parting words.

"Ella, Martinsville isn't the same without the bakery. It was an anchor in the town. I hope you and Tom will take a trip to Martinsville and look into this opportunity. You may find it to be the perfect future for you."

Her words jolt me with a different perspective, and I am momentarily dumbfounded to understand it would be more than operating a bakery. We would be part of something bigger than ourselves. As Sharon walks toward the depot and mounts the steps, it occurs to me that she never mentioned the bakery's name, and then I find my voice. "Sharon. Wait. What's the name of the bakery?"

"Devlin, it's the Devlin Bakery." She then gives me the victory sign and disappears into the depot.

Night after night, I lie in bed, rerunning Sharon's parting words. Tom and I have not spoken much about the bakery since Sharon left for home, and I don't want to pressure him for a decision, so I patiently wait for Tom to bring up the subject. If running a bakery is the answer to how we spend the rest of our lives, I would be doing something I genuinely enjoy and in which Tom could participate.

It has been two weeks since Sharon brought us the news of the shuttered bakery. I can see Tom has been turning it over in his mind. He walks around the house with a faraway look in his eyes. Lately, I see him seated at the corner desk, talking on the telephone far more than usual, jotting notes on a tablet pad, then putting them into the desk drawer. At this point, my patience has finally reached its limit. I can no longer wait for him to bring up the subject. We need to talk about this now.

"Look, Tom, about the bakery. I know you don't know anything about baking, and I understand operating a bakery would be nice for me; it's a good fit, but I don't want to pursue the opportunity if you are not on board. I want you to be content with whatever we do with the rest of our lives if we decide to sell the farm."

Tom puts a finger to his lips to quiet me, then puts his arms around my waist. "Ella Marie, the farm has consumed my time throughout our lives. All I want is to spend the rest of my life with you, have more time with you, and if running a bakery gives us that, then I will learn."

"Tom, I can't envision you measuring flour and sugar."

Tom chuckles at the mental image of himself, clad in a long white apron, measuring, stirring, and kneading dough.

"Me neither, but I can manage the equipment when repairs are needed, I can manage the finances while you run the bakery, and I can purchase the supplies. I can do the heavy lifting. All I want is more time with my sweet and sexy wife." With that, Tom plants a big, sloppy kiss on my mouth. It could be that the bakery business is what this couple needs.

It is decided. We will be taking a trip to Martinsville to investigate the bakery. Tom is making plans for additional help at the farm during our absence. He called his long-time friend, Bob Jamison, and asked him to come by the farm this afternoon, and he has arrived. Standing in the middle of the yard, Tom explains the favor he needs from him.

"Hey, Jamison. Thanks for coming."

"You're welcome, Tom. What can I do fir ya?"

"Bob, Ella and I are planning a trip to Martinsville soon, and I want to know if you and your boy can stay here at the farm for two or three days while we are gone. I know I can trust you and Bob Jr. to oversee the place. What do you say? Can you help me out?"

Jamison takes his time pondering the request, staring at the ground, digging the toe of his boot in the dirt. Geez, what's there to think about? It's a farm; it isn't that complicated. I patiently wait for his response.

Jamison finally looks up at me, head tilted, peering over the top rim of his glasses. Now squinting at me, Jamison flashes that dirty little grin of his. "So, you and the missus are taking a trip to Martinsville, ya say. Hmmm, a kind of second honeymoon, huh?"

"Look, Bob, it's a business trip. I can't give you any details right now, but I would be more at ease knowing that you and your boy are here to keep an eye on things. Nothing needs tending; the horses and cattle are in good shape. The fences are all mended. You and Bob Jr. can stay in the bunkhouse. I will clear it with Ella so you can use the kitchen in the main house. What do you say, Bob?"

"Sure, Tom, we'll be willing to help you out for a few days. Let me know when, and we'll be here."

"Thanks, Bob. I'll get back to you as soon as we have made our plans."

As I turn and walk toward the house, Jamison shouts after me. "You and the missus are taking a second honeymoon, ain'tcha? Ain'tcha? Why you old cuss, admit it, admit it, you old son of a bitch. Guess I don't need to tell you to have fun, do I?"

All the while, Jamison is laughing like hell. I love the old guy, but sometimes I wish he would shut his mouth.

I ignore his heckling and walk up the steps and across the porch; I let the screen door slam behind me even though I know Ella hates when I do. I see her shoulders flinch. "Sorry, honey."

"What's with Jamison? What is so funny?"

"Nothing, nothing. Pay no attention to the old guy. Bob has agreed that he and Bob Jr. will oversee the farm for a few days when we are in Martinsville. They can stay in the bunkhouse, and if it's OK with you, can they have the use of the kitchen?"

"Sure, why not."

I walk away, satisfied that I have the arrangements set in place. Now, I need to look at the calendar and pick the dates.

Ella returns to her cooking, and I hear her utter a comment.

"They better not make a mess of my kitchen."

"What did you say?"

"You heard me."

It is late afternoon two weeks later, and we have been on the road for almost four hours. The weather is hot and humid. It has been raining; the sun is now out, the roads are wet, and the air is heavy with moisture. My hair is sticking to the back of my neck, and circles of sweat dot Tom's shirt from bending over the steering wheel. In the south, this kind of weather is called "sultry."

As we approach the outskirts of the quaint town of Martinsville, we notice a white wooden sign on a post pointing to the office of Doctor Morgan, General Practice & Care. Next, we come upon The Good Shephard Lutheran Church with an expansive green lawn and tall spire. I'm sure there must be more than one denomination in town, although Lutheran suits me.

Now driving along the brick-paved main street, we pass Cummings & Son Hardware. Next to it is Gallagher's Pharmacy, which advertises it has "Cold Coca-Cola" at its soda fountain, then a lady's dress shop called Brook's; her sign boasts, "The Latest in

Women's Fashion." Across the street, we see Wong's Tailoring, and next to it is Martinsville Dry Cleaner. The sign in the window says they do laundry and offer a folding service. Next to the dry cleaners is a small furniture store, Ames Furniture, and on the corner is an old but well-maintained gasoline station, Speedway 79.

Farther down the street, we come upon the town square, its outer edges bordered by magnificent eastern white pine and oak trees; the fullness of their branches shade the entire city block. We see the occasional park bench strategically placed so people can sit and take in the beauty of the square.

On one corner of the lawn is a large white gazebo, a place to seek shelter when it rains, shade on a hot sunny day, or for a band to play for special events. I can tell that the people of Martinsville take pride in their community; the streets are clean, and the courthouse grounds are well-tended.

In the center of the square sits the Martinsville Courthouse. A long sidewalk and a series of wide steps lead up to the porch, with a deep overhanging roof and tall white columns. As we pass the town square, I see a sign on the corner that reads, City Jail – Turn Right Here. On the next block sits a hair salon, its name in bright pink lettering; Emma's Hair Boutique.

Then I see it, and I am overwhelmed. I start shouting, "Stop the truck, stop the truck."

"What in the world, woman?"

Pointing across Tom's face, I almost poke him in the eye. Tom slows down only for a moment, then continues on past.

"Did you see it? Do you see the sign in the window? Bakery Available."

"Calm down, don't get all worked up. We don't know a darn thing about it yet."

I flop back into my seat, overcome by the heat and my rising blood pressure. I unbutton the top two buttons of my blouse, lay the cotton material back and away from my chest, and fan myself with my most recent copy of Good Housekeeping magazine. I'm hot, I'm tired, and I'm giddy with excitement.

"How do we get to Sharon's house? I need to get a cool drink down your throat."

I pull Sharon's handwritten directions from my pocketbook and hand them to Tom. He alternates between reading Sharon's notes and keeping an eye on the road. We continue through downtown Martinsville, then drive another five miles until we find ourselves at the edge of the little town of Cooper.

Tom slows the car as we enter Cooper's quiet, narrow, tree-lined main street. I watch the trees sway in the breeze as rays of sunlight flicker as they beam down through the branches. The air temperature seems to have dropped, and instantly, so does my blood pressure. Cooper is a world unto itself, quiet, calming, and pastoral. As we slowly approach Sharon's house, we see her sitting on her porch in one of a line of tall-back rocking chairs. Sharon jumps up, starts waving her arms, and breaks the calming atmosphere by shouting, "Yoo-hoo. Yoo-hoo."

No sooner has Tom stopped the truck and put the gear in park than I leap out and fly up the porch steps. "I saw it, I saw it, Sharon. I saw the bakery, the Devlin Bakery. We saw a sign in the window that says, AVAILABLE."

"Yes, I know, dear. Come in, sit, cool off, and we'll talk about it after dinner." Tom and Sharon roll their eyes at each other behind my back.

Once in the house, I follow Tom, carrying the duffle, up the creaking stairs to the guest room. Its expansive windows overlook Sharon's lush backyard. She sowed her garden with an imaginative assortment of flowering plants and bushes amid the tall trees that have been growing for over a hundred years. I pause to take in the view and watch birds flit from tree to tree.

In the bathroom, I draw cool water into the claw foot tub, peel my clothing off my clammy skin, step into the tub, and sink up to my neck. I close my eyes. The cool water refreshes me. I can finally relax after the long drive. After an extended soak, I open my eyes and breathe deeply. I am ready to join Tom and Sharon downstairs. I put on a loose-fitting shift and slippers and pin my hair in a twist.

Sharon has prepared a light dinner of cold cuts, salads, and sliced fruit. After dinner, we sit in the parlor, where the air temperature is cooler than in the rest of the house; I can't figure out why, but it is a welcome change from the heavy heat in the back rooms.

A parlor is a traditional, formal sitting room. According to rules of etiquette, one never enters the parlor without an invitation. Its doors remain closed and are opened when visitors come to call, at the homeowner's discretion, of course. Nevertheless, over the years, people began to have difficulty determining which folks were worthy of an invitation.

Nowadays, the parlor's tall double pocket doors are kept open, but do not be mistaken. Common courtesy and rules of polite protocol stand fast. Folks, do not enter unless your host invites you. It is acceptable to look in and admire the décor, but never enter and sit on the homeowner's furniture, finger their books, touch or play with their curiosities. And a note to parents; please control your rowdy children. Keep them away from the parlor.

Tom and I are seated comfortably in the parlor when Sharon walks in with our dessert, plates of Brown Butter Cake. This cake was famous during the war when the government rationed sugar. It's still a favorite of most women who baked it while their men were overseas. After a few savory bites, Sharon informs us of her findings.

"I have managed to do a little investigation for you, and I know who you need to see to get all the details about owning and operating the bakery. I made an appointment for you to meet with the mayor tomorrow in his office at two o'clock, located on the first floor of the courthouse in the center of town. You can't miss it unless you're a dodo, and I know, Tom, you are no dodo."

"So, are you saying that I am? Thanks a lot." I stick my tongue out at her.

"Ella, I hope you will act like a civilized woman tomorrow, not like the one I have seen in the last few hours.

"Don't worry. I'll win people over with my buttermilk biscuits."

"Really? Did you bring some for me?"

"Heck no."

Sharon rolls her eyes again as Tom gets up from the downy sofa.

"I'm going to bed. I need to get some sleep, and you do too, Ella, if you know what's good for you."

"I'm right behind you."

Now snuggled under the covers in this soft bed, light rain falling on the roof and tapping against the windowpanes lulls Tom and me to sleep.

The rain clouds have cleared overnight, and the sun is shining brightly. Tom and I are excited about our meeting today with the mayor, which could be a turning point in our lives. I believe how I present myself to the mayor is crucial to the possibility of us becoming the bakery's next operator and owner.

The mayor doesn't know I am more than a wife and a mother. He doesn't know I have been running the farm operation for so many years that I could do it blindfolded. He doesn't know that I keep the books and make financial decisions while Tom runs all other aspects of the farm. He needs to know and understand that I am a businesswoman; therefore, my first objective is to look the part.

I have put much thought into my appearance for this meeting. I brought along a simple navy blue dress with tiny gold buttons down the front, three-quarter sleeves, and a matching belt. I give my hair a good hard brushing and put on some lipstick. I finish my look with my mother's gold watch on my left wrist and a short string of my grandma's pearls around my neck. Today is not the day to wear some prairie print frock.

We arrive in front of the courthouse five minutes before the hour, enter through the tall wooden doors, and find ourselves at the back of a courtroom. With no one in sight, we look around for clues as to where to find the mayor's office, and then we hear a slow dull voice coming from behind us.

"May I help you?" We spin around and encounter an older woman with a dour expression.

"Yes, please; we have an appointment with the mayor at two o'clock. Names are Tom and Ella Watson."

The odd woman slowly lowers her eyes, looks down her nose, juts out her chin, then gradually turns and walks toward a door to the left of the judge's bench and disappears. Without saying a word, I might add.

Now out of sight, Tom leans down and whispers, "I wonder where they dug her up; a rare fossil, indeed."

I adore Tom's sense of humor and his timing. I want to break into laughter, but I manage to control myself. A moment later, a short, portly man appears with a booming voice, changing the atmosphere from odd to friendly.

He offers his handshake to Tom and me.

"Welcome, welcome, the name's John Bigby. I'm the mayor of this fine little town. Let's go to my office."

We follow Mayor Bigby back through the same door the strange woman went through, down a long corridor, and enter another door leading into his office. "Have a seat, you two."

We sit on stiff wooden chairs, and Mayor Bigby plops himself into a tall, tufted leather chair that makes him appear to be even shorter and portlier than he is. I glance at Tom, his face serious, which helps me to keep my emotions in check. I'm nervous and want to giggle.

"What can I do for the two of you?"

"Mr. Bigby, Mr. Mayor, sir."

Now, I can tell that Tom is nervous, too.

"We have come to find out about the bakery in town that is for sale."

"Is that so." Bigby leans back in his chair. "Tell me about yourselves, where ya from, and why you're interested in the bakery."

"My wife, Ella, and I are from Naperville, about five miles beyond, to be exact. We live on a large farm, which has been in Ella's family for several generations. As an only child, Ella's father schooled her in every aspect of farming, from planting to tending the livestock, including handling the farm's finances.

"Ella inherited the farm when her father passed. She keeps the books for the farm and makes financial decisions while I manage the farmhands, oversee the crops and fields, and tend to the animals. I, too, was raised on a family farm; however, after Ella and I married, I relinquished my rights to that farm so my brothers could inherit the land.

"That's our background, and it may be too much information, but the point is that farming is strenuous and an all-consuming way of life. We have contemplated making a change for some time now and have decided to pass the farm to our children and create a new life for ourselves."

Tom takes a breath, allowing Mayor Bigby to ask again why we are interested in the bakery.

"Ella is famous for her baked goods, buttermilk biscuits, pies, and cakes. She's a whiz at baking. I guess you could say she's gifted."

Mayor Bigby stares at us for a moment. "How'd you find out about our little bakery so far from your place?"

"Ella's cousin, Sharon Hansen, who lives in Cooper, came to the farm for a visit a while ago.

"Ah, yes, I know, Miss Hansen. Lovely woman."

"Sharon told us about the local bakery being closed. She explained how important it was to the town and that the townsfolk would be excited to have it reopened. Ella and I would like to have something we can do together for the rest of our days. Running a bakery would be a logical business for us." Tom reaches over and squeezes my hand.

Mayor Bigby sits in silence, absorbing all of Tom's words, and finally, he speaks. "All right. What do you want to know about the bakery? You are talking about the Devlin Bakery, I assume."

"Yes, sir. We would like to see what the bakery looks like, see the setup, check out the equipment, perhaps have a chance to review the accounting records, and I would like to know the asking price."

A long silence covers the room. It appears that Mayor Bigby is mulling over Tom's answer. The mayor continues to stare at us as he pushes back farther in his big leather chair, throws one dusty, worn leather boot on the desk, and then crosses over that boot with the other. He picks up a spent wood matchstick from an ashtray, puts it in the corner of his mouth, and begins gnawing on it. All we can do is sit patiently and wait for him to reply. And then it came.

"Well, folks, ya see, the bakery's not for sale."

Holy Toledo, we are shocked. Neither Tom nor I know what to say; we are speechless.

Finally, I ask, "But Mr. Mayor, we saw a sign in the window that says the bakery is available."

"That's right, little lady, it's not for sale, but it's available."

I wonder what the heck kind of game this man is playing. He must have read my mind, for he removes the matchstick from his mouth and explains.

"I know that sounds a little strange, so let me fill you in on the story about the Devlin bakery. The bakery and the Devlin family were pretty precious to our fine town. The bakery was the gathering spot for our townsfolk. Folks made going into the bakery a part of their daily lives for a favorite treat and some good, clean fellowship.

People would walk back and forth in front of the display case, select a favorite muffin, a scone, or a cookie, then gather 'round and eat while talking with their neighbors. I guess you could say it was the anchor of the town.

"Then, early in the autumn of 1945, Mrs. Devlin closed the bakery. She told me she was getting too old and too tired to keep up with the daily routine. Don't get me wrong, Mrs. Devlin did her darndest to find appropriate folks to take over the operation before she made the difficult decision to close its doors, but unfortunately, no one stepped up to the plate.

"A few months after the bakery shut down, the war ended. Our veterans came home hoping to taste their favorite baked goods, but that wasn't to be, sad to say. I remember seeing a few of them standing on the sidewalk outside the bakery, dressed in their uniforms, in disbelief that the doors were closed. Yes siree, when it folded, a bit of the town's spirit flew out of this place. It felt like the heart of the town stopped beating. Martinsville hasn't been the same since."

Tom and I glance at each other, fascinated by the mayor's words; we wait for him to continue the story of the Devlin family.

Mayor Bigby removes his boots from the desk one at a time; slowly and with some effort, he swings around in his chair to face a drawered cabinet, opens it, and fumbles through the files until he finds the right folder. He then turns back toward us, slaps the folder on the desk, folds back the cover, and clears his throat.

"Ahem, pardon me. Well now, before Miss Devlin left town, she laid out instructions for the bakery's future in her trust. Let me read this to ya.

"We, the Devlin family, owners of the Devlin Bakery located on Main Street in Martinsville, Illinois, request that the mayor and the citizens of this fine town find suitable folks to operate the bakery. They must be upstanding citizens, honest, trustworthy, qualified, and passionate about baking. Once selected and approved by the mayor and the town's sitting judge, the new tenants may operate the bakery for one year.

"If, at the end of that one year, the bakery is a financial success and the tenant has received the townspeople's approval, the bakery and the building will become their sole possession, free and clear. No purchase price is intended or required.

"The Devlin family trust will pay the taxes on the property and maintain the building structure for ten years from the date it permanently closed at the hands of the members of the Devlin family."

Mayor Bigby closes the folder and leans back in his chair. His dusty boots go back onto the desk, one at a time, and he starts gnawing on that spent matchstick again. Bigby stares at the two of us with furrowed brows. Then his demeanor changes, and he starts grinning, big, broad grinning, as he eyes Tom and me.

After a prolonged pause, the mayor removes his boots from the desk once more, faces the desk, lays his arms flat in front of him, leans forward, lowers his head, and pauses, then, in a sincere voice, speaks the most heart-warming words I have ever heard.

"Mr. Tom, Miss Ella, I like you two. I know you are fine people. I have good instincts, and I'm rarely wrong. If I were to lay a ten-dollar bill on this desk, I know I wouldn't lose it. I feel certain that you two can make a go of the Devlin Bakery."

Nothing could have surprised me more. I don't know how to react, cry, or laugh.

Mayor Bigby then pushes back in his chair, pulls the desk's top drawer out to his belly, and reaches in, fishing around for something. Then, a wad of keys comes sliding across the desk toward me with a clatter.

"Those are the keys to the bakery. Go have a look. Take your time and come back here to see me tomorrow at three o'clock. I'll introduce you to Judge Garfield. We'll all have a beer together to celebrate if you want it."

I pick up the keys. The three of us rise from our chairs and shake hands. "Thank you very much, Mayor Bigby. We truly appreciate your confidence in us. Ella and I are excited about the opportunity; we can't wait to see the bakery. We'll be there early tomorrow morning."

Tom and I leave the courthouse, walk down the long sidewalk to the street, and cross it without looking back or at each other. We climb into the truck and sit for a moment, gazing out the windshield, then turn and stare into each other's eyes. Is this real? Can this be happening? My head is spinning.

Tom starts the truck. "Let's head on back to Cooper."

We had no way of knowing that the woman sporting the dour expression was watching us from the corner window of the courthouse.

Now, back in the little town of Cooper, we walk into Sharon's house, and she immediately begins firing questions at us. "What happened, what happened, what did he say? Tell me, tell me."

"Hold on a second, Sharon. We need a cold drink, and then we'll sit and tell you about our meeting with Mayor Bigby."

Taking me by the elbow, Tom leads me to a comfortable chair in the parlor, kneels in front of me, and removes my shoes. He then pulls the footstool over to me and places my legs on it; my, what a caring and attentive husband I have.

An hour later, the three of us sit in silence. Sharon is as amazed as we are. "You are saying the bakery can be yours. Is that right?"

"It looks like it can be. The mayor thinks we are a good fit to run the bakery. Tomorrow, we will see the layout, look over the equipment, and examine the accounting records. We will have until three o'clock to learn as much as possible, and then we will meet the mayor at his office. He wants to introduce us to the judge. He said we'll all have a beer to celebrate if we want it."

MARTINSVILLE, ILLINOIS

Martinsville, Illinois, in Clark County, was founded in 1832 by Joseph Martin. Joseph purchased the land in 1833 and planned a village along the National Road that attracted settlers. Martinsville was granted a United Post Office in April 1834 and became a city in 1905.

As of the 2023 census, Martinsville's population is just over 1,000 residents. The population has been on a continuous decline over many years.

CHAPTER II

The Investigation

I am well-rested and prepared to inspect the bakery this morning. The bakery may be dusty and dirty; after all, it has been vacant for three years; however, we have a second meeting with Mayor Bigby in his office at three o'clock, where we will meet the judge for the first time. Once again, I want to look my professional best.

I select a white long-sleeved blouse, my favorite mid-calf denim skirt, cinch my waist with a leather belt, and lace up my most practical shoes. I give my hair a good brushing, then wind it in a twist. Sharon brings me a comb with ivory inlay to secure it and add a finishing touch. A touch of lipstick, and I am ready. Sharon wants to come along, but Tom says it would be best for us to go alone. She can come another day, perhaps tomorrow.

I am so excited as Tom puts the key in the lock, opens the door, and we step over the threshold. A flick of the light switch reveals a glass-front display case to the left, running lengthwise in the room, and a shorter similar counter faces the front of the store to form an "L." Another tall cabinet with glass-paneled double doors stands against the wall on the right toward the back of the room. Nearer the front on the right are two small tables with chairs around them for customers to sit and munch on their baked goods and talk with their neighbors.

Natural light from the expansive front windows flanking the door, plus a third on the side of the building, lends a bright and cheery atmosphere to the bakery. At the back of the bakery are two doors; the one on the right leads into the kitchen, and the other leads to a small office.

Tom and I enter the kitchen to find a long worktable with several stools occupying the middle of the kitchen floor. Situated on the store's back wall are two long deep sinks for washing large trays or mixing bowls. On the outside back wall stand two deep and wide ovens for baking loaves of bread. Next to them is a tall, narrow oven with multiple racks for baking trays of biscuits, muffins, or layer cakes. We find bins for flour and sugar, a wide refrigerated cabinet, and two large mixers on stands in the middle of the floor next to the worktable.

Tom proceeds to look over the assortment of equipment while I head back to the office and sit at the old oak desk where I imagine Mrs. Devlin and other members of the Devlin family ran the business side of the bakery for many years.

Opening the desk drawers and the filing cabinets, I find Mrs. Devlin's meticulously kept records; lists of purchases, suppliers, and ledgers filled with the costs of goods and supplies, inventories, daily receipts, and bank deposits.

This information will provide the financial side of the business we want and need to review. I had wondered from whom the Devlins purchased essential ingredients such as flour, sugar, butter, milk, eggs, and lard; all the things I know we will need in bulk to run a bakery business daily.

What I don't find are any of Mrs. Devlin's recipes. I am concerned about making large batches of biscuit dough. Doubling or tripling a recipe doesn't always produce the same taste and texture as the original recipe. I need them to be as light, flaky, and as tasty as the biscuits I have always made.

My immediate concern is the quality and flavor of the dough, which can easily be affected by two factors. The grasses and hay the cows eat differ from region to region, which will determine the taste of their milk. The taste of the local water and the minerals it carries can also affect the taste of the dough. It makes sense that we will need to bake some test batches before opening the bakery.

Next, I find a bank book, and as I open it, an envelope falls to the floor. Picking it up, I see it is a letter from the Devlin family welcoming potential new tenants, stating they can contact them if they have any questions. I look through the bank book and the register; it appears that $1,000.00 is in the account. That is a lot of money. Could they have forgotten to clear the bank account when they closed the bakery? I have a hard time believing this could be an oversight.

Soon, I have a pile of books and records on the desk and more stacked on the floor next to my feet. An hour later, my inspection is interrupted by the front door opening; I look up to see Mayor Bigby walk in. I glance at my watch; it is two-thirty.

"Good afternoon, Miss Ella. I see you two are busy getting to know the bakery business."

"Yes, we are, Mayor Bigby. I would like to know as much about the business as possible before we commit ourselves. I am a prudent person, Mayor Bigby; very organized, and I want to be efficient and make the bakery a great success."

"Of course, Ella. And a great success you will be. I am certain of your abilities. Please understand that I don't expect you to dive in without having a good viewpoint of the business. There's no rush to open the bakery. Take your time studying anything you want. Take all this with you, read it over, mull it over."

"Thank you, Mayor Bigby. It is a big undertaking, and I am eager to get started."

Leaning toward me, Mayor Bigby takes my hand and sandwiches it between his. "Miss Ella, please call me John. We all want you to be confident in your decision-making and are here to help in any way we can. Look things over and make a list of any questions you may have. I'm sure we can get all the answers you need."

"One thing I want to mention, John. It appears that the bank account holds a $1,000.00 balance. Could that be right? Did they leave money in the bank account?"

"Actually, yes, for the new owners in case they need funds to spruce up the place or purchase supplies. I'm a signer on the account at this time. Mrs. Devlin is a generous woman indeed."

"How kind of her to do that for the new owners."

"Not exactly. You see, the Devlins want the bakery to be a success for our town's people and the new owners. You will understand more when you are open and running. You will see how important this bakery is to the townsfolk, but maybe not as important as the building across the street." Mayor Bigby lets loose with a loud belly laugh. I'm not sure I know what building he is referring to.

Tom has joined us from the kitchen and is listening to our conversation. "Hello, Tom. Are we ready for a cold beer across the street?"

"Wait, aren't we going to your office? Aren't we supposed to meet the judge first?"

Grinning, Bigby says in a loud whisper, "The judge does what I tell him." Bigby belts out another belly laugh at his little joke. "Not really, but you see, as the mayor, I'm here to make sure the people of Martinsville are satisfied and get what they want. The judge is here to make sure no one gets in the way.

"This morning, the judge and I had a long talk, and I told him all about you folks. He is comfortable with my assessment of you and your ability to run the bakery. He will join us for a beer across the street in the bar. It is almost three o'clock; we best head over. But first, let's get these books and ledgers into your vehicle. Take them home and review them at your leisure."

I had not noticed the building across the street, given that it doesn't look like a typical bar; instead, it is a plain, broad, dark brown wood building in the middle of the block. High above the doors in scrolled letters are the words, "Martinsville's Finest," and below in block letters is a polite invitation, "Ladies & Gents Welcome." The name doesn't lead one to understand that it is a bar.

The interior of the bar resembles an old-time fancy saloon. A carved old-fashioned dark wood backbar, tall and ornate, graces the wall on the left side of the large room. In front of it stands a shiny wood mahogany bar that runs the length of the backbar with at least twenty stools in a row.

Tables and chairs fill the rest of the large room, scattered about for dining, stretching to the back of the deep space. At the table farthest back, we find the judge waiting for us.

"Judge Garfield, I want you to meet Tom and Ella Watson."

We shake hands and take our seats, and magically, a tray of glasses and a pitcher of ice-cold beer arrives at our table. All eyes in the room are on my back; I can feel them watching us. After all, we are the new kids in town.

Mayor Bigby notices my unease; he leans toward me and whispers, "Don't worry, Miss Ella. No one knows why you're here. We're keeping it under wraps for the time being. Let me know when you are ready to meet in my office. We have some papers to sign. And now, Cheers!"

Over the next few days, Tom and I spread all the books and ledgers across Sharon's dining room table and examine them with a fine-tooth comb. The Devlins kept all their records neat and organized. Tom prepares a list of the suppliers the Devlins traded with, in Martinsville and nearby areas, including their names, addresses, and telephone numbers.

Sharon is helping us review various files and papers to see what other information we need to scrutinize. Tom and I sit with Sharon several days later to discuss our findings.

"I have a list of the people we need to contact, learn how they want to conduct business, and set up contracts. Next is a list of monthly expenses based on when they ordered supplies. Here is a complete accounting of the bakery's income and expenses for the last three years of operation. We can make this work with a minimum cash outlay at the onset. So here, look it over and see if you agree or if I have missed anything."

Sharon has a good head for accounting, so a second analysis from her is important to us. I give her the ledgers and tax returns to study. Later, she confirms what Tom has determined are accurate numbers for the last three years the bakery was operating.

Tom arranged a meeting with Mayor Bigby to review the list of local and nearby suppliers. We will have him advise us with whom we should do business. The mayor studied Tom's list and checked off the companies we should contact and which ones to avoid. We also need a recommendation for someone qualified to inspect the kitchen equipment and ensure it is in good working order.

Mayor Bigby gave us the name and number of a local mechanic, Mr. Jim Nelson. The mayor said Mr. Nelson knows kitchen equipment like the back of his hand. Mayor Bigby called and arranged for him to meet us at the bakery the following day. He agreed to inspect the equipment and see if it is in good working order or needs repair. Jim offered to be at the bakery the first couple of days we run the equipment to ensure everything goes according to plan. Running a dough blender doesn't take an engineering degree, but I am grateful for his abilities and help.

We asked Jim what he charges for his services, and he replied that we could pay him $5.00 for the initial inspection of the equipment and any needed repairs but not for being with us for the first day or two when the bakery is open. He will be satisfied going home with a basket of baked goods. Piece of cake.

Dear Mayor Bigby,

With great anticipation, I received and read your letter informing me of the folks interested in the bakery. Where are they from, and how did they hear about it? Your note was relatively short, and I am anxious to know more. Please fill me in on the details.

Mrs. Devlin

Jim Nelson came by the other day and inspected the equipment. He informed us that everything was in good working order. Jim found two more mixers in the utility room, smaller in size, which we will use to blend batter for layer cakes or muffins. The large mixers will combine the ingredients for making loaves of bread and biscuits. I understand biscuits are popular with the folks around here, so making large batches is what we will be doing on a daily basis.

Tom went home to finalize arrangements for the children to take ownership of the farm. They are thrilled. The profits from the farm will adequately cover their monthly living expenses, plus a portion of the yearly profits are to be set aside for Tom and me to be paid semi-annually.

I am amazed at how much Tom and I have accomplished so quickly. We were on our farm only a few weeks ago, wondering what our future would hold. And now, here we are in Martinsville, fully committed to operating the bakery and are making progress toward opening it soon.

Today, I am working on basic chores at the bakery, mopping the floors and polishing the glass display cases. I have a few more tasks to do when the door opens, and a tall, smartly dressed, dark-haired woman enters.

"Hello, you must be Mrs. Watson?"

"Yes I am; how can I help you? I'm sorry, we're not open yet."

"Yes, I know, and I'm sorry to interrupt your work, Mrs. Watson. I'm Patricia Snyder. I want to talk with you, please. May we sit?"

We pull out two chairs from the table and sit face to face. The woman stares at me, then after a moment of silence, she repeats, "I'm Patricia Snyder."

The name means nothing to me. "I'm Ella Watson. I'm sorry, Mrs. Snyder, should I know you?"

"I beg your pardon. I assumed you had heard my name from Mayor Bigby."

"No, he has not mentioned it to me."

"Mrs. Watson, I worked for Mrs. Devlin for the last three years the bakery was operating. I have something for you." She reaches into a large tote bag, pulls out a black three-ring binder, and hands it to me. I open it to find pages and pages of recipes.

"Those are Mrs. Devlin's recipes. When the bakery closed, she gave me the binder. She wanted to be sure it was held in safekeeping, that it didn't get lost. She told me to give it to the new owners if Mayor Bigby happened to find the right people to operate the bakery someday. The mayor knows that I have the binder in my possession. I guess he forgot to tell you about me and the binder. I know you may have your own recipes, but these might help you, particularly when making large batches of dough for loaves of bread and biscuits. Folks here in Martinsville adored Mrs. Devlin's biscuits. It is my pleasure to give you the book."

"This is certainly unexpected. Thank you, Mrs. Snyder. I appreciate that you have taken the time to come in and give this to me. I wondered why I didn't find Mrs. Devlin's recipes in the files; I figured I would have to work out the recipes myself."

"I am more than happy to help. One more thing I want to talk about with you, Mrs. Watson. I have truly missed this bakery and would like to work here. I know you don't know me from Adam, but I could be a tremendous help to you, a righthand person, shall we say? And you don't have to pay me. I understand you are just getting started. What do you think?"

"You are right. I could use some help, but it is only right that I pay you for your time. I don't know how much, but something."

"Let's see how things go first; I don't need the money. I had a wonderful experience working with the Devlin family. Mrs. Devlin was like a mother to me. Working here would give me great pleasure. It would be like being back where I belong."

Patricia then hands me a piece of paper with her name and telephone number. "Call me when you know when you want to open the bakery. We can get together several days in advance and bake a bunch of goodies."

"This is a great surprise, Mrs. Snyder. I can see how you would be a great help to me. I'll call you when I am ready to bake the sample batches."

As she heads out the door, she looks over her shoulder and says, "Oh, and call me Patricia."

"Call me, Ella."

A couple of hours later, I am getting ready to lock up, but first, I want to sweep the dust and leaves from the sidewalk in front of the bakery. Before I can finish, a beat-up dark blue truck slows down, and an older man shouts out his window at me.

"Howdy, ma'am. You must be the new owner of the bakery. Be opening soon, I reckon, now that you've signed all the papers."

He drives away, leaving me speechless. How on earth did he know that Tom and I had signed the papers two days ago? I have a good idea of how he knew about them.

Madder than a wet hen, I grab my shawl and the keys, lock the door, and head toward the courthouse. With no one in sight, I walk to Mayor Bigby's office and rap on the door.

"Come in. Welcome, Miss Ella. What brings you here this afternoon? Sit down, sit down."

It takes all my effort not to blow my top as angry as I am; I am fuming.

"Thank you, but I'd rather stand if it's all right with you. Look, Mayor Bigby, it is evident that new tenants will open the Devlin Bakery soon. You would have to be blind not to notice all the activity going on and us being new to town. But how on earth could someone know that we signed those papers? I would hope that some things of a legal nature are personal and private, but it is obvious that a leak is coming out of this office, and I am pretty darned upset. Where is the confidentiality and privacy for one's business affairs? Don't you have some degree of decency around here, or is our business spread all over town?"

Bigby looks startled. I can see the gears going around in his head. His face starts turning red, very red. He stands, slams his fist on his desk, and shouts louder than I have ever heard anyone shout.

"*HENDERSON. H E N - D E R - S O N? GET IN HERE.*"

Then another fist slams on the desk; it scares the heck out of me. I fall into the chair in a slump. Then I hear the door behind me open, and a meek voice says, "Yes, Mayor Bigby?"

"Henderson, you're fired. Do you hear me, Henderson? You're fired. "*YOU'RE FIRED.*"

I dare not turn and look, but I know who it is standing behind me.

Bigby starts around from behind his desk in a fit of outrage, his face redder than a beet; nevertheless, he manages to pause at my chair, puts a gentle hand on my shoulder, and says in a hushed tone, "Wait here, Ella. I'll be right back."

A door slams behind me, jolting me in my chair and leaving me alone in the mayor's office. I hear a muffled conversation, the mayor raising his voice repeatedly, but I can't make out the words; then, silence. Finally, Mayor Bigby returns to the room, throws a wad of keys on his desk, and plops into his chair. He is breathing heavily, his face is still beet red, and dots of sweat cover his forehead.

"John, I didn't mean for anyone to get fired."

Short of breath, he spits out, "Ella, you did me a favor. You did all of us a favor. I should have fired that woman years ago. What she did is unforgivable. I know she has snooped around my desk in the past. I know she saw the Devlin file in my side drawer. She's been a problem for a long time, but I couldn't bring myself to get rid of the old bat. Your confidence to come in here and tell me what happened gave me the willpower to get rid of her finally, once and for all. Good riddance to her. I'm glad she's gone."

The mayor and I sit in long silence and soak in the whole scene. Finally calmer, his face not so red, Mayor Bigby rises from his chair, comes around the desk, and stands beside me.

"Give me your hand, Miss Ella. Please forgive me. I apologize for what has happened. I hope I can, in some way, restore your faith in me and my position as mayor." With that, he bends over and kisses the back of my hand.

I stand up. "Thank you, John." I then give a sideways glance toward the keys on the desk. "Those are her keys to the whole place, aren't they?"

"You bet they are, Ella." We both break into laughter. "Now go home and make dinner for your handsome husband." Still holding my hand, he pats it and says, "Have a good evening."

Mayor Bigby,

My goodness, these folks sound like they are the right fit for taking on the bakery business. Did you say they are here from Naperville? And they have a cousin who lives in Cooper; I remember Sharon Hansen, a lovely woman with a pleasant personality. As I recall, she never married. She didn't come in often, but I never forget a face.

Where on earth will the folks from Naperville live? You know I have set aside funds to help new owners get settled, so be sure to help them with their living expenses. I can't take it all with me to heaven's gate. Be gracious to them and treat them right. They are going to take care of my bakery.

Mrs. Devlin

Tom and I have been so busy making plans for the bakery that we haven't given one thought to where we will be living once the bakery is open. I will need to be up early in the morning to start baking loaves of bread and dozens of biscuits, so living with Sharon in Cooper, five miles outside of town, isn't practical.

I figure my best bet is to walk to the courthouse and ask Mayor Bigby for advice on housing. It has been a couple of days since the scene in the mayor's office, and this will give me a chance to be sure our relationship is back on a friendly footing. Mayor Bigby welcomes me into his office like an old friend; the past is in the past. I take a seat and tell him what I need.

"Yes, Ella, I have an idea that will give you and Tom a nice place to live for an economical price until you decide where to make your permanent residence. May I take you to see it?"

John rises and offers me his arm. We walk several blocks together down Main Street; soon, he stops and opens the door to Martinsville's Finest. Yes, the bar. It is early; three people are seated in the dining room. Daniel Warner, the bar owner, is polishing glassware behind the backbar and whistling an unfamiliar tune.

"Daniel, this is Miss Ella Watson. She and her husband, Tom, are the Devlin Bakery's new tenants. As of now, they are living out in Cooper with her cousin Sharon; however, they will need a place here in town once the bakery is open. Is the apartment on the third floor available?"

"It sure is."

Daniel gets the key and hands it to Bigby. The mayor and I walk to the rear of the building, where we take an elevator to the third floor. It opens onto a small foyer, with one door across from it. John puts the key in the lock and escorts me into the apartment, which is spacious and fully furnished with a bedroom and a separate sitting area in a bay window.

The bathroom includes standard amenities, a toilet, a sink, a separate shower room, and a long bathtub. I can picture myself relaxing in it at the end of the day.

"John, I never expected anything like this over the bar. This apartment is so pleasant and cozy, but is it quiet?"

"Folks who have stayed here have had no complaints. It is the one accommodation on this floor, like a penthouse. Two more levels of apartments separate this floor from the bar. Daniel likes to keep this large suite for more long-term tenants."

"How much is the monthly rent?"

"First, Miss Ella, does it meet with your satisfaction?"

"Yes, it is perfect for Tom and me."

"Then don't worry about the cost. Mrs. Devlin has arranged for the trust to cover your monthly expense."

"How generous. That is so kind of Mrs. Devlin. Please extend our gratitude to her."

"My pleasure."

We ride the elevator down to the bar and meet with Daniel. I tell him we will want the apartment for at least six months, perhaps longer. Daniel agrees, pulls a preprinted contract from behind the bar, and John signs it for Tom and me. Daniel hands me the keys and says we can move in right away.

Daniel then escorts me to the back of the bar to show me a rear entrance beyond the elevator. Tom and I can get to our accommodations without walking through a crowded bar, which will be beneficial after a hectic day at the bakery.

Mayor Bigby takes a moment to check the time on his watch. "Miss Ella, I know it is a bit early, but if you have the time, would you do me the honor of having lunch with me?"

"Thank you, John; I would like to dine with you." I agree, as I haven't had a chance to tell him about my meeting with Patricia Snyder. I need and want his opinion about her working with me. We sit at a table nearest the back of the dining room and order vegetable soup and ham and cheese sandwiches.

"I want to tell you about a woman, Mrs. Snyder, who showed up at the bakery the other day. She gave me Mrs. Devlin's binder of recipes."

"Oh yes, Patricia, I should have mentioned her to you weeks ago; it completely slipped my mind. Sometimes I wonder about this old head of mine."

"Mayor Bigby, I understand Mrs. Snyder worked for Mrs. Devlin for several years. She has suggested that she work with me as my assistant. What is your opinion of that idea?"

"Let me tell you about Patricia. She is a responsible and honest woman and knows the bakery business inside and out. Patricia practically ran it single-handedly the last three years it was open. Mrs. Devlin was getting older and incapable of handling heavy items such as sacks of flour and sugar and no longer had the strength or the desire to run the machinery.

"Having Patricia on board will be an excellent opportunity to learn the bakery business firsthand from a real pro, Ella. I can assure you she will follow your directions and not act like the boss.

"And another plus; the people of Martinsville have a real fondness for Patricia for how she assisted the Devlins, keeping the bakery open long past the time Mrs. Devlin could have managed on her own. Our townsfolk will be thrilled to see Patricia back in the bakery. The two of you will make a great combination."

"Thank you, Mayor Bigby, for showing me such an amazing apartment, for lunch and for reassuring me that my instincts were right about Patricia."

Later that afternoon, I drive to Cooper to find Sharon and Tom sitting in the rocking chairs on the front porch. I sit in a chair beside Sharon and tell them the latest goings-on about our new home, a penthouse apartment above the bar. I then call Patricia.

"Patricia, this is Ella Watson. I would be grateful to have you working with me in the bakery. I know you will be a great asset. Tom and I are moving into the penthouse apartment above Martinsville's Finest tomorrow. Would you be available to meet us at the bakery around noon? I want to introduce you to my husband, Tom, and my cousin, Sharon."

"Yes, of course. I am excited to be working with you. See you tomorrow."

The following morning, Tom and I move what few belongings we had brought from Naperville into the penthouse. Sharon tags along and brings two sets of sheets, fluffy pillows, two large blankets, bath towels, and a few throw rugs for the bathroom. We are all set in our new surroundings.

From there, we go down the street to find Patricia waiting outside the bakery door. After polite introductions, the four of us review all the supplies in the kitchen and determine that we are ready for opening day. Sharon has agreed to pitch in when we need an extra pair of hands in the store.

Patricia and I decide to spend Saturday and Sunday baking trays of biscuits, loaves of bread, a few dozen cookies, and two-layer cakes. Testing out Mrs. Devlin's recipes before we open to the public will allow me to taste each item and decide if I need to alter the recipe before we open the bakery. I should mention that in addition to inspecting the kitchen equipment, Jim Nelson calibrated the ovens' thermostats. Good-tasting recipes and proper oven temperatures will ensure we produce baked goods that taste delicious and have a fresh-baked appearance.

Two days later, early Saturday morning, Patricia and I meet before the day gets too hot and begin baking biscuits using Mrs. Devlin's recipe book. If her recipe tastes as good as mine, I will use hers. I can always adjust the ingredients to suit my taste later. We bake four dozen biscuits, three-layer cakes, six loaves of bread, four white and two wheat, and three dozen sugar cookies.

I am amazed at how easy it was, primarily due to Patricia's expertise. Now, what do we do with all these baked goods? We plan to open the bakery this Thursday, and the whole lot will be stale by then.

We decide that the best place to show off our baking prowess is at Martinsville's Finest. We package all we have baked, stack the boxes on two large baking trays, and head down the street. I slip into the bar while Patricia stands guard outside over the two trays of baked goods. I spot Daniel immediately and motion for him to come to the end of the bar.

"Patricia and I have been baking all morning, and while we aren't officially opening the bakery until Thursday, we have baked dozens of biscuits, loaves of bread, and pastries. Would you mind if we offered your patrons samples of our baked goods?"

A couple of the men nearby realize something is up and let out a "whoop," which is all it takes. Daniel says yes. All eyes are on Patricia and me as we carry our trays into Martinsville's Finest. We set the trays on the bar top and spread our baked goods. We are ready. Daniel picks up a brass bell and rings it to quiet the room.

"Attention, folks. I want to introduce you to the Devlin Bakery's new proprietor, Miss Ella Watson, and her assistant, Miss Patricia Snyder, whom many of you already know. Today, you are the lucky recipients of Miss Ella and Miss Patricia's baking. They have brought samples for all of you to taste. The Devlin Bakery will reopen this coming Thursday."

Talk about a feeding frenzy. We greet the patrons as they taste our samples for the next two hours. People crowd around us and introduce themselves, telling me they are so thankful the bakery will reopen soon. People are licking their fingers and then shaking my hand; such a genuine welcome. Some ask if we are keeping the bakery's name the same, and of course, I tell them, "Yes." Sharing our samples with the patrons of Martinsville's Finest turns out to be the best way to announce the reopening of the bakery.

Sunday morning, Patricia and I meet to discuss preparations for opening day. We find several cartons of folding bakery boxes in the storage room, a large spool of twine, and the rod it sits on with a blade to cut the cord. Also, we find a small package of napkins on a shelf we will use when handing a biscuit or a cookie to a customer.

Unsure how busy we will be, our plan is for Tom to handle the cash register so that Patricia and I can greet and wait on the customers.

We will start the inventory on Thursday with five dozen biscuits, ten loaves of bread, and three two-layer cakes. Only three cakes, as cakes, are usually ordered in advance. We will also bake several dozen sugar cookies and two trays of cupcakes. We plan to bake what people want and see how fast they sell. We are now officially in the bakery business.

Mayor Bigby,

Oh, my goodness. Patricia will be working with Mrs. Watson; how delightful. Patricia was so valuable to me when I could barely run the place. It would never have been a success to the last day without her. Dear Patricia, give her my best regards when you see her. I sorely miss that woman. She was like a daughter to me.

Mrs. Devlin

CHAPTER III

Open For Business

It is opening day. Tom and I arrive at the bakery early; Patricia stands in the doorway, waiting for us. I am a little nervous, although I am not as nervous as I would be if Patricia weren't by my side. We are busy baking when my fun-loving cousin Sharon arrives, dressed as a lady of liberty.

She is wearing a long white garment that I'm pretty confident is an old nightgown. Her costume is complete, with a blue scarf tied around her waist and a red tablecloth knotted at her neck like a cape. A crown made of gold-colored construction paper, secured to her head with bobby pins, completes her outfit. She plans to stand on the sidewalk and wave the American flag at the townspeople. I am confident her costume will get the attention of passersby.

Mayor Bigby walks into the bakery toting a sandwich board he borrowed from Daniel. He has covered it with white construction paper. Sharon prints the words OPEN 7 AM to 2 PM Monday through Saturday on both sides. Mayor Bigby then places it at the curb outside the bakery.

Back in the kitchen, the large mixers blend the dough for five loaves of bread. Once we put the dough into the loaf pans, we place them on top of the ovens, where the heat will help the dough rise. Both large, wide ovens can hold five loaf pans side by side with enough space for good air circulation. Space and air circulation are the keys to baking loaves of bread evenly with a golden-brown crust. With two ovens, we can easily have ten loaves underway in no time at all.

We prepare more dough, fill more pans, and set them on top of the warm ovens to rise, ready to be baked when the first batch comes out of the oven.

Next, we combine the dry ingredients to make our signature biscuits, add the shortening, and then let the mixer blend the ingredients and form the dough into one large ball. We place the dough in the center of the table on parchment paper, roll it out, and cut it into circles. The circles are placed on shallow trays and baked in the tall, narrow oven.

While the loaves of bread and biscuits are baking, we mix the batter for the cakes. We already have containers of frosting in the cooler, made several days ago. Soon, all the baked goods have cooled and are ready to be put into the display cases. It makes for a beautiful assortment.

"Are we ready? It is time; the door is now open."

Tom props open the doors, and Sharon steps outside and starts waving her flag. Mayor Bigby stands next to her, smiling, waving, and calling to passersby. Tom and I look out the window and are amazed at the line of people in their cars and trucks coming down the street. More people are walking on the sidewalk, all coming to our opening day. Patricia and I are behind the counter, ready to serve our first customers. What a thrill.

Tom greets each new customer with a handshake, welcomes them into the bakery, and then introduces them to Patricia and me. In a matter of minutes, the bakery is packed with customers. An air of excitement fills the room as people gather in front of the display cases, chatting with their neighbors like it is old home week. They point fingers at the stacks of biscuits, rows of sugar cookies and muffins, and iced layer cakes.

It doesn't take long to see that our baked goods are selling faster than we could have expected. Patricia returns to the kitchen to mix the dough and bake more biscuits and loaves of bread, and Sharon comes in from her flag-waving duty to help me wait on the customers. She looks so cute working behind the counter in her costume; the gold crown is still securely attached to her head.

We had no earthly idea the response would be this great. Mayor Bigby remains on the sidewalk, calling people to enter and meet the new proprietors. Some people have inquired what other baked goods we might offer, reminiscing about their favorite cookie or muffin. The Devlins had not changed the selection in twenty years, so we begin a list of the baked goods our customers would like to see in our display cases.

Around eight o'clock, Daniel and one of the women from his kitchen arrive, toting an urn of hot coffee and a large plastic tub full of coffee cups. Daniel also remembered to bring a table to set up the coffee service.

"Ella, we want your customers to have hot coffee with their biscuits and cookies."

"Thank you, Daniel. I am sure they will appreciate your thoughtfulness."

Who doesn't appreciate free coffee? Of course, we have only two small tables with four chairs, not near enough to support the crowd, so people drink their coffee and eat their biscuits and cookies while standing on the sidewalk chatting with each other, enjoying the fresh morning air.

I am surprised at the number of folks who stop in that I had not seen around town; apparently, word has worked its way through the neighborhoods. What surprises me a bit more is all the women who you would expect to bake their own bread and biscuits come in and purchase ours.

"Patricia, we are almost out of biscuits. Will you please go and make more?"

"I have the dough already mixed. I need to roll it out, cut it, and put the trays in the oven. It won't take long."

Around eleven o'clock, the flow of customers slows, and we have our first chance to take a break and analyze what has happened so far. We both look a bit spent, so we sit to have some over-heated coffee and do some much-needed planning.

"This has been exciting. I had no earthly idea that the response would be this great."

"Me too, although when I look back on my working days, I can see why people would be excited to have the bakery reopened. Buying something delicious from a bakery is one way to pamper yourself."

Many folks no longer desire to bake loaves of bread and biscuits. It's easier to come into town and buy from the bakery. Think of men living alone, older men with no wife to bake for them. The bakery fills their need for sweets and provides a place to socialize with fellow townspeople.

Patricia tells me two customers will be in tomorrow to purchase three loaves of bread each, so we will have to bake extra. We have a growing list of sweets people have mentioned they would like to see us offer.

During the war, the government diverted the limited amount of sugar available in the states to support the troops, which resulted in sugar rationing throughout American households. The lack of sugar limited the variety and number of baked goods people could make; however, women put on their thinking caps and created recipes for baked goods without sugar, recipes many women still use today.

Sugar rationing ended in 1947, and with sugar now plentiful, we can bake more sweet treats in addition to loaves of bread and biscuits. How soon we can add to our menu will determine how much time we can devote to baking new items. Their requests tell me the townspeople are interested in the bakery, which pleases me greatly.

Our doorbells chime, new customers arrive, and we are busy with a steady stream of customers for the next two hours. Whenever someone I have not met comes in, I come from behind the counter, greet them with a handshake, and introduce myself. I try to engage them in a short conversation and make our initial meeting pleasant. If Patricia knows anything about them, she fills me in after they leave.

Biscuits and loaves of bread are the main staples we sell day in and day out. It doesn't take long to notice that most people don't want to buy a whole cake unless they need one for a particular occasion. For an older couple or someone living alone, having a slice or two of cake in the house is a treat, but a whole cake sitting on their kitchen counter? Too much.

I heard one woman talking to herself as she leaned over and tapped her finger on the glass display case, "I would give anything to have one slice of that cake, that one, right there." The woman's comment made me realize that just because people don't want to purchase a whole cake doesn't mean they don't like cake; they want less cake.

So, Patricia and I decide to change our way of selling layer cakes, and we now offer cake by one-half, one-quarter, or by the slice. We make and sell more cakes now that the proportion fits people's needs, which puts a smile on our customers' faces and ours, too.

The first two weeks have been lots of work and fun for us. It is now Saturday, and as Patricia and I are cleaning up before closing, Tom walks in and hands me an envelope addressed to the new owners of the Devlin Bakery, Main St. Martinsville, Ill.

"Daniel gave this to me."

I open the envelope to find a small note, the words written in a scrawled hand. "Please open the bakery at six o'clock." No signature. I show the message to Tom, who shrugs his shoulders.

"Patricia, look at this note. Open the bakery at six o'clock. Why would this be important or even something we want to do?"

"Truthfully, Ella, Mrs. Devlin did open the bakery at six o'clock. I never mentioned an earlier start time to you; seven o'clock was perfect for me."

"What would be the advantage of opening one hour earlier?"

"You see, two different groups live in and around Martinsville; the folks who live in town, the homeowners, and the store owners. Then we have the folks you probably have not met, those who work for the farms in the outlying areas. We have some beautiful farms nearby. You get milk, eggs, and butter from one farm and flour from another farm with a mill.

"A large and prestigious horse farm is not far from here. All the farms have farmhands and seasonal workers who begin work early. A few of them live on local farms, but most don't. They don't have much money, and an early breakfast means a lot to them."

"Early breakfast. You mean we are the workers' early breakfast?"

"Yes, of course. A big part of the Devlin bakery was selling biscuits to the farmhands. They are a mix of people, I guess you could say diverse, but a polite and appreciative group of men for the most part."

"And they mainly buy the biscuits, right?"

"Yes. Biscuits are easy to carry and go with whatever else the men can find to eat. Ella, it wouldn't take much to open an hour earlier. We can easily make a few dozen biscuits in the afternoon before we close. They would be ready for the farmhands when they get here at six o'clock. They would still be fresh, so we wouldn't have to arrive earlier. The farm workers will line up outside and wait for you to open the door. You can hand out biscuits in the store, and I can finish in the back."

I look at Tom standing behind me and then back at Patricia. "OK then, we are good to go at six." Before leaving, we change the sandwich board to read, "Open at six o'clock."

Dear Mayor Bigby,

It sounds like the opening day was a huge success, and I'm so thankful that Patricia remembered to give Mrs. Watson the binder with my recipes. Please congratulate them. This note will be short as I'm under the weather today.

Yours truly, Marion

It is now Sunday morning, and Tom and I have no plans except to rest and relax. Later, I will stop by the bakery, check on the inventory, and make sure we look in tip-top shape for the beginning of the week. I arrive at the bakery around two o'clock, and the next thing I know, the door opens, and Patricia walks in.

"I thought I might find you here."

"So nice of you to stop; have a seat. Now that you are here, do you have time to review the customer request list? Since the beginning of last week, our customers have added more ideas for baked goods to the list."

After a quick review, we find that chocolate is on the minds of many of the townspeople. A pie sounds good, but we quickly decided it would fall into the same category as a layer cake; therefore, chocolate chip cookies and chocolate muffins will have to satisfy folks craving something chocolate; that is what we will bake.

We will purchase what we need on Monday morning and start baking the chocolate goods on Tuesday.

To announce our new offerings, we grab one of the white placard signs from the storage room, the kind used for advertising in a window. On it, I write, "Buttermilk Biscuits, 10 Cents," and on another, "Chocolate Chip Cookies 10 Cents, Chocolate Muffins 10 Cents." You may have guessed I have altered the biscuit recipe, now making them with buttermilk. The combination of ingredients makes them sweeter, larger, and heavier without falling apart; the farmhands are sure to like them.

Arriving at the bakery the following day at our usual time, Patricia and I arrange the biscuits in a layered pile, staggering them neatly on a large tray. It looks like a cute little biscuit mountain. I then push the shorter counter forward, facing the front of the store, giving me a convenient opening to walk to the front of the bakery without looping back and around the longer display case.

Patricia and I found a stainless-steel bowl for the farmhands to drop their dimes in for their thick, fluffy buttermilk biscuits. We set the bowl and the tray on the shorter counter. We are working in the kitchen when Patricia looks up and shouts, "It's five minutes before six." I run into the store, and to my amazement, I see ten men standing in line at the front door.

Fishing in my apron pocket, I shout, "The key, where's my key?"

Patricia hands me hers. "Here, Ella, open the door; your audience awaits."

I don't suppose I have ever met a more polite group of men, a diverse group; many are white, some of color, and several are from Asian lands. Some are relatively short; some are tall, some are tan, and others are pale. All are wearing jeans, shirts, and boots.

One at a time, the men step to the counter and make their request; "Biscuit please, thank you, ma'am," or "Biscuit please, thank you, Miss Ella." One Asian man bows with his hands in front of his chest as he asks for his biscuit. I return the bow; he is surprised and pleased with my response and smiles.

I am amazed at their gentle manner. A simple biscuit feeds these hardworking men; a simple biscuit touches my heart. Their weathered faces, worn hands, demeanor, and politeness stir my emotions. Their faces have a history etched onto them, reflecting some unknown, untold story. I wonder where these men came from, how they got here, and who they left behind.

As the last one walks out the door, I turn around to find Patricia leaning on the doorway to the office.

She is smiling at me. "It was worth it, wasn't it?"

Overcome with emotion, I start to cry and run to hug her. "Thank you, thank you, Patricia. Now I understand."

The rest of the day is busy with customers purchasing everything in the display cases.

Tom and I have dinner in the bar at a table for two this evening. The room is filled with people laughing, having fun, and perhaps celebrating some event; however, the farmhands are all that is on my mind. I want to tell Tom all about them, but this is not the place for a touching story amid all this fun and laughter.

"You are rather quiet tonight. Is something wrong, Ella?"

"No, nothing is wrong, but I did have a moving experience today. I will tell you about it when we get upstairs."

Before I tell Tom about my experience meeting the farmhands, I prepare for bed by soaking in the deep bathtub. The tub is like my personal spa; it is very relaxing. The length is perfect and has the ideal slant to the end where I lean back and rest my head. Then, dressed in my nightgown and wrapped in my cotton robe, I slide into bed beside Tom.

Lying in bed in the dark, I relate the story of the farm workers. Tom is moved by the story, too. He takes my hand in his and squeezes it.

"What a blessing," he says softly.

"Yes, they are, those dear sweet men."

"No, Ella, I was referring to you."

I soon discovered that not all our patrons want a buttermilk biscuit, so we now bake regular ones and the buttermilk kind. Most farmhands prefer buttermilk biscuits, probably due to their rich flavor and size, which are big and fluffy. Then, one day, after handing out biscuits to the farm workers, it occurred to me that I was putting a biscuit in their old, worn hands. I don't know if they eat their biscuits right away or save them for later, so Patricia and I head into the utility room and start looking in the cabinets and shelves for something to set the biscuits on as I hand them out.

Eventually, we discover a large roll of brown Kraft paper, the paper butchers use to wrap meat, in a previously uninspected corner. After we close our doors, we unroll the paper onto the worktable and cut it into four-inch squares.

The following day, when the men arrive, I add the motion of plopping their biscuit on a square of Kraft paper before handing it to them. The men are surprised, but only one or two of them comment. "Why, Miss Ella, thank you so much." A simple four-inch Kraft paper square to hold their biscuit pleases them. It shows you that it doesn't take much to make a difference in this world.

We have been open for one month now. Patricia and I have developed a rhythm and a methodology for prepping and baking our baked goods like a well-oiled machine. I recently purchased all the stainless-steel containers on the Cummings Hardware Store shelf and have them lined along one end of the long worktable.

In the afternoons, Patricia goes into the kitchen, measures the dry ingredients for various baked goods, and puts them into the containers while I tend to the customers. When ready to bake an item, we blend in the wet ingredients, then refill the containers with more dry ingredients, ready for baking the next batch.

We bake our chocolate chip cookies late in the afternoon for no reason other than it is one less item to bake first thing in the morning. If the cookies are warm at closing time, we leave them on their trays overnight, covered with thin cloths, so they don't sweat.

Most customers, except the farmhands, come between eight o'clock and eleven, with another rush of business around one o'clock, closer to closing. We use the time with no customers to prepare the dry ingredients for the next batch of biscuits or loaves of bread.

Our kitchen equipment mechanic-extraordinaire, Jim Nelson, shows up periodically to ensure the equipment runs smoothly and to get a taste of what has recently come out of the ovens. This morning, Jim comes by early, and while watching us bake, he asks if we would like the worktable to be raised higher off the floor.

"You see that? You're bending too much at the waist. Don't your backs get sore?" Before I can answer, he says, "I'll be right back." He returns with a tape measure from his truck.

"Ladies, please stand straight and bend your arms at the elbow, 90'." Jim measures from the floor to our elbows and then the height of the table.

"Yup, that's what the problem is. This worktable is too low for the two of you. It would help you if this table were at least seven inches higher. It won't take much to make the adjustments. I can add wood blocks to the bottom of the legs and then put the casters into the blocks. It will make a world of difference. You will be more efficient, and your back won't be so sore.

"And there is something else I'd like to mention, Miss Ella. I would be mighty pleased to help you by cleaning these floors daily. Moppin's a hard job, hard on the back. That kinda work you two ladies shouldn't be doing."

"Oh, would you please? That will be a huge help. Thank you for offering, Jim. One more thing; look at these rolling carts. Can you raise them higher, too?"

Jim takes a long look at the wheels of the carts as he scratches his chin. "Shore nuf', can do. When can I work on them?"

"Saturday afternoon would be best after we close. I will leave you with a key to lock up, and you can come back on Sunday if you need the time." Bless him. The man is a world of information and ideas.

Jim is retired from what business we don't know, but we do know his head is full of logic and mechanical know-how. He frequently stops in the local hardware store and makes himself useful when the store gets busy. Jim walks around, helps the customers find items, and makes suggestions to solve their problems, doing whatever he can to help.

Old Mr. Cummings, first name Walter, and his son, Jeff, own and operate the hardware, and they view Jim's presence as a great benefit to the customers and themselves. Someday, the business will be Jeff's solely, and you can bet he will benefit from Jim's great ideas and his knack for solving problems. Every small town needs a Jim Nelson; we are lucky to have ours.

Saturday has come to an end. When Patricia and I leave, Jim is sitting on the kitchen floor, his tools spread out around him. He begins by measuring, then sawing, drilling holes, and hammering. I decide not to stop by on Sunday but will wait until Monday morning to see the newly altered table and carts.

When Patricia and I arrive Monday morning, we find the work table and the rolling carts at their new height. The floors have been mopped clean as a whistle, leaving no trace of Jim's efforts.

"Wow, the difference is so obvious. I cannot wait to get going and see how much better it is to work with our improved tables."

We value Jim's abilities and know-how.

Mayor Bigby,

If you don't mind me telling you, you should have fired that Henderson woman years ago. Sorry, I don't mean to scold you, but spreading people's business all over town is shameful. She was a devious female with an insincere smile pasted on her face. Goodness me, I shouldn't go on like this, but she was not your best asset or the town's. She'll find another place to land. That kind will always find a way. Did you give her severance money?

Mrs. Watson has gumption; I like that in a woman.

Mrs. Devlin

Today has been a rather hectic day. I practically drag my feet as I walk back to the apartment. Usually, I take the long way around the block to enter from the back of the bar, but today, I am too tired and take the shorter route through the bar. It is busy, crowded, and noisy. As soon as I enter, I recognize Mayor Bigby sitting at the end of the bar, first by his big laugh and then by the back of his head. Not wanting to delay getting upstairs, I walk on past, hoping he won't see me, but sure enough, he does.

"Now, Miss Ella. You aren't going to walk past without stoppin' to say "Hello," are you?"

I backtrack a couple of steps. "I am sorry, Mayor Bigby; I did not want to interrupt you with your friends, and to tell you the truth, I am quite tired. I want to get upstairs and rest."

Ignoring my plea, he reaches out and takes my hand in his usual manner. "How's the bakery comin' along, my dear? I hear you're doing lots of business."

"Yes, we are doing quite nicely. How come we haven't seen you lately? A free buttermilk biscuit to the mayor of the town."

"Been busy myself, frankly, but I will be in soon. Say, how are you and Patricia gettin' along?"

"Fantastic, she is a godsend; so easy to work with and helpful. It is a pleasure to have her with me."

"Ya know, you should get to know each other better, outside of the bakery, that is." Bigby leans in toward me and continues in a low voice. "What I mean to say is, you'll find she's a fascinating person."

Hmmm. I wonder what it could be that makes Patricia fascinating in the mayor's mind.

"Thank you for the suggestion, Mayor Bigby. Since Tom and I arrived in Martinsville, the bakery has consumed our lives, and I could use a break from work. Besides, I need a good friend. Patricia and I should get to know each other on a more friend-to-friend basis. I will suggest that to her right away. Good day, Mayor Bigby."

I turn to walk away and have taken five steps when I hear the mayor holler, "Did ya get my note?"

Nothing could have stopped me deader in my tracks. I should have known, of course; the note was from Mayor Bigby.

I slow my walk and turn my head to call over my shoulder, "I knew it was from you."

"You did not."

"Yes, I did."

"You did not."

"Yes, I did."

"Don't lie to me, Ella," Bigby's voice booms, and he roars his belly laugh. He thinks he is so funny.

Now, I stop and turn to face Mayor Bigby. "I knew it was from you. It was that left-handed scrawl from a right-handed person that gave it away. You can't fool me."

"I knew you were a smart woman, Miss Ella. Yes, I shor' did."

I turn and wave as I get on the elevator, and Bigby continues to roar.

Now lying across the bed, I tell Tom about my conversation with the mayor, and we laugh.

"He knew better than to tell me what to do, so he came up with the note with scrawled handwriting as if someone had never learned to write properly."

"You must admit it did the trick, and now you have the reputation as the kindest woman in town, and I love you." Tom leans in and kisses me on the neck.

"Tom, please. I'm tired, Tom, Tom, I'm tired, later maybe…" More laughter.

The following day, we get things rolling in the kitchen and open our doors to a steady stream of customers until eleven o'clock, when Patricia and I have a chance to sit and catch our breath. I tell her that Bigby was the one who wrote the note.

"No kidding. I would not have guessed, but it makes sense now that I recall how it arrived."

"Bigby asked about you. He suggested we spend time together away from the bakery. I have had the same idea, Patricia. I would like for us to have more than a working relationship. I would like for us to be friends, best friends."

"Oh, Ella, I have had the same thoughts. I need someone to have fun with, a good friend. Perhaps we can spend time together soon?"

"Sure. Tom is returning to the farm next weekend and will be gone for about a week, possibly longer. Will that work for you?"

"Yes. I want to take you over to my house. I live in one of our best neighborhoods. We can leave here after we close on Saturday. Do we have a plan?"

It is Saturday morning, and I am excited to have the afternoon with Patricia. I will spend the day learning more about her private life and seeing her home. There is no one I would rather spend time with than Patricia.

At two o'clock sharp, we close the bakery, jump in Patricia's car, and head to the neighborhood due south of the main street.

"I will start by driving you through the oldest neighborhoods and then take you to my street."

"I would like that. I haven't seen much of the residential neighborhoods except those we pass on the way to Sharon's house in Cooper. Eventually, Tom and I will want our own house; however, I can say that our current living quarters are perfect. The one thing missing is that Tom and I have nowhere to sit outside and relax. I would like to have my own backyard again someday."

We drive up and down several streets with older homes; most are small and neatly kept. I miss the grassy front yards, tall trees, and branches overhanging the road, creating a canopy of greenery.

"Look. That house is for sale; it sure is cute."

"You do not want that one."

"Why not? It looks well kept."

"It has bad juju, you know, bad spirit. The woman who lives in that house is not very nice. She is why Martinsville doesn't have a newspaper."

"What are you talking about?"

"Our town is too small to have a newspaper, it's true, but some folks say we don't need one. Somehow, Lila, who owns that house, knows everybody's business and spreads it around town. She should wear a white top painted with a big red letter, 'B.'"

"You mean like Hester Prynne with the letter "A" on her chest? Hawthorne. What would the "B" stand for?"

"B stands for blabbermouth."

"That is too funny. But the house is for sale, so she is moving somewhere, I guess."

"Yes, and no one knows where. No one has seen Lila in over a month, not even at the grocery store. I try to avoid listening to talk on the street, but sometimes, that is where you get the best information. Here is what I have heard. After a big blow-up with Mayor Bigby, she lost her job at the courthouse.

"A friend of mine was recently in the courthouse and walked past her office; it was empty, cleared out, and her nameplate was no longer on the door. No one knows any of the details about what happened."

"Wait a minute. Lila worked at the courthouse?"

"Yes. You met Lila, didn't you? When you had your meetings with Mayor Bigby."

Now, it was all starting to come together. "Patricia, pull over. I have a story to tell you, and I think you will get a kick out of what I have to say."

Patricia slows the car and parks in a shady spot along the curb. I remind her of the day she came to see me in the bakery. I told her that after she left, I went outside to sweep the sidewalk, and an older man in a truck slowed down and shouted at me. He knew we were the new tenants of the bakery, and somehow, he knew we had signed the papers and would open the bakery soon.

I told her how furious I was, how I marched over to Bigby's office, told him a leak was coming from somewhere in his office, and that I did not appreciate my business being blabbed all over town. I tell Patricia how Mayor Bigby became livid, slammed his fist on the desk several times, screamed at the top of his lungs for Henderson, and fired her.

"Wow, wow, so that is what happened; incredible. Bigby should have fired Lila a long time ago. Had Bigby known what she has blabbed all over town, he would have fired her sooner."

"Frankly, I am not sure he didn't know. He did say he knew Miss Henderson was snooping around his desk, going through his files, but I cannot imagine he didn't know about her tendency to peddle people's business affairs. Anyway, I guess it was the last straw. He was screaming her last name, Henderson, over and over. I never knew her first name."

"That is one heck of a story, Miss Ella."

"Patricia, please do not tell anyone. I do not want it to spread all over town. Some folks may not like that I was what caused the mayor to fire her, and I prefer to be known as the nicest person in town. Get it?"

"Of course, I will never tell a soul, but that is one story I won't soon forget."

Patricia starts the engine, pulls away from the curb, drives a couple of blocks, and then turns onto a street lined with beautiful tall trees. The homes are mostly two stories with wrap-around front porches. White tall-back rocking chairs, gently moving in the afternoon breeze, complete the look. The lush green lawns are perfectly mowed and edged with neatly clipped hedges set off by beds of blooming begonias.

"Patricia, this is so beautiful. Is your house on this street?"

"Yes. I am privileged to live here. My house is one of the smaller ones but has lots of charm." Patricia drives into the driveway and stops the car a few feet beyond the sidewalk. "Hurry; I need to hit the bathroom." She dashes around the car and runs up the steps and into the front door. Hmm, so this is one of those neighborhoods where no one locks their doors.

I follow behind Patricia and hear her holler, "Make yourself at home. I will be right out."

I step in the doorway, and I am in awe. In front of me is a regal curved staircase with white balusters and a shiny black handrail. The bottom few steps widen as they descend, forming a curve as they meet the foyer floor. I look to my left and see a tall, wide archway leading into a formal living room. I enter.

The room is welcoming and emits the spirit of someone who cherishes their belongings and delights in being here at home. I take in the beauty of the room, tastefully decorated, eyeing the deep blue velvet wingback chairs by the bay window, the matching ottoman, the heavy gold damask draperies, and the cream-colored camelback sofa. A sizeable Asian rug, in colors of bright blue, deep red, and light beige, anchors the furniture to the old cherry wood floor.

I walk over to the fireplace and am captivated by a row of framed family photos that stretch the length of the traditional mantle. One of them, in particular, catches my eye; a picture of a woman, smiling, in her mid-50s, perhaps. Her dark, curly hair frames her face perfectly. Her facial expression suggests the photographer has caught her by surprise.

Patricia walks up behind me; "She is lovely, isn't she?"

"Yes, very much so. Is this your mother?"

"No, that's not my mother, but she treated me like a daughter. I love her dearly."

"Who is she?"

"That's Marion, you know, Marion Devlin."

I almost drop the photo. "This is Mrs. Devlin? The bakery Devlin? And this house?"

"Yes, this was the Devlin house. Sometimes it feels like it still is. Better take a seat, Ella. You look a bit pale."

We sit in the wingback chairs by the bay window, and Patricia tells me the whole story.

"Marion's husband died about ten years ago, and my husband died almost a year later. Losing her husband was a massive blow to Marion. She couldn't get out of bed and open the bakery the next day, so one of her daughters called and asked if I could go in and work with the other two employees. I said yes, of course. I worked throughout the funeral services and her grieving period and never left.

"As time passed, the three of us did all the work, and Marion took on more of a figurehead role at the bakery. The entire town adored her and often came in to see Marion. The sad part is that she knew her daughters would never want to run the bakery. It was too much work, for heaven's sake. Both daughters now live in Reedsburg, Wisconsin, and have husbands and children. In the end, neither daughter wanted the house nor the furnishings.

"Jake and I lived in a smaller house several blocks from here. After he died, I intended to stay there. It meant something to me to remain where we had lived our lives together. But then, one day, Marion invited me to come by on a Sunday afternoon.

"With tears in her eyes, she wanted to know if I would like to buy the house from her. She knew how much I adored this house. I knew of no other answer than a resounding YES. I was thrilled, to say the least."

"Marion's daughters didn't have a problem with you purchasing the house from her?"

"Not at all."

We sit in silence for a few minutes. Hearing this remarkable story of how life's transitions worked out for Mrs. Devlin and Patricia makes my heart feel good.

"Would you like to see the rest of the house?"

"Of course, lead the way."

I follow Patricia across the foyer floor and along a wide hallway, where she leads me into the dining room through its tall paneled mahogany double pocket doors. A formal mahogany dining table surrounded by ten tall-back chairs stretches down the middle of the room, adorned with a large round crystal chandelier. The walls are papered in a deep gold damask pattern. A long buffet, topped with a gold-framed mirror and several pairs of candlesticks, anchors the room's far end.

We leave the dining room and continue along the hall, where we enter the kitchen. Tall white cabinets line the high kitchen walls, many with clear beveled glass panels, and all have crystal knobs. A large island stands in the middle of the kitchen with stools along one side. I walk around the room, admiring it all, then stop at the kitchen sink and lean forward to glance out the window. Patricia's backyard is as lush as her front yard. And then I notice something.

"Patricia, do you know that a gray-haired woman is sitting in your backyard?"

Patricia leans over my shoulder and peers out the window. "Why yes, that's Delia. I suppose now you would like to know who Delia is?"

"Of course, and let me guess, this will be another captivating story?"

"Yes, it will be."

We laugh and simultaneously say, "We had better sit." I sit at the island while Patricia fills the kettle with water to brew hot tea.

"Delia, the lady in my backyard, was in Marion's employ for nearly thirty years. Originally hired as Marion's personal assistant, they soon became close friends, making the word "companion" a better title for their relationship. No one referred to her as a housemaid or an assistant. Marion always introduced or referred to Delia as her companion.

"Marion didn't like the idea of Delia being responsible for any of the household tasks. She knew it was too much of a burden and wanted Delia to be her companion, so she hired a separate person as the housekeeper. Delia cooked all her meals, managed her medications, handled her correspondence, and made sure her clothes were clean.

"When Marion finally came to the difficult decision to close the bakery, her daughters insisted she move to Wisconsin and live with one of them. Marion desperately wanted Delia to come with her and live in her daughter's home, but Delia knew Marion's daughters would see her as an outsider and likely treat her like one. It was the breakup of a long and deep friendship."

"What happened next?"

"Both Marion and Delia were so sad. Marion deeply cared for Delia and knew Delia cared deeply for her. After I told Marion I wanted to purchase her home, the ball started rolling, and her daughters came to collect her. I had already talked privately with Delia about living with me in this house. Where else should she live? I couldn't see her renting a room at the back of some drab boarding house. At first, she wasn't sure if she should, but then she realized that living with me was the perfect arrangement for her.

"It would take a few more weeks for the house transaction to close, so Delia came to live with me in my little house. Then we moved in together when I got the keys to this elegant home."

"Wow, that is a fascinating story. I don't want to sound condescending, but I am proud of you."

"Ella, it made sense and was the right thing to do. Why should Delia be thrown out of the house that had been her home for thirty years? We needed to be together. She is always sweet and sometimes funny, and she and I get along like sisters. I guess you could say I love her. Yes, I do."

Patricia's story moves me, and I have difficulty keeping my emotions in check.

"It is a wonderful story, isn't it?"

"Yes, the best, the very best."

"Would you like to meet her?"

Dabbing at my eyes with my handkerchief, then my nose, "Oh yes, I would."

We follow the stone path from Patricia's back door into the lush garden in her backyard to where Delia sits at a table, a large umbrella shading her from the late afternoon sunlight, a book in her hand.

I am startled by her beautiful, thick white hair, crystal blue eyes, and tanned complexion. She is wearing a blue and white print chemise with a white lace shawl draped loosely across her shoulders. She smiles up at me, waiting for an introduction.

"Delia, I would like you to meet Ella Watson. She is the new proprietor of the Devlin Bakery." Delia puts down her book and extends her hand toward me, and I lean forward to take it in mine.

"Nice to meet you, Miss Ella. I suppose Patricia has told my story to you?"

I glance at Patricia, then back to Delia. "Why yes, she has, and an intriguing story it is. It is a pleasure to meet you."

"I hope you make good biscuits."

I am captivated by the lilt in Delia's voice. "I have been told they are good. People buy a lot of them."

"Then you will be a roaring success."

We sit in the garden with Delia as the sunlight begins to fade. We keep the conversation light and are comfortable with the occasional long pause. The air has already started to cool, and the sky is turning shades of orange and red. So much history is here, such respect and kindness for other people. I am relaxed and at peace. I don't want to return to the apartment, but it is getting late, and I probably should go.

"I don't know about the two of you, but I am getting hungry. I will see what I can find in the kitchen to make a light dinner for us. I will be right back."

Patricia leaves me sitting in the garden with Delia. I am unsure how to continue the conversation, so we sit in comfortable silence for several minutes. Finally, Delia speaks.

"Would you like to know where I come from?"

"Yes, Delia, I would."

"My family comes from Jamaica. My mother, father, and I left the country at the height of a government rebellion. My father worked for the government. It was challenging to work with the regime, as he disagreed with their policies. Of course, he had to be quiet about his opinion of the government to keep us all safe. The authorities were a bad bunch, harsh and cruel to anyone who disagreed with their ideology. Folks were in danger of being arrested if they didn't obey the oppressive rules.

"We were some of the lucky ones to leave the country. The opposition came to our house in the middle of the night and told us there was room on a ship that would take us to America. We left with the clothes on our backs. It was a hard trip with little to eat, but we were grateful for the passage."

Delia pauses and stares into the distance, remembering the escape in the middle of the night, the fear of being caught, and the possibility of being executed. I reach for her hand; my touch brings her back to the present. Her countenance changes, and she changes the subject. She now has a smile on her face.

"I don't sound Jamaican, do I?"

"No, you don't, Delia. Your accent could be from almost anywhere in the South."

"When we came to this country, I was ten years old. We settled in the South, and a church helped by giving us a small house. That's where I picked up my accent, from the local population, and received my education in their schools. Members of the church found jobs for my father and mother; those kind people gave us our start.

"Later in my teen years, I headed north and worked for one family after another for many years until I saw an ad in a newspaper about a woman who needed help with her home and daily care. After years of working for families with small children, which is backbreaking work, I believed I would like to work for an adult woman very much.

"The next day, I sent a letter telling them as much about myself as I could think to write. Several weeks later, I received a reply with a money order to pay for my transportation. And that is how I came to be in Martinsville."

"What was it like when you first arrived? You hadn't met Mrs. Devlin or knew anything about her. What if it wasn't what you wanted?"

"I can see how that could have been an awkward situation, but I had many years of experience and knew if it didn't work out, I could secure a position almost anywhere I went; however, I immediately liked Miss Marion. I guess you could say we clicked. I saw a certain look in her eyes and knew I had found my new home."

"I see you two are having a nice chat. Come in the house. I have put together some dinner for us, a few leftovers, and made toasted cheese sandwiches. I hope that will satisfy both of you."

I offer to help Delia out of her chair by extending my hand, which she accepts. Then, to my surprise and delight, she links her arm tight to mine as we walk along the path back to the house. We eat our dinner, and then Patricia drives me home.

I spend the next day, Sunday, by myself. I decide it is time to find things to do, so I rearrange the clothing in the bureau drawers and organize the clothes hanging in the closet. I change the bed linens and take them to the Wong laundry across the street.

Next, I go into the hardware store to look around, poke around, and waste time. Beyond the door on the floor is a box of old books someone dropped off. Had I not looked down, I would have tripped over the box. Come to think of it, I haven't seen a library in Martinsville. I wonder if one exists. Mr. Cummings looks up and notices me eying the box.

"Help yourself, Ella, to whatever you want. There are a few classics in the bunch."

"Thank you, Mr. Cummings."

Selecting five books, I head back to the apartment and spend the rest of the afternoon comfortably seated by the bay window, reading until the light is so dim that I no longer can. I am relaxed and content. I know Monday is always a busy day at the bakery. I can't wait to see Patricia again, my new best friend.

It is early morning, and the streets are dark. The sky is cloudy. There's a light breeze in the air. I see the lights are on as I approach the bakery; Patricia has already arrived. She and Delia go to bed early; therefore, Patricia wakes up early. Not one to lie around, she prefers to get a head start on the day and often will arrive ahead of me. We always have lots of preparation to do first thing in the morning, so whenever we can begin our routine a little earlier, it makes our work more manageable.

"Thank you for a wonderful Saturday afternoon and for sharing the stories about Marion and Delia with me."

I stand over my tray of biscuits, staring into space, recalling my conversation with Delia and her story of how she came to America and then to Martinsville.

"Delia intrigues me. She has that beautiful smooth skin, the color of coffee with too much cream. Her eyes are like crystals, a blue-gray color. And oh, that head of hair, thick snow-white hair, so beautiful. She told me how her family fled their country at the height of a rebellion in Jamaica."

"There will be another rebellion here in Martinsville if you don't get those biscuits into the oven soon."

Her comment makes me laugh. "Yeah, you are right." I set aside my reverie and get back to the task at hand.

At six o'clock sharp, we are ready for the farmhands to come and get their fresh, warm biscuits. Soon after the last farmhand has left, we see someone's backside pushing the door open, backing into the bakery. I easily recognize it; it is Mayor Bigby's. He finally squeezes past the door jamb, and I see he is struggling with a bushel basket overflowing with apples. He plunks the basket onto the floor.

"Good morning, Ella, Patricia. Look what I have here for you."

"How nice of you, Mayor. Hmm, that is a whole lot of apples."

"Perhaps it's time to start baking pies. Might be good for the business." Bigby makes his point by flashing a toothy grin, his eyebrows bobbing up and down.

"That number of apples would make dozens of pies, but we could make a few."

"Good, good, and if you have time, you might want to bake some extra and sell them to Daniel to offer to his diners. Nice hot apple pie for dessert, yum, doesn't that sound tasty?"

With arms folded across my chest, tapping my foot, I face Bigby.

"Let me guess; you already spoke with Daniel about us baking pies for him?"

"Well, yes, I suppose I did. You see, you two ladies are terrific bakers, and his kitchen crew isn't the quality of bakers you are, to be honest. Selling pies and biscuits to Daniel would be a nice way to make extra money for the bakery. I hope you don't mind my stepping in for you, Miss Ella."

"And you can have hot apple pie for your dessert, right?"

"It does sound mighty good. So why don't you drop in on Daniel after you close up and see what you can work out with him?"

"Mayor Bigby, you are always looking out for me." I give him a pat on the back, which is long overdue. He has done so much for Tom and me.

"Good day, ladies. Have fun baking."

Patricia and I look at the apples, trying to figure out how many are in the basket.

"How fast can we peel apples and make pies?"

"Let's see. We can start by making pastry dough in the small mixers. We can refrigerate the dough and start peeling the apples when we have a break from customers. I will call Sharon and see if she is available to come and help us."

"I have an idea. Why don't we take the apples, sugar, spices, and pans to my house and sit around the big island? We can take the big stainless bowls and blend the ingredients."

"That's a much better idea. We will be much more comfortable peeling apples in your kitchen than in this kitchen. When do you want to start?"

"Tomorrow is as good as any day. Call Sharon and ask if she can meet us at my house after we close. But first, let's find out how many pies Daniel would like us to bake."

Daniel ordered ten pies. I told him we would deliver them in two batches, five on Friday and the rest on Saturday afternoon.

Peeling apples with Sharon and Patricia around the large island with a breeze blowing in the open windows makes all our efforts feel less like work. And with Delia keeping us supplied with hot tea and sandwiches and some great conversation, we have bowls of apples ready to fill pie crusts in no time.

The townspeople relish the aroma of freshly baked goods in the early morning. Waking to the smell of apple, cinnamon, and nutmeg must drive folks in town crazy and the cows in nearby pastures, too.

Five pies are ready for the bakery and will go into the display cases on Wednesday. I must admit apple pie will be a delicious addition to our usual offerings, and in no time, people come in and buy an apple pie; although not all of our patrons want a whole pie, so we will cut slices the size they want for those who want a smaller portion.

We mix the dough for the pies we promised Daniel on Thursday morning. Friday morning, while I tend to the farmhands, Patricia rolls out the dough, fills the pie shells with apples, and bakes them in the oven. Saturday, we bake two pies with streusel topping and three with double crusts and deliver them to the bar after closing.

No doubt, a lot of finger-licking and lip-smacking will be going on throughout Martinsville for at least the next few days.

Bits of morning light creep into our room from around the edge of the curtain and the window frame, waking me. Sunday is a day of rest for most folks, although many will head to an early church service. I'm crossing my fingers; I hope God will forgive my weakness for staying in bed.

I expect Tom to return to Martinsville sometime today. I don't know when he will arrive, but I am not leaving this bed. I remain snuggled under the covers. I occasionally turn over, tuck the blanket around my shoulders, and squish my big fluffy pillow under my neck. Twenty minutes later, the telephone on the nightstand rings, and I answer it. It is Mabel from the kitchen downstairs.

"Oh, good morning, Mable. No, I wasn't sleeping. That's not a problem. I would like that, yes, regular. Uh, hmm. Lots of cream, please. No, that sounds great. Yes, yes, thank you so much."

I lie back on my pillow, perfectly still, and wait for the sound of the elevator coming up the shaft. A light rap on the door signals the arrival of Mabel's tray. I slip out of my cocoon and retrieve it from the table in the hall outside my door.

Arranged on the tray is a big pot of coffee, a pitcher of cream, two slices of coffee cake, and an orange. Propped up in bed, eating coffee cake and an orange feels like paradise. And nothing beats a cup of hot coffee with lots of fresh cream, and Mabel knows how to brew it perfectly.

I finish my breakfast, and now I need to decide whether to get up or not to get up. I choose not to get up. I fall into a deep sleep, and two hours later, someone interrupts my sleep by shaking my shoulder.

"Wake up, sleepyhead; your husband is back. What's been going on while I was away? Anything interesting?"

Where does one begin to answer those questions? How much time do you have, pal? I don't know where to start, and I don't want to talk. Talk can wait, Tom can wait, the whole world outside this bedroom can wait; however, I manage to greet my husband with a slight smile.

"Hi, honey. It's nice to have you back. But please, I need my rest." Tom gets my drift. There will be no conversation while I am in this bed.

Hours later, I finally get out of bed, shower, dress, fix my hair, and go downstairs to the dining room to find it almost empty except for Tom, Mayor Bigby, and Judge Garfield seated at a table at the far end. I don't want to talk to anyone, but it is too late; they wave at me to sit with them.

"Darling, nice to see you. Did you get enough sleep? You look refreshed."

Tom never calls me darling. Tom never uses the word, refreshed. Who are you? I'm cranky, but I don't want my irritation to show. A simple smile of acknowledgment will have to do.

I sit at the table with the men and listen to ol' Bigby blowing a lot of wind, filling the air with all the details he can recall about this week's events, including the bushel basket of apples and the pies we made. The judge, the mayor, and Tom's conversation, their voices pass through my head, in one ear and out the other.

I sit here wrapped in silence and bathe in the memories of this past week. No amount of chatter can intrude on my thoughts as I reflect on my experiences with the world's most caring and loving people. Those experiences are mine, and I cherish them. My life with these caring and giving people is joyful. I am one lucky woman.

CHAPTER IV

The Mystery Begins

Back from the farm, Tom reports that the Naperville area has had plenty of rain. The wheat and corn fields are green and lush, the buildings are in good shape, and the kids are healthy. The horses, cows, and chickens expressed their delight at the sight of Tom by neighing, mooing, and loudly clucking as they ran around the yard.

Now that Tom is back, he can participate by helping with duties around the bakery. I have put him in charge of organizing our deliveries, which consist of sacks of flour and sugar, dozens of eggs, buckets of butter, large tins of cocoa, and other essential ingredients. He can do the heavy lifting, fill the flour and sugar bins, and put the rest of the goods in their proper places while we bake.

Tom will have plenty of time to find other pursuits if he wants them. As talented as Tom is with people and animals, plus his knowledge of machinery, he should have no problem finding something to occupy his time in Martinsville.

Jim Nelson continues to mop the floors for us daily. Tom is plenty thankful that duty didn't fall to him. Jim arrives moments before closing time and locks the door when finished. We pay him for his service, plus prepare a basket of baked goods for him to take home. He is happier than a lark with this arrangement.

Patricia and I arrive early and bake our usual offerings, bread, biscuits, muffins, and several layer cakes. I take the tray of biscuits into the store and place it on the end of the counter, along with the bowl for the dimes and the stack of four-inch Kraft paper squares.

I return to the kitchen, whip a bowl of soft butter, and notice it is time to open the doors one minute before six o'clock. With the bowl still tucked in my arm, I walk into the store, set the bowl on the counter, take the key from my apron pocket, and unlock the door.

"Good morning, gentlemen."

"Morning, Miss Ella." "Good morning, Miss Ella."

The men line up, and the morning ritual begins. The sound of boots shuffling on the old wood floor, the men repeating their request for a biscuit, the plop sound it makes as it lands on the Kraft paper square, the ting sound their dime makes as it drops into the steel bowl. The sounds produce a rhythm. You could rock a baby to sleep by it.

Then the rhythm abruptly stops, and I look up to see the shortest farmhand, Adam, smiling at me; he has the whitest teeth I have ever seen. His hair is always neatly combed, and his face is tan. A twinkle in his blue eyes leaves me with no doubt he must have been a real test of a teacher's patience, like you never know what he will do next.

"Yes, Adam?"

Flashing that pearly white smile at me, he nods toward the bowl of butter. "Miss Ella, may I have a dab of that butter on my biscuit?"

"Of course you can, Adam." I pick up the spatula knife, scoop a bit of butter, and smear it on top of his biscuit.

"Thank you, Miss Ella; you are the kindest woman I know."

"You are welcome, Adam."

That starts other farmhands requesting a dab of butter, but not all do. Nevertheless, I will be whipping some soft butter and offering it with our biscuits. As the last farmhand leaves the bakery, I stand at the window, peering out. I watch them walk away and head out to work on the farms. Patricia comes up behind me and rests her chin on my shoulder. I can feel her breath on my neck.

"They are an odd group, aren't they, Patricia?"

"Odd? Gee, I guess you could call them odd."

"Yes, odd, like, who are they? Do you know anything about any of them?"

"One or two of them. We know Adam's name, but I know nothing more about him. He is a curious little guy; what do you bet he gave his mother a run for her money?" We both snicker at the idea of him being a test of his mother's patience.

"What about the one man with his shoulders sorta' stooped? He edges slowly to the counter, keeps his head down, and murmurs "Thank you" under his breath. I don't know if he is shy or doesn't want anyone to notice him. It is as if he is hiding under the brim of his hat from something."

"You do have an imagination, don't you?"

"I guess I do, but I find them to be a curious lot. Don't get me wrong. I like all of them, but they all look like they need a little bit of kindness to come their way.

"Patricia, who is the tall, thin one? His clothes always look clean and fresh, and he wears that expensive-looking cowboy hat. He has an air about him as if he thinks he is better than the other men. Do you agree?"

"Yes, I agree. The man's name is William Jennings, but he tells people to call him Duke. I have heard him say, 'Duke, just call me Duke.'"

"That is weird. I wonder why? I assume that someday we will find out. Then again, maybe we will never know."

At that moment, Mrs. Parsons and Miss McClure enter the bakery; it is time to get busy.

Ever since Mayor Bigby brought us the bushel basket of apples, we have occasionally found a basket at the bakery door filled with fruit or vegetables when we arrive. We have no idea who leaves them, but we are always appreciative when we discover a present waiting for us at the bakery door. A bushel of fruit, such as apricots, peaches, or sometimes cherries, tells us we will be baking pies or turnovers to offer our customers.

Then, one day, it dawns on us that this fruit could benefit the farmhands. Once we have finished baking, we place the bushel basket near the door and tell them to help themselves. Their faces look as if we have given them a gift.

One morning late in July, we find an unusual basket waiting for us at the door; a bushel of sweet corn. Somewhat surprised, Patricia and I stare at it like we have never seen sweet corn. We can't help but laugh.

"My goodness, what will we do with a bushel basket of sweet corn?"

"I have no idea, but I think we can figure it out."

Patricia and I haul it into the store, then into the kitchen. We stand staring at the green-sheathed ears of corn, waiting for a bright idea to strike one of us.

"Hmm, a bushel of sweet corn. How about cornbread or corn muffins?

"Or corn pudding."

"Corn pudding? I don't know what that is, much less how to make corn pudding."

"I know someone who does."

"Who?"

"Delia."

Once again, thoughts of Delia cause me to stare off into space.

"Sweet Delia. Looking at her face, I see a mystery below the surface. I can't put my finger on it, but something about her fascinates me." My thoughts trail off, waiting for a reaction from Patricia, but she ignores that I am mesmerized by my mental images of Delia and redirects my attention to the task at hand.

"Ella, we need to get this corn to my house and start cooking. Can you come today after we close? Tom won't mind you being late?"

"Not at all. I will let Tom know I won't be home for dinner. Tom is getting to know more of the local guys, and occasionally, he likes to eat in the dining room with a few of them. It is good for him to socialize as he hasn't had many guy friends. Most of his friends have been the farm animals."

We arrive at Patricia's house with our basket of corn and several large pots and pans for cooking. Delia greets me with a big hug and kisses on my cheeks.

"Lordy, what in the world do we have here, a bushel of sweet corn? What are you planning on doing with dat?"

"Cook it, then make cornbread, muffins, and corn pudding. Patricia says you know how to make good corn pudding."

"You bet I do. Oh, I haven't had corn pudding in ages. It's one of my favorites. Let's get shuckin'."

We haul the bushel into the yard and entertain ourselves with small talk and laughter about our younger years while we shuck the leaves and pull the silks off the corn. We have a big pot of water coming to a boil on the stove. We can get about six or seven ears of corn in at a time, boil them for seven minutes, and then put in another batch.

Once all ears are cooked and cool enough to handle, we slice the kernels off the cobs, give them a good scrape to squeeze out the corn milk, and divide them into even batches. We aren't sure how much corn we will need for the cornbread or muffins, but Delia is looking forward to whipping up her recipe for corn pudding, so we begin by preparing that dish.

Cornmeal, flour, sugar, salt, and paprika come from the pantry, and milk, butter, cream, and eggs come from the refrigerator. A pile of corn goes back into a pot on the stove with the milk and cream. We cook, stir, and mush it, then add a handful of whole kernels. We whip in the eggs, add the dry ingredients, stir it all together, and pour the mixture into a large casserole dish.

While the pudding is baking, Delia and Patricia search the refrigerator for what food they can find to fix an impromptu dinner.

Meanwhile, the smell of that corn pudding baking in the oven is intoxicating. I cannot wait to take a bite. We will eat some of it now and leave the rest here for Delia and Patricia. Tomorrow, we will mix several batches of cornbread according to a recipe from Delia and bake it in shallow metal trays. When the cornbread has cooled, we will cut it into squares and arrange it in the display cases. The three of us working together this afternoon was such fun. I almost wish another bushel of sweet corn would appear at the bakery door.

The first thing I do when we open our doors at six o'clock in the morning is hand out biscuits to the farmhands while Patricia bakes in the kitchen. They are our earliest customers, and I enjoy giving them my undivided attention and sharing light banter with them. But today, a young woman walks in, right behind them, carrying a large flat basket on her arm. She inches her way toward me. I think it best that I acknowledge her presence.

"Thank you for coming in, Miss; I will be right with you." Ignoring my comment, she moves closer to the counter and interrupts my conversation with the farmhands.

"I would like to buy some of your biscuits."

"I will be with you as soon as I finish serving these gentlemen,"

Still, she moves closer, shifting from one foot to the other, seemingly oblivious that I am helping my farmhands. Apparently, she is in a hurry.

"Patricia, will you come out here, please? Would you finish serving the men? Excuse me, gentlemen."

I come around the counter, "Now, what can I do for you?" I am a bit annoyed with her already. She can see I am busy with my customers. Can't you wait your turn? For goodness' sake, woman.

"I would like to purchase some of your biscuits. I hear they are delicious. Can I get about three dozen?"

"Patricia, do we have three dozen biscuits in the back for this woman?"

"Yes, but not all of them are cool."

"I will take them anyway. I am in a bit of a hurry. You can stack the biscuits in this basket, please."

I take the basket from her, lined with several tea towels, and head toward the kitchen. I arrange the biscuits so the edges don't touch, stacking them so they can continue to cool and not get mushy.

"Here you are, miss. That will be $5.50." She hands me a ten-dollar bill, says thank you, tells me to keep the change, and then flies out the door.

After all the farmhands have gone on their way, Patricia and I turn and stare at each other.

"Who was that young woman? Have you ever seen her before?"

"No, I don't recognize her; however, I couldn't help but notice that you charged her more money, and she said to keep the change."

"I figured she could pay more for being in a hurry and acting as if she should be waited on ahead of my farmhands. I don't like that. You wait your turn. It looks like we need to put up another batch or two of biscuits. We are wiped out."

Halfway through serving our farmhands the next morning, the woman returns carrying her flat basket; this time, she waits her turn with a smile on her face.

"Good morning. I want to purchase another three dozen of your biscuits, please, if you have them ready. May I purchase a small container of butter, too?"

"Certainly, but all I have is a stainless-steel bowl. I will need the bowl back. So please be sure to return it next time you stop by."

"Yes ma'am, I will."

I tell her what she owes me, and this time, she hands me a ten-dollar bill and a five-dollar bill. "Thank you, ma'am. Keep the change."

I think, with pleasure, come back any time. I gaze out the window and watch the woman walk away.

"Patricia, are you sure you have never seen her before?"

"No, no, I'm positive I haven't. And what could she be doing with all of those biscuits?"

"Your guess is as good as mine; I haven't the slightest idea."

"Well, she can't possibly eat all of them herself."

We both laugh at the thought of this young woman stuffing three dozen biscuits down her throat in one sitting.

This unexpected purchase of dozens of biscuits to a single customer, two days in a row, has created a challenge. Our claim to fame is that we sell fresh-daily baked goods; that is what our customers expect. Every day, we prepare for what we think will be our customers' wants and needs and aim to have the right amount and variety of fresh baked goods to sell daily, with no leftovers that could become stale overnight.

I am busy counting pastries in the display case this morning when the doorbells chime. I look toward the door and see the same woman coming in for the third day in a row. She has my bowl with her. She has a smile on her face; she's cheery.

"Good morning. Please, I want to purchase another three dozen biscuits and a tub of butter if you can spare some."

This is getting to be an intriguing occurrence. Not knowing who this young woman is and what she is doing with all these biscuits is like waiting for the punch line to a joke; however, today, she has arrived a bit later. The farmhands have come and gone so I can pay closer attention to her. I am mighty curious about who she is and to whom she feeds all those dozens of biscuits.

"Patricia, will you fill this woman's basket, please, another three dozen biscuits and fill this tub with butter."

Now, I can keep an eye on her. I watch as she walks back and forth in front of the display cases, eyeing all our baked goods.

"What kind of pie is that one in the back?"

"Apple, apple pie, baked with nutmeg and cinnamon."

"And those muffins?"

"Blueberry, fresh-made this morning."

"Your baked goods look so delicious. Are you the owner of this bakery?"

"Yes, I am. I'm Ella Watson. We bake all the items you see in the cases fresh each morning. Our townsfolk love eating our baked goods."

"I want to purchase the pie and a dozen blueberry muffins."

"Certainly."

"How much will that be?"

I add it up on my pad of paper; $5.50 for biscuits, $5.00 for pie, $4.50 for muffins, and $2.00 for butter. "That comes to $17.00."

I box up her order, tie the boxes with twine, and place them in her arms. She hands me a twenty-dollar bill and a five-dollar bill and says to keep the change. I want to engage her in conversation and see if I can figure out who she is, but she is out the door and headed down the street in a flash. I see her get into the passenger side of a newer model truck. It is rare to see a newer model truck around town driven by a man I do not recognize, which adds to my curiosity. They make a U-turn and speed off down the street.

Patricia and I are pressed back in the window, heads together, wondering who she is and who the man is driving the truck.

Patricia whispers, "I forgot to give her the butter."

"You didn't."

"I did."

"Well, she is sure to be back."

The weekend is here, and the town will be busy with townsfolk shopping for food and necessities. Yesterday, we made blueberry muffins and chocolate chip cookies before closing. We have three pies left, so we slice them into good-sized pieces and place them on paper doilies in the display cases.

After serving biscuits to the farmhands, I glance out the window and see Mayor Bigby walking on the sidewalk. I step outside and wave a towel in the air.

"Mayor Bigby, Mayor Bigby." He sees me, tips his hat, and keeps on walking. And the mysterious young woman hasn't shown up yet, and to think we baked extra biscuits this morning. Back in the bakery, I tell Patricia that Bigby avoided me.

"He must be busy, Ella."

"Not on a Saturday. Plus, it is early. Where could he be going in a hurry? And nothing is more important to Bigby than a free cookie or a slice of pie. Something is going on around here. I know it; I can feel it in my bones."

This evening, while Tom and I eat dinner in the dining room, I tell him about the young woman buying a large number of our baked goods three days in a row and that she gets into a newer model truck driven by a man neither Patricia nor I recognize.

"She must be buying for a crowd of people. Three days in a row, three dozen biscuits, a dozen muffins, and an apple pie; that's a lot of baked goods."

"Why not check in with Bigby? He must know what's going on around here. After all, this is his town."

"That is another curious thing. I saw Mayor Bigby across from the bakery early this morning. I ran outside, called his name, and waved at him. He tipped his hat and then kept on walking. Something is happening around this town, and I aim to figure out what."

Tom looks at me with a straight face. "Good luck." With that, Tom rises and leaves the table.

I think, how odd. Tom knows something.

Dear Mayor Bigby,

I haven't heard from you lately, are you alright? Are you ill? It worries me when I haven't received a letter from you in weeks. So please let me know the latest goings-on in town and how the bakery is doing.

Mrs. Devlin

As I walk to the bakery this morning, images of this young woman keep popping into my mind. It is a mystery who this woman is who purchases large quantities of pastries. And what is she doing with all those baked goods? I wonder who she could be. I put the key in the lock, enter the bakery, flick on the lights, walk into the kitchen, and light the ovens. When Patricia arrives, I cannot help but express my curiosity.

"I wonder if we will see that woman today since she didn't come by on Saturday."

"Are you still thinking about her?"

"Of course I am. The woman is new in town. Her clothes and hairstyle tell you that she is from somewhere else. She buys dozens of baked goods, doesn't care about the price, hands over more than enough money, tells me to keep the change, and flies the coop. Then, she takes off in a newer model truck with a mysterious driver. On top of that, I wave to Bigby, who ignores me, then I tell Tom the whole story last night at dinner, and wait, come to think of it, something was strange about his response."

"What did he say?"

"I told him I would get to the bottom of this, and he said, 'Good luck.' Then he left me at the table."

"Oh, that is strange for sure, oohhh." Patricia waves her hands in the air, "Spooky." Then, mocking me, "He left me at the table."

"Patricia, it was weird, I tell you. Tom had a funny look on his face. But enough of that; look at the time; we must get ready for our farmhands."

At that moment, the telephone rings.

"Devlin Bakery… yes, this is she. Yes, I can take an order. Let me grab a pencil. Yes, I'm ready. Go ahead, please. Three dozen buttermilk biscuits, three dozen muffins, what kind? Any kind." I put my hand over the receiver. "Psst, Patricia, it's her."

"Oh yes, I'm here. Sorry, that was muffins. Will there be anything else? Yes, we can do that; two dozen chocolate chip cookies and two apple pies; what else? Yes, I am so sorry. Patricia mentioned it after you left the other day. I will make sure you have plenty of butter. When do you want to pick them up? No, I am sorry I can't have this order by this afternoon; that is a lot of baking in addition to our regular fare. How about tomorrow? For sure, about noon; will that be ok? Good, but before you go, I need your name, please. Sarah? Sarah Jones. Certainly, Sarah, we will be ready. Thank you, goodbye."

Patricia is standing beside me, listening to the entire conversation. I hang up the phone and flash the paper in front of her face. "You don't think this is strange, do you? Would you look at this list?"

"You are joshing me. That was the same woman on the telephone?" Patricia grabs the paper from my hand and skims the list of items. "Her name is Sarah Jones? Nice going, Mrs. Watson."

"That is NOT her name. I could tell by how she answered that she didn't expect me to ask her name. Like the gumshoe detective once said, 'Okay, schweet-heart, now why don't you tell me your real name?'"

"What? Who talks like that?"

"Humphrey Bogart in The Maltese Falcon. 1941. You never saw that movie?"

"Oh, yes. I love that movie. What was the woman's name, the one he fell for?"

"Brigid O'Shaughnessey, played by Mary Astor, I liked her paired with Humphrey Bogart. At the end of the movie, he sold her out, and she went to jail."

"Hey, look at the clock; we are two minutes past the hour."

I run into the store and see our farmhands lined up on the sidewalk. I put the key into the lock. It clicks over.

As the door swings open, I tell Patricia, "We will see Mayor Bigby this afternoon and make him tell us what is happening in this town."

"Ok, schweet-heart, if you say so." Patricia giggles.

"Patricia, hush, the farmhands will hear you."

After the farmhands leave, the bakery is bustling with no let-up in sight. Two hours into the rush, the door chimes ring again, and I see Tom walk in sporting a concerned look.

"Ella, may I have a word with you? Can you step outside for a moment, please?" I turn toward Patricia, shrug my shoulders, and follow Tom onto the sidewalk, leaving Patricia with a puzzled look on her face.

"What is going on, Tom?"

"I know you think something is happening around here, and you are right. So, here's what I know. This past Friday morning, I was headed to Mayor Bigby's office at the courthouse to show him the latest revenues and how the bakery is progressing financially.

"As I was walking down the hallway toward his office, I heard Mayor Bigby and Judge Garfield discussing something happening at the horse farm, the big one beyond Cooper. I heard him say he wanted it kept hush-hush. He said that he feared that if the people in Martinsville were to know about it, they would run out to the farm and cause a disturbance.

"I have no idea what that means, but that is what I heard him say. I didn't want them to know I overheard their conversation, so I backed out of the hallway as quickly and quietly as possible. I doubt they knew I was there. So, something is happening around here. I am not saying it is good or bad, but I wanted to tell you what I heard."

While Tom and I talk, several customers file past us and enter the bakery.

"Ah ha, I was right. Thanks for telling me. We're getting busy; I'd better get back in the bakery now. See you later." Tom kisses me on the cheek, squeezes my arm, and takes off down the street.

In between customers, I update Patricia.

"Patricia, we are not going over to the courthouse this afternoon. Tom overheard Mayor Bigby having a conversation with Judge Garfield. Something is going on, but it is best to wait a while before we question Bigby."

"Wait for what?"

"For Bigby to tell us himself. Meanwhile, we need to check if we have all the ingredients to fill Sarah's order for tomorrow. Noon, tomorrow at noon, is when we find out more. I hope."

We have been on our feet for hours; Patricia and I could use a break, so when the rush of morning customers finally slows, we sit at the little table for tea. I relate the story Tom told me earlier. Neither of us can guess what could be happening at the horse farm, but then we wonder if Sharon may know more. The horse farm is about ten miles southwest of Cooper, closer to Sharon's house than Martinsville. I ring her.

"Sharon? It is Ella. Fine, I am fine. Hey, I have a question for you. I'm glad you are fine, too. Sorry, I should have asked you. Listen, is something going on out at the big horse farm? The one beyond Cooper. Yes, the Lancaster Horse Farm, that's the one. I wasn't sure about the name, to be honest with you. You don't? Tom overheard Mayor Bigby talking with Judge Garfield. Yes, I know Cooper is a little drop in the bucket compared to Martinsville.

"Yes, we have had many new people coming into the bakery, but one woman has been dropping in and purchasing dozens of baked goods. Uh, hmm. It is strange. She hands over more money than I bill her, says to keep the change, and leaves. She ordered a long list of baked goods we need to have made by noon tomorrow. It's all a bit mysterious to me.

"Yes, I would like to have you here with us. I believe you can help figure out who this woman is. Okay, see you tomorrow. Wait. Sharon, come early. We might need an extra pair of hands. Patricia and I will be busy baking. Okay, bye." I hang up the phone and turn to Patricia.

"She is coming over in the morning."

Last week, we had a full complement of ingredients delivered; therefore, we have everything we need to bake our regular fare and the large order placed by Sarah Jones. Planning is the key to keeping our baked goods rolling from the kitchen into the display cases, which can be challenging; however, it is a rare occurrence when we run out of our most requested items. It is a game of balance; our baked goods must always be fresh. Patricia and I do a pretty good job making it happen.

This morning, Patricia and I arrive at the bakery to find a bushel basket of oranges waiting for us at the door. While oranges aren't grown in Illinois, the grocery store stocks them, but a whole bushel basket is another story. Patricia and I put our heads together and have several ideas for incorporating them into our baked goods. We will blend the grated rind and the juice into our muffin and scone recipes. Of course, we will set aside plenty of oranges to offer the farmhands.

In no time, we have ten loaves of bread rising on top of the warm ovens, and four trays of biscuits are baking in the tall oven. Next, we will bake the muffins and cookies for Sarah's order and then the pies.

I have a bill prepared for Sarah Jones; $5.50 for the biscuits, $5.00 for the two pies, $13.50 for three dozen muffins, $4.80 for the cookies, and $2.00 for butter, for a total of $30.80.

Sharon arrives as the last farmhands are in line for their biscuits. "Let me understand this. A woman is purchasing dozens of baked goods, and you two imagine something strange is happening around here?"

"It does sound rather dumb when you put it that way."

I then relate the conversation Tom overheard in the hall at the courthouse. Add that to my gut instinct that the woman lied about her name, and we have a real poser.

"I get it, I get it. I cannot wait to see this woman for myself."

"Remember, we need to remain calm and not let on that we are suspicious of who she is or what she is doing here in Martinsville."

Noon finally arrives, then five minutes after, ten minutes after, holy Toledo, I hope she doesn't stand us up, oh, here she comes; however, the bakery is teeming with customers, so Sarah will have to wait her turn.

"Good afternoon, Sarah." No response. "I will be with you in a minute, Sarah; make yourself comfortable." Still no response. She doesn't know I am talking to her.

Meanwhile, Patricia is busy packaging items for Mrs. Osborn, and Sharon and I are behind the counter, waiting on Mrs. Tisdale, Mrs. Hemming, and Mrs. Garfield. Finally, Mrs. Hemming leaves with her purchases. I come around the front of the counter, walk up behind Sarah, and repeat her name. Again, there was no response. Sarah is not her name.

"Excuse me, Miss; I have your baked goods ready." Now she realizes that I have been talking to her.

"Thank you, Ella. How much do I owe you?" I hand her the bill for $30.80. She fumbles in her purse and pulls out a fifty-dollar bill.

"By the way, I gave you double the amount of butter and charged you for half. I'll get your change."

"No, Ella, please keep the money. Thank you for making this order on short notice. May I call in orders over the telephone from now on?"

"Of course, and the earlier, the better. Suppose you have your favorite baked goods and want them daily. Let me know. That way, I can get them baked ahead of time, and you can pick them up as early as you like. I can also tell you if we have baked specialty goods that are not normally on our list of offerings."

"I appreciate that. I will check with the um, um." Sarah's voice trails off, "I will call you later today."

"We close at 2:00, so it will be best to let us know what you want by noontime. That way, we can be sure we have all the necessary ingredients. Thanks for coming today, Sarah." I swear I see the corners of her mouth curl up as she turns away.

Her driver comes through the door and helps carry the packages to the truck parked across the street. After the truck pulls away and heads down the road, we breathe a sigh. We know her name is not Sarah, but who is she, and why is she not using her real name? The three of us stand in the window, staring, not knowing what to think or say.

"Let's sit for a minute. Tell me, ladies, what are your thoughts about this young woman?"

"We don't know any more about her than we did last week."

"Yes, we do; we know her name is not Sarah."

"We need to find a way to trick her and find out what it is."

"I know she is more relaxed around you today, Ella, like she trusts you."

"Oh, nonsense. The woman does not trust me any more than the man on the moon. She likes our baked goods, that's all. And she is lonely. Don't look at me like I'm crazy. I can sense these things in people, but you are right; she did soften her approach with me today. And she knows that I know she gave a false name, and she appreciates that I didn't call her on it. And I won't."

"What do we do now?"

"We wait. All we can do is wait. And we bake. Let's make those orange muffins we talked about yesterday. Patricia, let's see what we can find in the kitchen. Sharon, you can stay out here and wait on the customers. If you need help, holler."

Patricia and I open all the cabinets and the refrigerator, looking for items we can use to bake something new and different.

"I found a bag of currants. They look dry but will plump again if we can soak them in water. And here are some raisins. Let's make scones with the currants, bake them in a deep pan, and then cut them diagonally. How about we add the raisins to our orange muffins? We can mix some confectioners' sugar with water and drizzle it on the muffins and the scones. Hmm, we haven't made chocolate muffins lately. Patricia, see how much cocoa powder we have in the bin."

"You are on a roll, sister. Nice to have Sharon here to handle the store so you and I can bake to our heart's desire."

"Sharon, prop open the front door. Let the aromas of our baking out into the street and spread across the town. And leave the sandwich board out on the walkway; don't bring it in at two o'clock."

I fetch a couple of the placard signs from the storage room and tell Sharon what to write on them, but first, I need to decide on a price for our baked goods.

"Write, Scones with Currants, ten cents, Chocolate Muffins, 5 cents, and Orange Muffins with Raisins, 5 cents. I have another idea. Let's make a small batch of bread dough, roll it into small balls, put three balls into each compartment of the muffin tins, and bake little cloverleaf rolls. We can mix honey with melted butter and brush it on their tops when they come out of the oven. Sharon, here is another placard. Write, Parker House Honey Rolls, 10 Cents.

"Do you mind if we bake past closing time, Patricia? You can take some of the baked goods home to Delia. Sharon, you can take some home with you, too."

Letting the enticing aromas from the ovens float out the door has paid off. Daniel comes across the street to ask what smells so delicious. He wants to buy all the Parker House Honey Rolls, but I need to keep a dozen or so for my morning customers.

The telephone rings a little before two o'clock, and it is Sarah. She starts by ordering three dozen biscuits but can't decide what else she wants.

"This afternoon, we got the itch to make some new baked goods, and you may want to include them in your order."

"Such as?"

"We baked scones with currents, orange muffins, and chocolate muffins. Sounds good, doesn't it?'

"It sure does. How many will you be giving me?

"First, I will need to see how many we have before I can tell you that, but I will set aside some for you and keep some to sell to my walk-in customers."

"Whatever you can give me will be fine, I am sure."

"Sarah, why not let me put together a nice package of various items when you place an order? I will include a few dozen biscuits and some muffins and then add the special items."

"I like that idea, Ella. It will be easier for both of us. I am sure that whatever you package, the whole crew, um, everyone, will be grateful to have."

"Come back tomorrow around ten o'clock, and I will have your packages ready for you."

"Thank you, Ella. I know having a nice variety is sure to please everyone."

The question of who the "everyone" people are remains unanswered.

It is almost four-thirty, and trays of freshly baked goods cover the worktable, rolling carts, countertops, and round tables.

"Sharon, please write this down; twenty scones, three dozen orange muffins, four dozen chocolate muffins, and three dozen Parker House Honey Rolls for Daniel. We have three dozen chocolate chip cookies, six apple turnovers, five dozen biscuits, and six loaves of bread. Holy Toledo. Let's give Sarah three dozen biscuits, two dozen chocolate muffins, ten scones, one dozen orange muffins, and one dozen chocolate chip cookies. What does that total, Sharon?"

"That comes to a total of $27.40."

"Hmm, add the apple turnovers to Sarah's package; there are only three. We can bake a dozen for the store when we get more apples. Charge 75 cents for each turnover. They are worth every penny."

"That comes to $31.90, plus you forgot the butter. I will add $2.00 for a tub of butter, OK? Now that comes to a total of $33.90."

"Very good. Please make a bill for all of this and put her name at the top."

"Okay, ladies, we are finished for the day. Let's package what is cooled and the items that aren't, leave them on the trays and cover them with the thin white cloths. Sharon, let me give you a big hug. Thank you for coming; you have been a tremendous help."

"You are welcome. I always look forward to seeing you and giving you a hand here at the bakery. I had fun. Keep me posted about Sarah or whatever her name is."

We aren't pressed for time this morning. The display case, filled with a variety of biscuits, muffins, and cookies, means we only need to bake loaves of bread and more of the Parker House Honey Rolls. All those round little heads peeking through the glass look so cute in the display cases.

Last night, when we closed, we put the bushel basket outside the door with a note addressed to the anonymous donor that we would appreciate having more oranges if possible. We have never done that before, but I figured it wouldn't hurt to try. I want to bake more orange muffins, as they are my favorite. I find the sweet yet tart flavor of oranges very appealing. It is the perfect foil for all the sugary sweetness you expect to find at any bakery.

As I approach the bakery this morning, I see that the mysterious gifter of oranges has fulfilled my request. The bushel basket is at our door, filled almost to overflowing with oranges, more for my farmhands and lots for the bakery. We busy ourselves in the kitchen; soon, the farmhands will be here.

"Good morning, gentlemen; so nice to see all of you. We have plenty of oranges today, so take a couple for yourselves. Did all of you enjoy them yesterday?"

"Yes, Miss Ella, we shor' did."

"So nice of you, Miss Ella."

"We thank you, Miss Ella."

These are the most enthusiastic responses from the farmhands, except for Adam. He is the friendliest and most outgoing of the bunch. He frequently will lean forward and pay me or the bakery a compliment.

The farmhands pick up the oranges and get in line for their biscuits. The group has grown to more than 15 men, and we are learning more about the work some of them perform at the local farms.

Many men work with horses and cattle, either assisting in training or caring for them, feeding, shoeing, and keeping them brushed and clean. It turns out Adam is quite a horse charmer. He often pauses to get my attention and gives me a big smile as I hand him his biscuit, so this morning, I asked him what his job is.

"Horse trainer, Miss Ella, the horses like me."

"I'm sure they do, Adam; you have an effortless way about you."

"Thank you, Miss Ella, and you do too."

The other farmhands are more relaxed as time passes, but none offer more about themselves or are as outgoing as Adam. They express their gratitude for the biscuits and occasional fruit we have for them with a simple "Thank you."

Then there is the tall man who stands out in the crowd with clean, pressed clothes and an expensive hat. He rarely says thank you or good morning. We often hear him say, "Duke, just call me Duke." I wonder what his story is and why he tells people to call him Duke. Patricia and I watch and wait until we can learn more about him.

"What time do we expect Sarah to come and get her order, Ella? It's all boxed and ready."

"I told her it would be ready at ten o'clock, so we will see her around then. It will be interesting to see how long this goes on. If this keeps up, we could be baking late into the afternoon, even beyond closing time."

"It is OK with me, Ella. The townsfolk look forward to seeing something new that we bake, and I see no reason we can't continue to be creative."

Ten o'clock rolls around, and we are busy with several customers ready to buy our muffins, cookies, and cakes when the door opens, and Sarah walks in.

"Good morning, Sarah. We will be right with you. I have your baked goods packaged for you." This time, she knows I am talking to her when I say Sarah. After my customer leaves, I go to the glass cabinet and bring out her packages.

"I've already tied the boxes with twine, or I would open them to show you what we baked. I included buttermilk biscuits, chocolate muffins, orange muffins, scones with currants, chocolate chip cookies, and apple turnovers. Hope that keeps your people satisfied."

"Oh, I am sure it will. They have a real fondness for your baked goods, and I will find out what their favorites are and call you later today."

"Will we be baking for you, everyone, for a while? Quite a while?"

Sarah finds herself involved in a conversation about who she is referring to when she says everyone, and she hesitates. "Yes, although I am not supposed to talk about them." She then leans in and whispers, "I wish I could."

"I understand, Sarah. Call me later and let me know your people's favorites. Patricia and I will be dreaming up new sweets to bake for you. Here is your bill."

Sarah hands me a fifty-dollar bill; we don't even bother to talk about making change anymore. Her driver enters the door, takes some of the packages, and whisks her away in his truck.

As I stand at the window watching them drive down the street, Patricia comes around the counter and stands behind me; she whispers, "You are softening up that girl quite nicely, Mrs. Watson."

"Gee whiz Patricia, I am trying to make her comfortable. Who knew running a bakery could be this much fun."

Later in the afternoon, Sarah calls and says that her people are thrilled with the selection of baked goods and that we should continue to decide what to include in the packages for them.

For the next two months, Sarah places orders several times a week for large quantities of baked goods. We no longer put any thought into who is receiving all the baked goods; we take it in stride. No suspicious hints or rumors are circulating in Martinsville, so whoever is eating all of our baked goods has not come to light. There must be a heightened level of activity somewhere, but there are no such changes in the activity level in town.

Patricia and I regularly make delicious variations to our customary fare to satisfy Sarah's people and the townsfolk. With our creative juices flowing every day, we have earned a reputation for being inventive with our baking. I added dill weed to one batch of biscuits; to another, I added some grated cheddar cheese and a few chopped jalapenos.

People have fallen in love with our baked goods, an assortment many have never tasted. When we make something different, we bake extra to sell to Daniel for his customers. Our baked goods are the perfect complement to his dining menu.

"Patricia, how about we mix the orange zest into a chocolate sheet cake? We won't frost it; it's too messy — we will cut it in squares - easy to eat with the fingers. Have you ever had Snickerdoodles? They are my favorite cookie. Let's bake dozens of them and more of the Parker House Honey Rolls. Sarah didn't get them in her last order, so that will be a new goodie for her and whoever she is feeding. And we need to make more orange muffins and oatmeal cookies. Do we have any more raisins in the cabinet?" Our conversation this morning is an ideal demonstration of putting our heads together.

As Tom and I eat our dinner this evening, he appears preoccupied. Something is on Tom's mind as he has hardly said a word throughout the whole meal. Finally, Tom admits he has something important to tell me when we get upstairs. While we prepare for bed, Tom explains.

"I was eating breakfast this morning when Mayor Bigby stopped at my table and asked if he could sit with me. I said yes, of course, and invited him to have breakfast with me. He said he had something to discuss with me and asked if I would walk to his office after we finished eating. Of course, I went along.

"Judge Garfield was waiting for us when we arrived, which surprised me. They started questioning me about the farm, our farm. They inquired about our animals, particularly the horses, and asked me to explain my expertise overseeing them. I went into detail about raising them, breaking them in, handling births, the whole nine yards."

"Why did they want to know all of this?"

"Remember I told you about Bigby and Garfield's conversation a while ago? I overheard them talking about keeping something hush-hush. It turns out that a production company is filming a Hollywood movie at the Lancaster Horse Farm. A continuous stream of bad weather on the west coast forced the studio to seek an alternate location for the movie set, and somehow, they discovered the Lancaster Horse Farm.

"But they have another problem; the horses have been acting skittishly even though the local handlers are on site. It is a substantial change for them with the crew, the actors, and the director. Bigby promised the movie director he would find someone to lend a hand, someone with a higher level of expertise."

"And that someone is you?"

"Apparently. Bigby recommended me to Mr. Lancaster, the owner of the horse farm. He wants me to go to the ranch tomorrow morning. If he hires me, I will be working on the ranch for the rest of the shoot. Bigby said to tell you I am working out at the horse farm but to say nothing about the movie shoot. Frankly, I am not about to lie to you to satisfy his desire to keep this from the townsfolk; however, please act like you know nothing about the movie shoot. Don't tell Patricia or anyone. Bigby is adamant about keeping it under wraps."

"Really? Bigby wants this kept a secret? Away from the townsfolk here? He is afraid they will run out to the horse farm and get in the way of the shoot?"

"That pretty much sums it up. And that is why you haven't seen much of Bigby lately. He is at the ranch having the time of his life with the movie stars and the crew."

"Wow, Tom, this is exciting. You are going to do it, aren't you?"

"Yes, I did tell Bigby I was available, but I wanted to be sure you were on board. Of course, I will need to examine the horses, evaluate them, and then make a recommendation for their management and care. If Mr. Lancaster decides to hire me, I will begin work early in the morning, perhaps stay late, and report directly to him as they are his horses. I am not sure what time we will finish the day."

"It is all right with me as long as I can see you before we go to bed. You will have a fantastic time. If Mr. Lancaster offers you the job, you should accept."

"Thanks, Ella. I knew I could count on you to make sense of it all. Tomorrow is an early rise. We had better hit the hay."

The next morning Tom and I head to the dining room for an early breakfast. Then, I am off to the bakery, and Tom heads to the Lancaster Horse Farm. I will tell Patricia about the movie shoot and Tom working with the horses regardless of what Mayor Bigby wants. I do not see any point in keeping this a secret from her.

After a long and busy day at the bakery, we close a little after two o'clock, and I head across the street. Martinsville's Finest is not terribly busy, and to my surprise, at the end of the bar sits Mayor Bigby. I have not seen him in weeks, but to inquire where he has been or what he has been doing would be prying and rude. I will leave it to him to explain his absence; however, I know the answer to his whereabouts.

"Mayor Bigby, how are you? Nice to see you. We have missed you lately."

"Miss Ella. I have missed seeing you and tasting your delicious offerings. I hear you have expanded your selection. Nice going. The folks around here are talking about the bakery more and more. I know I haven't been 'round town much. Um, I have a little project I have been working on." He leans in, "It is a little secret, ya see. I am not privileged to talk about it, but I can sooner or later. Do you mind waiting a bit longer?"

"Mayor Bigby, plenty of secrets have been floating around town the last few months. Maybe we will all gather 'round the table soon and spill the beans."

I cannot let him think he knows something I don't know. That is part of the game we play. I call it, "Can you top this?" With that, I walk away, and that is his cue to start hollering at my back, but before he gets the chance, I holler over my shoulder.

"Bigby, I have your number. You might want to check your boots. Horse manure. Stinks. Best to clean up before you come back into town."

I blanch. Could I have gone too far? Then I think, nah. Anyone can get horse manure on a pair of boots from any number of places around these parts; however, I am confident I know where Bigby got his dose; at the Lancaster Horse Farm.

"Why, Miss Ella, aren't you the smart one. You think you got me all figured out, don't ya?"

He starts with his booming laughter, so I guess I haven't put him off.

"Yup, Bigby, I am one smart cookie. Come by one day soon, and I will give you one." With that, I step into the elevator and wave as the door closes. It is best to give him a run for his money every chance I get.

Mayor Bigby,

My goodness, a studio movie shoot at the Lancaster Horse Farm? Oh, how I wish I could be in Martinsville right now. All I see around the countryside are cows and big bulls. The smell of butter and cheese can sometimes be overwhelming with this summer heat. Let me know the details. Who is in the movie? Are you watching them film it? Oh, that's why I don't hear from you. You are out at the farm watching, aren't you? Good for you, but you owe me a financial report, although I bet things are coming along swimmingly.

Mrs. Devlin

Regardless of when Tom arrives home, we share our day before bed. I tell him about Bigby being in the bar, our banter, and how Bigby thinks he has a secret from the entire town.

"Yes, he does, and he's trying to keep it that way. I'm surprised he was in the bar this afternoon. Something must have brought him back into town."

"Yeah, like taking care of the town's business. How was it out at the horse farm today?"

"I met with Mr. Lancaster and his crew of trainers to discuss the horses' behavior and what they have been doing to keep them at ease. Then I went to the stables, examined the horses, and worked with them. After that, I had a second meeting and gave my recommendations for making the horses more comfortable."

"And they liked your recommendations?"

"Oh yes, they did. And after I finished working with the horses, I walked over to talk with the director and actors, and there I saw something I am sure you will be interested in knowing."

"Well, don't keep me waiting, Tom. What did you see?"

"The entire crew, the actors, and the director are all eating baked goods from the Devlin Bakery."

"Whoa, oh my goodness. That explains it. Sarah has something to do with the movie shoot. Baked goods for the crew. Who else would eat huge amounts of biscuits, cookies, and muffins we sell her? Well, I'll be darned."

The following day, while we count the baked goods in the display cases and check the refrigerator and bins for ingredients needed for baking, I tell Patricia what Tom told me last night.

"So that answers who is eating all the baked goods. Sarah has a connection to the movie shoot in some way. Very interesting."

"Yes, and we must pretend we know nothing until she tells us herself."

Devlin Family Notes

Arthur McKinley Devlin and his cousin Luther Devlin attended school in Martinsville. The cousins were raised like brothers, as neither had siblings. Arthur met Hallie Marie Houpt in Merom and told friends that someday he would marry her, and he did on the 5th of May in 1917. Arthur started a grocery delivery, "Hucksters Truck," with Melvin Manifold, husband of his mother's sister, Aunt Martha Mills. Arthur drove the *Manifold and Devlin Huckster* truck until the early winter of 1919, when he and Hallie moved back to Martinsville to be near family.

It was about 1931 when Arthur and Hallie decided to work for Hallie's brothers, who owned bakeries. It was only a matter of time before Arthur and Hallie Devlin would follow in their footsteps and open their own bakery.

Submitted by Janice Wells Hood

CHAPTER V

The Prank

Sarah continues to call her requests for baked goods for another three weeks, with each order increasing the number of biscuits, muffins, and any new baked goods we can create. We now have a set time for her to pick up her order. Her driver always appears as I place the packages in her arms; he opens the door, helps her carry the boxes, and off they go in the truck.

Today has been a hectic day. It is two o'clock, and as I am about to lock the bakery door, it opens, and Sarah walks in.

"Hello, Sarah. I didn't expect you today. Was I supposed to have a package for you this afternoon?"

"No, Ella, but I want to share something with you and Patricia. Do you have time to talk?"

"Yes, have a seat at the table. I will lock the door and call Patricia from the kitchen."

Patricia and I sit with Sarah, wondering if she will reveal what we already know about her involvement with the movie shoot.

"I am sure you have wondered who I am and why I have purchased so many baked goods from you over the past several months. I figured it was time to tell you I am part of a movie crew from Hollywood, California. Our shoot is out at the Lancaster Horse Farm. Your baked goods are feeding the cast and the crew. When I arrive with the packages, the whole gang crowds around to see what is in the boxes, but one person really loves everything you bake. He is a famous person, and he would like to meet you."

Patricia and I are wide-eyed at her story. We wonder, who could this famous person be?

"Can you tell us who that person is?"

"John Wayne."

"John Wayne? The movie actor John Wayne? He wants to come here to the bakery and meet me?"

"Yes, you and Patricia. But we need to be discreet. Mayor Bigby told the director he prefers this movie shoot remain a secret from the people in the town."

"Any time Mr. Wayne would like to stop by is fine with us."

"Good. How about tomorrow morning when you open at six o'clock?"

That evening, while Tom and I are eating our dinner, I lean in toward him, and as he is wiping his mouth with his napkin, I blurt out, "Tomorrow morning at six o'clock, we have a notable person coming into the bakery, John Wayne."

Tom coughs into his napkin. Sorry, Tom, I didn't mean for you to choke.

"Wow, good for you, John Wayne, my favorite."

The following day, Patricia and I do our morning baking as usual; however, we want the bakery to look bright, shiny, and tidy before our notable visitor arrives, so we set time aside for cleaning and polishing. After finishing our chores, we neatly comb our hair and ensure our clothes are free of flour dust. It is getting close to six o'clock when the ranch hands will be here, the same time as John Wayne. This meeting should prove to be exciting.

As usual, I unlock the doors at six o'clock sharp, and our farmhands walk into the bakery. I greet them as always, then begin the ritual of serving them a biscuit, some with butter, set on a four-inch square of Kraft paper. I have a bushel basket full of apples at the door for them. My stomach has butterflies, anticipating the moment John Wayne walks in the door of my bakery; however, I intend to maintain my composure when he does. Ten minutes later, Sarah enters with John Wayne right behind her.

"Patricia, will you take over for me?" I come from behind the counter, and John Wayne walks up to me.

"Morning, Miss; you must be the owner of this bakery?"

"Yes, I am. My name is Ella Watson." I extend my hand, and he firmly yet softly shakes it, as you would expect from a true gentleman.

"Pleasure to meet you, ma'am. I am John Wayne, and I wanted to stop by to tell you how much we, the whole crew, and I especially enjoy all the delicious baked goods you send our way. You are an exceptionally talented woman, Miss Watson. I haven't had biscuits this good since my grandmother passed, and that was twenty years ago."

Mr. Wayne takes a moment to pause and look around the bakery. "Looks like a mighty fine establishment you have here, ma'am."

I cannot help but notice the farmhands staring, eyes wide with amazement, their mouths dropping open at the sight of the famous actor, John Wayne.

"Thank you very much. I am delighted to know how much you enjoy what we bake. Mr. Wayne, I would like you to meet our farmhands. They come here in the morning at six o'clock for a biscuit and fruit. Gentlemen, please introduce yourselves to Mr. Wayne."

Starting with Adam, the farmhands humbly approach John Wayne, extend their hand, state their name, and say, "Nice to meet you," or "Pleasure, sir," or "Good morning, sir." Then, the one I have been waiting for, the different one. Standing tall and erect, he begins.

"Good morning, John Wayne. I'm William Jennings; it's a pleasure to meet you, sir," to which John Wayne casually replics, "Nice to meet you too, William; just call me Duke."

Immediately, the air in the room feels suspended for a split second. I hear a snicker or two from within the group, and the look on the men's faces is priceless. The men shuffle, shake their heads, and grin at each other. A glimpse of curiosity crosses John Wayne's face as if he wonders, what just happened? It is all Patricia and I can do to contain ourselves. And William Jennings looks aghast. Duke. I doubt he will ever again tell anyone to call him Duke.

The farmhands continue to whisper and laugh low with each other. John Wayne still looks perplexed. I quickly recover from the awkward moment and distract John Wayne by changing the subject.

"Mr. Wayne, please come over to the display case and let me show you what we have fresh-baked this morning."

"Why, Miss Ella, all of your baked goods look so delicious; I believe I will need to take a few more pastries with me this morning."

"My pleasure, Mr. Wayne. Point out which ones, and I will box them for you."

While John Wayne slowly walks along the front of the display case, eyeing the trays of pastries, I sneak a quick peek out the window. I see several farmhands standing on the sidewalk with their heads together, talking and laughing. William Jennings is walking away as fast as possible. He must be humiliated. Then I remember I haven't introduced Mr. Wayne to Patricia.

"Mr. Wayne, I would like you to meet Patricia Snyder. Patricia worked for the previous owner of the bakery for the last several years when it was open. She has been with me since my husband and I reopened the bakery. Patricia is my right-hand person and best friend."

Patricia and John exchange pleasantries.

"Would you like to have a seat, John? Pardon me, may I call you John?"

"Of course, Miss Ella, please do."

"I have a question for you.

"Whatever it is, go ahead and ask me."

"John, are you a bit of a prankster?"

"Well," he drawls, reflecting on his past experiences. "I have been known to pull one over on a friend or two. What have you got in mind?"

"Mayor Bigby. He and I have a game we play, trying to trip each other with things we know. The mayor thinks he is the only person in town who knows about the movie shoot; it would be fun to call his bluff. Are you with me?"

"Why, Miss Ella, I like your style."

"Is it possible for you to be back here tomorrow at four o'clock?"

"Yes, I believe I can arrange to be here by then."

"If you don't mind, please come in the bakery's back door so no one sees you. I have a plan and want it to be a total surprise."

I then explain what I have in mind to amaze Mayor Bigby, who is adamant about keeping the movie shoot a secret from the whole town. The famous movie actor John Wayne has agreed to my plan. Tonight, I will ask Tom to be in the bar with Mayor Bigby tomorrow by four o'clock at the latest. We will watch from the bakery window, hoping the timing works out as planned. It doesn't get more exciting than this.

After Sarah and John Wayne leave with his box of pastries, Patricia and I turn toward each other and burst out laughing. We are both hysterical over the look on William Jennings's face when John Wayne told him to call him Duke. We fall into each other's arms, holding each other up; we cannot quit laughing. Then, as luck would have it, old Mrs. Parsons happens to be walking by the bakery windows, sees us with tears rolling down our cheeks, and mistakes the reason for them as something awful has happened. She pokes her head in the door.

"Goodness ladies, what on earth are you crying about?"

I lift my head from Patricia's shoulder; it takes a moment to compose myself, and finally, between giggles, I manage to spit out, "John… John Wayne is in town."

"Ladies, that is not the least bit funny." Annoyed, she slams the door shut and struts down the sidewalk with her nose in the air.

With that, I fall back toward Patricia. We slip and tumble onto the floor, laughing until our sides might split. Right then, the door opens, and Daniel walks in and stares at us with his hands on his hips.

"You two ladies are nuts."

I manage to reply, "Yes, Daniel, we are."

"Come on now, ladies, let me help you off the floor. Look here, Ella; I have another list of items I would like you to bake for me, that is, whenever you two can stop laughing."

I glance at the list as Daniel turns and walks out the door. He's trying to keep a straight face, but I can see he is trying to suppress a grin as he hurries away. Patricia and I are still giggling. We spend the rest of the day waiting on our customers and reliving our moments with John Wayne. What a thrill.

That night, I fill Tom in on the details about the meeting with John Wayne and that I have a plan to one-up Bigby.

"Please see that you and Bigby are at the bar no later than four o'clock tomorrow. John will arrange with the director to cut the shoot a bit short. Watch for us to enter the bar a moment or two after the hour."

"Ella, my darling scheming wife, I can't wait to see what you have dreamed up."

Our farmhands have an air of excitement about them this morning, leftover from yesterday's meet and greet with the great movie actor John Wayne. They all are wearing big smiles as I hand them their biscuit. The one who looks stiff and stoic is William Jennings. No doubt, the man has not yet recovered from yesterday's awkward and embarrassing moment.

After a busy day, we close the doors at two o'clock as usual and continue baking until four o'clock, when I expect John Wayne to arrive. While Patricia and I bake dozens of biscuits and cookies, I tell her my plan to surprise Mayor Bigby.

Minutes before the hour, Patricia stations herself at the window to watch for Tom and the mayor to enter Martinsville's Finest. Soon, Patricia looks over her shoulder and gives me the victory sign. Tom and Mayor Bigby are in the bar, and John Wayne walks through the back door at four o'clock on the dot.

I lock the doors, and we walk across the street to Martinsville's Finest, where I plan to walk in on the arm of John Wayne, one of the world's most beloved and famous actors and floor Mayor Bigby. John is up for the game.

Standing outside the door to the bar, I ask, "Ready, John?"

"Ready."

I link my arm in his, John pushes open the door, and we step into the bar. Then, with one swoop, his arm goes around my back, and he sweeps me up into his arms in the manner a groom would usher his bride over the threshold. A hush falls over the room as everyone looks toward the door in shock and surprise.

"LADIES AND GENTLEMEN. May I have your attention, please?" The room is instantly silent. John then looks into my face and, with great sincerity, announces to the crowd, "I have here the best little baker this side of the Mississippi, Miss Ella Watson."

Right then, Bigby takes a big gulp of his beer, and upon hearing my name, he turns and sees me in the arms of John Wayne. Shocked at the sight, he spurts beer all over the person sitting beside him. Judge Garfield.

"Jesus Christ, Bigby, what the hell?"

The whole room explodes in laughter. With me still in his arms, John saunters across the floor, weaving between the tables and chairs. The patrons are agog at the sight of their local baker in the arms of John Wayne. He then sets me on the bar top, turns toward the crowd, and raises his hands to quiet the room again.

"People of Martinsville, hear me out. This talented little lady, Miss Ella, is as fine a baker as my grandmother was; God rest her soul." He then removes his cowboy hat and bows low in front of me.

"Ladies, gentlemen, and ma'am, drinks are on me. BARKEEP, give this little lady a cold beer."

The whole room starts clapping, hooting, and hollering. Bigby is busy wiping beer from his chin, and Judge Garfield, his shirt soaked in beer, continues to grumble. John gently lifts me off the bar by my waist and sets me on the floor.

The crowd gathers around me, and holding their beer and whiskey glasses high, they start chanting, "To Ella, to Ella, to Ella." For the next three hours, the bar is one big party. Later, I realized I drank more beer than ever before, but I can't remember a time when I had more fun.

Not until I get back upstairs with Tom do I realize what I have done. My little trick on Mayor Bigby let a whole bunch of people in Martinsville know that the famous actor, John Wayne, is in town. Oh boy, the cat is out of the bag now. Stretched across the bed in my nightgown, I console myself. What the heck; we all had fun, and anyway, they would have found out eventually.

Lying next to me, Tom reflects on the evening's event.

"Ella, how in the world did you come up with this idea? I am amazed. I had no idea you would do something like this. Seeing you in the arms of none other than John Wayne was a thrill, and what a surprise for the townspeople, John Wayne, here in little Martinsville.

Then Bigby spewing beer on Judge Garfield, the poor guy. I must admit it was hilarious. I had a wonderful time tonight, honey."

"I had a wonderful time, too, but you must know that the plan was not for John Wayne to pick me up. We were supposed to walk in, arm in arm."

"So, it was his idea to pick you up?"

"Yes. It was a total surprise to me, but I guess it turned out to be a good idea. And now I desperately need some sleep. Good night, honey."

Tom and I spoon together under the heavy bedcovers and immediately fall into a deep sleep.

Mayor Bigby,

I about dropped to the floor when I read that John Wayne is playing the lead in the movie. Imagine John Wayne, there in our small town. The fact that he loves Ella and Patricia's baked goods pleases me so much. Oh, how I miss Martinsville. Perhaps someday I can return for a stay. I can hope.

Mrs. Devlin

Getting up on time this morning is a struggle; it is no surprise that my head is foggy. I lost count of the number of glasses of beer I drank. It doesn't take much to affect me; I'm not much of a drinker. I guess you could call me a lightweight.

Tom props himself up in bed and watches me struggle to get ready for the day with a big grin on his face. Finally, I am about to leave the apartment and see Tom still sporting his grin.

"You'll wipe that smirk off your face if you know what's good for you, wise guy."

While waiting for the elevator in the foyer, I hear Tom laughing loudly. When I get to the bakery, I'll look for aspirin in the cabinet.

As I enter the bakery, Patricia is waiting for me at the door.

"Why, Miss Ella, you look like you had a rough night." She snickers.

"Don't start, Patricia. Yes, I drank a bit too much beer."

"You're famous, Mrs. Watson. That was some surprise; if people didn't know you before last night, they do now."

"Patricia, you know that is not how I planned it. The plan was to walk into the bar on the arm of John Wayne, not in his arms. Guess it made a splash, huh?"

"Yeah, all over Judge Garfield. Poor fellow, he was soaked in beer. You sure put one over on the mayor, big time."

"Yes, I did. The best part was the look on Bigby's face; it was priceless. Talk about stopping a man in his tracks. But I had no idea that John Wayne would pick me up. Then, to be set on the bar like some showgirl. Oh gee, that was embarrassing."

"Ella, you are overreacting. The famous movie actor John Wayne held you in his arms. He honored you as the finest baker this side of the Mississippi, as good as his grandmother. He bowed low in front of you, very respectful. What is your problem, girl?"

"Oh, all right, but I am usually more conservative. I am not sure what got into me, but I must admit, I loved putting one over on Bigby. I will know his reaction the next time I see him."

"Wait and see the reactions from the townspeople. That is what I want to see. I bet you'll find they loved it. Come on, Ella, let it go, and let's get baking. We need a few things for the display cases."

And busy we did get, first with the farmhands, who I am sure have not heard anything about last night's adventure, then starting at around eight o'clock, we have a constant flow of customers that lasts until ten o'clock, when we finally have a chance to sit with a cup of tea, a scone, and a muffin.

Our late morning tea break is interrupted by the telephone ringing. It is Sarah. She wants us to prepare an order for her to pick up at ten o'clock tomorrow morning. Her request is good timing, as we need to bake more specialty items for the display cases. We need more muffins, a layer cake, or possibly some turnovers, depending on the fruit in the refrigerator, and dozens of biscuits. I must keep busy to get my mind off last night's scene.

I no sooner hang up the telephone when the door opens and in walks Daniel. He is sporting a grin but doesn't say a word about last night. He then hands me another list of baked goods he wants us to make for his dining room customers including turnovers and a few dozen cookies. Wow, baking for Daniel has become a big deal.

We will be baking all day, way past closing time. I call Sharon and ask her if she could come and help us today. If we stay this busy, we will need her to manage the store while we bake in the kitchen.

"Sure, I can come over. I will be there in about thirty minutes."

"Sharon will be here shortly. Patricia, please go back and see what ingredients we have on hand, then make a list of items we can bake and pull the recipe strips. I will stay in front and help the customers."

When Sharon arrives, I return to the kitchen with Patricia and start filling the bowls with ingredients for the goods we want to bake.

Good organization is the key to successful baking. We line up the stainless-steel bowls on the long worktable and put the dry ingredients in the mixing bowls for each pastry we will bake. To keep track of what is in the bowls, I have the recipe for each baked good written on a strip of paper and tuck it under the edge of the bowl. We add the wet ingredients when ready to mix and bake that batch. It may sound hectic, but having someone like Patricia with me, whose mind is so focused, makes it easy. She is amazing.

The entire afternoon is a whirlwind, but we manage to bake dozens of scones, muffins, sheet cakes, and turnovers, with Sharon keeping pace with the activity in the store.

We place the trays of baked goods on the rolling carts and set them in front of the back door, where they get a bit of a breeze to help with the cooling process. Since we will stay past closing time, I will call Jim Nelson to see if he can mop the floors later in the day. Jim is always flexible, especially considering the package of goodies we set out for him to take home. In the morning, we will package up items for Sarah.

"I don't know about you two, but I am exhausted. I can't recall baking this many items in one day. So why don't we package Daniel's goods and take them to him now? We have most of what he ordered, but he will have to wait for his pies until tomorrow. I will buy dinner for both of you. That way, we can relax before you go home."

At around four-thirty, we put the key in the lock and head across the street with Daniel's packages and trays of baked goods. We deliver them into the kitchen, return to the dining room, and sit at a table only to have customer after customer approach and tell me how much fun they had last night and how they loved being in the presence of John Wayne. After dinner, we say our goodbyes, and I go upstairs to prepare for bed. Tom arrives at eight-thirty.

"How did it go with the horses today? Did you see Bigby? I didn't see him here in town; he wasn't in the dining room this evening."

"The horses are doing much better now, thanks for asking. Bigby was at the shoot, all right. He wouldn't miss an opportunity to hang around the actors and the crew. He likes to keep close, right behind the director. The funny thing was that when John Wayne told the crew what the two of you did last night at the bar, Bigby looked slightly surprised. He didn't know how to react until he concluded that the crew was excited about John Wayne making a fuss over you, Ella. After that, Bigby chimed in about how much fun it was. If you are wondering if you embarrassed him, you didn't."

"That could be where my thinking went astray; thank goodness I didn't embarrass Bigby. It is my little secret, huh? I like it that way. Maybe he will show his face tomorrow."

"Don't count on seeing him. The mayor spends most nights at the horse farm, sleeping in the bunkhouse. But I know one person who is tired of sleeping in a trailer at the shoot. John Wayne. I told John about the lodgings above the bar and checked with Daniel before coming upstairs. It so happens that one room is available below our floor. As of tomorrow night, John will be sleeping here at Martinsville's Finest. Guess both of us will be seeing more of John Wayne now."

And Tom was right. Early each morning, he and John have breakfast, then drive out to the movie set, and when they return in the evening, the three of us have dinner together. John Wayne is a delightful man whose presence transforms a room. His voice, swagger, and his gentlemanly approach to men and women are infectious. He tells us of the funny happenings on the movie set. He asks about our family, our farm outside of Naperville, how we came to live in Martinsville, and how we came upon the bakery opportunity. He listens intently and is genuinely interested in other people's lives.

Many of the crew and actors are now finding their way to Martinsville several times a week for a satisfying meal, libations, and the friendly company of our townspeople. After dinner, John stays in the bar and chats with the townspeople. Mostly the men, including Mayor Bigby, like to ask him about his career and life in Hollywood, and John loves to share his stories with them. When John decides to turn in, the men shake his hand and thank him for his time. Tom has a new friend in John and is having the time of his life.

This morning, Patricia and I discover our supply of baked goods in the display cases is low, which surprised us with all we baked yesterday, but orders from Daniel and Sarah have left us short. Daniel orders more and more of our baked goods weekly, and the amount of baked goods we sell to our walk-in customers has dramatically increased. We bake several dozen muffins, chocolate and orange, and dozens of cookies, and while we are baking, Patricia has a bright idea to give the farmhands a treat; a sugar cookie.

Alongside the biscuits and the bowl of whipped butter, I add another tray piled high with sugar cookies. I hand them their biscuit on the paper square, then place a sugar cookie on top. The men stare at the cookie, smiling as they turn and walk out the door as if we have given them a present. Kindness, appreciation, and gratefulness can come in a small package.

Sarah arrives minutes before ten o'clock; we have all her packages wrapped and tied with twine. I gave her three dozen biscuits, two dozen bran muffins, two dozen orange muffins, a dozen Parker House Honey Rolls, two dozen Snickerdoodles, a dozen chocolate chip cookies, and half of the vanilla sheet cake.

"Do you have a minute, Ella? Can we sit?"

"Of course, have a seat. What is on your mind?"

"John Wayne told me what you and he did at the bar the other night. You made quite an impression on him. He said it was the most fun he has had in a long time. John also said you are an amazing lady; he admires your sense of adventure."

"Thank you for telling me, Sarah. I am pleased that John had a good time. We mid-westerners are a nice bunch of people, down-to-earth. It is hard not to like us, don't you agree?"

"Yes, I agree. The people from the West, some, most of them, are different. The atmosphere here in Martinsville is calm and refreshing. Have you always lived here?"

"No, my husband Tom and I lived on a family farm five miles east of Naperville. It is a four-hour drive from here."

"How did you come to live in Martinsville and own the bakery?"

"We decided it was time to retire and hand the farm down to our children now that they are grown. Farming is a hard life, Sarah. The work is all day, every day. My cousin Sharon, who lives in Cooper, came to the farm and told us that Martinsville's bakery was no longer in operation. The owner's two daughters had no interest in taking over the family business, so when Mrs. Devlin could no longer run it, she decided, sadly, that her only option was to close its doors.

"Sharon encouraged us to make a trip to Martinsville to see if running a bakery was what we wanted for the rest of our lives. We met with Mayor Bigby, and the next thing we knew, we were in the bakery business."

"What a remarkable story, but how did you learn to bake like this? Your loaves of bread, biscuits, rolls; everything is so delicious."

"I learned from my grandmother. She cooked and baked for the farmhands seven days a week, and I was always by her side; that is how I learned my craft. She also taught me how to read, write, and sew. She was a caring and giving woman and more of a mother to me than my biological mother. The day my dear grandmother died was one of the saddest days in my memory. My father was an extraordinary man, gentle and caring. I cannot tell you how much he loved and cared for my grandmother and me."

"Oh, Ella, how marvelous that you had a sweet grandmother and a loving father. What about your mother? You didn't mention her."

"We can leave that saga for another day; it's a long story."

By the look on Ella's face, Sarah can easily see that talking about her mother is a touchy subject and diverts the conversation back to herself. "Perhaps one day, I can share my story with you."

The door chimes ring at that moment, and the bakery is busy with customers.

"Looks like I had better go now; you are getting busy. I will call you tomorrow."

Sarah gives me a big hug and kisses my cheek. She is a special girl, and I like her very much.

CHAPTER VI

The Truth, The Whole Truth

"Ella, I have an idea I'd like to run by you; it is about Delia. I want to bring her in someday to spend time with us and meet our customers. I tell her what we do throughout the day, but it would be fun for her to experience it herself. She might even see some people she hasn't seen in years. Would that be ok with you?"

"Of course, that is a great idea. Any day you want to bring her in is fine with me."

"What I can do is go pick her up when the pace slows. If she gets too tired, I can always run her home. It will only take a few minutes."

"Whenever she wants to come, she is welcome."

That afternoon, we put together a package for Sarah and tell her it will be ready tomorrow at eleven o'clock. The next day, we are busy with customers until around nine-fifteen, when we have a pause, so Patricia heads out to get Delia.

I make a pot of coffee for her, and Delia sits at one of the tables, but first, we let her choose any treat she desires from the display cases. Our customers are surprised and delighted to see Delia. She is having a great time chatting with them. It is like old home week, catching up with old friends about past times.

We are busy when Sarah walks in, so she has to wait her turn to pick up her packages. Several minutes later, I notice that Sarah has struck up a conversation with Delia, and then I see her sit at the table with her. They appear to be taking great pleasure in each other's company, deep in conversation, so I decide not to interrupt them but let them continue their talk.

Finally, Sarah signals that she is ready to pay and collect her packages. As always, I hand her the bill, and she gives me a fifty. Her driver comes in the doorway, helps her with the boxes, and flies out the door; then, they drive off in the truck.

Delia decides to stay the rest of the afternoon until closing time; however, I can't help but notice that her demeanor has changed. She seems relatively quiet, possibly deep in thought. I wonder what has come over her. Later that evening, the telephone rings in our apartment. It is Patricia.

"Can you come over right now? Delia has something to tell me, and you should be here."

"I will be right over." Something tells me this is urgent.

"Tom, give me the keys to the truck, please. I am going over to Patricia's. I am not sure how long I will be gone, but don't worry. I will telephone you when I am on the way home."

I park the truck in front of Patricia's house. She has the porch lamp lit and is waiting for me at the door. "What is it, Patricia? Is Delia OK?"

"Yes, she is. Let's go in the kitchen." I follow Patricia along the hallway into the kitchen, anxious to see Delia, only to find her sitting at the island with Sarah beside her. I am taken aback.

"Sarah, what a surprise to see you here."

"Hello, Ella. I know this is unexpected; please give me a few minutes to explain why I am here this evening. First, I need to tell you that my name is not Sarah. Its Jessica. Jessica Roberts."

"I'm confused; somebody fill me in, please."

"Once I tell you my story, you will understand. Patricia and Ella, you know that I am here in Illinois with the movie crew from California, and if it weren't for the shoot, I would probably never have had the chance to come to Martinsville. In the bakery today, when I saw Delia, we made a connection almost instantly; that is why I wanted to come here tonight. Let me start at the beginning.

"I have always lived in the Los Angeles area with my parents. I am adopted. My parents adopted me when I was four months old; they never kept it a secret. I always knew I was adopted as far back as I can remember.

"My father is an electrician and works for the movie studios. My mother is a professional seamstress. She designs and makes clothing for people in the spotlight. My parents always instilled in me that working is what a responsible person does, so when I turned sixteen, I wanted to get my driver's license and find a part-time job, which would require me to show my birth certificate.

"When I told my mother I needed the certificate, she went into her office, opened her desk drawer, took out an envelope, and handed it to me. I didn't open it until a couple of weeks later, and when I did, I found another document with the certificate, a record of my adoption. I doubt that my mother knew what she was giving me, not that they wanted to keep any information from me, but I believe they would have preferred to show it to me someday and talk about it, not let it fall into my lap.

"Most of the wording was general, with few specifics except for my birth date, and it did say that my birth mother had named me Sarah. The place where I was born was a non-descript name that gave me no clues about the location. Black ink covered the name of the city and state. With no concrete information, I put it back in the envelope with my birth certificate and forgot about it. Sorry, I know this story is long, but this is the best way to get to where we are today.

"After graduating from college, I had the opportunity to interview for a position working on a movie set. It was a small-budget movie working with the actors and their scripts, which I still do today. Here is where it gets interesting. I met a film editor at the studio, and we became good friends. One day, I told him that my parents adopted me at four months, and I told him about the adoption paper, with much of the information blacked out. He said he would like to look at it to see if he could decipher any details.

"As it turned out, with the lights he uses and other equipment, he could read the name of the city and state where I was born, Martinsville, Illinois."

"Now we are getting somewhere."

"That was a few years ago. I honestly didn't think any more about it until I got the call from the studio that we were coming to Illinois to the Lancaster Horse Farm, so close to Martinsville. You can imagine my excitement at having the opportunity to be near the town where I was born. While here, I figured I would gather some facts and see what information I could dig up.

"That is where Delia enters my story. When I saw her sitting in the bakery today, I was taken aback. I looked into her eyes, and we made a connection. My heart started to beat fast. I said, "Hello," and she asked me to sit with her. After a brief conversation, I knew I needed more time with her. I asked if I could call her, and she gave me the telephone number. Delia invited me to the house when I called, and here I am."

"When I laid eyes on you, Jessica, I, too, was aware of the connection. Our eyes met, and it was like looking into eyes I had looked into only yesterday. I knew for certain. The truth was clear."

Delia turns to Patricia and me. "I wanted to talk to her. I could not risk never seeing her again, so I invited her to sit at the table. I introduced myself, and she said her name was Sarah. Hearing that name, oh my, I was overwhelmed. Then she told me her birth date, and I almost fainted. I knew it was her. I knew she was my baby."

Patricia and I look at each other in surprise at Delia's startling statement. Delia then starts to weep, deeply affected by this turn of events.

"Would you like to go lie down, Delia? It's late; we can talk more about this later, possibly on Sunday afternoon when we have more time."

"Yes, I am exhausted. I can't talk anymore, not right now. Jessica, will you come back on Sunday? I can tell you what all I know then."

Jessica stands and gives Delia a long hug. "Yes, Delia, the rest of the story can wait until Sunday. Have a good night's sleep."

After taking Delia to her room, Patricia returns to the kitchen. "I don't know about you, but I, too, am overwhelmed. Jessica, how did you get here this evening? Do you have a way of getting here on Sunday?"

"A friend brought me. He is outside, waiting in his car. I will manage to get here. It is obvious that Delia knows something about my birth and the circumstances surrounding my adoption. I need to hear the truth. I cannot wait to hear what she has to say."

"You will be all right getting back out to the farm?"

"Yes, Ella, and thank you, Patricia, for letting me come here tonight." With that, Patricia escorts Jessica to the door and then returns to the kitchen.

"When we came home from the bakery today, I thought Delia appeared distracted, or perhaps she was feeling ill, but she said she was not. Then she told me she had invited Sarah to the house this evening. With Jessica on her way here, Delia told me she had a story to tell from years ago, an old, buried story that came to life when Sarah walked into the bakery today. That is when I called you."

"She doesn't mean that Jessica is her baby, does she?"

"Good question, but no, Jessica can't be. Can she? No. I guess we will have to wait until Sunday to get the answer to that question."

"If you don't mind, I would like to call Tom and tell him I am on the way home. I told him I would."

Back at the apartment, Tom wants to hear the details of what happened at Patricia's house tonight. I try to be as brief as possible without omitting essential information, but I need to get my sleep. Even after we turn out the lights, I lie in the dark and rerun the whole evening in my head.

All I can imagine is that Jessica came to Martinsville hoping that by calling herself Sarah, somehow, someone would make the connection. It was a long shot, but it paid off. It was pure luck that Jessica and Delia met on the only day Delia was in the bakery, but it was more than luck; it was a miracle.

I never did get much sleep last night and am exhausted. I rise early and arrive at the bakery before Patricia, turn on the lights, and light the gas ovens. I take the pie dough out of the refrigerator; we must need it for a creation this morning. I place it at the far end of the long worktable to let it get warm. I hope Patricia arrives here soon; I need a distraction.

Finally, she walks in. "Good morning."

"Good morning."

And that is all for now. Patricia appears to be preoccupied and immediately immerses herself in our daily routine. I can see that something is on her mind as she is never this quiet. I can't ask or press her. She will talk to me when the time is right.

I return to the store, take inventory of the goods in the display cases, determine we have enough to offer our customers today, and fill in any special orders we may receive. Therefore, we don't need to bake more pastries, cookies, rolls, or pies, so I return to the kitchen and put the pie dough back into the refrigerator for another day. Today, we will bake what we usually bake; loaves of bread and dozens of biscuits.

At six o'clock, I unlock the doors and begin the day by greeting my farmworkers and serving them a biscuit on a four-inch square of Kraft paper. I look at their faces for any indication of what their last evening held for them; however, I cannot imagine any event could hold a candle to what Patricia and I learned from Delia and Jessica.

Soon, the bakery is teeming with customers, peering into the display cases, pointing their fingers at the drizzle of frosting on a muffin, mentioning how cute the Parker House Honey Rolls are, amazed at the size of the latest batch of chocolate chip cookies. Oohing and ahhing, they finally decide what tasty morsels to take home with them; what will be on their dining table this evening or their breakfast table in the morning.

Eventually, we have our first chance to take a break with a cup of tea and something to eat. I go to the kitchen, fill the tea kettle with water, and put it on the stove. Patricia and I sit at the table nearest the front window and sip. A hot cup of calming tea relaxes me.

"How is Delia this morning? Is she okay?"

"Yes, she is back to normal, but you can imagine the shock. First, to lay eyes on Jessica, be hit with a bolt of recognition, and then have her identity proven by mentioning Jessica's birth name and date; that would make anyone believe in miracles."

"It is a miracle, but we have to wait until Sunday to find out the pieces to this puzzle."

"Can you be over at the house by noon? I will have sandwiches and soup prepared for us. Having our tummies full will make Delia's story even more interesting, wouldn't you agree?"

I have to laugh at her logic. "Probably. Soup and sandwiches are my favorites. If we hear from Jessica today, I will tell her noon on Sunday is story-time."

The door chimes ring at that moment, and we have a bakery full of people. The pace keeps my mind from wandering, wondering what Delia's buried story will reveal.

Hours later, when the flow of customers slows, we busy ourselves in the kitchen, scouring the cabinets and the refrigerator for clues to something different we can bake to surprise our customers. We decide on oatmeal cookies with raisins, some with chocolate chips, and several dozen Snickerdoodles. None of these are unique, but if it pleases us, I am sure it will delight our customers.

The first batch is out of the oven and barely cool. I pop a Snickerdoodle into my mouth, munch down on the edge with my front teeth, and relish its smooth combination of sugar, nutmeg, and vanilla. Ah, my favorite. Snickerdoodles should be in the pantry of every house in Martinsville. Eating them makes me feel satisfied and relaxed.

Moments before closing, the telephone rings, and it is Jessica. "Sorry I haven't had a chance to call you earlier. We have been so busy on the shoot. Can you please put together a larger package of goodies for me in the morning, around ten o'clock?"

"Of course. Only at this minute did we finish baking several batches of oatmeal cookies and Snickerdoodles. I will package up a dozen of each, two dozen Parker House Honey Rolls, two dozen orange muffins, and dozens of our biscuits. I have both buttermilk and regular on hand. I will see what else I have that might be tempting for your folks. And about Sunday, can you be at Patricia's by noon? Lunch first, then the story we all are waiting to hear."

"I will make it work one way or another. I cannot wait to see Delia. Is she okay this morning?"

"Yes, Patricia says she is her usual self and is looking forward to seeing you."

"Ella, I want to tell you something. At one point, I honestly thought you might be my mother. You are an amazing lady, and I would have loved it if you were."

"Thank you, Jessica. You can be my daughter anytime you want to be." I hang up the telephone, wipe a tear from the corner of each eye with the edge of my apron, and then gather my emotions.

"Patricia, that was Jessica. She wants us to put together a larger package to be picked up tomorrow at ten o'clock. Let's start pulling things out of the display and package them. We may have to bake more pastries for the store in the morning. Will you prepare the dry ingredients for a couple of dozen cupcakes and two different kinds of muffins? I will pull the recipe strips. I will juice some oranges and grate the zest. A vanilla sheet cake enhanced with orange zest will be tasty, and when it is cool, we will cut it into squares, then top them with a half-round of an orange slice."

"Don't forget a sugar drizzle topping, or else that cake will look naked."

"I have an even better idea. Let's make a chocolate drizzle with cocoa powder, confectioner's sugar, and water. We can add zest to the cake batter and top it with a half-round of an orange slice; wow, that will look fabulous and taste fabulous, too."

My mind is finally back on my work, thank goodness. We continue to bake past closing time, and I am tired. We cover the trays of cookies and muffins with thin cloths and lock the door. I head home for a relaxing soak in my deep, long bathtub.

Dear Mayor,

I am amazed that Mrs. Ella offers so many different cookies and pastries in the bakery. My goodness, they make Snickerdoodles. Oh, how I wish I had a pile of them. They always were one of my favorites. Scones, muffins, orange cake - who is providing the fruit baskets? Is it anyone I know? She's taking good care of my farmhands, I see. That's how it should be. Those hardworking men are the backbone of our town and our country. God bless them.

Mrs. Devlin

Saturday morning comes around quickly, and we are busier than ever. The time has passed so fast; however, Jessica walked in the door just now, so it must be ten o'clock. The bakery is full of customers, so she will have to wait until I can gather her packages and hand them to her.

"I can see you are busy. I won't stay long. Ella, I want to tell you I meant what I said on the telephone yesterday. You are the woman I would pick for a mother if I had a choice. Do you think we can spend some time together outside the bakery? You know, someday after we meet with Delia. It would be fun."

"Thank you, Jessica. I am flattered that you could see me as your mother. I agree it would be nice to spend a little time together. We will figure something out, I promise. For now, here are all your packages. I hope you will be happy with the assortment."

Jessica hands me a fifty-dollar bill and plants a peck on my cheek. Her driver magically appears in the doorway, helps with her packages, and off they go in the truck. I love that girl.

While Jessica did not place another order for early next week, we decide it is best to bake extra pastries in anticipation of a greater-than-usual demand on Monday morning. We can never have too many baked goods on hand. If we have more than we need, we can always sell them to Daniel for Martinsville's Finest, one hop across the street where any number of hungry people are more than willing to indulge in a treat from the Devlin Bakery.

We keep the doors propped open, allowing the breeze to waft in and back out, carrying the aroma of our baking; the scent of cinnamon, nutmeg, orange, chocolate, baked bread, biscuits, honey and butter from the top of the cute little Parker House Honey Rolls. Then, my mind turns to the many flavors we have not tried. The one that comes to mind is almond. I'll put on my thinking cap for some new recipes.

When finished with our baking, we wrap or cover the baked goods to keep them fresh over the weekend. But now it is time to relax. I do not want to think about anything until Sunday, at noontime, at Patricia's house.

Back at the apartment, I find Tom sitting by the bay window, looking comfortable and reading a newspaper. I wonder where he got it? Hmm. Anyway, I sit in the chair opposite him, kick off my shoes, lean back, and close my eyes. Then, I have the feeling that something is hovering over me. I open my eyes to find Tom's sweet face staring down at me.

"How's my girl doing? How's my little bakery bunny?" He kisses me on the nose. "Would you like me to rub your feet?

"Are you kidding? No woman in her right mind passes up a foot rub from her husband. Oh man, that is so relaxing. When you finish with my feet, what do you say we go for a ride out to see Sharon? You have not seen her lately, and I know she misses both of us. We can sit on her back patio in the shade of the trees and let her wait on us." I giggle at the thought.

"That is a great idea. Give Sharon a call and see if we can come for dinner. I will call Daniel and see if I can buy steaks from him to cook on the grill."

I ring up Sharon. She is thrilled with the idea of us spending the afternoon with her and having a grilled steak for dinner.

"Why don't the two of you spend the night here? It would be a pleasant change of scenery. You will have the whole upstairs to yourselves. You can go to bed when you want and get up when you want. I will be your hostess and pamper the two of you."

"Fantastic. I will also see about getting a nice bottle of red wine from Daniel. We will arrive by five o'clock, OK?"

"For sure, I can't wait to see you."

While Tom calls Daniel about purchasing steaks and wine, I put together a duffel bag with a change of underwear for both of us, our toothbrushes, toothpaste, a jar of face cream, a change of clothes for both of us on hangers, and a nightshirt for me; Tom sleeps in the buff when it's hot. Before we head out, I change into a loose-fitting shift, comfortable open sandals, and leave my underwear on our bed. Sometimes, you must let nature be at one with nature, right? Off to Sharon's house we go.

Sharon lives about five or six miles from Martinsville, in the tiny town of Cooper, which is like being in another world. Cooper is charming, with one main street featuring a small grocery store, a hardware store, a gas station, and a few antique stores to browse through when you need a distraction. The town has a relaxed, tranquil atmosphere. The homes have been built haphazardly on a few tree-lined streets, with yards so large that one perceives being alone on the planet.

Sharon greets us with hugs and pours us glasses of fresh, cold lemonade. I run our clothes and the duffel upstairs to the large guest room whose expansive windows overlook Sharon's intriguing backyard. Covering the back wood fence is an array of flowering vines that grow thick and lush. A variety of thick, full bushes in front of the fence adds depth and interest. Three tall trees on the lot provide a canopy of shade and privacy.

If Tom and Sharon weren't expecting me to be downstairs, I would peel off my clothes, get under the cool white sheets, and nap. I decide against it, although it is tempting.

Downstairs, I find Sharon tossing a large bowl of lettuce greens in the kitchen. She then adds a pinch of mint from her garden and sliced strawberries she purchased at the corner market. We need nothing else to go with the steaks; the wine finishes off the menu. Had I known ahead of time we would be here, I would have brought a dessert or two from the bakery.

Tom lights the grill, and soon, the charcoals are glowing red hot, ready for the steaks. Idle chatter is all we are making; no questions about the bakery, Mayor Bigby, the horse farm, or anything about Sarah. Sharon doesn't know the story about Sarah's real name being Jessica, not yet. We will have plenty of time tomorrow morning to get caught up on details, but right now, all I need is peace and calm, the gentle sound of the wind rustling in the trees, the smell of damp earth, the shadows slowly creeping toward the house, a nice breeze to blow over me, and for someone to refill my wine glass.

Dinner was delicious. Tom grilled the steaks perfectly, and the salad is light and tender. I'm careful not to overeat. I want to sleep well tonight and far into the morning.

Before the sun gets low, Sharon and I walk around the backyard admiring the plants, shrubs, and flowering bushes planted over time and the thick bark on the mature trees. She gave no forethought to her planting, no particular arrangement or pattern planned. She planted as her intuition led her to plant, here and there, giving the garden wanderer surprises of foliage and flowers as you wend your way around, behind, and among the bushes. It's magical and inviting, as a nonconformist would want it to be. The interior of her home reflects the same manner of play.

At the end of the evening, I head upstairs and take a quick shower in tepid water to wash the day off my face and body. I let my lightweight nightshirt slide down over my damp shoulders. On tiptoe, I cross the smooth floral-patterned carpet to the big downy bed and slip into it next to Tom's naked form. He is already fast asleep. Should I wake him, pull him next to me, or let the sleeping giant sleep? I, too, am relaxed and sleepy. We will have time for togetherness in the morning.

Morning makes us content to be here in bed together. The sun has been shining for quite a while. I can hear the birds chirping in the trees outside our window. I should check the clock; after all, I would like to spend some time with Sharon on the back patio and fill her in on the newest Martinsville goings-on if she wants to hear all the details. Am I kidding? Of course, she does. Yum, I smell coffee brewing. Oh, that will get anyone out of the sack. Tom and I dress and head toward the kitchen. As I suspected, Sharon has a pot of coffee percolating and a pan of eggs scrambling on the stove.

"Good morning, sleepyheads. Please do me a favor and pop that bread in the toaster. These eggs will be ready soon. Do you have plans for today? How long can you stay?"

"The answer to that question is a long story, but the short answer is I need to be at Patricia's house by noon."

Sharon looks disappointed but knows I must have a good reason for leaving early. While keeping an eye on the toast, I tell Sharon of Sarah's chance encounter with Delia at the bakery and the meeting at Patricia's house when Sarah told us her real name is Jessica Roberts. I explain how the encounter leads to today's meeting at noon when Delia will reveal the Devlin family's buried secrets and the truth about Sarah's birth.

"It sounds like pretty heavy stuff, wouldn't you agree? Getting to know Jessica over the last few months has been an exciting journey, and now this girl will know what most adoptees will never know. All we are about to learn would most likely have gone to the grave if not for Delia. I have always thought she had a mystery buried under her skin, and today, we may find out what it is.

"But what reason could Delia have for carrying around this burden? It is interesting that the word, burden, comes to mind.

Perhaps this story goes much deeper than what appears on the surface."

"She is an intriguing woman, isn't she? Is it her unusual look? Her beautiful skin and those crystal eyes beg you to ask a question, but you don't know what the question ought to be. Is that what gives her that mysterious aura? Hmm, wait a second. I think I know what her eyes are saying, 'I know something you don't know.'"

"Geez, Sharon, you are giving me the creeps, but you may have hit on the real issue. I have been trying to figure out that look she carries ever since I met her. She is a bit mysterious but open, kind, and loving. She has a compassionate heart and wears it on her sleeve. I guess someday we will get it figured out. In the meantime, the toast is burning, and those eggs are getting dry. We best get this food plated."

"I think you will find out today."

"Oh my gosh, you have given me goosebumps."

Since we got on the road to Martinsville, I have been slumped in my seat, gazing out the truck's side window. I cannot help but wonder what Delia and Jessica have in common. Tom interrupts my train of thought.

"Ella, what is on your mind?"

"This meeting, this unveiling, if you will. I don't know if I am dreading it or what. Why are we digging up buried bones? Maybe they shouldn't be. How necessary is this?" Then, a realization hits me, and I sit straight and turn toward Tom. "You know what? This meeting will allow Jessica to learn the truth, and Delia can unburden herself, tell her story, and finally let her emotions out. That's it. Delia has a buried story, too. Oh my gosh, Tom, this meeting is more about Delia than Jessica."

As soon as we get home, I change my clothes and put on some underwear and sensible shoes, although I am not sure why. It could be that I'm bracing myself for what comes next.

"Tom, I will need the truck. You don't mind, do you?"

"Of course not. Take your time. I know this could be a long afternoon for you. I will stay here and relax. If I get bored, I will see if I can run into John or stop by the hardware store to see if Jeff or Mr. Cummings needs help. Take your time. I will see you later."

Tom plants a peck on my cheek, then pats me on my backside as I head for the door. "Good luck, honey."

Arriving before noon, Patricia answers the door and then leads me into the living room, where we sit in awkward silence for several minutes.

"Where is Delia?"

"Oh, she is back in her room; she will be here in a moment."

More silence.

"Do you have any idea what she will tell us?"

"Nope. Your guess is as good as mine."

Again, more silence.

The ringing of the doorbell breaks the stillness in the air. Patricia opens the door to an excited Jessica. Her presence uplifts us; she is eager to see Delia.

"Hi Ella, Patricia, where is Delia?"

Then, from behind us, "Right here, come hug me, darlin'. My, my, you look as pretty as a picture today."

"Thank you, Delia. You look pretty, too."

Patricia jumps up from her chair. "Are we ready for some lunch? I'm starving. I have it all laid out on the island."

Patricia has set the kitchen island with colorful placemats and matching napkins. She fills a tureen with tomato soup from a large pot on the stove and places it in the middle of the island next to a platter of grilled cheese, bacon, and tomato sandwiches, my favorite.

Lunch is delicious, but the conversation feels aimless; I think we are all anxious to hear what Delia has to say. To lighten the mood, I fill the air with details about Sharon's house in Cooper, how quaint the town is, how intriguing her backyard is, and how Sharon planted her yard using two key ingredients; her intuition and creativity. After eating our lunch, Delia suggests we sit in the living room, where she will tell us the story we are all eager to hear.

"Please sit down. Patricia, you and Ella sit in the chairs by the window, and Jessica, please sit on the sofa next to me, and I'll tell you everything you need to know; that is, everything I know. I will try to give you an understanding of what happened so many years ago.

"When I first came to Martinsville, Miss Marion hired me to do various jobs around the house; however, it didn't take long before I became more of a companion to her. She was busy with her bakery business; she enjoyed her work. She was in the bakery six days a week, and her two daughters, Natalie and Susan, were already out of the house; however, they both were living here in town. One afternoon, I walked into the kitchen from the back porch when I heard the front door open.

"I was startled. I hadn't expected anyone to be coming to the house. Then, a young woman came running in and sat at the kitchen table. She looked rugged; her clothing was dirty, and I could smell her dirty hair. I'm certain she had not bathed in a good while. She stared at me, then shouted and told me to call her mother. I thought, her mother? Who is her mother? I didn't know who she was talking about; then she shouted at me a second time, 'Call my mother, call Marion.'

"She stood, and I saw she was pregnant, very pregnant. She turned, ran out of the kitchen, and bounded up the stairs, big belly and all. I followed her, staring up at her from the bottom of the stairs. At the top, the girl looked at me and screamed, 'Call my mother, you....' I won't say the nasty words she called me. I realized she must be Miss Marion's daughter, a daughter I never knew she had. That was why I didn't pick up the telephone and call the sheriff.

"I knew Miss Marion would be home soon; it was nearly three o'clock. I stood there, not quite sure what to think, when I heard Miss Marion walk in the back door. I went back into the kitchen, and we greeted each other. When she started to walk past me, I had to stop her. I had to stop her before she went into the foyer.

"I said, 'Miss Marion, Miss Marion, there's something I must tell you. A young woman is upstairs. She says she is your daughter. Miss Marion looked struck, and I had to tell her. I could not let her see. I had to tell her the girl was pregnant.

"Miss Marion started to tremble. Her chin quivered, her eyes were blinking and darting around, and she grabbed her throat. She kept repeating the name, Evelyn, Evelyn. It was shocking to see her like that. I was so scared. I put my arms around her tightly and led her into this room. I sat her in the chair where you are sitting, Patricia."

Patricia and I stare at each other, shocked at this story; Delia pauses and wipes tears from her eyes.

"Delia, what did you do next?"

"All I could think to do was to call Miss Marion's doctor. I ran to the telephone in the foyer and called Dr. Morgan. His receptionist answered, and I told her who I was. I told her that a girl was upstairs and that she was pregnant. I told her Miss Marion was in a bad way and asked if he could come quick, quick. She said she would send him right away. As soon as I hung up from Doctor Morgan, I dialed The Reverend Alwardt, the pastor at the Lutheran church.

"I had to wait a few minutes for him to come on the line. I kept hoping that the girl would not come down the stairs. When he finally answered, I told him exactly what I had said to the doctor's office. He said he'd be over fast. He told me to keep Miss Marion safe. I wasn't sure what he meant; safe from the girl, I guessed. I hung up the phone, ran into the dining room, pulled three chairs into the foyer, and lined them in front of the staircase. It was frightening. I didn't know what else to do.

"I ran into the living room and saw Miss Marion with her head tilted back, her mouth hung open, and her eyes closed. Oh lord, I thought she had passed. I gently touched her arm, and she opened her eyes and said my name. Thank the Lord.

"I told her Dr. Morgan and The Reverend Alwardt were on their way to see her; they would be here soon. She smiled at me, then closed her eyes again. Miss Marion seemed calmer knowing the doctor and the reverend were on their way, so I returned to the foyer, sat on one of the chairs like a guard, and waited. What do you call those men? You know, the ones that guard the castle?

"When the doctor and the reverend arrived, they went into the living room to see Miss Marion. Thank the lord they arrived before Mr. Devlin walked in the door, but soon he came home and wanted to know what the fuss was about. I said, "A girl is upstairs. She's pregnant." He looked startled for a moment, then went into the living room.

"I could hear them talking, but I can't recall a word they said. I was too scared. After sitting in the foyer for a while, I went to the kitchen to put water on for tea; however, I kept an eye on the staircase. I knew I could not let that girl come down.

"I made the tea, and then an idea popped into my head. I went to the end cabinet, got out the bottle of bourbon, and put a big shot in Miss Marion's cup. I took it to her. At first, she refused and said I should give it to Dr. Morgan, and I had to say, 'No, Miss Marion, this is special for you.'

"She took a sip, her eyes got huge, and she smiled at me. She knew I was looking out for her. She thanked me, set the cup in the saucer, and took my hand. We have been the best of friends ever since that day. We love each other. Yes, we genuinely love each other."

Overcome with emotion, Delia weeps tears of release. Patricia reaches over and takes hold of Delia's hand while she attempts to regain her composure.

"Delia, take your time, dear. We understand that recalling this story is not easy for you. When you are ready, tell us what happened next."

"Thank you, Patricia. I am all right. Well, now, let me see. Where did I leave off? Oh, yes, after I served her the tea, the doctor went upstairs, and Mr. Devlin followed. They were there for quite a time. The Reverend Alwardt stayed with Miss Marion, consoling her. The next thing you know, Dr. Morgan and Mr. Devlin came down with the girl and went out the front door.

"A few days later, Miss Marion told me they had taken the girl to Dr. Morgan's office. The doctor and his wife, his nurse, operate a clinic on the first floor of their home. The doctor and Mrs. Morgan have their living quarters on the second floor. Dr. Morgan has several rooms where patients can stay overnight or for several days when they need extended care. Dr. Morgan and Mr. Devlin decided Evelyn should give birth at the clinic so the doctor and his nurse could watch her due to her unpredictable nature."

Jessica is having a tough time wrapping her mind around all this information. She is in disbelief and feels the need to ask the obvious question. "The girl, Evelyn, she is Marion's daughter? She is my mother?"

Delia had no choice but to answer Jessica's questions; she could not avoid the truth. Delia nodded her head. With a look of bewilderment, Jessica stares straight ahead, startled by the reality of this new information.

"The next two days dragged on forever. I didn't know what was happening, and then Miss Marion invited me into the living room and asked me to sit with her in the chairs by the window. She confided that Evelyn was her youngest daughter.

"Miss Marion told me the girl had been a problem since age five. Nobody could figure out what to do with her; she was uncontrollable. Evelyn wouldn't do anything her mother or father told her to do. She sassed Marion, slapped her, and punched her. They sent her to many doctors in Chicago who gave her medications, but nothing helped.

"Eventually, when she became a teenager, she ran away from home, and then she'd come back, stay a day or two, then run away again. After she was about sixteen years old, they rarely saw her. She never called or asked for anything. Sometimes, she would be gone for a year at a time.

"The doctors said her head wasn't wired correctly and would be better on medication, but she refused to take the pills. The doctor said it would be best to put her out of their minds, not to worry, that this type of girl would always find a way to survive.

"Miss Marion and Mr. Devlin finally let go of the notion that they could help her, and eventually, their lives became much more manageable. No one had heard from her in years. And then, that day in the kitchen, it was all so shocking.

"The next day, Dr. Morgan's office called and said the baby was due soon and that Evelyn wanted to keep the baby. Of course, we knew that was not going to happen. Dr. Morgan asked Evelyn three times who the father of her baby was. He said that Evelyn turned her head aside and refused to answer.

"Three days after the baby was born, Doctor Morgan and his wife brought the baby to the house. They told Mr. and Mrs. Devlin that Evelyn had left in the middle of the night, abandoning her child. The doctor advised putting the baby up for adoption but stated it might be a challenge to accomplish, not having the mother present to sign off on the papers. That's when they told us that Evelyn had named you Sarah.

"Mr. and Mrs. Devlin went to see the judge, not Judge Garfield, a different judge, who said he could make the paperwork get done. He advised them to find parents who lived far from Martinsville to adopt the child. Marion and George contacted a lawyer in Chicago to oversee the search for parents to adopt the baby. It took four months to find the right people, and during those months, the baby lived here while they waited. And the baby became my little girl."

Delia now turns to speak directly to Jessica to continue her story.

"For four glorious months, I cared for that beautiful precious child. I rocked you, fed you, bathed you, changed your diaper, and loved you. I sat with you at night when you were fussy. You, Jessica, you were my child, not Miss Marion's. Mine. Jessica, you were my baby, and I loved you more than any mother could."

Delia wraps both arms around Jessica and hugs her tight, so overjoyed to have her child with her again.

With tears in her eyes, Jessica responds to Delia's confession.

"Delia, I know it wasn't easy for you to relive this story, but I appreciate that you did. Thank you for taking such loving care of me."

Overwhelmed by her birth story, Jessica is thankful that she wasn't left to languish in a room alone in the clinic. She leans her head on Delia, crying softly against her chest. Delia comforts Jessica and then continues her story.

"Several months later, Miss Marion told me the judge was coming to the house soon. On the day he arrived, he had a nice-looking couple with him. He introduced them as Mr. James Roberts and his wife, Claire. I carried you into this room and placed you in Mrs. Robert's arms. I had no other choice but to give you to them. It was hurtful, and it was beautiful all at the same time. I had to give you up; I couldn't keep you even though you were mine."

Delia pauses to sob and wipe tears of sadness and regret from her face. Once again, Delia composes herself and continues.

"I have something to show you, Jessica. Ella, please open the top drawer of the secretary next to you. You'll find an envelope; would you hand it to me? Thank you.

"Look, Jessica, these are photos of you and your parents in this living room. See? That is your momma holding you. I wanted proof in case a girl, a woman, would come looking someday. I have no other way to show what happened except by a photo of them holding you right here in this house."

"Delia, that is my mother. And look, that is my father; how fantastic. Thank you for being my mother for four whole months. I hope I didn't cry during the night and keep you awake, did I?"

"No, baby, you didn't. Would you like me to take you upstairs and show you the room where you lived with me?"

"Yes, please, I would like that."

Delia and Jessica ascend the stairs and stay for almost an hour. Patricia and I return to the kitchen and sit at the island, sipping iced tea.

"So that answers the mystery of the look in Delia's eyes. It was the searching and a longing for the baby she lost."

I take our empty tea glasses to the kitchen sink and look out the window into the backyard.

"Patricia, look, Delia and Jessica are walking together in the garden. It's wonderful that they have this time together. Delia needed this as much, if not more, than Jessica."

"Ella, after all the years of living with Delia, I had no idea she was keeping this story bottled up inside her. Marion never mentioned that she had a third daughter. Of course, she had no reason to tell me, but I can't imagine Marion and Delia living all these years not knowing what had become of Jessica. Poor Delia. I can't comprehend the pain of giving up Jessica, her baby. Hearing the story brings tears to my eyes."

Delia and Jessica look relaxed and peaceful when they return to the house.

"We had a long talk. Delia showed me where I slept in my cradle next to her. She showed me my baby clothes, a blanket, and pictures of us she had kept all these years. Look, here is one of Delia holding me. I am smiling. I guess I was a happy baby."

"Yes, you were, darlin', a very happy baby. I gave you all my attention day and night. Miss Marion told me my sole responsibility was to tend to you while you were in this house. It was the best time of my life, being your mama."

"Didn't my grandmother tend to me at all?"

"No, she didn't, not that she didn't care for you. You see, Ms. Marion knew you would be adopted, and she had so much heartache with Evelyn that she could not stand more. To fall in love with you, knowing that in a few months, some fortunate couple would adopt you, knowing that she would never see you again; the idea of it hurt her so. I know how upset she was when your new parents came to get you.

"When Mr. and Mrs. Roberts walked out the door with you, Miss Marion went to her room and stayed there the rest of the day. That night and a couple more, I heard her crying her eyes out in her bed. She was inconsolable. Jessica, please know she loved you as much as I did and still do."

"Will I ever get to see her? My grandmother?"

"I knew you would ask that question; here is my answer. Jessica, you have a nice momma, a nice daddy, and two sets of grandparents who love you. You have come this far and solved your mystery. You have your answers, and soon you will return to your home in California. Miss Marion is old, and she lives with her daughter in Wisconsin. Even I don't see her or talk to her anymore. To bring all this up would be upsetting. My advice, dear daughter, is to be satisfied with what you have. You have much more than most people. Let it go."

Tears well up in Jessica's eyes as Delia's words sink into her soul. Delia opens her arms to Jessica, wraps them around her shoulders, and gently rocks her. Jessica knows Delia is right. She has her parents and grandparents, and now she has the woman who loved and cared for her for four months. We sit in silence for quite a long time. Finally, I go to the refrigerator and break the stillness with a question.

"Don't you have ice cream in this freezer? I could use something cold and creamy."

"Look toward the back right corner, Ella. You will find a gallon of vanilla. We'll need the chocolate syrup, too."

The four of us sit around the island, eating big bowls of ice cream smothered in chocolate sauce. I don't care about the calories now; I need something cold and refreshing.

"Now that we have had our dessert, we can eat the leftover sandwiches if anyone is still hungry. I can reheat them on the griddle."

We all agree that the second round of grilled cheese with bacon and tomato sounds delicious.

Around the island, we sit, and Jessica tells us more about her life in California. She tells us about the clothing her mother is talented at designing and sewing. Her father is an analytical person with a penchant for playing jokes on her friends and family. Her grandparents live nearby, and she sees them regularly.

"Ladies, I need to get back to Tom. Delia, I thank you for being so open about the past. Good night, Jessica. I am overjoyed for you. Patricia, see you tomorrow morning bright and early."

Back at the apartment, I tell Tom the majority of the story and that I was right; the bones unearthed this afternoon were Jessica's and Delia's. Delia gave baby Sarah all her love and attention, hour after hour, day and night, for four months. Even though the child was not born of her body, in Delia's heart and mind, the baby became hers, was hers. Then, to willingly place the child in another woman's arms, to have the baby taken from her after four months of love and care was tantamount to ripping her heart out. I can't imagine the heartache she suffered. The meeting was essential for Delia's heart to begin to heal, that was for sure.

CHAPTER VII

Changes

It is intriguing, even a bit strange, how deeply someone else's story can affect you. The world should be different now, yet the sun rose in the east this morning and will set in the west later today. I believe it.

Patricia and I start the day following our usual routine by letting the pastry dough warm on the worktable while the mixers stir and blend our bread and biscuit dough, and the ovens make the "whoosh" sound as the pilot light ignites the gas in the burner into flame.

We find the farmhands lined up on the walkway outside our door at six o'clock, ready for their biscuits and fruit. After the last one leaves, I find myself standing at the counter, staring out the windows into the street.

"What is on your mind, Ella? I can see you are deep in thought."

"I want to make a change, Patricia."

"What kind of change?"

"We should have more time to ourselves before we get any older. I want to change our Saturday hours; open at eight o'clock and close at noon. The farmhands no longer come by on Saturday, but we can leave a basket of fruit at the door in case they do or for anyone who needs something to eat. We work hard and need a bit more time off starting immediately."

"That's it? I was afraid you had something more drastic in mind. I will change the sandwich board and put a sign in the window with our new Saturday hours."

"Yes, please do that for me. Plus, a time may arise when we want to take time away for ourselves or something important arises. After all, we do have lives outside of the bakery. Do you know anyone who could fill in for us if the other takes a day off? You must know someone, don't you? I would pay them for their time, of course."

"Yes, two other women were here with me when I worked with Marion; Kate Matthews and Janice Wells. Both live in town and are retired. One or the other might like to earn extra money. I will give the ladies a call."

"No, I should do the calling. See if you can find the ladies' telephone numbers, please. I will call and see if they are available for an occasional workday.

"One more thing, Patricia. My favorite time of year, the fall season, is around the corner. Tom tells me the movie shoot will end soon due to the changing landscape. Jessica has said more than once that she would like to spend time with me before she heads back to California, and while I am not sure what we would do together in this fine little town, I want to spend time with her."

At that moment, the door opens, interrupting our conversation, and Daniel walks in with a list.

"Good morning, Ella, Patricia. I need your help. Our breakfast menu includes a variety of toast, but people constantly want to know if we serve biscuits. They might as well ask if we have Devlin Bakery biscuits, as not any ol' kind of biscuits will do. Therefore, I would like to make a standing order for three dozen biscuits every morning. Is that okay with you ladies?"

We agree and send Daniel on his way with three dozen biscuits in a box. We will need to bake more biscuits daily and deliver them to Daniel early in the morning or after closing. Either way, they hold their freshness for a day or two. We agree to start the new delivery the day after tomorrow.

Before our conversation continues, Jessica walks through the bakery door dressed in a heavy cable knit sweater, blue jeans, and boots, sporting a thick red scarf wound around her neck. Her cheeks are rosy, and she is rubbing her cold hands together.

"Morning Patricia, Ella. Boy, it is starting to get cold in the mornings. We have to rise so early to prepare for the shoot. I know I didn't call in an order, but I would like to take some baked goods out to the crew. What can you spare?"

"We have plenty of freshly baked biscuits, bran muffins with raisins, oatmeal cookies, half an apple pie, and chocolate cupcakes. How does that sound?"

"Perfect, of course."

"Tom tells me the shoot will be coming to an end soon. How much longer will you all be in town?" My heart beats faster as I ask the question and await her answer.

"Another month possibly, but probably not past the end of October. It might depend on the weather, but we have all we need from the farm with the horses."

Patricia brings the packages from the kitchen wrapped in paper and neatly tied with twine. She hands them to me, and as I turn to hand them to Jessica, we simultaneously say the other's name. We laugh, and then both say, "You go first."

"What did you want to say, Jessica?"

"Do you think we can have lunch together before we all leave? I will miss Martinsville, but I need to get back to California and my parents. They are expecting me. They miss me."

"Yes, I would like that very much. We could get together on a Saturday at noon or Sunday."

The door opens before we can plan a time; her driver stands impatiently waiting for her. "Oops, gotta go. I will call you." Jessica turns and sweeps out the door as her driver leans in and holds it open for her.

My emotions well up in me, knowing Jessica will leave soon for California, never to be seen again. I am about to cry. The calendar marks the end of summer, the movie shoot is coming to a close, and Jessica will no longer be a part of my day but will remain in my heart and mind.

I pick up the corners of my apron and dab my eyes as I hurriedly walk into the office, leaving Patricia alone in the middle of the floor. I hear our door chime, signaling we have customers, for which I am thankful; I need a distraction. I must set my emotions aside and return to the store.

People are buying our latest creations, almond cookies and scones made with almond paste blended into the dough and topped with slivered almonds. I added a pinch of cinnamon to the mix to make it even tastier. The pace finally begins to slow around eleven o'clock, so while Patricia helps the last few customers with their selection, I head into the kitchen and put the tea kettle on the burner. We sit at the table in silence for a few restful minutes with our hot tea and chocolate muffins.

"Jessica cares about you. You two have a connection, don't you?"

"Yes, Patricia, we do. I cannot explain it, but Jessica is an amazing girl, and although we know little about one another, we are connected. I think she sees me as a mother figure, more so than her mother. I firmly believe that when a mother works outside the home, it leaves less time for a deeper relationship to foster, and a child needs love and attention beyond basic daily caretaking.

"On the other hand, I am not sure why I have such a connection to her. It could be that I miss my daughter, and Jessica fills that need. No matter the reason, I will not question it; I will appreciate what we have together, this space and time, whatever it means, or if it means nothing, I will relish it."

Patricia is readily aware of my mood and understands that Jessica's absence will leave an empty place in my heart. Staying busy is what I need right now. We end the day baking dozens of biscuits, both plain and buttermilk. There are a few scones in the display cases; all the cookies are gone.

We close the doors and decide to take the first biscuit delivery to Daniel a day ahead of schedule. Patricia and I make our way across the street to Martinsville's Finest to find the bar and dining room buzzing with patrons, and in his usual spot at the end of the bar sits Mayor Bigby.

"Miss Ella, how nice to see you this afternoon. How is the bakery business coming along?"

"Fine, Mayor Bigby. We frequently add new items to the list of offerings, and our customers love coming to the bakery to see what is new in the display cases."

"That is what I hear. And what do we have here in these boxes? Goodies for Daniel?"

"Yes, we are going to bake biscuits for him daily. Now his diners can choose biscuits or toast with breakfast."

"Terrific for all of Martinsville and me, too. Say, can you and Tom stop by the office soon? I want to review the financial reports, and I would like you to join us. I have something to show you, something I should have shown you a while ago."

"And what would that be, Mr. Mayor?"

"You will have to wait and see. Let me know when you and Tom can stop by." Bigby turns towards the bar and takes a huge gulp of his foamy beer.

It rained overnight. As I step out into the brisk morning air, a damp, earthy smell fills my senses. It relaxes me. I am well-rested and less pensive as I walk to the bakery. Today, I want to bake something different for our customers.

"Patricia, what can we make today? What have we got in the kitchen we haven't used before? Com'on, let's get creative. We need to make something that will surprise our customers."

We begin searching the pantry to see if we have some spices and some ingredients we haven't used until now. Then, we come across a container of maple syrup.

"I didn't know we had this here, did you?"

"It was in the bottom of a fruit basket about a month ago. I guess I forgot to show it to you. I have an idea; let's make sugar cookies with maple glaze. And how about adding a tablespoon of syrup and a few chopped walnuts to our bran muffins? Here is a whole bag I brought from my house yesterday."

It is decided. We bake our usual fare, and while I wait on the farmhands, Patricia stays in the kitchen and puts together the ingredients for maple syrup muffins. Talk about an aroma. When maple syrup hits the hot ovens, the aroma explodes. We open the doors and let the scent roll out into the street. Our customers get excited when we bake something they have not tasted before. We end our day baking dozens of chocolate chip cookies, a sure treat everyone will want, at least one or two.

"Wow, what a fun day this has been. Thanks for being creative with me. Now, let's close and get out of here. I am tired."

That night at dinner, I tell Tom that Bigby wants us to stop by his office soon to review the financial reports with both of us, and he has something he wants to show me.

"Can we meet tomorrow after you close the bakery at 2:00?"

"Sure, why not? I can be at the mayor's office at about 2:15."

The following day, Tom and I arrive at the mayor's office on time, and Mayor Bigby is waiting for us.

"Welcome, Tom, Ella. Please have a seat. Has it been seven or eight months since you opened the bakery? Yes, eight, I believe. After reviewing your most recent monthly report, Tom, I must say that the bakery has become a real money-maker thanks to your ingenuity and hard work, Ella.

"I have been reporting the bakery's financial progress and the reputation you have earned in the community to Miss Marion every month. She is pleased that the two of you, especially you, Miss Ella, have brought the bakery back to life. Our townsfolk treasure having the bakery open again, and your kindness has not gone unnoticed. I haven't shared Miss Marion's replies to my letters, and it is high time I do. That is my surprise for you, Miss Marion's letters."

Bigby leans back in his chair, slides open a side drawer, reaches in, and pulls out a stack of letters from Marion Devlin. Bigby stands, comes around the front of his desk, and puts the notes in my hand.

"Miss Ella, you have become one of my favorite women I have ever met. I want you to read how grateful Marion is that the bakery has once again become a success for the townspeople and how she appreciates your efforts to bring it back to life."

It never crossed my mind that Bigby would communicate with Mrs. Devlin about the bakery, but it stands to reason that he would. After all, he and the judge were responsible for selecting the next owner who could make the bakery a success and be the right fit for the town.

"Why, thank you, Mayor Bigby. I look forward to reading them."

"Now, you two skedaddle and have a nice early supper at Daniel's place, and I will be in soon to get some of your new offerings, okay, Miss Ella?"

"Of course, Mayor. You are most welcome to sample any of our new creations. You know that, so please stop in soon."

Tom and I rise from our chairs, shake hands with Bigby, and leave the courthouse.

Over dinner, I read Marion Devlin's letters. "Tom, you have got to read these letters. They reveal Mrs. Devlin's personality. I wish I could have known her. She sounds like such a charming person." I return the letters to their envelopes to show Patricia tomorrow.

Dear Mayor,

Sorry for the delay in responding to your last few letters. I have finally recovered from whatever is going around in this town. The grandchildren are so sweet and adore being around their Granny, but they breed germs, constantly coughing without covering their faces and picking their noses in public. You would think Natalie would know better than to let them get away with such bad manners.

Here I go again, going on about my surroundings. I know I need to be here, but I sorely miss Martinsville. Would you please give my best regards to all my friends for me? Oh, and thank you for the financial report. Fantastic.

Mrs. Devlin

Patricia and I have been on our feet for hours and finally have a moment to rest with a cup of hot tea and a scone.

"Patricia, look what Mayor Bigby had for me, letters from Marion Devlin. He has been sending her financial reports about the bakery regularly. These letters are her responses."

Patricia reads them one at a time. "These are like hearing Marion's voice, Ella. So personal. I miss her terribly, but I doubt I will ever see her again. It is such a shame."

"You don't think you will ever see her?"

"No, I can't see that happening. When Marion left Martinsville, she wasn't in good health. I know nothing about her condition anymore, but I am certain she wouldn't come alone on the train. Plus, I feel certain I would not be welcome at her daughter's house."

"After she moved to Wisconsin, didn't you or Delia keep in touch by writing letters?"

"Yes, actually, we did, but soon her replies stopped. Neither of us knew the reason. We simply figured that she wasn't well enough to write anymore."

Patricia's comment gives me cause to be concerned for Marion. Taking a few moments to write a simple reply, why would that be difficult?

Patricia reaches into her apron pocket and hands me a slip of paper. "Before I forget, here are the telephone numbers for Kate Matthews and Janice Wells. Having someone else working with us will feel strange, but I understand your point in having extra help lined up."

"All I want to know is if they are willing to help when we need it. You never know when a situation will arise, and one of us can't be here or may want a day off."

I called Kate and Janice later in the afternoon, and both ladies said they would love to have something to do with their time. With a day or two notice, either is more than willing to fill in for us.

Mid-October has come and gone; the days are getting shorter, and it is more challenging than ever to wake in the wee hours of the morning, especially with the temperatures so chilly. Tom has started setting the alarm clock so I don't oversleep. The shrill sound of the bell will rock any sound sleeper straight upright in the bed. It is grating on the nerves.

The pace of the bakery business has not slowed at all. Apples are in plentiful supply, so we find bushel baskets at the door two or three times a week. We cannot use all of them, so we have more than enough to offer the farmhands. We encourage them to take several with them whenever we find another bushel waiting at the bakery door.

"It looks like we need to have another apple peeling party. Sharon might want to join us. We can certainly use her help, and if you don't mind, can we work in your kitchen again? We had so much fun last time, and frankly, I have not seen much of Delia lately, and I miss her."

"Of course. Let's invite Jessica to join us, too. When she calls in her next order, find out if she is available Saturday afternoon and Sunday."

"I have an idea. We can make apple sauce and sell it to Daniel for his diners. Or we could jar a few batches and sell them from the display cases. Who doesn't love homemade apple sauce?"

"Great idea and less work, to be honest with you. Then it's agreed, we are on for this coming weekend?"

"You bet."

Jessica doesn't stop by the bakery today but calls to place an order for tomorrow morning, a much smaller one, nonetheless, an order for our baked goods.

"Patricia and I are planning an apple peeling party this Saturday afternoon at her home. Sharon will be there, too, and we would love for you to spend time with us. Delia will surely whip up something delicious to eat, so how about it? Would you like to join us?"

Before Jessica can reply, Patricia leans toward the telephone receiver and, in a loud voice, says, "Bring your overnight bag and stay the weekend."

"Fantastic. Thank you so much for asking me to join you. I cannot wait to see Delia."

After we close and clean the bakery, I head down the street to Mr. Cummings hardware store and buy all the small canning jars, lids, rings, and hot water bath equipment on the shelves.

It's another busy Saturday morning, and as soon as noon rolls around, we lock the door and load Patricia's car with the bushels of apples and all the items we need to make pies, premade pie dough, spices, sugar, stainless-steel bowls, and several rolling pins.

At Patricia's house, we find Delia standing at the stove, stirring a large pot of vegetable soup. Bowls of tuna and egg salad are on the table, along with stacks of sliced bread. We have our choice of sandwiches to go along with the soup.

Sharon and Jessica arrive at Patricia's house right on time. Jessica's fresh face is void of makeup, her long brown hair pinned in a knot at the nape of her neck. She looks adorable, dressed in her blue jeans, heavy cable knit sweater, and signature red scarf looped around her neck. Jessica greets Delia with a big hug and kisses on her cheek.

"It has been busy at the movie shoot, but it is finally winding down, and I will have more free time soon. Patricia invited me to spend the weekend with you, and I hope that's okay. I brought my overnight bag with me."

"Of course, darlin'. Put your bag in the room down the hall, the last one on the right. It is next to mine. We can stay up all night talking if we want." Jessica and Delia hug each other again; their relationship is endearing.

"Okay ladies, please take a seat. I am starving, so let's eat first. Then, we can start peeling and cutting up the apples. We will be doing well if we can make about ten pies."

"Sounds like a good plan. Daniel said he would take as many as we can provide, but we certainly want some for our display cases. I also told him we will make applesauce, and he liked that idea; he said applesauce would complement the new dinners he has planned for his fall menu."

We all sit down with bowls of hot soup and make our sandwiches. Midway through lunch, Jessica says she has an announcement. We all stop chewing and look in her direction, our attention piqued.

"I have decided to stay in Martinsville a little longer, past the end of the movie shoot. I love this town and the people I have come to know. I will miss my parents, but I need to be here a bit longer, on my own, to figure out what I want to do with the rest of my life."

Jessica pauses and looks to see the reaction on our faces. We glance at each other. We are all a bit stunned by her decision. None of us expected this from her; we congratulate her. We continue eating our meal, and Jessica tells us more about her plans with a big smile.

"I have already arranged for my lodging at Martinsville's Finest. John Wayne still has the room on the second floor, and he told Daniel not to refund him for rent paid after he leaves town but to allow me to use the balance of his rental agreement. Daniel says I can stay even longer if I want. I have a good amount of money saved, and my manager, the director, is okay with my not returning to California now. He doesn't have any work lined up for me after we finish the movie shoot."

I put down my sandwich, reach for Jessica's arm, and squeeze it. "Jessica, you have made me a happy woman today." Sometimes the world knows what you want and gives it to you.

"Thank you, Ella. I was hoping that would please you. Now we can spend time together, yes?"

"Yes, of course. We will make plans soon. There isn't much to do here in town, but if you want to stay awhile, you will get to know it better."

"Why don't the two of you come and stay a couple of days with me? We can go hiking and rummage around in the antique stores. That is the best my tiny town offers, but it would be a change of scenery for both of you."

Jessica and I look at each other and nod in affirmation. We will spend a long weekend at Sharon's house in Cooper.

We spend the rest of the day rolling out pie crusts, filling them with apples mixed with spices and sugar. Jessica has never used a rolling pin, but it doesn't take long for her to get the hang of it. She manages to roll out a reasonably even pie crust.

Sitting at the island, Sharon, Delia, and I continue to peel apples while Patricia is at the stove, stirring the large pot of apples to make apple sauce. The whole house smells like hot apples, cinnamon, and nutmeg. We bake ten pies and fill fifteen pint-size jars with applesauce.

It is getting late; I finally decide to head home. I am exhausted. I roll into bed next to Tom, who has spent the entire day at the Lancaster Horse Farm having a good ol' horseback ride and a barbecue with the director, the last of the crew, and John Wayne. I am not sure which of us is the luckier, but it doesn't matter.

This morning, we prepare and bake our standard fare; loaves of bread and biscuits. Then, I take a moment to review the lengthy list of treats we need to make and get into the display cases. I glance at the clock, which tells me I am late opening our door. I rush into the store and see a long line of farmhands waiting patiently on the sidewalk.

"Good morning, gentlemen. Sorry to be late opening the door; please come in out of the cold."

"Hello, Miss Ella. Yes, it is getting mighty chilly these mornings," says Adam. His usual rosy cheeks are bright red now.

The men all look stiff from the cold despite their warm coats. What else can we do for these hardworking men? Then, I have a bright idea. I will talk to Daniel about providing hot coffee for them now that fall is here; it will only get colder as the months go forward.

After some head-scratching, I decide to talk with Mr. Cummings and see what he could contribute to my plan to help the farmhands. After I explain my idea to Mr. Cummings, he stares at the floor, rubbing his chin, and then offers a suggestion. He has agreed to order a case or two of thermos bottles and donate them to the farmhands.

Yesterday morning, the thermos bottles arrived, and before we closed for the day, Daniel brought in a table, a coffee urn, and a bowl of sugar and set up the coffee service.

As the farmhands enter the bakery this morning, I find the look on their faces amusing; like little animals, they sniff the air and recognize the rich aroma of hot brewed coffee. Patricia satisfies their curiosity by announcing that we will be serving hot coffee every morning, compliments of Daniel, in a thermos bottle donated by Mr. Cummings.

As the men receive their biscuits, Patricia calls each farmhand over to the table, hands them a thermos filled with coffee, the cap on tight, and reminds them to bring it tomorrow morning for a refill. The men utter, "Thank you, ma'am," or "Thank you, Miss Patricia." The generosity of the people of our community has struck the men's hearts.

As the last of the farmhands leave, Mayor Bigby walks in the door, brushing past them as if they were invisible.

"Ella, can you and Tom come to my office after you close today? I have an important issue to discuss with you."

"Yes, I guess so." I pause. "Wait, Mayor Bigby, please see if you can find Tom for me. I don't know what he had planned to do today."

"I sure will. See you about two-fifteen."

Oddly, the mayor leaves without asking for a sweet to take with him. Patricia and I stand and stare, neither knowing what to make of Bigby's request nor the solemn look on his face.

We spend the rest of the day waiting on customers and selling almost all the baked goods in the display cases. Patricia bakes more biscuits and anything else she can whip up quickly. I walk out the door precisely at two o'clock, leaving Patricia to clean the kitchen and close the bakery. I walk to Bigby's office as fast as possible to find Tom, Mayor Bigby, and Judge Garfield waiting for me.

"Ella, Tom, we have a situation that we need to handle as soon as possible. Judge Garfield received a call from Marion Devlin early this morning. Arthur, would you please tell Tom and Ella what she had to say?"

"As you know, Mrs. Devlin established her will and trust with specific stipulations for transferring the bakery to a potential new owner. After one year of operation by a new tenant, the transfer would occur if the bakery has been a financial success and the new tenants have met with the approval of the townspeople. We all know you have met both of those criteria already. The bakery has revenues far exceeding what John and I had expected, and the townspeople admire and respect both of you.

"Unfortunately, Mrs. Devlin's daughters are privy to your success, and they are pressuring their mother to change the trust so that the new owner will need to purchase the bakery instead of taking ownership at no cost.

"Marion is distraught over her two daughters' demands. I might add that she has sought the help of her lawyer in Reedsburg without their knowledge; however, before this goes any further, Marion wants the bakery to be legally turned over to you now, Tom and Ella. Marion doesn't want to wait for the one-year term to arrive. She has the authority to alter the terms. The trust is hers."

We sit in disbelief, not sure what to say. Finally, Tom speaks, "Judge Garfield, what do we do now?"

"We go to Reedsburg, meet her lawyer, and handle this situation immediately. We need to get the transfer of ownership finalized and prevent those greedy women from running roughshod over their mother. Excuse me, I should not have said it that way, but we all highly respect Marion Devlin, and we do not want to see her pushed around like this, nor do we want any problems to arise in the future for the two of you. Miss Marion knows she needs this transaction handled as soon as possible to end this conflict with her daughters."

"When can we get this resolved?"

"Tomorrow morning. The train to Reedsburg leaves at eight a.m. Go home and start packing."

I'm in a bit of a daze as we leave the courthouse, and then it begins to sink into my head what difficulties we may face with Marion Devlin's daughters. How much power do they have? Is Marion strong enough to stand up to her daughters? My next concern is the bakery, with me being gone for several days. Patricia is a competent woman, but handling the bakery solo is impossible.

"Tom, please drive me over to Patricia's house. I need to tell her what has happened and have her call Kate and Janice to come and help while we are gone."

Patricia, surprised to find Tom and me at her doorstep, takes one look at our grim faces and exclaims, "Oh my gosh, what is wrong?"

I can hardly speak for fear of breaking down in tears. I look at Tom; he understands; he'll take it from here.

Patricia ushers us into the living room, and Tom tells her what Judge Garfield told us about the situation with Marion and her daughters. I sit in silence with tears running down my cheeks.

"We leave on the train to Reedsburg tomorrow morning at eight o'clock. I need you to call Kate and Janice and see if they can come and help you. If, for some reason, they cannot, then close the bakery. Put a sign in the window. I do not care. I do not want you working alone."

"I will call them right now. You two go home and get ready. And let me say this; try not to worry too much. Marion is a strong woman who won't let her daughters walk on her. I am surprised at their actions as her daughters are quite affluent. Frankly, their greedy attitudes don't make any sense to me."

"One last thing I would like you to do for me. Let Jessica know we are on our way to Reedsburg. I am not sure if I will see her this evening. There is no need to give her any of the details. Tell her it is about business."

As tears continue to roll down my cheeks, Patricia hugs me and reminds me not to worry. She will call Kate and Janice and talk to Jessica.

It is early and dark when Judge Garfield's wife arrives, driving their car with Mayor Bigby and the judge in tow. We put our suitcase in the trunk and head to the train station, about a ten-minute drive. The car heater isn't emitting enough heat, but Mrs. Garfield came prepared with two big blankets to wrap around us. Thank goodness, or I would freeze to death before we get to the depot.

"After you left the office yesterday, I arranged for our train tickets and reservations at a charming old hotel in the center of Reedsburg. We will all be comfortable there. The hotel has private rooms where we can meet with Marion's lawyer.

"She has also become friends with her lawyer's secretary, a young woman named Sophia, who has helped with their confidential communications. If it feels like we are conducting ourselves clandestinely, we are. Keeping the process under wraps until the legal papers are signed and sealed is paramount to ward off any interference from outsiders."

I am at ease knowing that Judge Garfield has handled all the arrangements. I drift off to sleep for the rest of the drive. The next thing I know, Tom is shaking my shoulder. "Wake up, honey; we are at the train station."

Minutes later, we are seated in the train car and on our way to Reedsburg. I begin to relax, and then I am struck with a realization that had not crossed my mind until now. Tomorrow, I am going to meet Marion Devlin.

DEVLIN FAMILY NOTES

Arthur's Uncle William Devlin and his son Luther Devlin operated a bakery in Martinsville from 1895 to 1953. Hallie's brothers, Donald and Burl, had a bakery in Palestine, Illinois, and Olney, Indiana. 1935-1966. It was Donald who patented the *Revolving Donut Cutter* and pastry cutters. The *Cutter* business was transferred in 1966 to his brother Byrl and his son Kenneth; they were still manufacturing cutters 40 years later. Hallie's youngest brother, Jessie Houpt, lived in Indianapolis, Indiana, and was the Plant Manager at the Sugar Creek Creamery.

Submitted by Janice Wells Hood

CHAPTER VIII

The Meeting

Four hours later, our train pulls into the depot on the outskirts of Reedsburg and glides to a halt. We stand, retrieve our bags from the overhead luggage rack, and take the porter's offered hand to steady us as we step down onto the platform.

A waiting taxicab takes us to the Old Reedsburg Hotel, bypasses the main entrance, and pulls up to a door on the side of the hotel. The cabby toots the horn twice, and the side door immediately opens and is held for us by a hotel bellman.

We emerge from the cab and quickly enter the hotel at the bellman's behest while the taxi driver pulls our suitcases from the trunk of the cab and rapidly places them beyond the doorway. He jumps back into the cab and drives away in haste. The swiftness of this arrival has my mind in a whirl. It appears this entire mission is under wraps.

The bellman escorts Tom, Mayor Bigby, and me to a small private room off the side of the lobby while Judge Garfield continues to the main desk to sign us into the register. I take a deep breath and relax. I must be tired, for a silly idea pops into my head. I wonder if he is registering us using our real names. It's all I can do not to snicker out loud.

Soon, Judge Garfield returns to the room where we are waiting and hands us our room keys. Two bellhops carry our luggage to our rooms on the second floor via a back staircase. Judge Garfield's room is on our right, and Mayor Bigby's is on our left. We no sooner get settled in our room than there is a knock on the door. Tom cautiously opens it to find Judge Garfield wearing his, I'm in charge, expression.

"I recommend we all order room service for dinner and plan to get a good night's sleep in preparation for tomorrow's meeting. We will all meet for breakfast in the dining room at nine o'clock. Our meeting with the lawyer is at ten o'clock. Goodnight, Tom; goodnight, Ella."

Tom and I rise early the following morning. We shower, dress, and go downstairs to the restaurant. Only two tables in the dining room are occupied with guests eating breakfast; nonetheless, we choose a table in the far corner to afford us as much privacy as possible. With all these precautions, it feels like we are playing a part in a who-done-it movie.

While sipping our coffee, Judge Garfield and Mayor Bigby join us at the table. They chat while Tom and I sit silently and eat eggs, bacon, and toast.

"Hope you all had a good night's sleep. Our meeting with Marion's lawyer, Mr. Alexander Schroeder, is on the ballroom floor level in a private room called The Rose Room. We will sign the transfer documents this morning, so please remember to bring your identification papers to the meeting.

"Marion will not be joining us as she has already signed her name on all the documents. She will arrive this afternoon around one o'clock for a brief meeting with Mr. Schroeder."

We are all sitting around a table in The Rose Room at precisely ten o'clock. The judge introduces us to Mr. Schroeder, and the meeting begins.

"Good morning to all of you. Thank you for traveling such a long distance to attend this meeting and coming on short notice. With Mrs. Devlin's permission, I will now tell you of the changes made to her will and revocable trust.

"First, Tom and Ella, the ownership of the Devlin Bakery located in Martinsville, Illinois, can be transferred to you at any time forward, as you have met the requirements to become the owners of the bakery, short of the one-year waiting period stipulated initially in the trust by Miss Marion. The signing of the documents to transfer ownership of the bakery is what we will be addressing today. Congratulations. The passage stating that no purchase price is intended or required remains in the trust.

"Miss Marion signed the documents late yesterday afternoon to transfer ownership of the Devlin Bakery to the two of you. All that is left is for you to sign those documents here today.

"Miss Marion's second alteration concerns the section of her will and trust pertaining to those parties who stand to share an inheritance or receive proceeds from her estate when she passes. I might add here that the wording of a will or trust is specific, and it is not unusual for people to amend a will or trust constructed years ago.

"The new amendment states that any form of objection, written or verbal, to the contents or directives, from parties of a familial relationship or otherwise will result in those parties, upon her death, receiving compensation of $1.00.

"You may wonder how this amendment pertains to you, Tom and Ella. It does. The will and the trust are inextricably linked together. Miss Marion and I have taken every conceivable step to ensure that no one, including her daughters, has worthy cause to contest the will and trust or refute any specific part by claiming she is incompetent; however, a protest is always possible even after the papers have been signed and recorded. Objections to any section of either document could adversely affect the ownership of the Devlin Bakery.

"We have obtained signed, witnessed, and notarized sworn statements from her doctor and those collaborating with her on societal projects. Most notable is her fundraising work with The Reedsburg Library Society. The sworn statement attests to her physical and mental capability and competency. Not one person to whom we presented the document did not willingly sign their name.

"We want no confusion or misunderstanding about the execution of the will or trust upon her death. In the future, I will arrange to meet with Miss Marion's two daughters to present and explain the amendments added by Miss Marion.

"And do not worry about Miss Marion and her care. She is well situated monetarily to have someone look after her if her relationship with her daughters deteriorates; however, I doubt that will happen. They have too much to lose, and I am also here to meet her needs if necessary."

Mr. Schroeder reaches across the table and hands Tom a folder of papers for us to review. Mayor Bigby, Judge Garfield, Tom, and I carefully read over the details of the documents. Marion and this competent, savvy lawyer have closed every loophole that could derail Marion's wishes as laid out in her will and trust. When finished, Tom hands the folder back to Mr. Schroeder.

"I should point out that included in the transfer of ownership is your lawful right to use the name Devlin Bakery for the next hundred years. Miss Marion wants to ensure your right to use the family name and would very much appreciate it if you would continue to call it the Devlin Bakery.

"Now, if you have questions, please ask them. If you have none, we are ready to sign the document transferring the title and ownership of the Devlin Bakery to Thomas Edward and Ella Marie Watson, a married couple residing in Martinsville, Illinois."

Tom responds without hesitation. "We are ready, Mr. Schroeder."

Mr. Schroeder then rises from his chair, walks over to a table in the corner of the room, picks up a telephone, and quietly speaks into the receiver. He returns to his seat, and we wait in silence for several minutes when the door opens, and a woman enters the room carrying her notary book and stamp.

We sign the documents, and Judge Arthur Garfield and Mayor John Bigby sign as witnesses. Then, all of us sign our names in the notary's book. The process is finished in a matter of minutes.

"The amendments to the will and trust will now be recorded here in Reedsburg and then in Martinsville, Illinois. The transfer of the ownership of the Devlin Bakery will be recorded in both jurisdictions immediately following the recording of the newly amended will and trust. Thank you for coming, Tom and Ella, and once again, congratulations. Miss Marion will be relieved that this transaction is now complete."

We all stand and shake hands. Mayor Bigby and Judge Garfield congratulate Tom and me, slap Tom on the back, and hug me. The bakery is on its way to officially and legally being ours. Tom and I are thrilled. Meanwhile, Mr. Schroeder is organizing and packing his papers, but I want to speak with him before he leaves.

"Mr. Schroeder, I am looking forward to meeting Marion this afternoon. You do know we have never met?"

"No, I did not know. Excuse me, but I assumed you two had met in the past. Miss Marion is a charming woman, and I have no doubt you will get along fine. She should arrive around one o'clock for a brief meeting to review the documents, which will not take long. If I were you, I would be waiting in the hotel reception area."

"Thank you, Mr. Schroeder; Tom and I will be there."

It is close to noontime, so Tom, Mayor Bigby, Judge Garfield, and I head to the dining room for a light lunch.

"Mayor Bigby, today is a big day for a second reason. I finally get to meet Marion Devlin."

"You must be excited about that, Ella. I hope you get a chance to get to know her before we return to Martinsville. Our train leaves tomorrow afternoon at 2:00."

"That should be plenty of time, although I am not sure how much time she has to herself. I know she lives with her daughter, who might wonder where she is if she's gone from the house too long. I will let her figure that out and be thankful for the time we have together."

Tom and I finish our lunch and return to the lobby area. Unlike most hotel lobbies, the room resembles an elegant traditional living room. Two camelback sofas facing each other anchor the middle of the room and are centered in front of tall, multi-paned windows that reach almost to the floor. The windows, dressed with rose-colored damask draperies, frame the view of the park across the street. Multiple deep green velvet wingback chairs paired with tables and lamps are off to the sides for more intimate conversations. Soft, low lighting creates a relaxed atmosphere.

Tom and I sit on the sofa, comfortable and content to be here; I have time to think. I can hardly wait to meet Marion. I had always assumed that my sole image of her would be the photo on Patricia's mantel, but now all that will change.

I am relieved that the legal affairs are now final; nevertheless, I cannot help but wonder what Marion's daughters' reactions will be to the changes made to her will and trust. How will they respond to the transfer of ownership of the bakery? It will be final before they hear about the transfer. I hope this does not cause an immense rift between Marion and her daughters, but after all, they didn't even want the bakery.

Voices coming from behind us interrupt my random thoughts. Tom takes my hand; we rise and turn to see Mr. Schroeder and Marion Devlin walking toward us, and I am stunned.

I lean toward Tom and whisper, "Look, Tom, who does she look like?"

"Well, I'll be darned. Marion is an older version of Jessica; it's amazing."

"Miss Marion, I would like you to meet Tom and Ella Watson, the new, not quite official, owners of the Devlin Bakery."

Marion smiles at Mr. Schroeder's little joke. "Tom and Ella, what a great pleasure to finally meet you, although I wish it were under different circumstances. I hope this spur-of-the-moment trip did not inconvenience you."

"No, no, not at all." I am stumbling on my words a bit. I cannot take my eyes off that face, a vision of Jessica. It is uncanny.

"Shall we all sit a while?"

The four of us make ourselves comfortable on the sofas. I am not sure why Mr. Schroeder is staying. Is he protecting Marion? The circumstances feel awkward, to say the least, stiff. I cannot talk to Marion in this setting. I want to spend one-on-one time with her so we can bond. A little conversation lasts a few minutes, and then Mr. Schroeder speaks.

"I will run along now if you don't mind. Marion, I leave you in good hands. Ella, may I speak with you for a moment?"

Curious, I follow Mr. Schroeder to the lobby door, where he stops, turns, and leans into me. "Ella, you look like you have seen a ghost. Is something wrong?"

"No, nothing is wrong, but you are right; I believe I have. I can't explain now. Can we talk another time?"

Schroeder stands erect and stares into my face with a perplexed look. "I will meet you for coffee tomorrow morning, around nine o'clock?"

"Of course, I'll be in the restaurant." As Mr. Schroeder turns to leave, I have another idea. "Wait, Mr. Schroeder, can we meet this evening after dinner? Is that too much to ask?"

"Of course not. Shall we say eight o'clock? We can meet in The Rose Room." It appears that I am going to have to explain myself tonight.

I return to the lobby to find Marion standing, talking to Tom. "So sorry for the interruption. Marion, do you have time to stay and talk for a while?"

"No, I don't. I must get back to the house, but can I meet you here tomorrow, say, at ten o'clock? That way, we can get better acquainted. You know, you are caring for my baby, the bakery."

"That is perfect. I will meet you here in the lobby."

"Until then, have a good evening, Ella. You too, Tom."

With that, Marion walks out the front doors of the hotel. Once she is out of sight, I turn back to Tom. A bit annoyed, he confronts me.

"What the heck was that about? What did Schroeder want? You left me sitting here alone with Marion."

"Sit down, Tom, and be quiet, for goodness' sake. Mr. Schroeder noticed the look on my face. He said I looked like I had seen a ghost, and I had to tell him, yes, I believe I have."

"Oh no, Ella, why did you say that?"

"Because it was so obvious," I spit out from clenched teeth. "Here I am, meeting a woman who has no idea I know so much about her, including everything about her long-lost granddaughter who has shown up in the town where she was born. They look exactly alike, and you wonder why I look like I have seen a ghost. I'm pretty sure I have. And what do I do about it? I can't simply blurt out, oh, by the way, your long-lost granddaughter is in town, and she would like to meet you, now, can I?"

"Oh geez, so now what?"

"Mr. Schroeder is meeting me in The Rose Room at eight o'clock this evening. I will tell him the whole story. He will know what to do."

"Ok, but you are not meeting him alone; I am going with you."

Later that evening, dinner time is a bit awkward. Tom remains peeved with me. We should be in a good mood after how the meeting with the lawyer went today, but neither of us is in a reasonable frame of mind. Judge Garfield and Mayor Bigby have joined us; they are in an upbeat mood.

"Ella, will you and Marion have time together tomorrow before we leave?"

"Yes, she will be here at ten o'clock. We are meeting in the lobby."

"Out the back of the hotel is a garden. You can walk around together and have a pleasant conversation if the weather holds up."

"What a great idea; we can walk and talk, and if the conversation lags, we can admire the plants." Mayor Bigby stares at me, unsure of what to make of my sarcasm.

It is now almost eight o'clock. Tom and I walk up the stairs to the ballroom level and find The Rose Room door ajar. Mr. Schroeder is waiting for us. We take our seats.

"Now, what is all this about seeing a ghost, Ella?"

"Mr. Schroeder, I have a story to tell you, and it is a long story but one worth hearing. But first, do you know Mrs. Devlin's history, all about her family and background?"

"Yes, I suppose I could say I do."

"I know quite a bit about her, too. Her employee, Patricia Snyder, works for me. I have been to Patricia's home, which was once Marion's home. I have met Delia, Marion's long-time companion. I know how they met and how Delia came to live with Patricia."

Mr. Schroeder listens intently, probably wondering what more I may know.

"I also know about Marion's daughter, Evelyn." I check Mr. Schroeder's face and see my words have struck a chord.

"Several months ago, a young woman from California came to Illinois as a member of a Hollywood movie crew. Being adopted and discovering she was born in Martinsville, the woman was ecstatic to be near the town. Her birth certificate shows her birth date and her given name, Sarah. She introduced herself to people in town as Sarah, hoping to uncover details of her birth and adoption.

"One day, Sarah walked into the Devlin bakery to pick up her packages, which happened to be the only day Delia had been to the bakery since we had reopened it. When Sarah saw Delia, when their eyes met, they said, "Hello," and Delia offered for Sarah to sit at the table with her. They made an instant connection.

"Delia asked Sarah who she was, and Sarah told her she was from California, was born in Martinsville, and was adopted at four months. Delia couldn't resist asking for her birth date; Sarah told her and added that her birth mother had named her Sarah. All this information struck Delia profoundly; she immediately knew that Sarah was Evelyn's daughter.

"A few days later, we met at Patricia's house, and Delia told us the story about the birth and adoption. That is when Sarah told us her parents had named her Jessica."

"How do you know she is telling the truth, the girl, I mean?"

"Delia showed us photos of baby Sarah cradled in the arms of Mr. and Mrs. Roberts sitting in Marion's living room, which looks the same today as it did then. Delia kept the photos in case a girl arrived someday and needed proof.

"I should also tell you that Jessica asked if she would ever meet her grandmother. I know not all people want to search for adopted children. I understand it can be painful, but what if Marion wants to meet her? What if giving the baby up for adoption is the one thing in her life she regrets?

"Mr. Schroeder, I cannot walk into Marion's life and tell her what I know. That is not something I would ever do. Neither can I walk away without somehow knowing what she would want. I leave it to you, sir, to know what Marion would want."

Alex sits, tugging his chin. He then leans back in his chair and breathes a huge sigh. I can see he is weighing all the information I have given him.

"What is the girl's name?"

"Jessica Roberts."

"Her parents' names again, please."

"James and Claire Roberts. They live in Los Angeles."

"Tell me the part where the ghost comes in."

At this point, Tom speaks. "The girl is the perfect image of a younger version of Marion. No one could deny the resemblance."

We sit in silence while Mr. Schroeder continues to digest all this information. I hope he will know what to do and how to handle this with Marion. Soon, he leans forward, arms resting on the table.

"I can tell you that I know the story about Marion's daughter, Evelyn, and the adoption of a baby girl. I know it was a great loss in Marion's life, but I cannot say I know what she would want. When she first came to Reedsburg, Marion hired me as her lawyer. She transferred her will and trust to me, and at that time, she told me about her family history and her daughter, Evelyn. She thought the day might arrive when Evelyn would reappear. That has not happened thus far, but as her lawyer, I needed to know the whole story."

"Then you know Evelyn had a baby girl that was placed for adoption." I need to hear him confirm.

"Yes."

"And you know the baby lived in Marion's home for four months, and during that time, Delia was in charge of the baby's care?"

"Yes."

"Thank goodness, so you do know the story. Where do we go from here, Mr. Schroeder?"

"That is a good question. I need time to consider my approach with Marion, and then I will get back to you. In the meantime, please get to know her. I doubt the subject will come up, but if it does, please do not say anything until I have had the chance to work on this, OK?"

"Of course, Mr. Schroeder, thank you so much. You have taken this burden off my shoulders."

"You are welcome; I will be in touch."

I am in the lobby precisely at ten o'clock the following morning. The weather is clear but chilly, so I have my long coat with me in case we want to walk outside. I hear the doors of the hotel open and the bellman welcoming Marion.

"Good morning, Ella." "Good morning, Marion." We greet each other with a warm hug.

"Shall we sit a while? How about the two chairs in the front window?"

"That is perfect, Ella. I am grateful we have this time to get to know each other. I am sorry it had to be under these circumstances.

Now tell me all about yourselves, you and Tom. Tell me the details of how you learned about the bakery. Your cousin Sharon, she is the one who told you?"

And that is where our conversation begins. I tell Marion about the farm, the work involved, and that Tom and I had been contemplating making a change in our lives. I tell her Sharon came to the farm and told us the Devlin Bakery had been closed for three years and how the townsfolk longed for it to be open again.

I tell her about our first meeting with Mayor Bigby and how he stumped me when he said, 'Ya see, it is not for sale, but it is available.' Marion has a good laugh over that one.

"He can be a card at times, but he is a fair and honest man. He has done so much for the town of Martinsville. In many ways, his personality has become the town's personality. He is astute, too. Do not be fooled by his good ol' boy demeanor."

"Oh, I have no doubts about his intelligence."

"And Patricia works with you every day?"

"Oh yes, and she is a godsend. We work together so well. She came to the bakery several days before we opened and introduced herself to me. She gave me the binder of your recipes, which helped me make larger batches of dough for bread and biscuits. Now we have become friends, quite close friends."

"And I hear you have expanded your offerings; so smart of you to do that. I simply did not have the energy to do much more than we had been doing for so long."

"Patricia and I have so much fun putting our heads together to create new baked goods. We have a board where customers can post what they would like to see us offer, which got us started making a wide variety of items; cookies, cupcakes, scones, muffins, cakes, and pies. We now sell a good number of our baked goods to Daniel for his dining customers. When we have a new idea and start baking, we open all the doors and let the aromas float out into the town. That lets people know a new treat will soon be in our display cases. We get a kick out of wondering what people may be thinking."

"I can see from the financial reports Mayor Bigby sends me that you have made the bakery a tremendous success. Congratulations, I am thrilled for you and Tom, and of course, Patricia, and I am proud of you, too."

"Thank you, Marion. It has been a welcome change in our lives. Tom and I both love Martinsville and the townspeople. We thank you for your generosity in covering the cost of our lodging at Martinsville's Finest. The apartment is comfortable and quiet, and we are content to stay there for now. Eventually, we will find a home to purchase."

"Please know there is no rush on my account to find a house, Ella. I am more than willing to cover your lodging expenses. I set up the trust to ensure that whoever Mayor Bigby and Judge Garfield approved as the new tenants would have every advantage in getting started. I left the money in the bank account to get the bakery up and running if needed. It was the least I could do. You are taking care of my baby, my bakery."

"You probably know that Tom and I were able to get started without touching the bank account, and with your recipes and Patricia's help, we were profitable in short order."

"Yes, I know, Ella. You have done an excellent job bringing the bakery back to life, but enough talk about the bakery. Tell me about the movie shoot at the Lancaster Horse Farm. That must have stirred up the town for sure."

"No one knew about it for quite a while. Mayor Bigby wanted the movie shoot kept a secret; he tried his best to keep it quiet. He feared the townspeople would run out to the farm and create a disturbance. It took Bigby a while to realize that folks were not as curious as he imagined they would be. Instead, they kept to their usual routine when they heard about it, although Mayor Bigby was always at the farm. Eventually, John Wayne came into town with other crew members. They certainly added a flair to evenings at Martinsville's Finest. Now, tell me about yourself, Marion; how do you like living here in Reedsburg?"

"It is a delightful town, and as you may know, I have become entrenched in many fundraising events, primarily for The Reedsburg Library Society. That keeps me busy, and of course, there are the grandchildren. Suppose I had not retired and moved here. Who knows when I would get a chance to see them, although I miss Martinsville, Patricia, my friends, and my old home. It is lovely, isn't it?"

"Yes, it is. I love spending time with Patricia and Delia in that beautiful home. They both miss you very much, Marion."

"Thank you for telling me that, Ella. I am afraid I don't have much time left; I am growing older. When I look back on my life in Martinsville, I remember how wonderful it was with my dear husband, George, God rest his soul, and raising my daughters in that home. Such precious memories. I have only one regret, which is not bad for a lifetime."

A shiver runs up my spine. I try not to show any reaction to Marion's statement. There is a long pause, and I sense a shadow cross Marion's face. It appears that she has reflected momentarily upon a tender subject. She doesn't offer more information, and I certainly can't ask. One regret; is it the one I believe she could have? It's time to come back to the present and change the subject.

"What do you say we have lunch in the dining room? It is getting close to noon, and we leave at 1:15 for the train station."

Marion looks relieved at my suggestion; it distracts her from her deep thoughts.

While we eat our lunch, I share more details about the baked goods we make, how fruit baskets magically appear at the door, and the day we received a bushel basket of sweet corn that we took to Patricia's house and Delia showed us how to make corn pudding.

I tell her about the day I understood how serving biscuits to the farmhands was so important, how my emotions swept over me, and that we now provide them with hot coffee each morning, compliments of Daniel, in thermos bottles contributed by Mr. Cummings. Marion is overjoyed, listening to my stories, and admires how we take such loving care of the farmhands. Soon, we hear the grandfather clock in the hall strike one o'clock. Knowing that our time together has ended, we rise, and Marion takes my hands in hers.

"Ella, it has been such a delight meeting you. Thank you for all your hard work bringing the bakery back to life. I know the townspeople appreciate that you bake so many tasty pastries. Let Patricia and Delia know I think of them often and miss them terribly. Hug them for me, please."

"Thank you, Marion. I am most grateful for our time together this morning. And I will tell the ladies you miss them."

We had a pleasant and predictable conversation. I didn't expect it would be any different from what it was.

The four of us are quiet on the train ride back to Martinsville, most likely tired from the day's events. I glance at Judge Garfield and Mayor Bigby and wonder what they know about Marion's daughter Evelyn, the adoption, and Jessica. How could they not see that Jessica is related to Marion? Jessica is the exact image, a much younger version, of Marion. You would think they would have a spark of recognition, wouldn't you? The resemblance is so obvious; am I missing something? I am suspicious.

Marion will be sure to see the likeness when she meets Jessica; if she meets Jessica, that is. I cannot wait to hear from Mr. Schroeder about the outcome of his future meeting with Marion when he tells her Jessica is in Martinsville.

The morning after returning to town, I enter the bakery to find Kate and Janice working alongside Patricia. I had not met the ladies before, and I tell them how much I value their ability to react on such short notice to come and help Patricia. They both say they would be willing to help again whenever we need them. Once more, I thank them and let them select anything they want from the display cases.

It is late morning before Patricia and I can finally sit at the round table with tea and a biscuit.

"Tell me about the trip, the meeting with the lawyer, and don't leave anything out."

"It went smoothly. Mr. Schroeder and Marion amended parts of her will and revocable trust so that no one, including her daughters, can contest her directives without suffering dire consequences. He had many signed and notarized sworn statements from people who were more than willing to attest to Marion's capabilities and competency. We reviewed all the paperwork, then signed our names to the document, transferring ownership of the bakery to Tom and me. Marion included a statement that we have the lawful right to use the Devlin Bakery name for the next hundred years."

"Bravo, Ella, the bakery is now officially yours and Tom's. And, what a great idea about using the family name. You never know what hair-brained reason someone may conjure up to take you to court. Did you and Marion meet and have a chance to talk?"

"Oh yes, we met the next morning. We had the usual conversation, sharing bits of our lives. I told Marion about the farm, how I met Tom, and when we married. She wanted to know how we came to know about the bakery. I told her that Sharon had come for a visit and urged us to investigate opening the bakery after being shuttered for three years. I also told her I have been to your home and have met Delia. Nothing unexpected, basic information sharing."

"Hmmm."

"Hmmm, what?"

"Did she ask about me?"

"Oh, oh yes, of course. Marion said to hug you and Delia and to tell you she misses both of you immensely."

"Are you exhausted? You seem pretty flat about all this."

"Yes, I guess I am. It was intense, not knowing if we would become the owners of the bakery, and wondering what would happen to our hard work and efforts. Marion and her lawyer wanted to dissuade anyone from contesting or raising objections that could disrupt the future ownership of the bakery. The way it reads now will protect us.

"I should also tell you that I almost dropped to my knees when I laid eyes on Marion. How come you never told me that she and Jessica look so much alike? When Mr. Schroeder saw the look on my face, he took me aside and said I looked like I had seen a ghost. We met later that evening, and I told him the story about Jessica and the day she came into the bakery and met Delia. Mr. Schroeder was skeptical at first, but then Tom told him Jessica is the mirror image of Marion.

"He knows I know all about Evelyn, the baby, the adoption, and that Jessica truly is Marion's granddaughter. I left it to him to find out if Marion would want to meet Jessica. Marion has a right to know the girl is here and decide whether they should meet. To lay eyes on her and know she has had a good life and loving parents. I would want to know, wouldn't you?"

"Wow, I bet that was some meeting. I would want to know; I would want to meet an adopted granddaughter, but I honestly don't know what Marion will want to do. Are you going to tell Jessica all of this?"

"Oh no, I won't say a word to Jessica. I will tell her if it comes to pass, and I'm sure she will be thrilled. I know she would jump at the opportunity to meet Marion."

"What do we do now?"

"We wait to hear from Mr. Schroeder."

I can't help but notice that Patricia has avoided my question about why she never mentioned Jessica's likeness to Marion.

Back in Reedsburg, Mr. Schroeder has called a meeting in The Rose Room with Marion and her daughters, Natalie and Susan. The women are surprised at the request and eager to hear what Mr. Schroeder has to say.

"Natalie, Susan, I have made several amendments to my will and trust. Mr. Schroeder, will you please explain the changes that I have made to my girls?"

"Certainly, Marion, although, if I may, I'd like to begin with the subject of the bakery."

"Oh yes, that's fine, Alex; please do."

"Natalie, Susan, you may recall, the original trust established the criteria for operating tenants to become legal owners. The process began with Mayor Bigby and Judge Garfield selecting and qualifying potential new tenants. Second, once up and running, they must make the bakery a financial success, and third, the townspeople must approve of them. The trust states that once the operating tenants meet those criteria, they will become the owners of the business and the property at the end of one year of operation at no cost to them.

"The Devlin Bakery is profitable, as I am sure the two of you are aware, and the townspeople of Martinsville highly approve of the Watsons. Having met the criteria in less time than expected, Miss Marion eliminated the one-year waiting period and proceeded with the transfer of ownership.

"The bakery is now legally in the hands of Thomas Edward and Ella Marie Watson of Martinsville, Illinois. That transfer includes the right to use the name Devlin Bakery for the next one hundred years. Rest assured that your mother is in full charge of these changes. They are her ideas."

Marion's daughters look a bit ashen at these announcements.

"The second amendment to the will states that if family members or anyone outside the family contests provisions of the will or trust in any way, verbally or written, they will receive an inheritance of $1.00."

"Mother, a $1.00 inheritance? Did you need to make such a statement? Really?"

"It is for your protection, girls."

"Let me address that question, Marion, if I may. Ladies, a will and trust are written with specific parameters and language to lessen the possibility of interference from anyone, either family members or outside the family, who may contest the meaning of the wording or make a claim on the estate. Your mother wants to ensure her wishes are followed and protected from potential challenges.

"As Miss Marion stated, these parameters are usually part of the initial language of a will and trust; therefore, this amendment is simply tying up loose ends.

"I should also add that we have sworn statements signed by her doctor and many other people well-known to Marion who were more than willing to attest to her physical capacity and mental competency. These documents leave no room for anyone to contest the new directives.

"The new will and trust are on file with the court system, and a copy is in my office. Marion, would you like a copy of the will and trust to be in your possession?"

"Actually, no. Should something happen to me, the girls can see you."

"If you ladies have any questions, I would be willing to answer them." With no response from either daughter, Mr. Schroeder stands and offers to shake hands, which one daughter accepts.

"Thank you, Natalie and Susan, for coming."

Once Marion's daughters leave the room, Mr. Schroeder sits with Marion again.

"Alex, thank you for overseeing this delicate matter and making it appear to be a normal adjustment. I can see that the girls are surprised at these changes, but they were necessary. I apologize for their sullen attitude. Do you have anything else we need to go over?"

"Yes, actually, I do have a situation we need to address. If you have a few minutes, are you up to talking about a family matter right now?"

"Yes, Alex. It sounds quite important. What is this all about?"

Alex pauses and gathers his thoughts before speaking about the delicate subject of the adoption of Evelyne's baby.

"This is about the child born to your daughter Evelyn twenty-six years ago. While adopted into a family, she is your blood. What if this child should appear someday?"

"Alex, I am not surprised that one day the subject of this child would arise, and as you said, she is my blood. I do not know what the chances are that she would make an appearance. How does this affect the will and trust?"

"That would be up to you, Marion, but the young woman is in Illinois right now."

"She is in Illinois?"

"Yes, Marion, she is in Martinsville."

"Oh, my goodness. My granddaughter is in Martinsville. How did you find this out?"

"Ella Watson told me. The girl came to Martinsville as a member of the crew working on the movie at the Lancaster Horse Farm. She began purchasing a good deal of baked goods from the bakery for the crew, which continued for a good portion of the year. One day, she went into the bakery when your friend Delia was visiting, and they met. It is quite an interesting story how it all came about, but now she knows about her background and adoption with Delia's help, of course."

"Ella Watson told you, my goodness. I understand why she didn't say anything to me. And dear Delia told her the story. It is wonderful, isn't it, Alex?"

"Yes, Marion, it certainly is."

Mr. Schroeder smiles, reaches across the table, and takes Marion's hand. The impact of this revelation is beginning to affect Marion's emotions. Her chin starts to quiver, and tears fill her eyes. After all these years of wondering about the baby girl. What was the quality of her home life? Did she have loving parents? And what does she look like?

"Alex, does she want to meet me? Do you know?"

"Yes, Marion. She would like to meet you. Her name is Jessica Roberts. If you would like, I can arrange a meeting for the two of you."

"Yes, I would like that. After all these years, I am amazed that our baby girl has shown up. Should I go to Martinsville, or what should I do?"

"In my opinion, she should come here. I can book her a room at the hotel. You do not have to tell Natalie or Susan if you don't want to. That is for you to decide."

"Oh yes, that is probably best. This news takes my breath away. Natalie and Susan have never mentioned her. They were already living here in Wisconsin when Evelyn showed up pregnant. And to think that Jessica has met Delia. I can imagine Delia's delight in seeing the child again after all these years; what an extraordinary meeting that must have been. Go ahead and make telephone calls. Do whatever it takes, Alex. I would love to meet my long-lost granddaughter."

Mr. Schroeder helps Marion to her feet and walks her down the stairs to the lobby. At the curb, his secretary is waiting in her car to drive Marion home.

"Thank you, Alex. I never imagined this day would come, and I am so thankful it did. Let me know when you get in touch with Jessica."

Devlin Family Notes

Arthur and Hallie Devlin opened their bakery around 1943, The Devlin Pastry Shop, on West Cumberland Street in Martinsville. It was 1959 when Arthur and Hallie moved their business to a larger building on the north side of Main Street and lived in the apartment above the bakery. It was now called the Devlin Bakery. The Delvin's were bakers for over 40 years, operating their bakery in Martinsville for about 30 years, retiring in 1973 to Arizona.

Submitted by Janice Wells Hood

CHAPTER IX

The Reward

The fall season is officially here. The leaves from the trees, no longer green, are shades of gold, red, and tan. They have fallen to the ground and are swirling across the landscape, blown by a chilly autumn wind. Some folks think the fall season looks and feels bleak, but not me; it is my favorite time of year. I love the sound of rustling leaves, the refreshing sensation of the cool, crisp autumn air on my skin, and how the wind plays with my hair.

The movie shoot has ended, and the entire troupe has returned to California, except Jessica, who has moved into the room below ours. Her parents are not particularly thrilled that she has no immediate plans for returning to California; however, she explained her desire to remain in Martinsville to figure out what she wants to do with the rest of her life. How long she will stay in our little town is unknown.

Jessica and I spend an occasional evening together, mostly going for a long walk after dinner, often arm in arm. Tom recently returned to the farm to meet with the children and review the latest revenues, allowing Jessica and me to spend an entire weekend together. We went to the library, which is in total disarray.

No one works regular hours. It needs serious organizing, but we managed to walk among the stacks, selecting books to read and discuss.

Mr. Cummings offered to lend us two old bicycles he had stashed in the hardware storeroom. I hadn't been on a bike in years, but I managed to stay upright and not fall on my head. We toured the neighborhood near where Patricia lives, looking at the houses, a few of which are for sale. Jessica is a caring girl, and I love spending time with her. She truly is like a second daughter to me.

Daniel recently hired Jessica as his assistant to handle the jobs a business owner often finds bothersome and time-consuming; sorting, organizing, and filing paperwork. She is surprisingly good at putting things in order and has streamlined a method for keeping track of employees' hours, the payroll process, and paying bills on time. She has made two separate ledger sheets, one listing all the supplies used in the bar and another for the kitchen.

Daniel can rest assured that Jessica will promptly order the products and supplies needed for both areas. Daniel is happier and more relaxed, having Jessica's expert eye overseeing the office. With the burden of paperwork off his shoulders, Daniel will be able to devote more time to his patrons in the bar. And Jessica will have the financial support she needs while she decides how long she will remain in Martinsville.

Dawn has not broken as I head to the bakery with a thick wool shawl wrapped loosely around my shoulders. The air is chilly this morning; the short walk to the bakery energizes me.

By six-thirty, the farmhands have come and gone with a biscuit, an apple, and a thermos filled with hot coffee. Not until hours later do Patricia and I finally have time to sit with a cup of tea, she with a muffin and I with a scone.

"Sometimes, I imagine a little corner in heaven set aside for us for how we treat those hardworking men. I am not looking for a reward, but I see in their faces how much it means to them that we think of them and provide for them."

"If you knew more about my background, you might wonder if the good Lord would let me into heaven."

"What the heck does that mean? Were you a wild child, Patricia? I cannot imagine you were anything but the perfect daughter."

"I guess I wasn't that bad, but I did defy my parents' rules more than a time or two. Nothing harmful. I would call them mischievous acts of kindness."

"Oh yeah? What is a mischievous act of kindness? What are you talking about?"

"When I first met Jake, we were so in love. We couldn't keep our hands to ourselves. Fortunately for both of us, he had a degree of self-control, and his father held him with a tight rein. His father would have long talks with him about us. Then, one night, it got so intense that Jake ran from me. I couldn't figure out why. I didn't hear from him for three days. I wondered if he no longer loved me or had found someone else. I feared that I had lost the love of my life.

"Then, on the fourth day, he came to my house, dressed up like he was on his way to church. He knelt on the living room floor before my parents and proposed to me. I couldn't say yes fast enough. He was an exceptional person, Ella. No man could have loved more, and he was a good provider."

"I'm so happy for you, Patricia. Thanks for sharing your story with me. Did you have children, Patricia? It has occurred to me that I have never heard you talk about children."

"No, for all the passion in our marriage, we never conceived. The doctors could not figure it out. Their recommendation was to keep trying. That bit of advice we didn't need."

"You would have made a great mother, Patricia."

"Ella, I have something I want to tell you. When Evelyn's baby was born, Jake and I wanted to adopt her. We saw the judge, told him we were interested in adopting her, and wanted to know if it was possible. He sat there and said nothing except that he would get back to us. We waited several days for his reply; then, he told us that he had already advised Marion and George to have the baby adopted by people who lived far away from Martinsville.

"We begged the judge to talk to Marion and George and see if they would accept our offer, but he refused to speak to them, so that was the end of the discussion. I don't believe Marion and George ever knew we wanted her."

"Oh Patricia, I am so sorry, so sorry. It must have hurt you tremendously that the judge wouldn't even talk to them; see if they would consider letting you adopt her."

"Yes, it was a letdown, but we had to put the idea aside and continue our married life as it always had been. I was upset for a long time but did my best to hide my disappointment from Jake. I didn't want him to know how I longed to be a mother."

Patricia and I sit in silence. I can see tears welling in Patricia's eyes; the hurt and disappointment remain after all these years. I can't help but wonder what Patricia's life would have been like if she had raised Jessica as her daughter. It would have been a different life for both of them.

And then I recall the evening we met in Patricia's kitchen, and Jessica told us her story. My goodness, now I know why Patricia was unusually quiet the following morning. It must have been a shock to realize that the young woman sitting next to her at her kitchen table was the child she wanted to be her daughter. Heartbreaking.

Our moments of rest are cut short by the sound of the door chimes, and we are busy for the next several hours. Amid all the chatter with our customers, the telephone is ringing off the hook.

"Patricia, can you grab the phone for me, please?"

"Devlin Bakery; yes, she is here. Ella, Ella, come quick; it is a long-distance call for you from Reedsburg, Wisconsin."

I rush to the telephone, leaving Mrs. Parsons at the counter with a half-filled box of cookies and a piece of pie partially cut.

"Hello? Yes, this is Ella Watson. Long distance? A telephone call from who? Operator, I can barely hear you. Can you speak louder? I can hear you now. Mr. Schroeder? Yes, I will take the call. Hello, Alex. Yes, I can hear you. Really? That's wonderful news. Yes, I will find her. No, I know where she is. I will have Jessica call you. Please give me your number; ok, got it. Thanks so much for calling. Goodbye."

I hang up the phone and turn to Mrs. Parsons. "Patricia will help you with the rest of your purchase. I have to run an errand; it's urgent."

Mrs. Parsons gives me her usual 'humph,' with her nose in the air and that look of disapproval on her face. Watching it is painful, but I could not care less about her attitude. Nothing else matters. I need to find Jessica right now.

Flinging open the door, I run across the street, hair flying, skirt flying, apron flapping. I burst through the doors of Martinsville's Finest. Daniel looks at me like I am on fire.

"Where is Jessica?" No answer. "WHERE IS JESSICA?" At that moment, she comes through the service door behind the bar.

"Jessica, Jessica, your grandmother wants to meet you." We throw our arms around each other, laughing, crying, and jumping up and down. I am overwhelmed, and so is she. People in the bar perceive something good has happened, and several patrons clap their hands.

"She wants to meet me? She wants to meet me. How do you know this?"

"Yes, Jessica. I just received a call from her lawyer. Marion would like to meet you in Reedsburg. Oh my gosh, let's sit; let me catch my breath."

"You met my grandmother when you were in Wisconsin?"

"Yes, Tom and I met her, of course. She changed her will and trust, so the bakery is legally ours now. She is a genuinely nice lady."

"Did you tell her about me? Did you tell her I am in Martinsville?"

"No, it would not have been my place to tell her about your presence in Martinsville; however, I did meet with her lawyer. I told him how you came here with the movie crew and met Delia. I left it to him to broach the subject with Marion. I decided not to mention it to you in case nothing came of it."

"Oh my gosh, this is like a dream come true. Thank you, Ella, for telling the lawyer about me. I wasn't sure if I would ever meet my grandmother, and now I can, now I will. So how do I get to meet her?"

"Marion's lawyer is Mr. Alexander Schroeder. He advised Marion that it would be best for you to come to Reedsburg. He will book you a room at The Old Reedsburg Hotel, where Tom and I, the judge, and the mayor stayed. It is a stately old hotel right in the middle of town. It has a restaurant and a private park in the back. Rooms are available where you and your grandmother can sit, talk, and have all the privacy you need."

"Ella, would you be willing to go along with me? I would be more at ease having you by my side."

I had not even imagined that Jessica would make such a request, but I immediately had another idea. "What if Delia went with you?"

"Ella, I am not sure. I am close to her, but I have a closer relationship with you. You are like a mom to me, and I would rather have you with me."

"Jessica, dear, why do you need anyone with you? You will have private time with your grandmother. I would not be in on your conversations, so why do you want me to go with you?"

Jessica sits quietly, mulling over my words. "What if something goes wrong? What if she doesn't like me?"

"Jessica, of course, she will like you, you silly goose. You will figure this out, but I must get back to the bakery now. Patricia is probably going crazy all by herself."

I wrap my arms around her neck and kiss her cheek. I do love this girl. She is so dear, so naïve at times, and so reflective.

I walk across the street to find Patricia relaxing at one of the round tables. All the patrons have come and gone. She has a cup of my favorite tea waiting for me. I tell her Jessica wants me to go with her to meet Marion.

"Go ahead and go with her, Ella. I can get Kate or Janice to help here; it is not a problem."

"That is not the issue. Jessica needs to do this on her own, and I do not want to take more time away from the bakery. I don't. I did suggest she take Delia with her, but she wasn't too fond of that idea."

Later that day, close to closing time, Jessica walks into the bakery. "Ella, do you have a minute?"

"Of course, honey. What is on your mind?"

"I have decided about the trip; I am going alone."

That evening, Jessica has dinner with Tom and me in the dining room. Tom takes the opportunity to tell her what a splendid idea it is for her to make the trip on her own.

"Jessica, you will be comfortable in Reedsburg. It is a delightful small town. Marion's lawyer, Alexander Schroeder, will arrange for his secretary, Sophia, to pick you up at the train station and take you to the hotel. She is a good friend of Marion's. You will be safe there, in case you were wondering."

"Tell me, what does my grandmother look like?"

Tom rises from his chair, takes Jessica by the arm, and leads her to the big mirror on the back wall. "See that girl? You look so much like her; Jessica, you are a younger version of Marion."

A week later, Tom drives Jessica to the train station in time for the eight o'clock a.m. to Reedsburg. I saw her before I went to the bakery to say goodbye and to have a great trip. She appeared a bit nervous, but that will take care of itself once she boards the train.

Now seated on the train to Reedsburg, I can finally relax, knowing I will soon meet my grandmother. I have hoped for this day almost all my life. Tom says I look like her. Mr. Schroeder's secretary will have no trouble recognizing me if the resemblance is that strong.

Four hours later, the train wheels begin to grind to a halt, steam hissing and blowing from them as the engineer applies the brakes. I press my cheek against the window and see the sign on the side of the depot come into view. REEDSBURG.

A gentleman passenger helps me by taking my valise from the overhead luggage rack. The train conductor offers me his hand; I am careful with my footing as I descend the narrow steps. Once standing on the platform, I see a woman waving her arms.

"Hello, you must be Jessica."

"Yes, I am, and you must be Sophia?"

"Yes, Mr. Schroeder's secretary. I am here to take you to the hotel and see you get checked in and safely to your room. I know Marion is thrilled that you are here. I have arranged an early dinner for you and Miss Marion, but first, a private room so you can meet for the first time."

"Thank you, Sophia, for your help and kindness."

It is a short ride into town. I could have easily walked if it weren't for toting my valise. Sophia ushers me into the hotel and introduces me to the desk clerk, Mr. Raymond Krug.

"Welcome to the Old Reedsburg Hotel, Miss Roberts. We are pleased to have you here with us."

By the way he smiles at me, I'm sure he knows why I am here; to meet my grandmother, Marion Devlin. He hands me the key to my room, and a bellman carries my suitcase to the second floor.

Once in my room, I unpack my belongings, hang my clothes in the closet, and sit in the comfortable chair near the bedroom window.

Next to the bed is a small nightstand, and on it is a bowl of oranges. I lean back and find myself almost asleep when the telephone rings; it jolts me awake.

"Miss Jessica, this is Raymond at the front desk. Miss Marion is in the lobby waiting for you."

In the lobby? Sophia said we would meet in a private room. I quickly brush my teeth and my hair and smooth my dress. I am ready. I decide to take the stairs instead of the elevator to the first floor. I can see the entire living room from the top step of the staircase. My footsteps are silent on the dark floral carpet as I descend.

"Mrs. Devlin, it is me. Jessica."

My grandmother turns, and I see her face for the first glorious time. She stands, and we embrace. We break into sobs, and with tears rolling down our cheeks, we hold each other tight. We inhale deeply to catch our breath and sit together on the sofa.

"Jessica, dear, let me have a good look at your face. My goodness, you do look like me. None of my daughters look as much like me as you do. I could not deny you even if I wanted to."

"Thank you so much, Marion. But first, what would you like me to call you?"

"You can call me grandmother or grandma. The little children call me granny; don't tell anyone, but I'm not too fond of being called granny; that sounds too old-fashioned. What would you like to call me?"

"I would like to call you Grandma if that is okay with you."

"Of course, Grandma, it is, and why not?"

We both giggle over that question. It eases our nervousness and takes the edge off this solemn moment. I have faithful, loving parents and grandparents who could not care for me more, but this is different. There is a connection when you see your image reflected in another person's face. It's a connection between the eyes and the heart, as if they beat together. It creates a rhythm, a pulse. It is hard to describe unless you have experienced it for yourself, but take it from me; nothing else can compare.

"I do not know about you, Jessica, but I want a drink. Would you like to join me in a brandy? Apricot brandy over shaved ice is my favorite."

Arm in arm, we walk across the living room floor to the tiny bar area outside the main dining room.

"Sit here next to me, Jessica. Tell me about yourself now, dear."

"First, Grandma, I want you to know I have loving parents. My dad is a logical man and funny, too. My mother is a talented seamstress.

"I have always known I was adopted, and from the start, my parents treated me like I was of their flesh and blood. Being an only child, I had a close relationship with my folks. They talked to me like an adult, even when I was little. They gave me a good understanding of the world. They never hid the realities of it from me.

"My parents always trusted me, and I followed their rules even though sometimes I did not agree with them, but I never wanted to let them down or disappoint them.

"After high school, I went to college and got a degree in liberal arts. It's a general degree but an interesting one. I had no idea what career I wanted to pursue. A friend of mine was working part-time at a small movie studio. He introduced me to the owner, who hired me as a script aide part-time; that is my full-time job now. I work on the set with the actors and actresses. Now, tell me about your life in Martinsville."

We pause to sip our brandy, and Marion talks. She tells me about her family, the bakery, and her loving husband, George, my grandfather. She tells me about her first meeting with Delia and how they became friends.

"Jessica, you must tell me how you came to know about your birth. It must have excited you to discover your history."

I tell Grandma about the envelope with my birth certificate and the adoption paper with so much information blacked out and how my friend at the movie studio deciphered the details with his equipment, which is how I came to know I was born in Martinsville.

Then, I describe the day I met Delia in the bakery, how we looked at each other and instantly felt a connection, and how shocked Delia was when I told her my birth date and given name. Grandma is fascinated when I tell her about the meeting in Patricia's living room the following Sunday. She is grateful that Delia revealed the details surrounding my birth to Patricia, Ella, and me. The whole story is sheer luck; she is relieved and thankful that I know.

Marion takes hold of Jessica's hands. She looks down at them and recognizes the familiar shape and size of her fingers and thumbs. She smiles. For a moment, Marion has returned to the past, recalling, remembering.

"Grandma? Is something wrong?"

"No, of course not. Sorry dear, I was thinking. Now, Jessica, you are my granddaughter, and I want you to be a part of my family if you want to be. I have waited twenty-six years to see you again, to find you. I always hoped I would. We may not have raised you, but you are a part of us. You are a Devlin, Jessica."

"Thank you, Grandma; I would like that very much."

We sit silently over the next few minutes, relishing our first meeting and heartfelt connection while sipping our brandy. We then move into the dining room, order dinner, linger over our food, and stay until almost nine o'clock. We are exhausted from the emotions running through us. We call it a night and plan to spend the day together tomorrow.

It didn't take long for me to fall asleep last night. It's as if a milestone has been climbed and reached. I slept soundly until eight o'clock this morning. I shower, fix my hair, and head to the dining room for breakfast. Today, Grandma has a meeting and luncheon with The Reedsburg Library Society and invited me to attend.

"Good morning, Miss Jessica."

"Good morning, Mr. Krug."

"I have information about the location of today's luncheon, where you will meet Miss Marion at eleven o'clock. It is in the conference auditorium at The Reedsburg Library, within walking distance, two blocks away. She is the keynote speaker."

"Thank you, Mr. Krug."

I finish breakfast, walk across the street, and sit in the park until it is time to head down the street to the library. I arrive minutes before the meeting starts. My grandma is waiting beyond the doors, and she hugs me tightly.

"I'm sorry we couldn't have breakfast together. I had a last-minute meeting to review the schedule and presentation about the newest fundraising event. Come with me. I have your seat at a table in the front of the room.

"Jessica, I would like you to meet my associates; Mrs. Wilson, Mr. McCarthy, Miss Engles, and Mr. Smilee. Ladies, please meet my granddaughter, Jessica Roberts, from California. Jessica, dear, here is your seat next to mine."

Everyone makes polite small talk. Grandma soon excuses herself and leaves the table. Seconds later, the lights in the auditorium dim, and the room becomes silent. A gentleman walks to the podium and introduces Grandmother as the keynote speaker, Mrs. Marion Devlin, Director of the Reedsburg Library Society. The lights go back up, and Grandma appears on stage. Mrs. Wilson leans over as the meeting begins and speaks softly to me.

"You will be impressed with your grandmother; she is an excellent speaker, community leader, and fundraiser."

"Thank you for telling me so, Mrs. Wilson."

Grandma receives a rousing round of applause as she approaches the podium. She speaks for twenty minutes with no notes to aid her. Her eye contact with the audience is remarkable. Her speech is clear, concise, and enthusiastic.

At the end of her speech, waiters and waitresses, attired in white coats and gloves, serve our lunch; it is all very formal. After lunch, she escorts me around the room and introduces me to her friends and colleagues as her granddaughter from Los Angeles.

It's easy to see that the library has become a vital center in Reedsburg. People linger and chat; they are in no rush to leave the auditorium. The library is always busy; it has become the town's anchor.

Reflecting on the day, I can easily say my grandmother is the most gracious person I have ever known. It is as if I have always been in her life. We return to the hotel and spend an hour of the afternoon leisurely walking, arm in arm, through the gardens. What a day this had been for me.

Sophia drives Grandma home for a rest. We will meet again this evening for a late supper in the hotel's dining room, but first, an apricot brandy over shaved ice in the bar.

"Jessica, I have been wondering how you would like it if I introduced you to my daughters, Natalie and Susan. They are your two aunts."

"I must admit I don't have an answer to that question. I didn't expect to meet your daughters on this trip, or not ever. I leave it to you to know what is best for them and me."

"The idea of you meeting them has been on my mind ever since I heard you were in Martinsville. If you are to be a part of my life, it is logical that they would eventually meet you. I believe there is no time like the present. I don't want to make you feel awkward, but they need to know of your presence."

It is agreed. The next day, Sophia's car arrives in front of the hotel and drives me to Natalie's home. Grandma introduces me to her daughters, Natalie and Susan, and at first, they are polite, but I can tell they are more than uneasy. Grandma and I sit on the sofa, and Natalie and Susan sit in chairs across from us. We tried to make small talk, but Natalie and Susan had nothing to say, and after ten minutes, they stood and left the room while Grandma was in mid-sentence. It was strange, if not rude.

In hindsight, it would have been better to inform Natalie and Susan of my presence and not make their acquaintance. It will take a while for them to get accustomed to having another member in the family, and then I realized they may never accept me as a member of the family. Nevertheless, I have my grandma's support; as she said, I am a Devlin. I did meet my grandma's grandchildren. All three are so cute and polite.

Grandma and I remain seated in the living room until noon when Sophia arrives in her vehicle to take us on a motor tour of Reedsburg and the surrounding areas. Then, at Grandma's suggestion, we return to mid-town, where Sophie slows the car, drives up to a building, and parks. The sign on the building says Mr. Alexander Schroeder, Attorney at Law. Grandma and I take a seat in the reception area while Sophia enters Alex's office to announce that we would like to speak with him if he has a free moment.

"Alex, pardon the impromptu visit, but I was wondering if you have time to meet with Marion and her granddaughter, Jessica. I believe she has something specific on her mind."

"Of course, I'm not working on anything at the moment; tell the ladies I'll be right out." Soon, Alex comes out from his office and greets Marion and Jessica.

"Good to see you, Marion. Hello, Jessica. It's a pleasure to meet you; I've heard so much about you. I can surmise that you and your grandmother are having a grand time getting acquainted."

"Yes, Mr. Schroeder. Grandmother and I are so incredibly grateful to be together."

"Please, come into the office. Sophia, will you bring coffee and join us when you return."

Now seated, Alex continues. "Marion, it's nice to see you again. Is there something in particular you want to discuss today?"

Marion reaches over and takes Jessica's hand in hers.

"Yes, Alex, yes, there is. Meeting Jessica, having her with me, and knowing she wants to be a part of my life has brought me great joy. What I am about to tell you, which I haven't mentioned to Jessica, is that I want to include her in my will. We don't need to discuss the details now; that would take too long. Nevertheless, I wanted you to meet Jessica. Once she returns to Martinsville, you and I can get together to rewrite my will."

"Jessica, we will need a few personal details to identify you in the will. Sophia, please take Jessica to your office and fill out the forms."

Sophia's instincts tell her to close Alex's office door behind her as she and Jessica depart. She surmises Alex will want to talk with Marion in private.

In a kindly voice, Alex broaches the subject of Marion adding Jessica to her will. "Marion, are you sure you want to do this? I'm not looking to dissuade you from adding Jessica to the will, but I want to be certain that the timing of this decision is appropriate. After all, you and Jessica have only recently met. What do you know about her? Devil's advocate, if you will."

"Alex, it is true that we have been together for only two days, but she is my granddaughter, Evelyn's child. She has a right to be included; after all, I have plenty of investments and assets. Natalie and Susan need not know about this change, and frankly, I wouldn't care if they did. It is my money and none of their business. I am certain that Jessica will become a more significant part of my life as time passes. We can discuss it at length someday, but I know I want her in my will."

Marion and Alex sit in silence for a moment. Something in Alex's gut tells him there is more to this conversation than meets the eye, and he has learned never to ignore his intuition. If she has something to say to him, she will explain it in good time. Meanwhile, Alex will file this distinct feeling in the back of his mind for the future.

Finally, Marion speaks. "Alex, I have my reasons."

"I understand this is private, Marion. I am truly elated that you and Jessica have found each other. Say the word when you are ready to add Jessica to the will. It will be my pleasure."

Alex rises, comes around his desk, and sits in the chair beside Marion. They clasp hands. Yes, Alex can tell by the look on Marion's face and in her eyes that there is a situation here that we will not speak about today.

I have one more opportunity to have an evening meal with my grandma before my time here comes to a close. It's hard to comprehend that tomorrow, I will return to Martinsville. Mr. Krug has offered to call Ella at the bakery, tell her I will be home on the six o'clock train tomorrow afternoon, and ask if someone can pick me up at the station.

Our last dinner together is bitter-sweet. We hold hands throughout most of the dinner. We don't want to say goodbye, so we avoid the subject, and when we know we need to part, we sit in the hotel living room, still holding hands, tears streaming down our cheeks.

"Don't worry, my darling granddaughter; this is not our last meeting. We have the rest of our lives to be together, that is, the rest of mine. We will remain close; we will see each other again soon. I'll have Alex send for you. I love you, Jessica. Now, let's not say goodbye. Let's say goodnight."

We stand, wrap our arms around each other, and kiss each other goodbye. Watching Grandma walk out the hotel doors was a tremendously sad moment for me. Much later, we were to find out that Susan was in town this afternoon and saw Grandma and me enter the office of Mr. Alexander Schroeder.

"Tom, would you be so kind as to pick up Jessica at the train station this afternoon? She should be arriving on the six o'clock train."

I have these few minutes to myself, sitting near the bay window in our apartment, waiting for Tom to bring Jessica home from the station. I reflect on how my life has changed since coming to Martinsville; I am leading a second life without having left the first one. It may sound silly, but it is true.

My life in Naperville and here in Martinsville has been extraordinary. I was born, raised, and lived a satisfying and productive life on the family farm; even so, life in this cozy town is refreshing and energizing. I genuinely love living in Martinsville and owning the bakery. Not that one life is better than the other; they are different, and I have no complaints about either one.

The whirring sound of the elevator coming up the shaft interrupts my reflection. Tom and Jessica burst through the door; she runs into my arms, and we embrace.

"Jessica, oh honey, you look terrific, I must say."

"Ella, meeting my grandma was more amazing than I could have imagined. I was a bit stressed before the moment arrived, but all that tension left when I laid my eyes on her. She hugged me, and we both cried. She was so welcoming; we decided I could call her grandma."

"Were you able to spend much time with her?"

"Yes. We had dinner together in the hotel's dining room every evening. We had long talks. I can tell you more of the details later."

"Yes, save the whole story for when we get to Sharon's house in Cooper tomorrow. You remember we have a weekend planned with her?"

"Oh yes, I did not forget. I am looking forward to being with all of you. I can tell you about the trip when we are all together and what happened the last day I was with Grandma."

"You are home now; get some rest. We plan to leave around nine o'clock tomorrow morning. Pack a few items; comfortable clothes, PJs, shoes, and a light jacket. That is all you will need."

Patricia and Delia will join Jessica and me at Sharon's house in Cooper for a long weekend. Jessica will tell the group of us about her meeting with Marion. I look forward to hearing the details; I imagine it was magical.

Sharon is preparing an early Thanksgiving dinner for us, including roasted turkey with bread stuffing, mashed potatoes, gravy, a selection of vegetables, and probably plenty of wine. I love spending time at Sharon's house.

She has made the entire home relaxing and comfortable with her eye for decorating. I especially admire her kitchen, her parlor, and the guest bedroom upstairs, with the expansive windows overlooking the backyard. It is my favorite place to have a getaway. I'm confident the other women will find it as warm and welcoming as I do.

Before we leave, Patricia and I pass out biscuits to the farmhands early Saturday morning, deliver dozens of biscuits and three pies to Daniel, then close the bakery early. We are now ready to head out to Sharon's house.

As we start toward the tiny town of Cooper, something beckons me to turn and look out the truck's back window. And in the air, trailing behind us, floating and tumbling in the dust kicked up by the tires, are several four-inch squares of Kraft paper. The sight tugs at my heart.

It didn't take long to get to Sharon's house in Cooper, considering four women had to get their belongings in order first. As we approach Cooper, the air is different, lighter, easier to breathe, and smells like mown grass and damp soil. We see Sharon sitting on her front porch as we round the bend. Dressed in her standard attire, blue jeans, ankle boots, and a feminine blouse, she is wrapped in a heavy shawl to ward off the brisk morning air. She rises and begins waving both arms.

"So good to have all of us together, especially you, Jessica. Having someone your age with us will be a pleasant change of pace."

"Sharon, we are so looking forward to this weekend with you. Thank you for inviting us. Now, where do you want us to put our bags?"

"Ella, take the large guest room upstairs at the back of the house. Jessica, you sleep in the smaller room upstairs in the front of the house, and if you don't mind sharing, Patricia and Delia can take the bedroom at the back of the house on this floor. Twin beds should provide plenty of space for all of you. Once you get settled, I'll meet you in the kitchen. Does anyone want coffee? I'll brew a fresh pot."

We all agree we could use a cup. Within minutes, we are all gathered in Sharon's kitchen with full coffee cups.

"Would you like to sit on the back porch? It is cool right now, but it should warm up shortly. I'll grab a few shawls for us."

The five of us sit and sip hot coffee, our porch rocking chairs creaking in unison.

"Jessica, are you ready to tell us about your trip to Reedsburg to meet your grandmother?"

Jessica pauses her rocking and leans forward, ready and willing to give us the details.

"Meeting my grandma was the best experience of my life. We met in the hotel living room; we hugged and shed tears and sat for a while to get acquainted. We talked about our lives, mine, with my parents, and she told me about her life in Reedsburg. She said her life has changed since moving to Wisconsin, and her health has dramatically improved. Her blood pressure is under control now that she doesn't have the stress of working in the bakery.

"After a while, Grandma suggested we move to the bar for an apricot brandy over shaved ice, where we talked more about our lives. We then moved into the dining room, had dinner, and stayed until it was late."

"It sounds like she is in great spirits. How does she look?"

"She looks terrific. Of course, I didn't know her before, but she appears to enjoy her life in Reedsburg. She has met and become friends with many people in the community. She is the director of The Reedsburg Library Society. On the second day, I attended a luncheon at the library, where she was the keynote speaker. A woman sitting next to me at lunch told me how much the people of the Reedsburg admire and respect her."

"This is a remarkable turn of events. When Marion left Martinsville, folks assumed she was down for the count. I am so thankful to hear that she is doing much better. What great news for all of us, Jessica."

"Did you meet her daughters, Natalie and Susan? If you did, how did it go?" Delia is curious.

"Yes, I did. Grandma took me to the house where she lives with Natalie. Susan was there, too, and both women said hello to me, but they didn't engage me in any conversation. So, Grandma and I held the chat and told them how we met and about having dinner together. Natalie and Susan sat there and stared at the two of us without saying a word.

"After about five minutes, they stood and left the living room. They never returned or said goodbye. I doubt they ever expected to meet me, much less have Grandma invite me into Natalie's home. I'm afraid it was too much too soon."

"I don't mind telling you that the girls didn't like their mother having you come live in the house when you were born. They said their mother should have left you at Doctor Morgan's clinic under a stranger's care." Delia tears up at the mere thought of not caring for the baby girl, the child abandoned.

"But Ms. Marion wouldn't have had it any other way, such a kind soul, that woman. Oh, I'm sorry. I shouldn't have told you how they disapproved, but it is true. If I live to be a hundred, I will never understand those two women."

Patricia adds her two cents. "I'll tell you more truth, Jessica. Marion's daughters believe they know what is best; the world should revolve around their wants and desires."

"That certainly paints a telling picture of Natalie and Susan. I do have something else to tell you, though." Jessica pauses.

"Speak up, child. Don't keep us waiting."

"After we left Natalie's house that afternoon, Sophia drove us around Reedsburg, and then we went to see the lawyer, Mr. Schroeder. Grandma said she wanted him to meet me, and then told him she wants to add me to her will."

Silence hangs in the air.

"I think I shouldn't have mentioned this to you."

"No, no, it is ok, darlin'." Delia bursts out laughing and claps her hands. "Oh, my. Wait until those two girls hear about this. I want to be a mouse in a corner to witness their reactions. Oh, lordy, what a fuss that will stir up."

Jessica slumps in her rocker. "It might be better for me to tell her not to include me; after all, we haven't had time to build a relationship, and while we are connected, she doesn't know me well. Our relationship is happening so fast; it is a bit confusing."

Delia leans over and rubs Jessica's arm. "No, baby, don't do that. Miss Marion knows what she is doing. I'm telling you, she doesn't care what Natalie and Susan think or want. It is great news that she loves you enough to include you."

"Thank you, Delia. I don't want to cause problems for grandmother and her daughters; that would never be my intention."

Delia bursts out laughing again, the sound tinged with a bit of revenge. "Nothing on this earth can prevent it. Natalie and Susan will have to get over it."

Sitting silently listening to the conversation, Ella now adds her thoughts. "Jessica, you should be honored that she wants to include you. You deserve it as much as anyone else."

"OK, so I won't worry anymore. Grandma will let me know if and when she makes the change, but it doesn't matter to me one way or the other. I am sure she needs time to think and decide what she wants to do.

"I am so thrilled that we have had the opportunity to meet. I have always wondered about my grandmother and if I would ever meet her. Her telling me she wants to include me in her family means so much to me."

With that settled, their coffees finished, Sharon rises from her chair and stretches her body toward the ceiling. "How would the four of you like to check out our tiny town of Cooper? It is three blocks away. We can putter around in the antique stores. You may find something you can't live without."

"I'm on board."

"Me, too."

We walk into town and browse the little shops along Cooper's main street. At noon, we stop and have a light lunch in a small café at the back of an antique store, and then we slowly make our way back to the house. Delia excuses herself and heads to the bedroom for her daily nap.

We pass the rest of the afternoon, lazily, idly, and pleasantly. Jessica offers to help Sharon in the kitchen to begin preparations for this evening's dinner.

"Patricia, how about you and I take a walk around Sharon's backyard? She has done a marvelous job with her planting."

Once out in the yard and away from the house, Patricia can ask a question. She whispers, "Ella, do you have something you want to talk about?"

"Yes, I do. Patricia, it's wonderful that Marion wants to add Jessica to her will. My one concern is that this may backfire on Marion. Do you think her daughters will find a way to retaliate?"

"I have no doubt her two daughters will pitch a fit when they discover that Jessica is in Marion's will, but I doubt they can back Marion into a corner. Those girls act like Marion is sitting on a ton of money."

"And she isn't?'

"Marion has a sizable estate compared to many people, but it is not sizable as opposed to Natalie's and Susan's estates. Those two girls are wealthy beyond imagination, and they want more. Marion has enough assets to take care of herself through the end of her life. I assume she has minimal expenses now that she lives with Natalie."

"Natalie and Susan must know what their mother is worth, right?"

"I doubt they do. Marion is not one to talk about her assets, not even to her daughters. She is a very private person. It is easy to assume that Marion is rich, even wealthy, by how she carries herself. I don't know the exact numbers, but I would use moderate, to describe her financial situation."

"What did Marion's husband do for a living?"

"He worked for a large engineering company located near Chicago. He traveled a good deal during their marriage. I'm sure he made a good living. Marion told me herself. She said, 'The bakery paid most of our living expenses, and George was a frugal man. He invested wisely.' Those were her exact words when she sold her home to me."

Squatting down and snatching a few stray weeds, Ella is pensive.

"This is all rather intriguing. Hmm, so Marion wants to put our little Jessica in her will. Now, that's something."

"Yeah, it sure is."

Something distracts me; I look up to find Jessica standing behind Patricia and me.

"Are you two talking about Marion and her will?" Jessica still has a look of concern on her face.

Ella rises and puts her hands on Jessica's shoulders, then, with her finger, lifts her chin to look her in the eyes.

"Look at me, Jessica. Please relax and make the most of your relationship with Marion. You longed to meet her, and now that you have, don't let this situation overshadow your joy. Jessica, Jessica, do you understand that this is not a problem you have created? Marion and her daughters established a pattern of interaction long ago. Come on now, put this out of your mind, and have fun this weekend."

"You are right; I will let it go and build a relationship with my grandma."

I hug Jessica. "That's my girl."

With my arm around Jessica's shoulders, the three of us walk back toward the house, the aroma of delicious food floating toward us and surrounding us as we enter.

"What smells so delicious?"

"I am roasting a turkey with bread stuffing. The red potatoes are boiling, I'm roasting Brussels sprouts and yams and baking a casserole of creamed corn with cheese sauce. Before you arrived yesterday, I made cranberry sauce and baked a pumpkin pie. Dinner will be ready in about thirty minutes. Ella, will you check the table and make sure I have enough serving utensils laid out?"

The evening meal is one of the best I have had in years. A meal such as this tastes delicious; even better, I did not have to make it myself. Our stomachs are so full that dessert will have to wait until later this evening. We retire to the parlor and set up a double-deck pinochle game.

I woke early this morning and can't get back to sleep. It must be from all the rich food I ate last evening. I roll over and stare at the clock on the nightstand; it's ten minutes to six and still dark outside. After twenty minutes of tossing and turning, I decide there is no longer any point in lying here, so I tiptoe down the stairs and make a pot of coffee. Brrr, the kitchen is icy cold; it must be freezing outside. The house is quiet except for the bubbling sound of the percolator. Then I hear a whisper.

"Good morning."

"Jessica, what are you doing up? It is early."

"I could ask you the same question. I've been lying awake for some time now, then I heard creaking on the stairs, so I decided to investigate."

"That makes two of us. The coffee is ready. Care to go to my room and talk?"

Snuggled in my big bed, we sip our hot coffee with quilts pulled up to our necks.

"Ella, remember when I told you I needed time to figure out what I wanted to do with the rest of my life?"

"Yes, Jessica, I do."

"I have given a great deal of thought to my future and have made some decisions."

"Would you like to tell me about them?"

"Yes, I trust your judgment, so please feel free to offer an opinion or make a suggestion."

"Alright, I will. So, tell me, what are your plans?"

"First, I am sure that I want to make my home in Martinsville. I met my grandma and Delia, two crucial reasons for this decision. Plus, I have you, Patricia, and Sharon. Ella, I don't fit in California. I'm not sure I ever did. My friends all act so childish, so silly. I fit better here in Martinsville; I am comfortable in Martinsville. I don't see why I can't make a life here, especially now that I have a way to support myself."

Jessica pauses, and I wait for her to continue.

"I just realized something, Ella; do you know what I think?"

"Tell me, Jessica."

Jessica gets up on one elbow and, with a look of excitement on her face, exclaims, "I'm a Midwesterner, Ella. I was born here."

"Oh my, what an intriguing observation. You are right; you have Midwestern blood in your veins."

"Yes, I do, Ella. I'm sure that must be why I am so at ease in Martinsville."

"You never told me how you came to work for Daniel."

"Yes, that was certainly an unexpected event. I knew if I were to stay here, I would need to find a way to make an income. Shortly after the troupe left for California, Daniel and I were talking in the restaurant, and he asked why I had stayed behind. I told him I had been thinking seriously about making my home here in Martinsville but didn't know what work I could find.

"That is when he told me that he had been thinking about hiring an assistant to help with his office work, and then he offered me the position. He is paying me well, and I can keep the tiny apartment on the second floor rent-free as part of my compensation. He said he has more responsibilities he could eventually give me.

"Ella, even more changes will come; somehow, I know it, so I want to stay here and see where life takes me. That's all I can tell you right now, so tell me, what do you think about all this?"

"I love hearing your observations. You are smart, and you are trusting your God-given instincts. You have your entire future ahead of you, and now is the time to explore your options before it is too late."

"Thank you, Ella. You know I think of you as my Midwestern mom." Jessica sets her coffee cup on the nightstand, leans back onto the pillow, and lets out a big yawn. "I am sleepy. Do you mind if I stay here and close my eyes?"

"Not at all. It's early; let's see if we can get some shuteye."

I roll over, reflect on everything Jessica said, smile, and close my eyes. Two hours later, I wake to the sound of chatter coming from the first floor.

I nudge Jessica and whisper, "Hey, sleepyhead, time to get up."

We quickly put on blue jeans and sweatshirts and descend the stairs in our slippers. Sharon and Patricia greet us in the kitchen.

"Good morning, you two. I see someone has already been in the kitchen."

"Yes, I woke early and couldn't get back to sleep, so I came downstairs to make coffee. Jessica heard my footsteps on the stairs and joined me. It was so cold here in the kitchen that we decided to take our mugs upstairs and get back in bed. We had a long talk, then went back to sleep. It was so nice to sleep in."

"Where is Delia?"

"She is awake now. She will be here in a minute."

"Let's start making breakfast and then plan our day."

Breakfast consists of scrambled eggs blended with a good amount of cheese and chopped chives, a frying pan sizzling with bacon and link sausage, and a stack of toast in the warm oven. Arranged on a platter, Sharon has a selection of scones with currents and bran muffins with raisins.

We serve ourselves and sink into our rocking chairs on the back porch, wrapped in blankets and shawls.

"I like starting the day like this. Breakfast, coffee, and a morning chat on the porch, although it is a bit chilly. What were the two of you talking about early this morning, or is that territory private?"

Jessica glances at me, a question in her eye. I nod my agreement that now is the time to tell everyone about her plans for the future.

"Ladies, I have made many decisions about my life's course involving all of you. I have decided I cannot leave Martinsville. I cannot go away and leave you adorable ladies. My new home is now this midwestern town of Martinsville."

We all clap and congratulate Jessica on the new course of her life. Delia is overwhelmed by Jessica's announcement. Joyful, she stands and hugs Jessica.

"Now that we found each other, we get to keep each other, right, darlin'?"

"Yes, Delia. you are a primary reason for my staying here. Plus, now that I have met my grandma, I want to be close enough to see her whenever possible. Patricia, Sharon, and Ella, you are fine examples of clever, funny, and independent women. I admire your lives and want to stay and learn from you."

"Aren't we all flattered, huh, girls? Jessica, you are now officially one of the women of Martinsville. Pick up your coffee cups, ladies, and let us toast to our newest member of the town."

We raise our cups, clink them all around, and drink hot coffee to our Jessica.

"Ladies, I had plans for us to decorate the house for the coming holidays, but I have changed my mind. It's too much like work, so let's be lazy today. We can go for a long walk, read a book, eat, or take a nap. Let's do whatever we want for the next day or two."

"You don't have to convince me. I want to do a lot of nothing for the next two days. Kate and Janice have control of the bakery."

So, that is how we spend the rest of the day. Hours later, when the clock in the hall strikes three, Sharon announces it is time for wine and prepping for our dinner in the kitchen.

"What's for dinner tonight?"

"My favorite day-after-Thanksgiving dinner; turkey ala king on homemade biscuits. We have leftover vegetables I can warm, too."

"Come on, Jessica. It's time for you to have a cooking lesson, number one."

Jessica glances at me.

"Hey, don't look at me. You're the one who wants to be a midwestern woman; you'll have to learn how to cook."

Devlin Family Notes

My siblings and I have fond memories of our grandfather Arthur getting up every morning at 3 AM to start making donuts, pecan, and cinnamon rolls for early morning delivery to the National Restaurant that his cousin Luther ran on Main Street. Luther no longer had a bakery; he only had the restaurant, The National Café. We believe he most likely gave up the bakery business when his cousin Arthur came to town and opened The Pastry Shop.

It is noteworthy that Arthur became famous in Martinsville and surrounding areas for baking wedding cakes and his ability to decorate them to meet the bride's desire.

Submitted by Janice Wells Hood

CHAPTER X

The Confrontation

Sophia raps softly on Mr. Schroeder's office door.

"Come in, Sophia."

Sophia walks to Mr. Schroeder's desk and leans over to whisper, "Mr. Schroeder, Marion's daughters are here, Natalie Fairbanks and Susan Strauss. They want to see you."

"You don't say. Did the women tell you what they want?"

"No, but we can easily guess."

"They don't have an appointment. Tell the ladies I'm busy."

"But Mr. Schroeder, you aren't," teases Sophia.

"All right, but if the women are here to talk about what I suspect they want to talk about, I want a witness to the meeting and for you to take shorthand. Tell them I'll be with them momentarily. Then, seat the women in the office down the hall. Be sure to close the door. I'll call Marvin Thomas's office and see if he can come over immediately."

Sophia leaves the room as Alex picks up the telephone and dials Marvin's office.

"Hello, Marvin. I have a situation in my office and need a witness to a meeting. Yes, a lawyer, a non-partisan one. Can you come over right away? Thanks, Marvin. You know how much I appreciate this. Yes, it might get sticky. It is Natalie Fairbanks and Susan Strauss, Marion Devlin's daughters. I have them seated behind closed doors. Right. Thanks, I owe you one."

Alex presses the intercom button and speaks in a hushed tone. "Sophia, pick up the telephone. Marvin is on his way here, and when he gets here, be very quiet and show him into my office. I need to talk with Marv before meeting with Natalie and Susan."

Ten minutes later, Marvin Thomas arrives. "That was fast work. Thanks for coming on such short notice."

"You'd do the same for me. What's the situation?"

"Marion Devlin recently met her long-lost adopted granddaughter, a young lady named Jessica Roberts. They hit it off quite nicely, and Marion loves the girl. I arranged for them to meet here in Reedsburg a few weeks ago. During that visit, Marion brought Jessica into the office to meet me. Marion wants to include the young woman in her will."

"Then what's the problem?"

"Before meeting Jessica, Marion transferred the ownership of the Devlin Bakery to Tom and Ella Watson in Martinsville. She also amended her will and trust to state that anyone who contests her will, either verbally or in writing, will inherit $1.00. The amendment is partly to protect the new owners of the bakery but also to avoid the directives from being contested after she passes.

"Suppose Marion's daughters are here to discuss the granddaughter, Jessica. Under the updated terms, they could create a real problem if they object to her receiving an inheritance."

"Yes, I see what you mean. Has Marion already added the girl to her will?"

"No, not yet, but the women may not know that, and I don't have to tell them either way without Marion's permission."

"Usually, people either attend the reading of the will or receive a copy from an attorney, discover the distribution of the assets, and then contest the will. Do the women know of this amendment?"

"Yes. We met after the changes were made and filed with the courts. It is solid."

"How did they take it?"

"They were annoyed with their mother."

"The best thing we can do now is listen to what they have to say; however, I might add, whether Marion changes her will, now or in the future, an objection made is an objection made."

"I agree. I hope these women know what they are doing. Let's see what they have to say." Pressing the intercom, Alex speaks, "Sophia, bring the ladies into my office.

"Hello, Natalie, Susan. I'd like you to meet a colleague of mine, Mr. Marvin Thomas. Mr. Thomas is an attorney. He is here to witness this meeting. Marvin, please meet Natalie Fairbanks and Susan Strauss. Have a seat, ladies. Sophia, please join us with your steno pad. Now, to what do I owe this visit?"

"Frankly, Mr. Schroeder, Natalie, and I are concerned over the recent appearance of our sister Evelyn's daughter, Jessica."

"What about it?"

"We know she was here weeks ago and spent time with our mother. Mother brought her over to the house so we could meet her. Later that same afternoon, I was in town and saw Mother and the girl walking into your office."

"Please continue."

"Our point is, we are concerned that this girl, Jessica, may have been added to the will, that she may stand to inherit some of our mother's assets."

"Mr. Schroeder, Susan, and I have a right to know if our mother added this girl to her will and trust. Has she done that?"

"Natalie, Susan, this is not a matter of rights, of which you have none. I cannot answer or comment on any part of this conversation regarding Marion's will or trust without her permission."

Natalie and Susan appear taken aback at my reluctance to participate in the conversation or answer their questions. They bend their heads toward each other and whisper for several minutes, then sit back in their chairs, ready with their next question.

"Mr. Schroeder, if you are unwilling to tell us, how do we find out?"

"I guess you'll have to ask your mother." My answer riles the women. They didn't expect to receive such an answer.

Natalie, obviously annoyed, blurts out, "We did, and she won't tell us."

"Then you have your answer. Marion doesn't want you to know her business."

Natalie and Susan are indignant at my answer and are now suspicious about Marvin Thomas's presence and uneasy with Sophia recording the conversation using shorthand. Their tone turns demanding.

"Why is Mr. Thomas here? Why is your secretary taking notes?"

"A matter of protocol. I record all my meetings with clients or, in your case, relatives of my clients to ensure there are no misunderstandings."

"We want to go on record with our objections about this girl and her possible share in an inheritance. How do we do that, Mr. Schroeder?"

"Your mother, Marion Devlin, is my client; therefore, I cannot advise you what to do or say. You should seek a lawyer and get some good legal advice. Then, if you want to object, you may enter a document in your language of choice, and I will put it in Marion's file with her will and trust.

"That is all that needs to be said today. I suggest you go home and put a great deal of thought into how you want to proceed. Come back if you want to take this matter to the next level. One more thing, ladies, please make an appointment next time."

Natalie and Susan rise and head toward the door without uttering another word. Sophia, Marvin, and Alex follow and stand in the window, watching them get into their car and drive off.

"They think they are pretty smart."

"I think they are pretty stupid."

"Sophia, how long will it take to type up this meeting? I need it signed by all three of us and notarized. Then file it with Marion's papers."

"Give me twenty minutes."

"Atta, girl."

Sitting at my desk, I run the meeting details through my mind. I conclude that Natalie and Susan have not objected in a manner that causes their inheritance to be $1.00. They have questioned Marion's choices but have not hung themselves so far.

"Sophia, I need to contact Marion, but I don't want to call the house. When will you see her again?"

"Next week, possibly. If I see Marion in town or the library, I will tell her to contact you."

Alex murmurs, "I'm beginning to think I need a carrier pigeon to do my work lately."

"What's that?"

"Nothing, nothing. I need to speak to Marion soon. Watch for her, and don't tell anyone I am looking for her."

"Aye, aye, sir."

It has been three days since the scene in Alex's office, and I can't help but be incensed that Natalie and Susan want to know the particulars of Marion's will. Why the nerve they have, thinking they should be privy to Miss Marion's will and trust. It is none of their business how Miss Marion wants her assets divided. I have a plan; I am bound and determined to get in touch with Marion, but first, I need to telephone the office.

"Mr. Schroeder, it is Sophia. I hope you don't mind if I am late for work. Oh, nothing, a little errand I need to run. Yes. I will make it quick. Nothing is wrong, sir. I need a couple of extra minutes, that's all. Ok, ok, goodbye."

Natalie takes the children to school early on Tuesday and Thursday mornings for music practice, so I park my car down the block from Natalie's house. If I park closer, she is sure to recognize my car. I patiently sit slumped in my seat, waiting and watching for Natalie to leave with the children. Then, it should be safe to go to the house and talk to Marion.

Okay, I see Natalie is leaving. I wait until she turns the corner at the end of their street, then jump out of my car, run to the house, and knock on the front door. No answer. I bang harder. Marion, come on, come on, answer the door. Darn. I go around the back of the house and knock on her bedroom window—tap, tap, tap. Finally, Marion appears in the window and lifts the sash.

"Sophia, what in the world are you doing in the backyard? Why didn't you come to the front door?"

"I did. You didn't hear me knocking? Marion, Mr. Schroeder wants to talk to you."

"He could call me. We do have a telephone, you know."

"No, you don't understand. Mr. Schroeder doesn't want to chance Natalie knowing he is calling."

"Oh."

"Marion, I must get out of Natalie's backyard before she returns and catches me chatting with you at your bedroom window. Please, get in touch with Mr. Schroeder."

Minutes later, I'm back at the office. I smooth my dress and hair, hoping I don't look like I've been running down the street.

"Good morning, Mr. Schroeder."

"Sophia, come in here, please. Do you want to let me in on your little escapade?"

"I couldn't help myself, Mr. Schroeder. I went to Natalie's house and knocked on Marion's bedroom window. I told her that you want to talk to her."

Alex makes a significant effort to stifle a grin from growing on his face. "Keep this up, and I will have to increase your wages for detective work."

"Yes, Mr. Schroeder, I am sorry I was late, Mr. Schroeder."

"Sophia, how long have we worked together?"

"About five years now, Mr. Schroeder."

"You can dispense with Mr. Schroeder. That is my father. Please call me Alex unless a new client is present."

"Thank you very much, Mr. Schroeder; I mean Alex."

"Now go get the Phillips file for me, please. Oh, and Sophia, if the coffee is ready, would you mind bringing me a cup?"

"Aye, Aye, sir." Sophia heads to the tiny kitchen.

Murmuring to himself, "What would I do without that woman."

"Did you say something, Alex?"

"Um, yes, cream, no sugar, please." Murmuring again, "The girl has the ears of a rabbit."

"I heard that."

Two hours later, the telephone rings and Marion is on the line.

"Alex, I have Marion Devlin on the line, number two."

"Marion, good morning. I'm fine, thank you. How are you? Terrific. Marion, I would like you to come to the office soon. Yes, it is somewhat important. Yes, yes, it does. Yes, they were here several days ago. Both Natalie and Susan. No, of course not. You are my client, and your business is strictly confidential. Yes, they were quite annoying. OK, any time this afternoon that is convenient for you. Two o'clock? Fine, see you then."

"Sophia, Marion will be here about two o'clock. Show her in immediately, don't keep her waiting, and please hold all my calls."

"Aye, aye, sir."

At precisely two o'clock, Marion walks in the door to Alex's office. "Hello, Sophia; Alex is expecting me."

Sophia presses the intercom key. "Alex, Miss Marion is here to see you."

"Send her in, and Sophia, please join us and bring your steno pad."

"You may go in, Miss Marion."

Marion settles into a chair and rolls her eyes at Alex. "Ok, tell me what happened."

Schroeder relates the entire scenario to Marion, including that non-partisan lawyer Marvin Thomas attended as a witness and that Sophia took shorthand. Schroeder concludes that the conversation has been typed, signed, notarized, and put into her file.

"How efficient of you. Thank you for handling it the way you did. What do you recommend I do now?"

"Marion, you should discuss this with Natalie and Susan. They are bound and determined to find out if you have added Jessica to the will and trust. They should hear your position regarding Jessica as an heir and tell them that your affairs are private."

"That is good advice, and I will heed your suggestions. It doesn't surprise me that they would try to discover more about my relationship with Jessica. The atmosphere in the house has been tense ever since I introduced Jessica to them. I have opened Pandora's box, so it seems, and now I must deal with the consequences."

"What do you want to do now? Are your plans to add Jessica to your will?"

"Alex, I have given this a great deal of thought. I have lost sleep over it, but I cannot help but love the girl. I have provided for my two daughters and grandchildren; moreover, Jessica is also my grandchild. We look alike. We think alike. We even finish each other's sentences on occasion. I love the girl; I do. And I see no reason not to include her.

"Of course, who knows what will be left of my assets when I die. Conceivably not much, it is hard to tell; nonetheless, I do not want to ignore Jessica, and I won't, regardless of anyone's opinion."

Alex pauses and digests Marion's words, waiting for more direction from her.

"Let's get it done. Let's get it done right now. There is no point in any further delay, especially if I need to have a conversation with Natalie and Susan. And I want it to be airtight. If the girls balk in the slightest, the amendment reducing their inheritance to $1.00 goes into effect."

Alex hesitates with a dubious expression on his face. "Whatever you say, Marion."

"Alex, don't give me that look. I know what I am doing. I know my daughters better than anyone else. It galls me that they think they are better, more deserving than other kin. They have a cockeyed idea that my pockets are loaded, and for all one knows, they are, as opposed to other people on the planet, but Natalie and Susan are wealthy beyond belief. I can no longer stand to be around them with their bossy, greedy attitudes; I have had my fill."

"I apologize, Marion, if I came across as doubting your choices. I know you have your reasons, and I am here to serve you faithfully. Please forgive me if my tone sounded off base."

"You are forgiven. Now, let's get on with amending the will."

"Do you have particular wording you want to add, or will Jessica inherit the same percentage as the other grandchildren?"

"Here is what I want. Currently, the will is structured so that if Natalie and Susan object and fall into the $1.00 inheritance pit, the estate goes directly to their children. They receive and inherit equally. However, I am changing that and want this to be clear. The grandchildren's inheritance will vanish from the will and trust at the same time as their mother's. I am not the least bit concerned about my grandchildren, as dear as they are to me, as they will inherit sizable estates from their parents someday."

"Alright, Marion, what about Jessica?"

"If Natalie and Susan object, the entire estate falls to Jessica, whatever it is worth. I see your eyebrows raised. You are surprised, aren't you? Alex, this arrangement may sound uncaring, but I have another plan up my sleeve."

Alex looks wide-eyed, and Sophia stops notetaking, dropping her pencil to the floor.

"What would that be, Marion?"

"All this planning is worthless no matter what Natalie and Susan do."

"I am sorry, Marion. I don't understand. Can you please be clearer?"

"Alex, I may not have much left when I die. I plan to spend as much money as possible before I kick the bucket."

Taken aback, Alex and Sophia break into gales of laughter, dissolving the tension in the room. Finally, able to catch his breath, Alex speaks.

"Marion, I have to hand it to you. You know how to solve a problem, don't you?"

"I don't think of it as solving a problem. I see it as a reality. George and I worked hard all our lives, and now I plan to live my life to the hilt. I am going out on top."

"Marion, please tell us your plans for living to the hilt."

"Thank you for asking that question, Sophia. I have been looking back on my life since I came to Reedsburg. My health improved, and I found an outlet for my newfound energy, though limited, with satisfactory results. Look at the Reedsburg library; now renovated, it is clean, bright, and bustling. It has colorful rooms for children to read and study and programs to teach them history, math, and science. Companies hold their monthly meetings at the library. Our townsfolk have donated thousands of books; many are about local family history."

"You have not found your involvement gratifying, Marion?"

"Oh yes, I have."

"What is the problem?"

"While I like it here, it isn't home. I am trapped living with Natalie; I often feel confined to my bedroom, a fifth wheel, and a babysitter. I miss Martinsville, Mayor Bigby, Patricia, Delia, and Irene Garfield. I want to live the rest of my life in Martinsville."

A jaw-dropping silence pervades the room.

"Oh, Marion," Sophia chokes, tears beginning to pool in her eyes, "I will miss you terribly, and so will the town. Are you sure you want to leave us?"

"Sophia, I will miss you, the townspeople, and the library, but Martinsville still haunts my dreams to this day. When I left, I wasn't physically or mentally in good shape and needed to distance myself from the bakery. Seeing it closed and vacant saddened me and kept me emotionally tied to a past that can never be.

"With it open and prospering under new ownership, I need to give Martinsville another chance before it is too late. I will come back here to see the grandchildren, and you and I can spend time together."

"You can stay at my house with me whenever you return."

"Marion, is there a chance that your daughters will be angry enough to prevent you from seeing the grandchildren now that you have included Jessica in your will?"

"Not if they don't know all the details."

"I am beginning to believe you are smarter than the rest of us. What is cooking in that head of yours now?"

"I am not sure, but I will know when I see their reactions to adding Jessica to the will. I plan to tell them that much but nothing more. I won't tell them I plan to live my life to the fullest, doing with my money what I please. Both the high school and library building in Martinsville are in dire need of renovation. Someone needs to begin the improvement process, and it might as well be me. I will be satisfied if I can accomplish half of what I achieved here in Reedsburg, in Martinsville."

"Where will you live, Marion? You sold your beautiful home to Patricia." Sophia eyes remain teary.

"I have a very best friend in Irene Garfield. She is the judge's wife. We have been best friends all our lives. She has repeatedly offered me rooms in their home, a few blocks from my old home. If that doesn't work for some unforeseen reason, I will buy a little house."

"Marion, I admire your energy, your desire to live the rest of your life to the fullest. If more clients had your attitude, they might live longer and happier lives. Let me know how the conversation goes with Natalie and Susan. Sophia and I are here for you. Please let us know if we can do anything for you once you move back to Martinsville."

"Thank you, Alex, thank you, Sophia. I love you both."

"We love you, too, Marion; Sophia, will you take Marion home now?"

Ten minutes later, I enter the front door of Natalie's house; she is standing in the foyer, waiting for me.

"So, I see Mr. Schroeder's secretary brought you home. You've been at his office again."

"Yes, I was, and yes, she did." The tension in the house feels even higher than usual. With my nerves on edge, I believe it best I go to my room, so I turn away and proceed down the hall, and then I hear Natalie's voice behind me.

"Mother, come here. We should talk."

I stop and turn to face Natalie. I know we need to talk; however, I fear how the conversation might end.

"Alright, Natalie, let's talk. Go ahead, you start."

"Susan and I are upset about this, Jessica girl."

"You mean my granddaughter Jessica."

"Alright then, granddaughter. Susan and I don't like the idea of her being in your will. We don't see why she should inherit any of your assets. She may be Evelyn's daughter, but she isn't part of this family; another family adopted her, so why would you include her?"

"Natalie, I have my point of view and beliefs about Jessica being a part of this family, which has nothing to do with your feelings or desires. Whether or not she is in my will should be of no concern to you. What I decide to do with my assets is my business. You and your sister are too invested in my affairs. Besides that, I haven't asked you to include her in your life. I'm not forcing her presence down your throats, although if you got to know her, you might have a different opinion; she is a sweet girl."

With a stony-eyed stare, Natalie pauses and then finishes her thoughts. "Sorry, Mother, but Susan and I want nothing to do with her. If you insist on including her in your will, you should pack your things and return to Martinsville."

"You are right; it would be better if I didn't live near you or your sister."

As often as I have pondered moving back to Martinsville, hearing those words from Natalie's lips cuts me to the core. Then again, this is no surprise. All my life, they have tried to run me and my affairs. To think they have the right to demand what I do with my assets, to whom I bequeath them, why the nerve they have. I wish this had never happened, but I can do nothing about their attitude. Again, I turn and walk toward my room.

"Mother, wait. I have one more subject to address."

Her words stop me cold. I can't imagine where this is heading. My heart is beating so fast that I fear it might jump out of my chest. I turn to face Natalie.

"What is it?"

"The bakery."

"What about the bakery?"

Wagging her finger in Marion's face, Natalie barks, "You gave it free and clear to those farmers from Naperville. They should have paid money for the bakery. They didn't have to work to become the owners. You merely handed the business to them."

Outraged, Marion defends her decisions about the bakery.

"Handed it to them? Are you out of your mind? Well, are you? Now you listen to me, Natalie. Those hardworking, dedicated folks from Naperville had to meet with Mayor Bigby's and Judge Garfield's approval, and the townspeople had to approve, too. They opened the bakery knowing they would need to operate it for an entire year before becoming the owners, and there was no guarantee that at the end of one year, they would.

"Nevertheless, they worked diligently out of their passion for the bakery business. They put their own money into it until it turned a profit. They put their hearts and souls into it, their time, hard work, and sweat each step along the way. It took a lot of faith, and you think they didn't work for it?

"Let me tell you something, dearie, you and your sister are the ones who have never worked for anything. What do you know about hard work? Nothing. Your father adored you. He gave you everything you wanted, and you ridiculed him behind his back. You looked at him with disdain, and yet he left both of you a sizable amount of money when he died. Talk about undeserving? You and your sister have never done a damn thing to deserve what your father gave you. You had better watch your step, Natalie. You have crossed the line with me."

Red-faced and teary-eyed, I turn and head down the hallway to my bedroom and close the door behind me, leaving Natalie standing with her mouth gapped. I can hardly breathe. My heart is pounding in my ears. I've said my piece, and I meant every word. I gasp to catch my breath. I feel weak. My legs are shaking.

You can best believe that Natalie never expected me to come back at her with such brutal honesty. I have tried to reason with Natalie and Susan for years. No matter what approach I have taken, words, or logic I have used, they brush them aside like so much trash.

There is no way to describe how long overdue this confrontation was. People have no idea what I have had to put up with; I have taken and taken from those girls. I will no longer let them push me to live according to their rules and wishes. They are self-centered, demanding, rude, and ruthless.

I realize this is my fault; I let them get away with bad behavior, even as children. George and I spoiled them. I failed to teach them to be gracious, humble, and thankful, and it has backfired on me. They don't understand how to behave if you want to get ahead, have a pleasant life, be recognized, be admired, and have friends. Where is their humanity?

Our confrontation overshadows my night's sleep. I lie here without rest; nevertheless, I do not regret what I said. I realize I cannot remain in this house any longer; I must leave immediately. This is Natalie's home, and living here has given her even more power over me; coming here was a mistake. After many dark hours of reliving our clash, sleep finally finds me.

Hours later, the early morning light creeps into my room through the gap where the drapery hangs before the window frame. I glance at the clock next to me on the nightstand; it is too early to rise.

Thankfully, my mind has quieted, and I lie here hoping that sleep will find me again. If it does, and when I wake, I will stay in my room until I know Natalie has left to drive the children to school. I do not need to come face-to-face with her, not this morning, for all one knows, maybe never. Then and only then will I pick up the telephone.

"Sophia? It is Marion. No, frankly, I am not. Yes, last night with Natalie. Susan wasn't there. Is that invitation to come and stay with you still open? Is it? Sophia, I don't want to intrude. That's so nice of you. I can be ready at any time. Okay, I'll watch for you. One more thing, Sophia, thanks a million."

As I hang up the telephone, the gravity of the situation stirs my emotions and brings tears to my eyes. There is no turning back, no time to waste, and no time for self-pity. I must pack as many of my belongings in my small suitcase as will fit, and as quickly as possible.

Now ready, the idea of walking out of Natalie's home without leaving her a note puts a sly smile on my face. Let her wonder where I am or how long I'll be gone. Something tells me she wouldn't care, but then my sense of what is right emerges; I will not stoop low. I write a note to leave on the foyer table. It reads, "I need a break and will be in touch to arrange my move-out."

Moments later, I hear the familiar beep-beep of Sophia's car horn. I rush to the front door with my suitcase in hand, open it, and find Sophia standing there, ready to help me. She greets me with a smile and a comforting hug, then carries my bag to her car and puts it in the back seat. Together, we speed away from Natalie's house toward her own. A sense of relief flows over me as I escape the environs of Natalie's home. From now on, my life will be different once more.

Sophia's house is on a quiet street five minutes from Alex's office.

"Come in, Marion, and make yourself at home. The guest bedroom is down the hall on the left. It has its own bathroom. The sheets and towels in the bathroom are clean. It appears as if I was waiting for your arrival."

"You are most generous, Sophia, but I must tell you I don't know what I'll do next. Talking with Natalie last night turned ugly. I need time to absorb what has happened. I'm not sure how long I will need to be here with you; however, I don't want to inconvenience you."

"Marion, you are no bother. I will love having you here with me. Take your time. You may stay as long as it takes to decide what to do. Now, I need to get to work. Should I relay what has happened to Alex, or would you prefer to tell him yourself?"

"Go ahead and tell him what has transpired. He needs to know about this turn of events. I don't know if Natalie and Susan will contact him, but he needs to know we had a parting of ways. I can fill him in on the details after I have calmed down and had time to figure out where I go from here.

"Oh, one last thing; if my daughters come to the office, I don't want them to know I am staying with you. I don't want them to come here and upset you and your household. Frankly, I don't have any reason to see or speak to either of them for a long while."

"I understand, Marion. I need to get to the office. You will find coffee in the pantry and plenty of food in the icebox. Help yourself. I mean it."

I arrive on time for work and immediately head for the kitchenette to put on a pot of coffee for Alex and me.

"Good morning, Sophia."

"Good morning, Alex. If you have a few minutes, I need to talk to you about Marion."

"Of course. What is going on?"

"Early this morning, Marion called me. She wanted to know if my invitation to come and stay with me was still open. I told her it was, went to Natalie's house, and picked her up. Last night, she and Natalie had a blow-up. I guess it got heated. She will stay with me until she decides what her next step will be. She expects her daughters will come to see you, and she prefers you not tell them she is staying at my house."

"Hmm. I'll handle that part if Marion's daughters ask. If they show up here, tell them they need an appointment to see me. I will need to have Marvin as a witness, and next time, he may not be able to drop what he is doing and come running. No excuses. I will not see them without an appointment, so handle them if they drop by the office. On second thought, Sophia, it's best to lock the front door. I don't want those two women barging in here."

Sophia turns on her heels and heads to the front door.

Standing in the kitchenette, listening to the coffee pot percolate, Alex murmurs, "All I need are those two wet hens coming in here and creating a scene."

Giggling under her breath, Sophia pretends she didn't hear his comment. "What did you say, Alex?"

"Nothing, nothing. Geez. Did you lock the door?"

"Aye, aye, sir."

I have been expecting a telephone call from Natalie all day and am surprised that it took her until late afternoon to ring the office.

"Hello, Sophia, this is Natalie Fairbanks. Do you know where my mother is? It is almost four o'clock, and I haven't seen her all day."

"Please hold a moment, Natalie. I'll see if Mr. Schroeder has a moment to talk to you."

Sophia puts Natalie on hold and runs into Alex's office.

"Alex, Natalie Fairbanks is on line one, and she asked if I know where her mother is. She says she hasn't seen her all day. You should talk to her."

Alex picks up the receiver and punches the button on the telephone with the flashing light. "Hello, Natalie. Alex Schroeder, here. How can I help you? I'm sorry, Natalie, I haven't seen or spoken to her all day. If I do, I'll let her know you called." Alex hangs up the telephone.

"That was short and sweet. You didn't tell Natalie anything at all."

"Right. Natalie wanted to know if I had seen or spoken to Marion, and I said I had not, which is the truth. I didn't give her a chance to ask any other questions. Wait a minute. Hmm. I don't want Natalie to report her as missing to the police. Wouldn't that be a mess? Get Marion on the telephone. I need to talk to her."

Sophia dials her residence multiple times, letting the telephone ring and ring, but Marion does not answer. A moment later, the telephone rings in Alex's office.

"Alex, Marion is on line two."

"Hello, Alex. Sophia's telephone has been ringing and ringing, and while I have no business answering it, I figured it most likely was you calling."

"Yes, Marion, it was me. Natalie called to ask if I had seen or spoken to you today, and I said, "No." How did you leave it with her when you left the house?"

"I placed a note on the foyer table stating that I needed a break and would be in touch to arrange my move-out."

"So that is what your discussion came to last night? You'll be moving out of her house?"

"Yes. Natalie told me that she and Susan do not want anything to do with Jessica, and that if I put her in my will, I should pack my belongings and return to Martinsville. I was shocked, even though I expected Natalie and her sister to take that stance. Then, I told her she was too invested in my private affairs. My options are moving back to Martinsville or making a new home here; however, I need time to think.

"Alex, I want to get all of this behind me, and if I do leave Reedsburg, I will need to contact the people I value and with whom I have worked. Of course, I will meet with the library society board and give them my resignation. I wouldn't think of slipping out of town without a proper goodbye.

"Furthermore, I never want to talk to Natalie or Susan again. There is nothing left to say. I am one hundred percent done trying to please my girls. They are selfish, nasty, and greedy, and they try to push me into doing what they want. Then it got awful."

"What happened?"

"Natalie brought up the bakery. She said I handed it to the Watsons, that they didn't work for it, and that they should have paid money for the bakery. I was incensed at her attitude and told Natalie she had crossed the line with me. Then I got honest and told Natalie that she and Susan had never worked hard for anything. I will never understand how I raised two daughters with such self-centered dispositions, but I cannot be around it anymore. I simply cannot."

"I believe it would be best if you moved all your belongings as soon as possible. That way, Natalie won't expect to see you at the house anymore. It would be advantageous to have me go with you. I can go tomorrow evening if you like. I'll bring Sophia with me. I can stand in the living room while she helps you pack.

"In the meantime, I would call Natalie and tell her you have a safe and secure place to live, tell her not to worry about you, and then hang up immediately. Please do not allow her to find out where you are staying. Do you still have the key to Natalie's house?"

"Yes."

"Good, then we won't have to knock."

The following morning, I am up early and brewing a pot of coffee when Marion strolls into the kitchen, clad in her robe and slippers.

"Good morning, Marion. Have a seat at the table. I have the coffee on for us. I will go out and get the morning paper."

Minutes later, Sophia returns with a large cardboard box in her arms.

"Look what I found on my front porch; two more are on the porch like this one. Come help me, Marion."

We bring the other two boxes into the house and set them on the kitchen floor. Sophia grabs the scissors from the drawer, slices through the masking tape, and opens the box.

"What in the world is all this?"

"Those are my clothes, Sophia. Guess I do not need to go to Natalie's house this evening." Marion plops into the kitchen chair. She looks stunned and hurt all at the same time, with tears welling up in her eyes.

"Oh no, Marion. I am so sorry. Let me pour you a cup of coffee; it will help."

"I will be alright, Sophia; sooner or later, I will be alright."

"Do you want me to stay home with you? I can call Alex and tell him you need my company. He will have to get along without me today."

"No, no, Sophia, but thank you for your concern. I should find something to do and not sit here wasting the day wallowing in this mess. Can you drop me off at the hotel on your way to the office? I will walk to the library when it opens at nine o'clock."

"Of course, Marion. If that is what you want, of course."

The clock on the wall strikes the hour of nine as I unlock the door and let myself into the office. Alex is already busy on the phone. I wait until he finishes his call and rush to tell him the latest news about Marion.

"Excuse me, sir; I need to talk to you about Marion. This morning, I went out to get the newspaper and found three cardboard boxes on my front porch. They are full of Marion's clothes and belongings."

Alex's face instantly turns beet red. He stands and shouts, "Holy mother of God. Marion is at your house, right?"

"No sir. She asked me to drop her at the hotel on my way to work. She plans to walk to the library when it opens at nine o'clock. She should be there by now."

"*NO. NO.* Find Marion, Sophia, get her now, and don't come back without her."

"Aye, aye, sir."

Alex starts to pace the floor in his office. "Those bitches, those bloody bitches!

Alex continues to pace until Sophia returns with Marion twenty minutes later. He walks up to her and takes her hands in his.

"Marion, Marion, please accept my deepest sympathy. No human being should receive such treatment. Come and have a seat in my office." Alex puts a gentle arm around Marion's shoulders and leads her to a chair. "Would you care for a calming cup of tea? It may help to relax the nerves."

"Why not? It will do me good." Alex gives Sophia the go-ahead sign. Moments later, she returns with three cups of tea.

"I figured you would want me in on this conversation?"

"Yes, of course, Sophia. Please join us and bring your steno pad."

"Here is your tea, Marion." She whispers, "And something extra for the nerves."

The three of us take a few sips of our tea, letting it soothe our throats and calm our nerves. Marion looks up and smiles at Sophia for the something extra in her cup.

"Marion, I know this happened only a couple of hours ago, and you are upset, but I need to know if this changes the terms of the will we made a few days ago. Given this morning's event, do you want to make other changes before finalizing the revisions?"

"Alex, I know I may be in shock, but I am not a stupid woman. I know exactly where this is heading; the handwriting is on the wall. Natalie and Susan are already furious that I welcomed Jessica into my life, and one way or another, they will make trouble when they know of my recent revisions to the will and trust. While they have not yet formalized objections in writing or verbally, the outcome is apparent, so why wait for the inevitable."

Marion pauses, and Sophia and Alex wait for her to continue.

"Alex, tear up the will. Start a new one. I want no mention of Natalie, Susan, their children, or Evelyn. Instead, write it so all my assets go to my granddaughter, Jessica Roberts. She will be the trustee."

"As you wish, Marion. Sophia, please start a new will immediately. We can have it finished by the end of the day."

"Right away, sir. If you will excuse me, Miss Marion, Mr. Schroeder."

Marion smiles as, moments later, she hears Sophia's Remmington clicking away in the outer office. She is a caring and efficient secretary.

"One more thing, Alex; I have made a decision. I will be moving back to Martinsville soon. I've told you in the past that Martinsville haunts my dreams. I have been giving this move careful thought and consideration for quite some time now, and considering recent events, I know I am doing the right thing by returning to what I call home.

"My good friend Irene Garfield and her husband, the judge, have always said I would have a place to live in their home if I returned to Martinsville. I will write Irene and the judge a letter and one to Mayor Bigby, informing them of my plans.

"Martinsville has several community projects that need attention. I want to do the same fundraising work for Martinsville that I did for the community of Reedsburg. Of course, I will meet with Mayor Bigby and Judge Garfield and get their opinions about what I have in mind. Alex, we all need a purpose in life regardless of our age. While my body may not serve me as well as it once did, my mind is still sharp as a tack."

Marion pushes forward in her chair.

"I have been doing a great deal of thinking, Alex. I need you with me for my plans to work as well as I expect. According to the law, I need you to write and negotiate contracts and oversee the projects. I need to be sure that the community is legally protected. I know I can count on your legal expertise. Go with me to Martinsville, Alex. Say you will."

CHAPTER XI

The Farewell

Dearest Irene,

I have some good news and some not-so-good news to share with you. I have often dreamed of returning to Martinsville, and that opportunity has presented itself. My girls and I have had a falling out over the details of my will. It turned nasty, and I no longer live at Natalie's house. I doubt I will ever again have a relationship with my daughters or grandchildren. For now, I am living with Mr. Schroeder's secretary, Sophia, until I can make other arrangements.

In the past, you have generously offered me lodging in your home. My inquiry is this. Is the invitation still open? We have been friends for so many years, and while we get along famously, I would never want anything to come between us. So please let me know what you and the judge may think about these living arrangements.

Your devoted friend,

Marion

My dear friend Marion,

While it pains me to hear of the undoing of your relationship with the girls, the good news is your return to Martinsville. The judge and I have talked about you living with us, and we are most definitely in favor of having you in our home. We have more than enough room, especially for a dear friend. So let us know your plans, and we will welcome you with open arms.

Love to you, your friend,

Irene

After three days of leisure at Sharon's house, returning to my daily routine is challenging; however, upon entering the bakery, I am surrounded by the aroma of baked goods, and it takes only a few minutes to get back into the swing of things.

Kate and Janice have done a marvelous job caring for the bakery; therefore, I have nothing to do this morning except greet the farmhands lined up on the walkway, waiting to come in for their biscuits and hot coffee.

I put on my apron and set the tray piled with biscuits on the counter, the container of whipped butter, the Kraft paper squares, and the bowl for their dimes.

The farmhands are eager to see me, greeting me with, "Hello, Miss Ella," or "We missed you, Miss Ella." You know you are back where you belong with so many cheerful responses.

"Patricia, will you please take inventory of the display cases while I write out checks to Kate and Janice?"

"Thank you, ladies, for coming and filling in for us. We had a relaxing and fun time at Sharon's home."

As before, both women chime in that it was not a problem, that they enjoyed chatting with the customers and appreciated making a little extra money.

Patricia counts dozens of sugar and oatmeal cookies and half a dozen chocolate muffins in the display case. We return to the kitchen to bake our usual fare, and hours later, we have the display cases filled with fresh baked goods.

Before you know it, we will be busy with customers requesting baked goods we don't have, so we will make a quick list. We promise our customers we will have their favorites in the display case by tomorrow afternoon.

Dear Mayor Bigby,

I have some surprising news to tell you. After residing for more than three years in Reedsburg, I am returning to Martinsville to live. I have contacted Irene Garfield, and she and the judge have offered me permanent lodging. What a blessing it is to have such devoted friends.

I have several improvement projects I would like to tackle in the community, namely the renovation of the high school and the relocation of the library. I am asking you and the judge for your endorsement of these projects. I will be traveling with my lawyer, Mr. Alexander Schroeder, whose help will be invaluable when setting up plans and contracts. I will advise you of our travel plans as soon as they are firm.

Yours truly,

Marion Devlin

P.S. Please check with Daniel about renting a small room for Mr. Schroeder. He refuses to accept lodging from Irene and the judge.

Irene Garfield rarely comes into the bakery, but today, she walks through the door while Patricia and I are taking a break with tea and muffins.

"Hello, Irene. How nice to see you. What can I get for you? We have fresh-baked buttermilk biscuits, muffins, scones, and a variety of cookies. Come over to the display case and have a look."

"Oh no, thank you so much, Ella. I have another reason for coming to see you and Patricia this morning. May I sit with you?"

"Of course, let me pull up a chair for you. What's on your mind?"

"Ladies, I'm certain you will find this bit of news very exciting. I recently received a letter from my dear friend, Marion, announcing she is moving back to Martinsville soon. Isn't that the best? I knew I needed to tell you, ladies, right away." Irene claps her small, delicate hands like a seal, wrinkles her nose like a mouse, and titters.

Patricia and I turn to face each other, wide-eyed, surprised at this announcement. Irene has piqued my curiosity, so rather than wondering what Marion's reasons are for her return to Martinsville, why not outright ask the bearer of good tidings?

"What wonderful news, Irene. Did Marion give a reason for moving back to Martinsville?"

"Yes, she did. She poured her heart out to me. You know that Marion and I have been remarkably close friends ever since we were little girls, and I know she will tell you her story when she sees you, so I don't believe it to be gossip to let you in on her business.

"Well, ladies, you may know that Marion's girls have a history of interfering with her personal affairs. This time, Marion and her girls had a nasty falling out over the terms of her will and trust, and it got heated. Natalie told Marion to pack her belongings and leave if she didn't do what she wanted her to do. In short, Natalie forced Marion to take a stand. Hence, Marion moved out of Natalie's house and is living with her lawyer's secretary while preparing to return to Martinsville."

I don't know about Patricia, but I am aghast at hearing about the daughters' treatment of their mother. I had no idea this was happening to Marion.

"Do you know her plans for where she will be living?"

"Oh yes, she will be living with the judge and me. Isn't that terrific? We have a big house with plenty of rooms. Marion will have her privacy, and we will have ours."

"Thank you for coming in and telling us the news, Irene. It will be such a big surprise for Martinsville to have Marion back in town."

"Yes, indeed, but now I must be getting back home to Arthur. I know how much he misses me when I am gone." Again, Irene titters and wrinkles her nose.

"Are you sure you don't want to take some baked goods home? What would the judge like to eat?"

"Oh, alright, let me take a look. Oh my, all of your baked goods look so delicious. I'll take two muffins and two scones."

I box the baked goods for Irene and tell her they are on the house. I figure her news about Marion's return to Martinsville is worth a few free sweets.

As Irene opens the door, she turns to add a parting comment.

"I should also tell you this; her lawyer will be traveling with her. She said his name is Alexander Schroeder. Goodbye, ladies, and thank you." Irene waves her tiny hand as she steps out the door.

As soon as Irene is out of earshot, Patricia and I start shouting, "Can you believe it? Marion and her girls must have come to blows for her to leave Natalie's house."

"Patricia, how come you never told me there was a problem with Marion and her girls? I had no idea."

"It is not as if it were crucial information I needed to share, but those girls were always creating havoc with Marion and George over the years. Once the girls married and moved to Wisconsin, the problems were less significant, but I often suspected that Marion living with Natalie would be a big mistake. I am surprised she managed to live with her this long, to be honest."

"That certainly paints a picture of her daughters for me, heartbreaking if I do say so."

"Marion and George gave those girls everything under the sun; they never appreciated or were grateful for anything. The good news is that her health must be better to be able to travel. Moving back to Martinsville will be good for Marion."

"What caring folks Irene and the judge are, inviting her into their home. It sounds like Marion will be content living with Irene and Arthur. And isn't that Irene Garfield the cat's pajamas? She is like a cute little granny and an innocent child rolled into one."

"She is the most admirable woman you will ever meet. You will never hear her speak badly of anyone, but you never know what will come out of her mouth. Every word she says comes across as innocent; she is always honest and often quite blunt without realizing it. Her words will shock you and make you laugh. I am not sure how she pulls it off."

Our conversation is cut short by the arrival of more customers. An hour later, we are back in the kitchen baking.

"Ella, tell me about this lawyer Marion will be bringing with her."

"What do you want to know about him?" Something in Patricia's manner makes me suspicious of her motive for asking the question.

"What does this man look like? Is he married?"

"Look at you, Patricia. Interested in a man these days? Well, I'll be darned."

"Oh, Ella, I am curious, that's all."

"Yes, and we all know what happened to the curious cat, but I will tell you what I know about Mr. Schroeder. I would guess he is fifty-two, give or take a few years. I have been in his presence a couple of times, and he was dressed in a nice suit and tie. You could say he is handsome. Yes, I would say he is rather good-looking. I never noticed a ring on his left hand. Anything else you want to know?"

"No. That will do, for a start."

Ella taunts Patricia by singing, "Patricia wants a boyfriend, Patricia wants a boyfriend."

"Knock it off, Ella; I don't want a boyfriend."

"Perhaps, then, a husband?"

Patricia glares at Ella.

"Okay, I'll knock it off. We will discover more about Mr. Schroeder when we have him under surveillance here in Martinsville. Let's be honest; we could use some excitement in this town."

Patricia and I decide not to speak to anyone about Marion's plans until we know she is definitely on her way to Martinsville. Although, I had better tell Jessica the news. Marion has been in touch with Irene, so, chances are she has contacted Mayor Bigby. Now, there is a man with a megaphone tucked under his arm. There is no telling how soon the neighborhood will be abuzz with this latest information.

Days later, Mayor Bigby receives a letter from Marion telling him of her plans to return to Martinsville. It is early morning, and Judge Garfield raps Mayor Bigby's office door.

"Good morning, John. Are you busy?"

"Good morning, Arthur. Not really. Please come in and have a seat. I was reviewing a recent letter I received from Marion. She says she will be moving back to Martinsville and will lodge with you and Irene."

"Yes, that's right. Irene is excited to have her best friend living under our roof."

"How extraordinary that the ladies will be together. She also mentioned that she will have her lawyer with her. His name is Mr. Alexander Schroeder. She writes to say she wants to tackle two projects: the renovation of the high school building and the relocation of the public library. Both projects are rather timely. We have been crossing our fingers that nothing disastrous would happen to the high school building for years. We should have had the structure evaluated ages ago.

"And the library isn't an enjoyable place to go. Books are piled here and there, on the floor and tables; there is no organization or categorization. Often, books are not returned and are never retrieved. It's a real mess. Disgusting. I'm certain Marion can improve it."

"John, you hit the nail on the head. The library needs someone to organize it, take care of it, and run it like a business. Marion is correct; the library would better serve the community if it were closer to the center of town, and bringing her lawyer with her is another brilliant idea. I am getting old, and I know little about the legalities of contracts anymore. Hiring the right people to get the job done, overseeing the work; thinking about it makes my head spin."

"Hmm. I see what you mean. If we like this fella, and if we act nice, maybe we can rope him into staying."

Both men chuckle at the thought.

Back in Reedsburg, Alex is reviewing his plans for the trip to Martinsville with Sophia.

"Alex, traveling to Martinsville with Marion is a clever idea. My question is, how long will you be gone?"

"Oh, I would say a couple of weeks at best, Sophia. I have arranged for Marvin to assist you if something critical arises with our clients. You can take calls and redirect them to him at your discretion. If a client requests changes to an existing will or trust or needs to construct a new one, you can send people to his office, or he can come here. Neither of us has a heavy workload, but new business does crop up from time to time."

Alex leans back in his chair and gazes at the ceiling. "I believe I should take a break and see another town. I haven't been away from Reedsburg in twenty years."

"Alex, Alex." Sophia snaps her fingers at him. "You are somewhere dreaming."

Alex sits forward. "No, no, I am not, Sophia. Look at my calendar, please. What is on the agenda for today?"

"I'll go to my desk and check it for you."

Alex leans back in his chair once more, stares into space, and murmurs, "I wonder what Martinsville smells like? I am tired of smelling old milk and old cheese."

"What did you say, Alex?"

"Nothing, nothing, Sophia. See if you can get Marion on the line, will you?"

"Aye, aye, sir.

In anticipation of today being a busy day at the bakery, Patricia and I have already loaded the last trays of biscuits and cookies into the oven when the telephone rings.

"Good morning, Devlin Bakery; Ella speaking."

"Hello, Ella. It is Marion."

"Marion, how nice to hear your voice."

"Thank you, dear. I'll try to make this quick. I called to tell you and Patricia that I plan to move back to Martinsville soon. Living here in Reedsburg with my children was not the best situation for me in the long term. I'll tell you more when I see you.

"The main reason for my call is I can't find a telephone number for Jessica. Would you mind letting her know? She will be thrilled to hear this news. I'll call back when I have an arrival date."

"Oh, you can bet she will be thrilled. I'll let her know as soon as I see her. What are your plans once you return to Martinsville?"

"I have several projects in mind, and my lawyer, Mr. Schroeder, will be traveling with me. I have him convinced that I can't set up projects without him. That's all for now. I'm running up Sophia's telephone bill. Goodbye, Ella."

Ella hangs up the phone and turns to Patricia.

"That was Marion. She wants me to tell Jessica about her future arrival, but she has not set a date."

"Having Marion back in Martinsville will revitalize the town. You will see how much she is loved and respected. I told Delia last night, and she burst into tears. The two pals can be reunited. Judge and Irene Garfield's house is a few blocks from mine. I am delighted for them both."

We have been so busy all morning that I have not had a chance to tell Jessica the news, but she should be here any minute to pick up Daniel's biscuits. Here she comes now.

Jessica arrives out of breath and in a hurry. "Good morning, Ella, Patricia. Are the biscuits ready?"

"Yes, they are, and I have a surprise for you. Guess what? Your grandma, Marion, will be moving back to Martinsville soon. She wants you to be among the first to know before word of her return spreads throughout town."

"Are you serious? Oh my gosh, that is so wonderful. I can hardly believe what I'm hearing. See? I told you changes were in the wind, didn't I?"

"Yes, you did. Keep that antenna of yours up. We need to know what is next to come."

"I will. I will. I'll see you later this afternoon. Bye." Jessica plants a kiss on my cheek and flies out the door, packages in her arms.

It has been two weeks since the unsettling event of Marion's belongings being boxed and left on Sophia's porch. Marion has resigned herself to the fact that her relationship with her daughters is over. It was shocking but no real surprise, as it was only a matter of time before the relationship frayed down to the last few threads. The people who will suffer the most loss are Natalie and Susan's children.

Marion has found comfort in Sophia's home. It is small and cozy. Sophia has an eye for color and a knack for arranging furniture. A few fine antiques, inherited from her mother and grandmother, dot the rooms. Wherever you look, one can see her decorative and creative touches. It is impossible to be in her home and be miserable.

Her home transports a person to a world where one can set worries aside. And Sophia couldn't be a more giving person. Knowing that people care about what happens to you, people who suffer with you and hold your hand, is what genuine humanity is all about. Sophia and Alex are that kind of people.

The law office of Alexander Schroeder is quiet this morning, except for the sound of Sophia's Remmington as she types up a new will and trust for Alex's latest client. When Alex finishes his telephone call, he pops his head out of his office.

"Did you get ahold of Marion?"

"Yes, she is waiting on line two, Alex."

"Good morning, Marion. How's my favorite client?"

"I am fine, as fine as can be expected. Alex, now that I have decided to return to Martinsville, I almost wish I hadn't moved here. I should have known better, but closing the bakery was a difficult time for me. Of course, that would mean I wouldn't have met you and Sophia. Perhaps that was why I came to Reedsburg, to find you and Sophia and a new purpose for my life."

"We certainly treasure knowing you. Reedsburg won't be the same without you. If you can stop by soon, Sophia has a new will and trust constructed and ready for your signature."

"I will be over on Monday. I have a luncheon at the library on my calendar today, after which I will speak to the library society board and tender my resignation. I must say, it doesn't bother me in the least. I have made marvelous friends here and set the library on a course of improvement others can assume and perpetuate. My work at the library was a vastly different accomplishment; I didn't know I could handle such things. Alex, it is never too late to reinvent yourself. Remember I told you so."

After the luncheon, I announced my resignation from the society, and explained that I was leaving Reedsburg and returning to my hometown of Martinsville. I could see the board members and the chairman were shocked; the air in the room stood eerily still for a brief moment.

"Congratulations to you, Miss Marion. We will miss you terribly; you have been a delight to know. I am sure you have your reasons, and we hope you find the same satisfaction in your endeavors in Martinsville as you did here in Reedsburg. Thank you for all you have done for Reedsburg and the library society."

So eloquent his words, spoken with a steady voice, as if the chairman knew what I was about to say. They are planning a going-away cocktail party in my honor this Friday at five o'clock in the ballroom of the Old Reedsburg Hotel.

I arrive at the old hotel late Friday afternoon and walk into the ballroom with Alex and Sophia at my side. It is as if the whole of Reedsburg is there to greet me. The entire room rises and applauds. I am speechless for the first time in my life.

All of the board members are present, including the people who assisted with fundraising, the community of workers I have known for the past three years, and many people whose children were positively affected by the changes made to the library.

I spend the next three hours walking around the room, talking with people, thanking them for their work, and receiving their good wishes for my future. I cannot imagine a better send-off. I am confident that I have made the right decision. I know I made it with heavenly guidance; the world is spinning in the right direction. Now I need to go home to Sophia's and go to bed. I am dog tired.

When Marion and Sophia arrive at the law office Monday morning, Alex is already reviewing the new will and trust typed by Sophia.

"Good morning, Alex.

"Hello, Marion. Please come in and have a seat. I have the new will processed as you requested. I want to review the details to ensure they align with your wishes.

"First, the will does not reference your children, Natalie Fairbanks or Susan Strauss, nor the progeny of either daughter. I have added a separate statement that refers to your daughter, Evelyn Devlin, and any progeny she may have, known or unknown, as not receiving an inheritance, except for her biological daughter, Jessica Roberts; for this, I needed to be precise.

"The trustee and recipient of all assets remaining when you pass are the sole property of Jessica Roberts, granddaughter. She is the sole person named in the will. I will be her advisor and attorney in case there is a dispute.

"I felt it best to retain the $1.00 inheritance clause for family members or anyone other than family who may want to contest the will. We both know that your daughters will file a challenge once the will's directives are known. Compensating them with $1.00 means you acknowledged them as family; therefore, they will have less basis to support a dispute.

"I didn't want to complicate the meaning of the terms, Marion; they are straightforward. Adding more wording would likely open the door for interpretation, for someone to question your intentions." Alex pauses and stares at Marion momentarily; "Is there anything else I need to know?"

Marion, too, pauses and then responds. "I don't think so, Alex, not now." Another brief pause, she is thinking, she continues. "I want to thank you, Alex. I can see you put much thought into this version of my will. Is there any other advice you'd care to give me?"

"Yes, Marion. I suggest you set up a joint bank account for you and Jessica as soon as you arrive in Martinsville; that way, you will have provided Jessica with ready cash outside of the trust to handle your bills and health care needs if you become temporarily or permanently disabled. Such responsibilities can be significant for anyone, especially for a woman the age of your granddaughter. Are you of the opinion that Jessica can manage your affairs?"

"Yes, I am. I will establish a joint bank account with Jessica right away. She is the only person I fully trust with my money. I will instruct her on the details of my projects. I will have you with me to write the legal paperwork, and Jessica will have the counsel of Mayor Bigby and Judge Garfield once you return to Reedsburg."

"I have another idea, Marion. Are your current bank accounts in Reedsburg joint with Natalie or Susan?"

"Oh why, yes. I should change that right now; it's a good idea before my daughters get a notion in their devious heads. There is only one account, my checking, but it holds a substantial amount of money. To remove the girls from the account, I will need to close it and reopen a new one."

"It will be worth your efforts; however, it's best that it not be a sole owner account in case something unexpected arises. You get my point. If you need another signer on the account, feel free to add Sophia or me. Once established in Martinsville, the joint signer can close the account and wire the monies to your new bank."

"Brilliant idea, Alex. You and I can go to the bank together tomorrow?"

"Yes, let us head there first thing in the morning. Now, let us get back to your plans for when you return to Martinsville. Fill me in on the details."

"I will talk with Mayor Bigby about my fundraising ideas. His responsibility is to see that the town and the buildings don't go to pot. All I want to do is get the ball rolling. I want to make him and the community aware of the needs. Of course, I will kick in a share of the renovations, but I can't support the entire cost. I need the community to support the projects, contribute to the cost, be accountable, admire the results, and be proud of the accomplishment."

"I know what all you accomplished here in Reedsburg. I see no reason you can't set the same goals and produce the same results in Martinsville."

"Martinsville may look like a sleepy little Podunk town, but I know people have money in their pockets. I need them to see the worth of donating funds to improve the community. That is how I accomplished it here in Reedsburg. I have no idea what improvements the high school building needs, whether structural or cosmetic, that will need to be analyzed.

"And the library is in such bad shape that one can hardly call it a library. It is in an old home on a residential street far from the center of town. The woman who owned the house died, and in her will she donated her home to the city to create a library. I want the mayor to find different quarters for the library so the townspeople can access our vast collection more readily.

"Of course, I will need to establish a staff to run it. A library is a good place for women to get involved. They will gain more self-respect if they put their energies into a worthwhile project instead of sitting around crocheting doilies all day."

"Marion, you make me laugh."

"Hmm. Come to think of it, what will the town do with the property once it no longer houses the library? The city will still own it; it sounds like another project on the horizon. I'll have to give it some thought."

"Oh boy, wait until you get to Martinsville. It won't take long, and the whole town will know the whirlwind has arrived."

CHAPTER XII

The Arrival

The weather is turning dramatically colder as the afternoon hours progress toward dusk. A sharp six o'clock wind whips Marion and Alex directly in the face as they disembark from the train, making the freezing temperatures harder to endure. Alex places a guiding hand on Marion's elbow to steady her.

The only possible temper to the cold is a warm welcome from Martinsville's mayor and judge; however, in light of the severe weather, a brief handshake will have to suffice as a substitute for proper introductions. The foursome hurries to the judge's vehicle and quickly gets in. Judge Garfield slowly drives the icy streets to his home, where his wife, Irene, waits with a blazing fire in the fireplace and a warm dinner in the oven.

When Marion walks in the door of the Garfield house, she is immediately hugged and welcomed by her childhood friend, Irene. The men stand aside and allow Marion and Irene their private moments. The women whisper intimate greetings and talk about how they have missed each other and how overjoyed they are to be together again. Minutes later, they all move into the living room, where Arthur begins the introductions.

"Let us start over now that we are out of the arctic blast. Marion, how nice to have you back in Martinsville. I must say you are looking fit as a fiddle. Let me take your coat. And, you are Mr. Schroeder, Marion's good friend and a lawyer? Welcome to our home, Mr. Schroeder. I am Arthur Garfield, Martinsville's judge; this is my wife, Irene. Alex, I would like you to meet our mayor, John Bigby. John, meet Mr. Alex Schroeder. Now, let us all have a seat by the fire."

Irene has a tray of small snifters filled with brandy on the sideboard. "I hope you like apricot brandy, Mr. Schroeder. It is Marion's favorite. I bought it to welcome her into our home."

"I do like it, Mrs. Garfield. Thank you for graciously inviting me to dinner."

"You are most welcome, Mr. Schroeder."

"Irene and I knew the two of you would be cold and tired from the long train trip, and sipping brandy by a roaring fire will relax you and cure the chill. It is Irene's and my favorite way to spend a brisk winter's evening, isn't that right, my dear?"

"Yes, Arthur, it is. Marion, Mr. Schroeder, Arthur and I felt it best to have dinner here this evening where we won't be bothered by all the folks in town. After being away more than three years, seeing our Marion will cause quite a stir. We will leave that to another day."

Raising his snifter, the judge proposes a toast. "To our beloved Marion, we welcome you back into the fold. And to you, Mr. Schroeder, welcome to the humble town of Martinsville. May your stay be a satisfying and fruitful one."

They all raise their glasses and drink in unison.

"I am overwhelmed with happiness to see my lifelong friend after three long years. I didn't want to be working in the kitchen on my first chance to be with Marion, so I asked Alicia to help prepare the dinner this evening. I want as much time with my very best friend as possible. Mr. Schroeder, Marion will be making her home with us. You are also welcome to stay in our home during your visit. We have more than enough room. I can assure you of your privacy."

"That is most kind of you, Mrs. Garfield, but I understand the mayor has secured accommodations for me above Martinsville's Finest?" Schroeder poses the question in Mayor Bigby's direction.

So far, Mayor Bigby hasn't spoken a word outside the obligatory introductions. He appears to be sizing up the situation, namely, Marion's attorney, Alex Schroeder, but now, he must answer the question.

"Yes, the best lodgings in town are the apartments above Martinsville's Finest. Ella and Tom Watson occupy the third-floor penthouse. I am having breakfast with Tom at eight o'clock tomorrow morning. If you would care to join Tom and me, Mr. Schroeder, please do. Ella won't be with us as she rises much earlier to get to the bakery and start her morning routine with Patricia."

The polite conversation carries us to when Alicia announces that dinner is ready and asks if we would please take our seats in the dining room. An hour later, Marion and Alex are satisfied and relaxed after one of the best meals they have had in a long time. They calmly sip their coffee as they eat their dessert, a large wedge of custard pie. Irene notices that Marion looks comfortable, even a bit sleepy.

"Marion, would you like me to show you your rooms now?"

"Yes, Irene, I would, and as delightful as this evening has been, I must admit I am fatigued. I would hate to fall asleep here at the dinner table. If you don't mind, I will excuse myself." All three men rise as Irene and Marion leave the dining room arm in arm.

The evening ends after the men have indulged in a nightcap and more conversation in front of the fireplace. The judge prepares to drive Mayor Bigby and Mr. Schroeder to Martinsville's Finest, which is a few blocks away, though walking would be most uncomfortable owing to the winter weather, such as it is.

As Mayor Bigby approaches the door, a sharp tug on his coat sleeve stops him in his tracks. Startled, he turns to find Marion standing there, clad in her robe.

"Relax, Bigby, if I say he is alright, he is alright."

It is early morning. I open my eyes and am confused by the unfamiliar surroundings; I don't know where I am. Then I remember I am in Martinsville, sleeping in my new lodgings at Irene and Arthur's home. I lie here, letting my body wake up, and the memories return.

So it did happen, all this moving, this upset; that is how life goes sometimes. I am sure I will get used to the changes sooner or later.

I don my robe and slippers and head to the kitchen to find Irene standing at the counter beside a large percolating pot of coffee.

"Good morning, my friend. Please have a seat at the table. The coffee will be ready in a few minutes. Did you sleep well last night?"

"Like a rock, I would say. Where is Arthur? Still asleep?"

"Oh my, no. Arthur left early for Martinsville's Finest to join your Mr. Schroeder and Mayor Bigby for breakfast. Arthur appreciates having a smart lawyer around who speaks his language. Your attorney's presence has energized my Arthur. His face is lit up like a Christmas tree."

"Oh, that's wonderful, Irene. I told Alex he could inform the judge and the mayor about the projects I have in mind for Martinsville. As for me, I am not sure what I want to do today. Where do I start? Get my sea legs, I guess."

"Yes, don't be in a rush, Marion. You arrived not even twenty-four hours ago. You will want to see many people before starting your projects. Relax and let the men handle the business discussion."

Irene pours two cups of coffee and sits at the breakfast table across from Marion.

"If I may change the subject, I understand Delia is thrilled that you are back with us, and we both know many women who would like to see you. I plan to invite the neighborhood ladies for a luncheon one day. It will have to be on a Saturday so we can include Patricia and Ella. If that sounds good, I will make telephone calls and arrange a date."

"What a good idea, Irene. With this wintry weather, having all the ladies together in one location will be best. Please include Ella's cousin, Sharon. She lives out in Cooper, but there is one person I need to see right away; Jessica."

"Who is Jessica? Do I know her?"

"I haven't had the chance to tell you the best news. Remember years ago when Evelyn gave birth to a baby girl? That baby girl is 26 years old now and is here in Martinsville. Her name is Jessica Roberts. Alex arranged for Jessica to visit Reedsburg; we spent a few days together. Irene, Jessica is my granddaughter, the light of my life, and I need to see her right away."

"Oh, my dear, Marion. After all these years, you have your granddaughter back." Marion and Irene rise, hug, and cry tears of joy.

When Mayor Bigby and Alex Schroeder arrive at Martinsville's Finest, the dining room is abuzz with people eating breakfast. They finally locate an empty table in the far back corner of the restaurant.

"Mayor Bigby, I met Marion shortly after she came to Reedsburg to live with her daughter, Natalie. When Marion first arrived, she needed time to recuperate from her years of working at her bakery. Eventually, with her health improved, Marion wanted something productive to do with her time. Over the next few months, she became friends with my secretary, Sophia, and they began spending time together at the library.

"You may be surprised to learn that in the three years that Marion has lived in Reedsburg, she has changed the complexion of the town. Marion couldn't help but notice that the library building was in dire need of an update, starting with better lighting and paint. After all, it is over a hundred years old. It wasn't long before she discovered the two upper floors of the library were not in use. Marion suggested establishing reading rooms for the children and areas where they could study history, science, and math.

"She met with the mayor, the library director, and the staff. She presented her ideas for updating the building and utilizing the upper floors for children's studies, which included hiring tutors for children who needed help after school. Of course, projects do cost money, but that didn't stop Marion. Instead, she became a leader in fundraising simply with her speeches and passion for the people of Reedsburg, especially the children. I'm sure you are aware of Marion's natural ability to connect with the townspeople.

"Now, people of all ages flock to the library. Companies hold monthly meetings in what is now the conference room, and children attend classes. Their grades have improved. The number of books loaned out has increased tenfold. It demonstrates what the efforts of one dynamic, determined, and persuasive person can accomplish."

"Quite impressive, Mr. Schroeder. I was not aware of the depth of Marion's accomplishments in Reedsburg. Now, let me guess; you are about to tell me that Marion has ideas for making changes here in Martinsville?"

Alex can't help but break into a smile.

"She wants to light a fire in the hearts of the people of Martinsville as she did in Reedsburg. Her main concern is that the high school's structure is solid and remains a safe learning center. Her second concern is the library. She feels the library would better serve the public if the location were more central to town. Of course, Mayor Bigby, Marion seeks your agreement and support in these efforts."

"No doubt about it, Alex. I will meet with Marion as soon as she is ready. I'm anxious to hear her thoughts and ideas."

A week later, Irene Garfield hosts a delightful luncheon for Marion to welcome her back to Martinsville. Patricia, Sharon, Delia, Jessica, and Ella attend, along with women from the neighborhood and several women business owners.

Marion proudly introduced Jessica to the ladies as her granddaughter from Los Angeles. I don't recall any faces sporting a look of bewilderment or curiosity unless you count the twisted expression on Mrs. Parson's face. Then again, she pretty much looks that way all the time.

It's possible that the older women of town put two and two together and remembered when Evelyn gave birth to a baby girl who lived in the Devlin household for four months until she was adopted. No one dared to question her reappearance.

While all the ladies were excited that Marion has returned to Martinsville, a pointed question hung in the air that no one had the nerve to ask. Why did Marion move back to Martinsville? What happened in Reedsburg to cause her to return? Instead, the ladies politely asked what she planned to do with her time.

Marion seized the opportunity to announce her intention to move the library to a more suitable, central location. The women agreed it was a good idea, but no one had a suggestion for a logical location. Several women said they would be willing to help run the library "When they have the time." Marion was momentarily annoyed with their reply, which was difficult to conceal. That precise attitude was what plunged the library into its current state of disarray. Many women are retired yet physically able to run a library, but apparently, they lack the necessary commitment. Marion managed to push their useless comments aside and delight in the ladies' company.

They spent the balance of the afternoon eating tea sandwiches and drinking coffee and punch, chatting and sharing the latest news about their lives. Jessica answered questions about the movie shoot and how she came to be in Martinsville. Jessica enchanted the women with her easy conversation, and Marion beamed with pride. Overall, it was a pleasant and relaxing afternoon.

Next on Marion's agenda is a plan for reconnecting with the shopkeepers in town. On the first day the weather is sunny and pleasant enough to be outdoors, Marion and Irene walk along the main street, enter the town's establishments, and greet the owners and the clientele. This plan will take time, of course.

Their first stop is the ladies' dress shop, Brook's, where they meet with the owner, Lucille Brooks. Surprised and overjoyed to see Marion, Lucille is proud to point out the latest fashions she has on display. Marion and Irene touch the fabrics and remark about the colors and designs. Marion purchases a new sweater she spotted on a mannequin in the window.

The next stop is the dry cleaners and laundromat, where Mr. and Mrs. Taylor are thrilled to see Marion. The room is steamy and noisy, but the joy on their faces says it all.

Next door, Mr. Wong stops measuring a man's inseam long enough to express his delight in seeing Marion in his tailor's shop. He holds her hands and bows, welcoming her back to Martinsville. He proudly shows her the tailor-made suits he is creating for his clientele.

The next stop is Gallagher's Pharmacy. The pharmacist, Doc Gallagher, Jesse the soda jerk, and at least ten patrons send up a roar upon seeing Marion. Irene and Marion sit on stools at the soda fountain where Jesse serves them root beer floats, complements of Doc Gallagher.

They spend the next hour sharing and updating each other about their lives and times since Marion left town three years ago. Marion and Irene have time for one more stop, the hardware store, to see Mr. Cummings and his son Jeff.

"Marion, I can hardly believe my old eyes. How delightful to have you back in town. Come, let's sit and get reacquainted."

Jeff provides chairs for Marion and Irene to sit behind the counter with the senior Cummings.

"You are looking so well, Marion. Word of your return has quickly spread throughout all of Martinsville. Everyone is so pleased to have you back in town. Have you been by the bakery yet?"

"Thank you, Walter. It is marvelous to see you and Jeff again. No, I haven't been to the bakery. It may be the hardest stop I intend to make. I started at the far end of the street, but I especially wanted to see you today; the bakery can wait until tomorrow. Walter, my condolences on your loss of Elizabeth. She was a fine woman and a good friend."

"Thank you, Marion. Our lives aren't the same without her." Walter pauses to dab his eyes with his handkerchief. "Jeff and I are slowly learning to manage life without her. We take turns cooking the evening meal but haven't figured out what made her meatloaf so delicious."

Marion laughs, "Yes, meatloaf was her specialty. Sorry, but I don't have any suggestions."

"What are you planning to do with your time now that you have returned to your hometown? I understand you were quite busy with the library in Reedsburg."

"Yes, I was, and it was a delightful way to pass the time. I met many people and made great friends; now, the library is busier than ever. I surprised myself with everything I was able to accomplish."

"Here is a suggestion; our library is in dire need of someone to organize it. Perhaps you can do something to improve it. Go and look; I'm sure you can come up with a list of solutions."

"Walter, the relocation and organization of the library are at the top of my list."

After an hour of conversation, Marion and Irene bid Walter and Jeff goodbye and head toward the door. As they leave, Marion's foot bumps into a box on the floor, almost causing her to fall. Little did she know it was full of books.

Standing on the sidewalk, both women notice deep gray clouds rolling across the sky, and with the wind starting to rise, Irene and Marion decide it is best to walk back to Irene's home before an impending storm breaks. Regardless, it is after two o'clock; the bakery is closed.

The news of Marion Devlin's arrival back into the community has indeed sent a hum throughout Martinsville, although the town is all abuzz for one more reason. Lately, the townsfolk have seen Marion entering the courthouse with the new stranger, none other than her lawyer, Mr. Alexander Schroeder. Anyone in the courthouse would surely notice the closed-door meetings with Marion, Alex, Mayor Bigby, and Judge Garfield.

Posters tacked onto the walls at the courthouse, hardware store, Martinsville's Finest, the bakery, and throughout the neighborhoods announce a town hall meeting scheduled for next Saturday afternoon. All the townsfolk are welcome to attend.

At our end of the street, the bakery business is flourishing. With the upcoming holidays, folks are ordering more cakes, pies, loaves of bread, and dozens of biscuits than usual. We send Tom for essential ingredients several times weekly to keep our bins full. Daniel has increased his standing orders for biscuits and pastries to two or three times a week. Sharon waits on our customers during the busiest times of the day so Patricia and I can stay in the kitchen and bake.

Of course, I will continue to greet the farmhands in the morning and serve their biscuits. That is a tradition that I cherish and will not relinquish. Sharon fills their thermos with hot coffee.

We need more than one person to wait on the customers while Patricia and I are baking up a storm in the kitchen, so I call Janice and Kate to see what hours they can work to help us with the morning rush. The atmosphere is energetic, with everyone working side-by-side and the steady influx of new customers.

Friday has finally arrived, and it is almost closing time. The last of the customers have left, and we all take a moment to breathe a sigh of relief when the door swings open one more time. Irene, Marion, and her lawyer, Mr. Alex Schroeder, are in the doorway, and time seems to stand still. I break the moment with applause, and all the women join me.

"Marion, Irene, welcome to the bakery. And you too, Alex. How nice to see all of you. Alex, let me introduce you to our staff."

Hearing Marion's voice, Kate and Janice run into the store from the kitchen. Greetings, hugs, and kisses take a while to pass around. Marion then finds herself in front of the display case, filled with enough pastries to impress the previous owner.

"My goodness, Ella and Patricia, you have transformed this bread and biscuit business into a real pastry shop. Congratulations, and I should add that I am not envious. It was time for a new owner, and you, Ella, were the perfect candidate."

"Thank you, Marion. That is quite the compliment. I couldn't have done it without Patricia's help."

I encourage Irene and Marion to select an array of goodies to take home for themselves and the judge. As Marion points to her favorites, Patricia and I describe the ingredients in the baked goods of her choice, and Kate carefully packages Marion's selection. I tell Marion the pastries are on the house, but she insists on paying for them. Meanwhile, no one notices the growing magnetism between Sharon and Alex Schroeder.

Now laden with pastry boxes and ready to brave the cold, windy weather, Irene and Marion walk toward the door; however, Alex Schroeder remains motionless, staring into the face of Sharon, who is sitting at one of the small tables. Sharon stares back at Alex.

"Come along, Alex. We are having dinner at Irene and the judge's house this evening."

Marion tugs on Alex's coat sleeve, oblivious to the attraction between him and Sharon. As Marion pulls on Alex's sleeve, his eye contact remains fixed on Sharon until his head finally has to follow the movement of his body at Marion's prodding.

A blast of frigid air blows through the bakery as the door opens, and they exit. With the door closed, Patricia and I stand in silence and pause to relish the moment Marion entered her long-time family business establishment. I had wondered how it would affect her, being back where she had spent most of her adult life. Would seeing the bakery again and breathing in the aromas of fresh baked goods stir her emotions? It appears that she handled it calmly, at least on the surface; what a moment this has been.

Then I notice the air in the bakery has changed; something is different, odd. Still sitting at the round table, Sharon has her head bowed down and her fingers thrust into her unruly hair.

"What? What happened? Sharon, are you alright?"

Sharon responds with a slight shake of her head, then turns toward me, a look of bewilderment on her face. Never have I seen her face hold that expression; I am confused. Behind the counter,

Patricia, leaning on the top of the display case with arms crossed, explains with a slight smile.

"I can tell you what happened; the love bug bit two people."

"Oh. Sharon, is she right?"

Head now lowered onto the table, with her hands still tangled in her hair, Sharon murmurs, "Well, yes, I think it did."

"Well, I'll be darned."

Irene, Marion, and Alex arrive at the Garfield home moments before the downpour begins. The savory aroma of roasting chicken, combined with a dusting of poultry seasoning, sage, and thyme, welcomes them. Alicia has been in the kitchen for the last few hours preparing a dinner feast.

Arthur is dutifully waiting in the living room with a tray of snifters filled with apricot brandy. The fire in the fireplace is crackling, emitting heat into the room. Arthur, full of energy and ecstatic to have Alex's company, begins with his usual comments about the weather.

"I love a good chilly winter day, don't you, Alex? I can't imagine a better time to relax with a snifter of brandy before a roaring fire. Please take a seat with me. Now, tell me more about yourself if you don't mind. I know about your work and education; however, I don't know anything about your personal life."

"Arthur, there isn't much to tell. I was born and raised outside of Milwaukee, and after I graduated from Harvard Law School, I established my practice in Reedsburg, where I have lived ever since. I do love my work."

"I take it you have no wife or children?"

"You are correct, sir."

"Married life is not meant for everyone, Alex, although young folks think it is, and finding a mate later in life isn't all that unusual. Sometimes, those are the best ones, but I wouldn't trade my sweetheart for anyone else. Irene and I have been married for over fifty years. I have lost track of the exact number; Irene can tell you for certain how many years it has been."

Then, leaning forward, Arthur lowers his voice and gives Alex a bit of fatherly advice. "A good woman is hard to find, and that's not merely a silly adage. Leading a single life has its advantages, but they increase once you marry. Even at our advanced age, I love to watch Irene running around, taking care of me and the house, and I know how lucky I am to have such a beautiful friend, lover, and companion. Think about it, Alex."

Finished with his fatherly advice, Arthur leans back in his chair, takes a deep puff on his cigar, blows the smoke into the air above their heads, and then turns to call into the kitchen. "Alicia, how long before you are serving dinner?"

"About another hour, sir."

"Good, plenty of time. Alex, what do you say we have a chat in my study?"

Alex can hardly wrap his mind around what came out of Arthur's mouth; women, marriage late in life, and coming only moments after I met a remarkable woman who intrigues me and causes my heart to race and where of all places? The Devlin Bakery. It must be fate.

Marion turns to Irene. "What do you suppose those two are up to?"

"Arthur loves being around Alex. It is rare for Arthur to find someone with an intellect like his; they have a real camaraderie. He has been much more energetic and enthused since he met Alex, but Arthur is getting older; he is seventy-five now, you know, and wants to retire from his position with the town. It takes so much of his time and is no longer a challenge. I can easily guess he wants to offer Alex his post. I'll know when the conversation turns serious."

Marion pauses to digest Irene's last comment. "Irene, how will you know when the conversation turns serious?"

"When I can smell the cigar smoke, silly."

Late that evening, Tom and Ella prepare for bed in their third-floor penthouse apartment. Martinsville's winter weather has arrived with a vengeance.

"Geez, it is so cold in here tonight. Is the window open? It isn't, is it?"

"No, dear, the window is not open. Here, put your cold feet against my legs; that will get them warmed up. YEOW. Where have you been keeping them, in the freezer at the bakery?

"I said I was cold."

"Let me get some of my thick socks to put on your feet; that should help, or you'll never be able to fall asleep."

Tom braves the cold wood floor to fetch socks from the bureau drawer, then fits them over Ella's ice-cold feet and jumps back into bed under the blankets.

"Ok, how is that? Get closer so we can cuddle and share some body heat."

Now set tight together, Tom and Ella lie under the heavy blankets, listening to the winter wind wash the windowpanes.

"Tom. I have something to tell you."

"You do?"

"Uh-huh."

"Speak up. What is it?"

Although already tucked tight in the covers, Ella turns to face Tom and props up on her elbow, allowing the warmth to escape from the blankets.

"Marion, Irene, and Alex came into the bakery today. On the surface, Marion appears to have adjusted to being back in her old stomping grounds without showing any sign of upset, and then something else happened."

"How long are you going to stay propped up on that elbow? You are letting the cold air get in between us."

"Tom, Sharon and Alex met, and something happened. I mean, something good. He, they both, connected in some starry cosmic way. Patricia said the love bug bit them."

"Good. It is about time that woman found herself a man."

"Tom, why do you say it like that?"

"She is overdue. She is beautiful, smart, and sexy even at her age. She needs someone with whom she can spend the rest of her life. I like the guy; he would be a good match for her, and she could be for him. Now get off that elbow and get under the covers. I am freezing."

The temperature in Martinsville feels doubly cold in the early morning hours; thank goodness it is not windy. A light dusting of snow covers the streets and sidewalks, and my shoes make a crunching sound with each step I take.

I put the key in the lock, let myself into the bakery, then turn and lock the door behind me. I switch the lights, quickly walk back to the kitchen, and light the ovens. They will help warm the entire bakery. Patricia arrives minutes later, and we begin our usual routine. It will be a busy morning, with no time to talk.

Soon, we have loaves of bread baking in the oven and more pans of bread dough resting on top to rise. Four dozen biscuits are baking in the tall oven, and the blender is mixing dough for a second batch.

It is now six o'clock, our usual time to open the bakery; however, the days are shorter now, and the darkness persists past seven o'clock. The farmhands cannot begin their work until it gets light, so I wait to unlock the door until they arrive for their biscuits and any fruit we may have on hand. We now have more time to bake loaves of bread, dozens of biscuits, muffins, tarts, pies, and Parker House Honey Rolls.

I recently told Sharon she need not arrive until around seven-thirty. She helps us load our baked goods into the display cases, stacks trays of cupcakes on top, and stores the rest in the glass-paned cabinet. We have a steady stream of customers by eight o'clock that continues all day. We have no time for long conversations, only our chatter with the customers. We close and lock the door precisely at two o'clock and head home. Suffice it to say that we are all dog-tired.

Even though I am exhausted, I walk around the block, the long way, to the back entrance of Martinsville's Finest rather than take the shorter route through the bar. The last thing I want is a conversation on my way to the apartment. Fortunately, no one sees or interrupts me before I can disappear into the elevator.

I enter the apartment to find Tom not around; I'm relieved to have some precious time alone. I peel off my dress and climb into bed for a restful afternoon nap. Two hours later, the sounds of Tom's key turning in the lock and creaking door hinges wake me. I open my eyes but remain as still as a mouse. Tom softly tiptoes over to the bed, peers down into my face, and whispers, "Ella, are you sick?"

"No, I am fine; I am tired. When I found you not here, I took advantage and laid down for a nap. What time is it?"

"About 4:30. What do you say we have an early dinner and get to bed? You look like you could use more sleep these days."

We take a table in the far corner of the dining room, away from the cold draft that blows through the dining room every time the front doors of Martinsville's Finest open. No sooner does the waitress set our plates in front of us than we look up to find Alex Schroeder standing next to our table.

"Good evening, Tom and Ella. May I join you for dinner?"

Tom and I glance at each other, most likely thinking the same thing.

"Of course, have a seat. The pot roast with potatoes, onions, and carrots is delicious tonight."

The waitress arrives and asks Alex, "What will it be, sir?"

Alex eyes the food on our plates. "I'll have the pot roast and coffee; thank you." He then turns to us. "Tom, Ella, I would like to talk to you about Miss Sharon if you don't mind. Is she your sister, Ella?"

"No, we are first cousins. Our mothers were sisters."

"What can you tell me about her? Is she married?"

Tom looks at me and gives me an imperceptible nod. I can't help but want to tell Alex of the conversation Tom and I had last night; however, it might embarrass a gentleman such as Alex. To answer his question, I begin with an in-depth description of Sharon.

"Alex, I will be more than happy to tell you about Sharon. She is sweet, kind, and independent. She is not married and never has been; she never found the right man. She has had a few beaus throughout her life, although no one captured her heart.

"The right man for Sharon will be someone who loves her personality and way of life. She marches to a different drummer, Alex. She is not one to be hemmed in by societal views or norms. That is not to say she is a rebel; she is not. She is honest and straightforward. She is perfect in her own way. So please, no one should try to change her. Many men have tried and have failed."

Alex sits in silence, staring into space, drinking in my words, the grin on his face growing wider. We wait for him to comment, and then it occurs to me that his mind is swimming with my description of Sharon. After a long pause, I continue.

"Alex, why don't you tell us about yourself? Have you ever been married?" My questions bring his attention back to the present.

"No, actually, no, I haven't. I have never met anyone with whom I wanted to be close, someone to share my everyday life with. Most women have bored me. Until now, that is. I don't even know Sharon, but somehow, I was drawn to her as I looked into her eyes. It may sound strange, but I can best describe it as a spiritual experience. Frankly, Tom and Ella, I would like your permission to see her. I want to get to know her. Perhaps a proper introduction is in order."

Listening to Alex's comments, I am as giddy as a little kid waiting to open Christmas presents. I want to jump up and down, but I might cause a disturbance in the dining room, so I think I'll act my age, maintain my composure, and respond to his request.

"Tom and I would like to arrange a proper introduction for you and Sharon. Nothing would make me happier than for you to get to know her."

With that issue decided, the three of us sit in silence and finish our dinners, and then I have an idea. I sit up straight, dab my mouth with my napkin, and lay it on my lap, hands folded on top.

"Here is what I propose. Why don't I arrange for us to meet at Sharon's home soon. Perhaps for lunch on a Saturday afternoon? If you can see Sharon in her surroundings, her home and her backyard, you will understand more about her than you can learn from what I tell you. I'll talk to her tomorrow after we close the bakery."

"Thank you, Ella; I appreciate it very much."

I cannot even describe my excitement over the next twenty-four hours. I want to get to the end of the day, close the door, turn the key, sit with Sharon, and tell her of her possible fate. Tom will be here at 2:00 to talk to her.

"Sharon, please don't be in a rush to leave; stay a few minutes."

Then, before I can lock the door, Tom walks into the bakery.

"Sharon, please have a seat. Ella and I have something we would like to discuss with you. Last night, Alex Schroeder stopped by our dinner table and asked several questions about you. He would like a proper introduction and the opportunity to get to know you if you are interested. Ella had the idea to meet at your home on a Saturday afternoon for lunch. Ella and I will be with you to be sure you are comfortable. Sharon, what are your thoughts about getting to know Alex?"

"Fine."

"Fine. That's all you have to say is, fine?"

"Ok, then; whaaaaa. I'm scared to death. Is that better?"

"You are nuts; you know that?

Sharon giggles like a schoolgirl. "You two are acting so serious; I couldn't help myself."

Ella chimes in, "Sharon, be serious for a moment; are you interested in meeting him? Are you interested in getting to know him? Alex certainly wants to get to know you."

"I have given it some thought, and yes, I want to meet this man. He is gorgeous, intelligent, and doesn't wear cowboy boots, although I imagine he would look great in tight blue jeans." Again, Sharon giggles and then gets serious. "At this point, I need to be open to a man in my life. What should I serve for lunch?"

Tom throws his hands in the air. "Hell, if I know, tuna sandwiches would be okay with me."

"Ok, you two, let's get serious. Really? Tuna sandwiches? Get acquainted with tuna on their breath? Why don't we chew on garlic cloves and get it over with?"

The three of us laugh at the thought of conversing with smelly tuna or garlic on our breath. Something tells me this will be a successful get-together; however, I'll find something to blame it on if it isn't.

It is Saturday morning, and big fluffy snowflakes are floating down from the sky by the bucket full. Once again, Mayor Bigby postponed today's town hall meeting at the courthouse until further notice. Tom tells me the mayor hasn't received the report from the Chicago engineering company he hired to analyze the structural integrity of the high school; however, this snowfall would likely have been a deterrent to a packed audience at the courthouse.

Nonetheless, we will not let the weather interfere with our plans to take Alex to Sharon's house for lunch. Sharon decided to serve chicken noodle soup and grilled cheese and tomato sandwiches. I can't imagine that the menu will result in bad breath issues. We knock on her front door precisely at one o'clock. Standing in the vestibule, we stamp the snow from our boots and hang our coats in the vestibule closet.

"Sharon, please meet Mr. Alexander Schroeder. Alex is Marion's lawyer from Reedsburg, Wisconsin. He is here to help Marion with her renovation plans."

"Alex, this is Ella's cousin, Sharon." Both parties extend their hands to greet one another formally.

"Please come in out of the cold. We weren't expecting this much of a snowstorm today. I hope we don't get snowed in, although there is no need to worry; I have enough food and drink for several days in case we do." Everyone chuckles nervously at her little joke.

"Sounds perfectly inviting, Sharon. It is a great pleasure to meet you."

"I brewed a fresh pot of coffee if you need to be warmed up."

We all agree to have hot coffee, take seats in the living room, and make small talk that somehow feels awkward; at least to me, it does. Running low on ideas for casual conversation, I make a suggestion.

"Sharon, why don't you give Alex a tour of the house, the first floor."

Alex and Sharon rise, and he follows her through the living room toward the front of the house, where she invites him into the parlor.

"Your home is warm and cozy, Sharon, so inviting and comfortable."

"Thank you. It was my parents' home, and I grew up here. Over the years, I've changed a few things and added my personal touch. I can't imagine living anywhere else. I love the back porch in the warm weather, but the parlor is my favorite room. So many special items here were gifts to my mother from my father. Would you like to have a seat?"

"Yes, I would. Tell me about your family, Sharon."

"My father was a farmer, a rancher. He owned property about three miles from here. We lived on the ranch for many years, but Mother didn't like it there, so they purchased this house when I was ten years old. Father wanted to come home after working all day on the ranch, put work out of his mind, and spend the evening with my mother and me.

"When Dad died, my mother sold the acreage to a neighboring rancher. It is now part of a large horse farm, the Lancaster Horse Farm."

"Tell me about your mother."

"She was charming. I could not have had a more nurturing mother. I was her little girl; she loved taking care of me, spending time with me, and teaching me about love and life. She and my dad set a good example for a successful marriage. She has been gone a long time. I miss her."

Alex listens intently to each word that flows from Sharon's expressive mouth, each word more captivating than the last. He thinks, I can hardly believe my luck. She is the most intriguing woman I have ever met. I love how she looks; tight blue jeans, ankle boots, an oversized sweater, smooth, creamy skin, and soft pink lips. Her eyes are a deep cinnamon color, and her hair is soft and wild, with a mind of its own. She is so sentimental and caring yet so independent and capable.

I can't believe that she is single. Any man in his right mind would have tried to win her over. I can't help but chuckle at the thought that she has waited all her life for me to appear. Then, my thoughts turn serious again. I would love to hold her in my arms but dare not try. I hope she is as attracted to me as I am to her.

Alex's mind returns to the present when he realizes that Sharon has stopped talking. They sit across from each other in silence, gazing into each other's eyes, sizing one another up, and wondering, is this the world's way of making magic? If so, then why has it taken so long for us to find each other?

Meanwhile, Ella is grilling cheese and tomato sandwiches in the kitchen. "Sharon, lunch is ready whenever you are."

Alex stands, takes a small step toward Sharon, and offers his hand. She places her hand in his and rises from the downy sofa. They now stand inches apart. He dreams of being closer soon; however, Alex could not have known, that if he had tried to kiss her, she would have willingly let him.

Without forethought, Alex whispers, "You are so beautiful." Hearing his words in his ears, Alex is now conscious that he spoke his thoughts aloud to the woman standing before him.

"Thank you, Alex. There is something you should know." Sharon leans in and whispers in his ear, "I make a fantastic chicken noodle soup." Her words break the moment's tension, and they both smile.

Ella ladles the soup into a tureen and places it and the platter of grilled cheese and tomato sandwiches in the middle of the table. Ella looks up as Alex and Sharon enter the dining room. Seeing the look on their faces, she does a double-take. Their eyes are glazed over as if in a trance; embarrassed, Ella has to look away. She thinks today will be a long day if this keeps up.

The atmosphere remains charged as we take our seats. Ella and Tom feel awkward, as if they have entered someone's private personal space. She glances at Tom; is he aware of the tension in the air? His eyes hold no sign. Men, how oblivious can they be? Finally, Ella thinks Tom is catching on when he asks, "Is it hot in here, or is it me?" Ella rolls her eyes at him.

Throughout lunch, Tom and Ella carry the conversation, asking Alex about his career and home in Reedsburg. Tom does most of the talking, ignoring the intense rapport building between Alex and Sharon. With lunch finished and the dishes cleared, Ella helps Sharon put the remaining food into the refrigerator and places the soup pot in the sink to soak. Neither woman utters a word until they have finished, then Ella turns to Sharon.

"My gosh, Sharon, he is smitten by you."

"Do you think so?"

"Why, yes, it is written all over him."

Overwhelmed, Sharon stands and stares into space, unsure what to think. She can hardly believe this is happening to her.

At Ella's suggestion, the four of them move to the seating area beyond the kitchen, which looks out onto Sharon's backyard, a snow-covered winter wonderland. Seeing that Sharon is still somewhat dazed, Ella takes it upon herself to direct Alex's attention to Sharon's array of plants and bushes, which now are nothing more than mounds of snow in various sizes and shapes. Nonetheless, she continues describing each snow-covered plant and bush in detail.

"Sharon's backyard is my favorite place to relax and unwind. She selected and planted every plant, bush, and tree to create a unique landscape regardless of the season. Oh my, look at the trees. The snow is piling high on the branches."

"Thank you, Ella; I know how much you love my yard. Alex, would you like to have a tour of the backyard?" Sharon, too, appears to be mindless of the weather.

Alex politely responds, "Yes, I would, although I'm not prepared for this amount of snowfall."

"Then, follow me." Sharon rises and leads Alex up the stairs to the second floor and into the guest room at the back of the house; its broad windows stretch the room's width. Sharon and Alex stand facing out the windows; the view of the snow-covered yard is breathtaking, white, and wintery. Sharon explains. "When Ella and Tom come for a visit, they stay in this room. Ella loves looking into my yard from this window. You'll have to see it when it is all in bloom."

"I would like that. Is this your bedroom, Sharon?"

"No, this was my parent's room. My room is on the first floor. Once they were both gone, I kept my bedroom downstairs. It never felt right to move into this room. Maybe someday, I will."

"Yes, someday."

Sharon and Alex continue to gaze across the snow-covered yard for several more moments, and then he breaks the silence. "I would like to see you again, Sharon. May I call on you?"

Now, Sharon and Alex turn from the window to face each other.

"Yes, of course. I would like that very much."

Alex reaches out to touch her hand; Sharon pulls back, much to his surprise.

"Alex, if you touch me, I am afraid I will melt. I hope you won't think I am being forward, but would you like to spend the day with me tomorrow, just the two of us?"

"Please. I mean, yes, yes, I would."

Sharon smiles, then turns to leave the room. Both are content, knowing they will have private, uninterrupted time together tomorrow. Alex follows her down the staircase. At the bottom, they find Tom and Ella standing in the vestibule.

"I think it's wise that we head back to Martinsville. It looks like this snowfall is not going to let up any time soon. We need to get back before the roads become impassable. I'm afraid that if we stay much longer, we will surely get snowed in."

Tom, Ella, and Alex put on their winter coats and scarves and thank Sharon for a delicious lunch and a pleasant afternoon. Tom and Ella step out the door and into the cold. As Alex is about to step over the threshold, he turns back and reaches for Sharon's hand.

This time, she doesn't resist. He takes her hand, leans down, and places a soft, lingering kiss on the back of it. Still holding her hand, he looks up into Sharon's face.

"Thank you, thank you so much." He then turns, steps over the threshold, and closes the door behind him.

Now alone in the vestibule, Sharon experiences a wave of exhilaration throughout her body. She closes her eyes, raises her hand, and gently presses the back of it against her lips, where Alex had placed his kiss.

In the car and on the road, Tom attempts to make conversation.

"So, Alex, what do you think of our cousin, Sharon?"

Again, Ella rolls her eyes at Tom for asking such an obvious question. Sitting alone in the back seat, Alex takes a moment to respond. One must be careful with one's innermost thoughts, especially of a personal nature. Finally, he gives a well-thought-out answer.

"She is the most beautiful woman I have ever met."

Amazed at Alex's response, Tom and Ella slowly turn toward each other, enough to catch each other's eye. Alex's words seem to remain hanging in mid-air. There is no more conversation for the rest of the drive until they are near the edge of Martinsville.

"Tom, would you mind driving me to the Garfield house instead of the apartment?"

"I can certainly do that. I assume Arthur and Irene are home, but we will wait in the driveway to be sure you get into the house."

Ten minutes later, Tom eases the car into the driveway at the Garfield home.

"Thank you, Tom and Ella, for taking me to meet Sharon."

Alex opens the door, steps into the blowing snowfall, and slogs through the snow piling high on the sidewalk. Carefully ascending the porch steps, Alex raps on the Garfield's door. Moments later, the door opens, and Alex disappears behind it.

With the engine idling, Tom leans forward, drapes his arms over the steering wheel, and stares out the windshield. He takes a moment to reflect on the afternoon's get-together. "Gosh, that was intense."

Ella leans back and sighs, "You're not just kidding."

Arthur closes the door and stands face to face with Alex in the vestibule, patiently waiting for him to collect his thoughts and state his mind.

"Good evening, Arthur; sorry for the interruption. I was hoping you might have a moment to speak with me in private?"

"Certainly, Alex, no imposition at all. Come, let's have a seat in my study. Would you care for a brandy?"

"Yes, sir. I could use one about now."

From their seats in the living room, Marion and Irene watch Alex follow Arthur down the hallway and disappear around the corner.

"I wonder what that is all about," Marion ponders.

"I don't know, but Alex appears rather serious this afternoon."

"Come in and have a seat, Alex."

Arthur pours Alex a dram of brandy from a cabinet and hands the glass to Alex. "Take a sip. Now, what's on your mind?"

"Judge Garfield, I want to accept your endorsement to take the post as the local judge when you retire. As discussed earlier, I have good reasons to accept it; however, I have one more reason."

"What is it, Alex? First, take another sip of that brandy. You look a bit flustered."

"Sir, this afternoon, I was formally introduced to Ella Watson's cousin, Sharon. I briefly met her the other day when Marion, Irene, and I stopped in the bakery. The next evening, I had dinner with Ella and Tom. I asked about Sharon. I told them I would like to meet and get to know her. I felt that a proper introduction was in order. Ella arranged for the three of us to go to her home in Cooper for lunch today.

"Judge Garfield, I have never met a woman like her. I am agog. I believe I love her. If I may confide in you, Sharon invited me to come to her home tomorrow, but before I go, do you know why she never married?"

Arthur Garfield leans forward in his chair, forearms propped on the edge of his desk, brandy snifter in his left hand and an unlit cigar in his right.

"Alex, Sharon is a unique woman. She is as beautiful a woman now as in her earlier years. Her parents had a very loving marriage, thus setting the bar high for Sharon's expectations for married life.

"Few men from these parts know how to interact with and treat a woman like Sharon. Just because a woman knows how to saddle a horse and ride doesn't mean you can roughhouse her. She's a woman, first and foremost. Oh, she is independent, strong, willful perhaps, yet delicate. Plenty of men have chased her, but none made the grade. If you two were to fall in love and marry, given what I know of your personalities and values, I have an idea you would be a perfectly matched couple."

"Thank you, Judge Garfield, for all your advice and insight. Now, I need to figure out how to get back to Cooper tomorrow. Where can I get a vehicle?"

"My boy, you can borrow mine."

"Thank you, sir."

"Now, let's sit here a while longer; get you calmed down."

Alex takes another sip of his brandy, and Arthur lights his cigar, takes a deep double draw, and blows the smoke into the air above their heads.

In the living room, Irene exclaims to Marion, "Oh my, Alex and Arthur are having a serious conversation.

"How do you know?"

"Arthur has lit up his cigar."

Sunday morning arrives with clearer skies. Sunbeams pour through the gaps in the clouds, their light reflecting off the snowdrifts. Another magical day, Alex observes as he views the landscape from his second-story window. Nothing like this ever happens in Reedsburg. He has to laugh at himself.

Once showered and dressed in fresh, warm clothes, he rides the elevator to the dining floor and looks for a table to order breakfast.

"Alex, Alex, come and join us," Tom calls as the waitress serves them scrambled eggs, bacon, homestyle potatoes, and a biscuit.

"You had quite a day yesterday. Are you and Sharon going to get together soon?"

Ella kicks Tom in the shins under the table. Geez, he asks the most prying questions. Alex looks surprised at Tom's inquiry and doesn't answer. Thank God Alex has the common sense to ignore him.

Ella changes the subject. "Good morning, Alex. How are the Garfields?"

"Fine, they are doing fine. Excuse me, Tom and Ella. I think I will take a brief walk before ordering breakfast." With that, Alex turns and heads out the front door of Martinsville's Finest.

"What's with him?"

"For goodness' sake, Tom, stop asking Alex questions. Surely, you can remember what it is like to be smitten by a woman. He has a lot on his mind and is not ready to talk about Sharon."

"Yes, Ella, I remember; I was trying to break the ice, sorry."

"That's not the way to do it."

"That bad, huh?"

"Yes. Your questions have put Alex on edge."

"I apologize, Ella. I won't do it again."

Carefully navigating the snow and ice, Alex's walk takes him straight to the Garfield house. He looks up as he approaches and sees Arthur standing in the front window holding a coffee cup. Arthur waves a welcoming hand.

"Good morning, Alex; please come into the house. Irene is fixing a big breakfast, so you are right on time." Arthur pauses to study Alex's face for a moment. "What's on your mind this morning?"

"I'm sorry for the intrusion, Arthur, but I need to be around someone who understands what I am going through. Tom Watson keeps asking questions about Sharon, and I'm not ready to talk about her right now. This morning, he asked again, and I had to walk away."

"Tom Watson is a very polite man, but apparently, he doesn't know how to address the situation properly. He appears to be uncomfortable?"

"I am the one that is uncomfortable."

"What do you say you stay here with Irene and me for a few days until you have had a chance to be with Sharon and sort out your thoughts and feelings. I didn't tell Irene about yesterday's conversation, and I won't. We need to keep this between us men."

Arthur gives Alex a solid slap on the back. "Now, come and join us for breakfast. Relax, then take my car and head out to see that charming woman waiting for you in Cooper." With that, Arthur leads Alex into the kitchen.

"Look who is here to join us for breakfast, Irene." Arthur gives her a look that says, don't ask questions.

"Hello, Alex. Sit down. You look hungry, and we have more than enough to eat. May I pour you some coffee?"

Arthur, Irene, and Alex sit in silence, eating their breakfast. Finally, Alex has found an atmosphere where he can relax and have someone with whom he can talk and share his desires and emotions. Arthur is like a father to him, a very comforting feeling.

"Alex, will you join me in my study? And bring your coffee with you." Arthur closes the door behind them.

"I've given your situation a bit more consideration, and I want you to know that you are welcome to stay with Irene and me for as long as you like. You will be more comfortable here than in the room over the bar. You and I can talk whenever you want or need to. Our conversations will be private and confidential.

"When you are ready to see Sharon today, why not stop at the apartment first and gather your belongings. Use the back entrance, and when you return, come here. You can use my car whenever you want to see Sharon."

"I would like to take you up on your generous offer if you believe it will be okay with Irene?"

"She will be delighted to have you here with us, guaranteed."

An hour later, Alex arrives at Sharon's house in Cooper. He wishes he had called before leaving Martinsville, but it simply never occurred to him. Alex barely finishes rapping on the door when it swings open.

Sharon is wearing blue jeans, an oversized navy blue sweater, and socks; no shoes. Her unruly hair frames her face and softly brushes her shoulders.

"Good morning. I would have called, but I didn't have your number. Sorry."

"Don't worry; it is not a problem. I have been awake since dawn, wondering when you would arrive. Let me take your coat, Alex. Would you like coffee, or have you had enough?"

"I would love some." Alex follows Sharon into the kitchen and watches her pour two large mugs of coffee.

"Come, let's sit in the parlor. No, don't sit in the chair, Alex. Join me on the sofa."

They sit in silence, sipping their hot coffee, each comfortably searching the other's face. Neither knows where to begin. Finally, Alex speaks.

"A woman has never struck me as you did when I first saw you. I can't explain what happened. It was as if the heavens opened up, and there you were. All I know is that I am intrigued and enthralled by your presence. You are different, not like the usual women I have ever met. I want to get to know you, and you to know me." Alex pauses, not knowing how far he should go with his thoughts, but it is now or never.

"Sharon, my life has been all about my work; however, I know there must be more to life than the law. I want companionship. I want to love and be loved, and I don't believe it is too late to find love."

"Have you ever been married?"

"No. Most of the women I have known were in the law profession. I didn't want to marry someone like me. I know that sounds funny, but it is true. I want someone to complement me and be on the same intellectual level. I'm looking for a woman who can use her head and think outside the box. I don't want a cookie-cutter wife. Sharon, I hope I am making myself clear."

Sharon takes Alex's coffee mug from him, sets it on the table, then takes his hands in hers.

"I have never been married either. I was determined not to settle; I wanted the kind of marriage my parents had. My mother adored and respected my father; he loved and admired her. Father treated my mother as a princess and was always a gentleman. Alex, I have seen too many men treat their wives like dirt. I won't tolerate treatment as if I'm a servant, and I always knew I would never be willing to live under the rule of some man's thumb. I am a woman; that does not make me a second-class citizen." Sharon pauses, then continues.

"When it came to the men in town, need I tell you the pickings were pathetic; overheated pimple-faced boys. I dated a little in high school, but they only wanted to get me in the backseat of their father's truck or a hayloft. I refused to be used by a man, and I certainly didn't want to be told how to live my life.

"Alex, I don't fit the mold of what society dictates; not that I am not a moral person, I am. From an early age, I knew I would not want to live a life pushed into how people said I should live. I have been living a satisfying solitary life, waiting for someone to come along who would understand and appreciate me. And here I am today, sitting across from you."

"Does that mean you believe there is hope for late bloomers like us?"

"It is never too late, Alex. May I sit next to you? I'm cold."

I open my arms, and Sharon moves closer and leans her head on my chest. I put my arms around her shoulders and think, I must have been a good boy sometime in my life to deserve this moment.

I don't know how long we sat, entwined in each other's arms. My one regret is not having this wholeness earlier in my life. Oh yes, I have held a woman before, but I never became part of a whole. We are as one, physically and spiritually. I can best describe this as finding the last jigsaw puzzle piece. It is painstaking, the dreaded searching, trying one piece after another, and never finding the right piece to complete the puzzle. My puzzle is complete now; peace and tranquility fill my soul.

"How long would you like us to sit like this, Sharon?"

"Not much longer. I've had too much coffee."

She looks up at me with a cute grin on her perfectly shaped mouth, a mouth I am dying to kiss, but I don't want to be another base-minded male and scare her away. I need to be a gentleman and wait until the time is right. Sharon reaches up and softly touches my cheek, and now it is my turn to melt into the sofa. My heart skips a beat.

"Come, I'll show you where the bathrooms are. You will need to know, won't you?"

Sharon runs out of the parlor, and I surprise myself by playfully chasing after her. When was the last time I acted playfully? Minutes later, I find her leaning against the counter in the kitchen.

"I love your house, Sharon. You said your mother didn't like living on a ranch?"

"No, she didn't, and later in life, I discovered her main reason for leaving the ranch; me. She knew the crude, egotistical, lust-filled men at the ranch could be dangerous to me someday. She wanted to keep me safe. She taught me to think for myself and get what I want out of life instead of being at the mercy of someone else's desires."

"Wow, your mother was intelligent and caring; you were lucky to have her for your mother."

"Yes, I was."

Sharon stares into my eyes, silent for a moment, and then, to my surprise, she steps toward me and puts her arms around my neck. I respond with my arms encircling her back.

"Alex, Alex," Sharon pleads as she looks up at me, "I don't want to appear forward, but if you don't kiss me right now, for God's sake, Alex, kiss me."

Until the day I die, I will never forget the sensation of the soft, tender kisses I laid on her beautiful mouth that day, standing in her kitchen. I didn't want to stop. I wanted the memory of them to last forever; I had to make it last.

Finally, I open my eyes, look down at her face, and stroke her hair. Then, I close my eyes again and plant more tender kisses on her lips, lightly, gently. I whisper, "Where have you been all my life?"

Sharon smiles up at me. "I was wondering the same thing about you. Shall we go sit on the sofa?"

I nod my consent. Moments later, we sit facing each other, silently captivated by the other's presence. Finally, Sharon speaks.

"I had to have you kiss me, Alex. I wanted to feel your lips on mine. I wanted to see how you would kiss me. Gently, passionately, or roughly. You can tell a lot about a man by how he kisses a woman."

"Do I get an 'A' for how I kiss?"

Sharon leans toward me and replies softly, "You get an A+."

Sharon moves closer and leans her head against my chest again, our arms wrapped around each other. I lightly stroke her hair. She is deep in thought.

"Alex, you live in Wisconsin."

"Yes, I do."

"It would break my heart if I never saw you again."

"Sharon, I have something to tell you, and it is confidential. The possibility that I will be moving to Martinsville is high. Since I have been here, Arthur Garfield and I have built a close relationship, and he wants to retire. He has mentioned my taking his seat as the judge, although my filling the position would need to be approved by the city council members. I can live anywhere, Sharon. I know we need to spend time with each other."

Sharon raises her head and turns toward me, then kisses me.

"That is good news."

"You love to kiss, don't you?"

"What do you think?"

"I think you do."

"It's your fault."

"My fault?"

"Yes, you started it."

"I started it? You begged me to kiss you in the kitchen."

"Yes, but you kissed me, so it's your fault. I am making up for lost time. You don't mind helping me make up for lost time, do you?"

"No, it is my pleasure."

"Then kiss me, Alex, kiss me."

CHAPTER XIII

Decisions, Decisions

"Irene and I weren't sure when you would return, so we went ahead and ate our dinner; we set aside a plate for you. You must be hungry, Alex, but first, let me help you with your suitcase and show you to your room."

Arthur leads Alex to a small, tasteful, warm and cozy room at the back of the house next to the space occupied by Marion. The pathway from Alex's room to Arthur's study does not pass through the central part of the house; it is a private walk, a bonus when Alex and Arthur need to talk.

"Thank you, Arthur, you are right. This arrangement is superior to sleeping in the apartment. Here, I can relax, think through my options in private, and make plans for the rest of my life without the intrusive curiosity of well-meaning people."

Returning to the kitchen, Alex doesn't take long to eat and wash up before joining Arthur in his office.

"How are you this evening, Alex? I trust you had yourself a good day."

"Arthur, I have never been more excited in my entire life. Sharon and I had a chance to talk about our backgrounds. I learned quite a bit about her. We drank coffee, we laughed, and she fed me lunch, more chicken noodle soup. She is an angel, and I am so in love with her." Alex dared not admit he kissed Sharon; it might sully Arthur's opinion of her.

Arthur is slow to respond; he is a cautious man. "Alex, Sharon is a quality woman. I am remarkably familiar with her; I knew her mother and father when they were alive. You could not have found a finer family in town. Lucky is the man who wins her heart."

"I know we need to spend more time together. We are in no rush to make decisions, but I have never met anyone like her. I admire her reasoning and her logic. She has always known what she wants from life. She is mature and funny, not to mention beautiful. And, if I may be frank, we are very attracted to each other. What else could I ask for in a wife?"

Leaning back in his chair, Arthur pauses to reflect on Alex's rationale. He then takes a deep double draw on his cigar, tilts his head back, looks toward the ceiling, and blows the smoke into the air above their heads. He watches as it floats, curls, and expands, then swings around to face Alex and changes the subject.

"Let's talk more about the judgeship. As I said earlier, I have been planning to retire for quite some time. The position is multifaceted, so it is not boring. And you will be able to bring your particular expertise to the community. Usually, a position such as this is elected; however, I can select my successor upon retirement. I will recommend that you hold the post to Mayor Bigby and the city council."

"Arthur, I want to assure you that I was interested in the position before I met Sharon. I have wanted to leave Reedsburg for some time but had no prospects. Thank you for the recommendation. Please keep me posted on the process."

"Certainly, and now, I have one other subject we need to discuss; your transportation. I know you want to spend as much time with Sharon as possible. You need to be free to come and go and not feel you are inconveniencing Irene and me.

"Two doors down the street, we have a neighbor lady who is a widow, Mrs. Snaddon. She has a car and rarely takes it out of the garage. I will ask her if she will let you borrow the car. Your other option is the gas station owner, Henry Gibbons, who has a variety of vehicles that locals or out-of-towners can rent. I recommend you drive the neighbor's car if she agrees. That would be your best and most economical option. I will speak with her about it tomorrow.

"Congratulations, Alex. I believe you and Sharon will make a delightful couple. Oh, and Alex, one more thing. Here is the key to the backdoor. Irene and I retire early and are sound sleepers."

At the beginning of a new week in December, Martinsville resembles any other cold, sleepy, small midwestern town. Although the sidewalks are now clear of ice and snow, few people venture out as the temperatures are uncommonly low. New posters appear in the courthouse and other establishments, announcing that the town hall meeting will take place next Saturday afternoon at one o'clock.

Patricia and I start baking as early as five o'clock. Kate and Janice will assist us, along with Sharon; the ladies will arrive at eight o'clock. Sharon sees that we are busy with multiple customers and immediately joins us behind the counter, helping the customers select their baked goods while Kate and Janice help Patricia with more prep work in the kitchen.

It is almost eleven o'clock before we have our first chance to sit with a cup of tea and something to eat. Eventually, I catch a moment alone with Sharon in the kitchen and ask her how she is with a question in my voice and a knowing look in my eyes.

"Alex came to my house yesterday. We spent the entire day together. Ella, I am in love with Alex. It is as if the past is gone, and I am a different person now. I know it sounds irrational; we hardly know each other, but we are so comfortable being together, and the chemistry is astounding." Sharon's cheeks become a bit rosy with this admission.

"Please don't say anything to Tom, or anyone else for that matter. Alex and I need to spend time together, quietly and secretly, to figure out what we want to do. His presence has turned my world upside down. Ella, he is what I have wanted all my life."

"I won't say a word to Tom or anyone, and if you need time away from the bakery, take the time. We can manage."

"Thank you for that, Ella, but I need to be here; otherwise, my head is filled with thoughts of Alex."

"I understand, Sharon. I remember what it feels like to meet the man of your dreams. Come here; let me hug you." I whisper in her ear, "I'm happy for you. Alex is a quality man."

I hear our door chimes ring and look to see who came in the door; Marion and Jessica. Jessica hugs me and kisses my cheek. She looks adorable with her wind-blown hair and her cheeks red from the cold.

"You ladies are braving the wintry weather, I see. How are the two of you? It has been a while since I have seen you."

"Good morning, Ella. My adorable granddaughter and I are having a grand time together, talking and relaxing. She is the light of my life. Besides getting something tasty from your display case, I came to tell you that Mayor Bigby has delayed the town hall meeting due to the frigid temperatures and the upcoming holidays. He has concluded that many folks will be getting ready for Christmas and, therefore, unable to attend. He will schedule the town hall meeting for after the new year, depending on the weather.

"I can tell you that Mayor Bigby will discuss finding a new location for the library. And I understand he now has the report from the engineering firm in Chicago regarding the structural integrity of the high school building."

"It makes total sense to wait until after the holidays when, more than likely, most all of the residents will be available. Thank you for stopping by to let us know. Please look over our pastries before you go. We have lots to choose from this morning. Take a few samples with you."

Jessica and Marion select an array of baked goods from the display case and head out the door into the cold. The rest of the day continues with customer after customer until closing time. Patricia and I decide to stay and do more baking while we have momentum. Working in the kitchen, I have time to think.

"Patricia, Christmas is next Wednesday, and I plan to close the bakery for several days. We both could use a few days off. Let's be closed on Tuesday, Wednesday, and Thursday. If people haven't prepared for the holiday, they will have to figure out some alternative to our baked goods. Does that sound good to you?"

"It certainly does. I could use the time to sleep in and time with Delia. You and Tom can come for Christmas dinner, and I will invite Marion and Jessica, too. Nothing fancy. It will be a simple meal with best friends.

"It is a deal."

Moments later, a realization strikes me. What will the farmhands do when we are closed for three days? Will they have enough to eat without what we provide for them every day?

"Patricia, the farmhands will miss out on their biscuits while we are closed. We need to do something extra for them on Monday. How about we bake extra biscuits or loaves of bread for them?"

"Ella, you have a heart of gold. What a clever idea; let's bake up a storm. I love the idea of giving them lots of baked goods; after all, it is the giving season; however, it is your bakery so you decide how much to give them."

Patricia and I spend Sunday afternoon baking loaves of bread, biscuits, and cookies. Monday morning, we have packages prepared for the fifteen farmhands; as the men enter, we hand out the boxes. There will be no bowl for dimes today.

The men are surprised and appreciative. I see several are teary-eyed. When the last one leaves, Patricia and I look at each other; we, too, are emotional.

"Did you see that? The men's faces looked like we had handed them a million dollars. Patricia, there must be more we can do for them, but I do not know what that could be."

"Sometimes, we forget how much we have, how much we take for granted. We need to give it some thought."

Alex spends the early part of the day settling in his new environment. Arthur knocks on his door and announces that lunch is ready and waiting in the kitchen. Afterward, Arthur and Alex retire to the study for an extended discussion about the duties and responsibilities of the judgeship. Then, Arthur explains that the neighbor, Mrs. Snaddon, has agreed to lend him her car. She appreciates having someone drive and run the motor and other parts. Arthur hands Alex the keys to Mrs. Snaddon's vehicle.

Mid-afternoon, Alex heads to Sharon's house in Cooper, driving the 1941 dark blue Ford sedan. He called Sharon in advance and asked if he could see her. She said yes.

Alex hangs his coat in the vestibule closet, turns, and lightly kisses Sharon on her lips. "Let's go have a seat in your parlor. How was your day, darling?"

"I spent the day at the bakery. It was hectic, busy all day."

Now seated on the sofa, I take Sharon's hands in mine. "Sharon, we hardly know each other; even so, I must tell you that my feelings for you are strong. You are always on my mind; however, I am a logical man. We need to put our emotions aside and discuss what each other wants for the future."

"What do you want, Alex?"

"I want what has been missing all my life. I want a wife to partner with, a comfortable home, someone to cook with, weed the garden, sit together and read, run the vacuum."

"Really? You would run the vacuum for me?"

"Yes, of course. I know about home life. I come from a good home with loving parents. I know what it takes to be a caring husband. The problem is I haven't had a chance to put it into practice."

"I can tell you what makes a good marriage; respect and admiration. Being on your best behavior and being kind throughout the day, at every turn, is important. You need to be a good listener, a good helper, and have patience. I saw these attributes in my parents every day of their married life. They made it look easy, and it can be if you keep your wits about you."

"Do you want to be married?"

"Yes, I do. Although, years ago I didn't. I never wanted the typical role of a wife that most women have. I will not cater to a husband who acts superior to me and won't put up with being bossed around. At this stage of my life, I don't need to worry about having children, one after the other. I want to take care of my man because he loves me, and I love him. I am looking for an equal partnership built on love, respect, and thoughtfulness."

"And that is what you shall have."

"You can give me something like that?"

"Yes, most definitely."

Sharon studies Alex's face and, with hesitancy, asks a question.

"Alex, what about the bedroom?"

"What about the bedroom?"

"Alex, I don't have any experience in lovemaking." Sharon looks away as her eyes fill with tears. "I had to tell you. I want to please you, Alex."

Alex reaches for Sharon's hands. "Sharon, I admire you for being forthright with me. We can take it slow. I will make sure you are comfortable. Frankly, I don't think you will have any trouble in the bedroom."

Sharon's cheeks flush bright pink, and she grins. "Alex. Now you are embarrassing me."

"You are a sensual woman, Sharon. You are passionate and compassionate. That's all it takes."

Alex calms Sharon's unease by putting his arms around her and pulling her to his chest. As he holds her, he thinks, dear God, please don't strike me dead. My life is only now beginning.

Hours later, Alex returns to the Garfield home; he lets himself in through the back door near his room. He finds an envelope on the bachelor's chest with a note that reads, "Alex, if you arrive not too late, come see me in my study." Alex heads down the hall to find the door to Arthur's study ajar. He raps softly.

"Come in. Good evening, Alex. Please, take a seat. How are you and Miss Sharon? I hope you don't mind my asking."

"Not at all, Arthur. I am more than willing to talk about Sharon with you. We had a good talk this evening. We needed to discuss our desires for our lives and what we expect from a relationship. We both agree we want marriage if the circumstances are right."

"Did you ask her to marry you?"

"No, I didn't. The point of the discussion was to tell each other how we view marriage and share our thoughts on what it takes for a marriage to succeed. I want to marry Sharon, but I have much to accomplish before proposing. We need more time together, although we are splendidly happy."

"Such good news, Alex." Arthur leans back in his chair, eyeing Alex. "Now, I want to inform you that I nominated you as my successor for the judgeship seat for Martinsville. I spoke to Mayor Bigby, and he polled the city council. They want to interview you.

Can you meet with them tomorrow at the courthouse? Ten o'clock? I will be with you, of course."

"Yes, sir."

"In many ways, the interview is a formality although a necessity. After the interview, you will wait in the courtroom while the mayor and the council members come to a resolution. They will then come out and inform you of their decision."

"If they approve, I will need to return to Reedsburg to finalize my affairs and sell my house. I have a longtime friend, Marvin, a lawyer overseeing my office, and I can merge my practice with his. Can we arrange a future date for the transition?"

"Of course; no rush. I will want to spend time with you in my office to familiarize you with the work I oversee. And, Alex, I thought you might like to know I will retain my authority to marry people. I would be honored to marry you and Sharon whenever you decide.

"On another subject, I know you and Sharon are trying to keep your relationship quiet; however, it became necessary to tell Irene as she was suspicious. You need not worry, Alex. Irene knows to stay silent. And as you know, next week is Christmas. We want to invite you and Sharon to celebrate Christmas Day with us and have a traditional turkey dinner in the dining room. Alicia will be here to help Irene. We will be pleased to share our home and a roaring fire with such a delightful couple.

"And, Alex, please feel free to show affection to Sharon; hold her hand and put your arm around her. You need not feel awkward or constrained in front of us. Irene will be thrilled to see the two of you together. She still strongly believes in love."

"Thank you, sir. I appreciate the offer. I'll check with Sharon, although I am certain she will be pleased with the invitation."

"One last thing, Alex. Martinsville is an easygoing town; however, reputation is important. It would be best if you arrived here from Sharon's house no later than eight o'clock in the evening. Come to think of it, the worst tongue wagger is no longer with us, but I want to protect you and Sharon from raised eyebrows."

"Sounds like good advice, sir. Thank you."

Under a bright and clear morning sky, minutes before ten o'clock, Alex Schroeder, Esquire, and Judge Arthur Garfield, dressed in suits and ties and wearing topcoats, walk side-by-side, their footsteps in unison, on the long sidewalk leading to the courthouse. The walk feels ceremonial. They climb the steps and pass through the tall, stately double doors. Now standing at the back of the courtroom, Arthur pauses and explains.

"Through those doors to the right of the judge's bench is the boardroom. The city council members and Mayor Bigby are waiting for us. You will walk around the table, introduce yourself to each member, shake hands, and then return to the end of the table, where you will sit in the vacant chair. I will take the seat on your right. The council members will ask about your education, experience, and expertise. Smile and try to look relaxed. They will also want to know why you are interested in the position. No answer is right or wrong. Take it easy and do your best. Are you ready?"

"Ready, sir."

Arthur lands a solid slap in the middle of Alex's back. "Good luck."

They enter the boardroom, and Mayor Bigby and the city council members all rise.

"Good morning, Mayor Bigby, council members. Allow me to present Mr. Alexander Schroeder, Esquire, from Reedsburg, Wisconsin." Arthur turns and nods to Alex, indicating that he may proceed.

Following Arthur's instructions, Alex walks around the conference table, introduces himself to each council member, and returns to the table's end.

Mayor Bigby picks up a gavel, smacks it on the table twice, and declares, "This Martinsville town council meeting is in session." Bang, one more time. "You may now be seated."

An hour later, with the interview over, Mayor Bigby asks Alex to retire to the courtroom to await the city council's decision. Alex thanks them for their time and courtesy and leaves the boardroom.

Waiting, waiting; it is the worst. Thank goodness I brought a book, although I wish I had a newspaper. I wonder if I can eventually get someone in this town to print one. Doesn't anything exciting worth reporting ever happen in Martinsville? Yes, of course, but it would most likely be the same non-important events as in

Reedsburg. Alex chuckles at himself. *What will my responsibilities be as the judge? How silly; I know the answer to that question.*

Twenty minutes later, Alex's thoughts are interrupted by the opening of the boardroom doors, and the council members, Mayor Bigby, and Judge Garfield file out, chatting amongst themselves. Arthur walks up to Alex and offers him his hand.

"Congratulations, Alex. You have been elected the new Judge of Martinsville, Illinois, by unanimous vote."

The city council members, Arthur and Mayor Bigby, break into a round of thunderous applause. Each council member congratulates Alex with a handshake and a clap on the shoulder. Then, Judge Garfield turns to the council members and the mayor, waving raised arms to get everyone's attention.

"Gentlemen, what do you say we all have a drink at Martinsville's Finest to celebrate the newest judge of Martinsville? Do we all agree?"

Everyone agrees by clapping and shouting, "Here, here."

Again, Arthur raises one arm high and points toward the door, "Gentlemen, follow me."

Later that afternoon, Alex drives Mrs. Snaddon's 1941 dark blue Ford to Sharon's house. Mounting the porch steps, two at a time, he pounds hard on her door until she answers. Alex sails through the open doorway, drops his briefcase on the floor, picks up Sharon, whirls her around the room a time or two, and then plants her feet on the floor.

"Alex, Alex, what is happening?"

"Sharon, my darling, when I am making passionate love to you in the future, there will be no need to call out my name. You can holler, Judge.

"Really? Oh, Alex, I mean Judge. Congratulations. Now you can be with me here in Cooper."

"Yes, my sweet. Cooper, Illinois, where I will live with my bride forever."

"What?"

Alex immediately falls to one knee. "Sharon, I love you. Will you do me the honor of marrying me?"

"Yes, yes. Yes, yes."

Then, the look on Sharon's face changes, and she starts to cry.

Alex stands. "Sharon, Sharon, why are you crying?"

Catching her breath, she explains. "I am crying out of happiness. All my life, I hoped to find the right man for me. I am so overwhelmed. It has taken forever, yet it happened so fast when it came. Will you take me to the sofa, please? I need to sit down."

I swoop Sharon up in my arms, carry her to the sofa, lay her down gently, and whisper in her ear, "I will always love you; I will always take care of you."

"Thank you, Alex. I love you too." We spend the next few minutes holding each other and planting kiss after kiss on each other's face and lips.

"Darling, I have a few things to tell you, but first, I need to know what time it is."

Sharon cranes her neck to look up at the wall clock and points. "It is five-thirty."

"Ah, yes. Speaking of time, that reminds me. Arthur has suggested that I return to town by eight o'clock in the evening. He doesn't want anyone to question our morals or integrity. It is Arthur's way of protecting us." Alex lets out a laugh. "And, at our age, I feel like a teenager with a curfew."

"Leave it to Arthur to think of such things; on the other hand, he is right. Reputation is important in any small town, and Martinsville is no exception." At that moment, Sharon's stomach produces a loud growl; Sharon clutches her stomach and giggles.

"Sorry. Are you hungry, Alex? I am."

"Yes, I am, come to think of it."

"Follow me to the kitchen. Let's see what we can find to eat."

Standing in the kitchen, as if we have done this before, we search the pantry and refrigerator and manage to put together a reasonably delicious meal.

While eating our dinner, I inform Sharon that Arthur will select a time to retire, after which I will formally occupy the position; however, first, I would need to return to Reedsburg to oversee my business and personal affairs. I will transfer my law practice to my lawyer friend, Marvin Thomas, sell my house, and move my belongings to Cooper. I also tell her that Arthur shared the news of our relationship with Irene and invited us to spend Christmas Day with them. Sharon smiles and agrees with the plan as we carry our empty plates to the kitchen sink.

The hour is approaching eight o'clock; Alex prepares to return to Martinsville. With his hand on the door handle, about to close it behind himself, Alex pauses to tell Sharon one last bit of information.

"Oh, and by the way, Arthur said he would be honored to marry us. Good night, my darling." Alex winks at Sharon, then disappears beyond the door, leaving her standing there with a smile.

Despite the cold, the town's main street is busier than ever, with folks buying last-minute gifts for relatives and food they need for Christmas dinner. People walk in and out of the hardware store, the laundromat, the ladies' dress shop, and the drug store. Ella and Patricia bake dozens of biscuits for Daniel's customers to cover the days the bakery will be closed around Christmas day.

Martinsville's Finest is busy with people eating their lunch and dinners accompanied by guests from out of town. Tom, Ella, Marion, and Jessica will have Christmas dinner at Patricia's house. Alex and Sharon will be the only dinner guests at Arthur and Irene's home.

It is Christmas Day, and the plan is for Alex to pick up Sharon at her home in Cooper and then drive back to Martinsville to the Garfield house. Alex and Sharon rap on the door, and Arthur answers. He has a pine garland draped around his neck, a highball glass in his right hand, and a lit cigar in his left. Above his head, a mistletoe nosegay hangs from the foyer chandelier.

"Come in, come in, and welcome. May I steal a little kiss from your girl, Alex?"

"Make it one and make it quick."

Arthur plants a peck on Sharon's cheek. "Hello, Sharon. Irene and I are pleased to have you and Alex here for Christmas dinner. Come, let's make ourselves comfortable in the living room."

"Sharon, it has been too long since I have seen you. Sit down and make yourself comfortable. Arthur has built a cozy fire to keep us warm, and I have snifters filled with apricot brandy. Arthur, would you do the honors?"

"A toast. To the most beautiful couple we know, we are so pleased that you found each other. Merry Christmas."

"Merry Christmas to you, too, and thank you for inviting us to dinner. Arthur and Irene, we have an announcement. I have proposed marriage to Sharon, and she has accepted."

"Then, a second toast. Congratulations to both of you. May your life together be joyous for many years to come." Snifters clink all around a second time, and we all sip our brandy.

The four of us sit in the living room, making small talk until Alicia announces dinner is served. Now, seated at the dining table, our engagement and marriage have become the main topics of discussion.

"Sharon, Alex, what are your plans for your marriage?"

Sharon glances at Alex with a slight shrug of her shoulders, so Alex proceeds to answer.

"I expect that after the new year, I will return to Reedsburg, manage my business affairs, and put my house on the market. I have a few items I want to bring to Sharon's house besides my personal belongings and one piece of furniture, a desk that belonged to my father. I hope I can find a place for it in Sharon's home. After I get back, we can make plans for the wedding."

"Why not get married first? Take the entire month of January getting close to each other before returning to Reedsburg. It's something to consider. I can marry you anytime. How about on New Year's Day?"

Sharon and I look at each other with a question in our eyes. We have barely decided to get married, much less had time to figure out the timeline. Irene chimes in with her thoughts on the subject.

"What a great idea, Arthur. You know, most young couples marry and then live with their family; a terrible idea, if I do say so. Fortunately, you can have a whole month of honeymooning in Cooper in private. You know the purpose of a honeymoon, don't you? Newlyweds need a honeymoon to get to know each other physically, without interruptions."

Arthur looks at Irene, amazed and quite surprised at his wife's topic of conversation.

"I have no idea where we would go for a honeymoon. Sharon and I have not discussed such matters." Alex's attempt to quash the conversation falls on deaf ears as Irene continues her narrative.

"A honeymoon out of town would be such a waste of money. Sharon's home in Cooper is warm and cozy; you will have all the privacy you need. Arthur and I went to Chicago and stayed at The Drake Hotel. We left the room only twice to have breakfast and dinner, then ordered all our food from room service. We let the housekeeper change the linens once or twice."

Wary of what Irene might say next, Arthur takes her by the hand and tries to quell the conversation. "Irene, Sharon, and Alex aren't interested in the details of our honeymoon."

Irene pulls her hand back. "Arthur, darling, let me finish." Irene turns back to Alex and Sharon. "You see, I was a virgin, and Arthur had to teach me about lovemaking. I will never forget that first night. Arthur came out of the bathroom, and I was amazed at his…"

"IRENE." Arthur is aghast.

"I was going to say his silk pajamas and smoking jacket; he looked so handsome."

Arthur groans, throws his head back, and closes his eyes while Alex figures he might as well climb aboard the train of thought the unabashed Irene is conducting.

"If you must know, Irene, I plan to take a quick shower and come out of the bathroom buck naked and amaze Sharon." His bold statement startles Arthur and Sharon but doesn't faze Irene in the least. It is fast becoming evident that nothing can divert her from continuing her honeymoon advice.

"It isn't easy at first. You have to get the hang of it. Then, it becomes so easy and pleasurable with plenty of practice." Irene wrinkles her nose and titters.

Groaning, Arthur places his face in his hands, elbows on the table, horrified that his wife's unfiltered persona has taken over.

"Well, it does, Arthur, and dear, please take your elbows off the table; it is bad manners."

Arthur looks up, "And, talking about lovemaking at the dinner table, isn't? Please, somebody, get the telephone operator on the line. I need to make a long-distance call."

"Who do you want to call, Arthur?"

"Emily Post. I want to ask her if talk of lovemaking is appropriate at the dinner table."

"Oh, Arthur, I doubt she would answer the telephone on Christmas Day. She must be with family."

Alex looks over at Sharon and realizes she is laughing hysterically into her napkin, tears running down her cheeks. Arthur puts his head back in his hands, elbows still on the table, and lets out another long groan.

Undaunted, Irene leans back in her dining chair. "Arthur is an amazing lover, even to this day."

"Irene, PLEASE, oh my gosh."

Irene picks up her fork and puts a chunk of pumpkin pie into her mouth that is bigger than it can reasonably hold. Despite the nugget, Irene manages to mumble, "But Arthur, you are darling." She then takes another bite of her pie, apparently finished with her advice for the newly engaged couple. A relieved Arthur, Sharon, and Alex sit silently and eat their dessert.

"Dinner was delicious, Irene. May I help you clear the table?"

Sharon helps Irene and Alicia with the kitchen cleanup while Arthur and Alex retire to the living room and sit in the chairs before the fireplace.

In an attempt to regain his composure, Arthur begins the conversation with his thoughts about the beliefs and values of the folks of Martinsville, the judgeship, and what Alex should expect when he holds the seat, all points previously discussed. Alex tries his best to keep a straight face and not burst out laughing while he listens to Arthur's solemn oration with the image of a youthful, dapper version of him dressed in silk pajamas and a smoking jacket stuck in his head.

As the evening ends, Alex and Sharon prepare to return to her home in Cooper. Bundled in their coats and scarves, Arthur escorts them to the door and thanks them for coming.

"I am certain this will be a Christmas day you will never forget." In Arthur's mind, he is referring to their engagement, but Alex and Sharon's thoughts immediately revert to Arthur and Irene's dinner table conversation and images of them on their honeymoon.

"Thank you for such a splendid dinner, Arthur and Irene; we appreciate your hospitality. Good night."

Alex drives two blocks and pulls the car to the curb; he and Sharon relive Irene's dinner conversation, laughing until their sides ache.

Back at Sharon's house, we sit on her sofa in the parlor, gazing into each other's eyes. I know we are thinking the same thing. Where do we go from here? We have not known each other for a long time, yet we are confident that a union is in our future.

We are not children; we are in our early fifties. I have experienced life more than she, but we both waited for marriage, dreaming of finding someone with the same hopes and aspirations for a successful, loving marriage. Holding her hands, I ask Sharon how she feels about marrying soon and taking the month of January to be together in private here in Cooper.

"Sharon, I am confident that I want to marry you. I want to spend my life with you. I love you dearly. The more time we spend together, the more certain I am; I haven't even a shred of doubt. I sincerely trust we can find happiness together. Frankly, I see no reason not to start our lives together sooner rather than later."

Sharon moves closer to Alex and cups his face in her hands. "I love you, Alex, and I agree; I can't think of any reason to wait. I want to start my life with you tomorrow if possible."

"Shall I speak to Arthur about marrying us?"

"Yes, please."

Alex wraps his arms around Sharon, and they begin a kissing and cuddling ritual that lasts for hours with nothing left to say. Finally, standing at her door, reluctant to leave, Alex realizes he has forgotten something significant.

"I need to get a ring for you, Sharon. What would you like it to be?"

"I have a ring that I want to be my wedding band. It was my mother's. Father gave it to her on their 25th wedding anniversary. She rarely wore it, and it is beautiful. You don't mind, do you?"

"Of course not. If that is what you want, then that is what I will slip on your finger."

"Thank you for understanding. Goodnight, Alex."

It is freezing in the car as I drive back to Martinsville; Arthur will have to give me a pass for not returning by eight o'clock.

"Marv, hello. Yes, I know you expected to hear from me sooner, but things have changed here in Martinsville. Marv, I am getting married, yes, that is right. I have met a wonderful woman, and she has changed my life. Another unexpected occurrence is that the local judge is retiring. The mayor and the city council have interviewed me and offered me the position.

"Marv, things are moving fast here, and I won't return to Reedsburg until later in January to tie up my business and sell my house. I want to merge my practice with yours since we oversee the same things. I thought you might like the idea.

"Yes, we plan to marry soon; New Year's Day is what we have thought about. Marv, I know this is short notice, but I have known you most of my life. You are my best friend, and I would be honored if you would come here and be my best man. Will you? Thank you, Marv. And I want you to meet this remarkable woman named Sharon. OK, I will call you when I have a few more details. Thanks, buddy."

Alex and I parted last night without making arrangements for today, which is probably best as I need to focus on planning a wedding. I could use some advice from Ella and Patricia. With the bakery closed today, my instincts tell me to drive past Patricia's house. Sure enough, Tom's truck is in front of her house.

"Hi Patricia, Ella, Delia, and Tom, I hope you don't mind my arriving unannounced, but I have some important news to share."

Sharon tells them about her engagement to Alex and Christmas dinner at Arthur and Irene's, omitting the details of Irene's story about their honeymoon at Chicago's Drake Hotel. What wonderful news. They all hug and congratulate Sharon on her upcoming nuptials. Sharon then tells Ella and Patricia that she needs help.

"Ladies, I have blue jeans, shirts, and cowboy boots; that's all. I have nothing to wear for my wedding."

"I think we can find something around here; let's see what's in our closets."

The women escort Sharon into the bedrooms to search the closets for a dress appropriate for her wedding. Delia finds a long white dress, somewhat simple and summery but suitable for the occasion. She helps Sharon slip into it; with a few minor alterations, it will be a perfect fit. Delia then retrieves a white lace shawl of soft fine wool from her dresser drawer, wraps it around Sharon's shoulders, and secures it with a pearl broach.

"Sharon, dear, you look like a bride. Now, we need to find something for your feet. Cowboy boots won't do, and going to Alex barefoot is not a good idea unless you are a peasant. Here, try on these slip-on shoes; they complement the dress."

"Thank you, Delia. They fit perfectly."

"Where do you plan on having the ceremony?" Patricia wants to know.

"At Irene and Arthur's home, I assume, although we haven't spoken about it."

"I have an idea; you and Alex can get married in my living room. Can you imagine how beautiful you will look descending the staircase?"

"I love the idea. Thank you for such a generous offer; I will speak to Alex."

"Let's see if we can get him on the telephone now."

After a few minutes of conversation with Irene, Alex gets on the line and agrees to come to Patricia's home several doors away.

"Hurry, get me back into my clothes. I don't want Alex to see me dressed like this."

Minutes later, Alex arrives, and we all congratulate him with hugs and kisses. Patricia suggests the delightful couple be married in front of the fireplace or the picture window. Alex then tells us that his best friend and colleague, Marvin Thomas, has agreed to travel to Martinsville to be his best man and plans to spend time with Marvin before they no longer live in the same town.

"I would like to descend the staircase on my own, and then I would like you, Tom, to escort me to Alex. Will you do that for me?"

"Of course, Sharon, it will be my pleasure to give away the bride."

"Ella, will you be my attendant? Delia, would you please help me dress? Patricia, thank you so much for offering your beautiful home for our wedding."

"Let's not forget that we need a wedding cake. Patricia and I can bake one for you and Alex."

"You would do that for me?"

"Of course, Sharon. Do you know of another bakery in town?"

Sharon giggles, "Sorry, I'm not thinking clearly. I would love for you to make a wedding cake for us. Thank you so much."

They all have tears in their eyes, imagining how exquisite this wedding will be for two people meant for each other.

Marvin Thomas arrives on December 29th on the six o'clock train and settles in Alex's old room at Martinsville's Finest. Marvin and Alex sit at the back of the dining room, drinking beer after their evening meal, while Alex tells Marvin how he met Sharon, how she entranced him, how they fell in love, and how they shared their hopes and dreams for married life.

"I am happy for you, my friend. Marriage is a big step, and I know you have always wanted to marry the right woman someday. Does she have any children?"

"No, no children."

"But she was married before?"

"No, she has never been married."

"You don't mean what I think you mean?"

"Yup, Marv, you got it right."

"Holy smokes, you have an assignment on your hands."

Alex and Marvin spend the next day together while Sharon meets again with Patricia, Ella, and Delia at Patricia's house.

"I need more help, gals. I will have a man in my house from now on. Marriage is unfamiliar territory for me. I don't know where to start; I'm overwhelmed and can't think straight."

Ella ponders for a moment, then comes up with a list of practical ideas.

"You should probably start by doing some housekeeping. Clean the bathrooms and launder the bed linens. Do you have decent towels?

Let me see, what else? Do you need to clean out the refrigerator? By the way, what does a girl like you wear to bed? You can't meet your husband the first night dressed in a gunny sack."

Ella and Patricia laugh at the mental image of our beautiful Sharon clad in coarse cloth.

"I have nice gowns to sleep in that were my mother's. They were too beautiful to give away. Thank goodness I kept them. Other than that, Alex will have to accept me as I am."

"Ella, why don't we go to Sharon's house on Sunday? We can help her get organized and ready for her honeymoon."

Sharon leans forward, arms hanging at her side, and lowers her forehead onto Patricia's kitchen island.

"Oh man, I need to get some food in the house."

CHAPTER XIV

Gatherings

New Year's Day is here, and we are about to have a wedding. Patricia has her home decorated with flowers and candles. A stringed quartet seated in the living room waits to play the bridal chorus.

We escort Sharon upstairs to Delia's room, where we will dress our bride. Delia couldn't be happier than if Sharon were her daughter; it is an honor, indeed. Delia helps Sharon slip into the white gown, arranges the lace shawl around her shoulders, and secures it with the pearl broach. She then gathers Sharon's trademark unruly hair away from her face, coils the ends around her finger, and pins it to the nape of her neck. Delia then places white rose buds among her unruly curls.

The result takes our breath away. Sharon looks delicate, ethereal, and angelic. We stand around her, quietly talking while waiting for the appointed hour. We hear sounds from the foyer; soft music has begun, and the guests are arriving. A light tap on our door tells us it is time for the ceremony to begin. Patricia, Delia, and I slip back down the staircase.

Once we join the others in the foyer, the music changes tempo, drawing the guest's attention to Sharon as she comes into view at the top of the staircase. Tom steps forward and extends his hand, letting her know it is time to begin her descent. The room is so quiet you can hear a pin drop.

Sharon joins Tom in the foyer, the guests move into the living room, and Alex, Marvin, and Arthur take their positions in front of the fireplace. Sharon looks down and finds she is holding a sweet bouquet, a combination of white roses, baby's breath, and orange blossom stems, so delicate and fragrant. Who handed them to her? She doesn't know.

Tom ushers Sharon into the living room and places her hand into Alex's. Arthur begins by quietly talking to Alex and Sharon, inaudible to the guests, and soon, the couple appears calm and settled. Arthur begins the ceremony, dearly beloved. Sharon manages to maintain her composure as she repeats her vows to Alex.

Now, it is his turn. With his emotions rising to the surface, Alex recounts his vows to Sharon while wiping tears from his cheeks. Vows, now spoken, and the ring on Sharon's finger, Arthur announces they are husband and wife and that Alex may now kiss his bride. Elated, Alex places a passionate kiss on Sharon's lips. The mood then shifts from ceremonial to celebratory as Alex and Sharon turn toward their guests, who congratulate and wish them a long, happy, and prosperous life together.

Janice and Kate serve the wedding cake and punch while Alex and Sharon open the gifts brought by their guests. Hours later, Alex and Sharon bid their guests farewell and thank them for attending their wedding. Their next stop is a cozy home in Cooper, Illinois.

Let me assure you that I am a private man, an appropriate man. I do not share confidential or personal information or talk about my private life with anyone other than my wife; however, a honeymoon for a man and his bride is an extraordinary experience. Ours was romantic and sensitive. Although not an ingenue, my bride had not had sexual experiences, so she was a bit shy and a little apprehensive.

I began our lovemaking experience by taking a quick shower. Then I entered the bedroom wrapped in my terry cloth robe. Sharon was sitting on the bed waiting for me, dressed in an ivory lace gown.

When she looked at me, I tilted my head toward the ceiling, closed my eyes, and dropped my robe to the floor. In the dim light cast by the dressing table lamp, I am confident my naked body made a remarkable impression on her. Indeed, Sharon gasped, not once but twice.

I won't expound on the rest of our togetherness, but I will tell you that I assured her I would be gentle with her. I did not want to overwhelm her with my lovemaking. I asked her to open her eyes and look into mine. I frequently whispered her name and told her I loved her. Later, I held her in my arms and let her sleep the night with her head on my chest. Love is a beautiful thing to have in your heart for another person; culminating it with the physical union is the frosting on the cake.

The following two weeks seem to fly by. Patricia and I continue to bake cakes, cookies, and biscuits for Daniel's dining patrons. Although we haven't had any substantial snowstorms, the temperatures have dipped to a record low. We have not heard a word from Sharon and Alex and can readily assume they enjoy being together as a newly married couple in Sharon's home in Cooper.

This past Friday morning, Arthur Garfield had the great pleasure of swearing in Alex as the new judge of Martinsville. Irene and Sharon attended as witnesses to the ceremony, along with Marion and Mayor Bigby. Sharon held the bible on which Alex placed his hand.

"Alexander Henry Schroeder, place your hand on the bible, and repeat after me; I, Alexander Henry Schroeder, do solemnly swear."

"I, Alexander Henry Schroeder, do solemnly swear that I will administer justice without respect to persons, and do equal right to the poor and to the rich, and that I will faithfully fulfill my duties and obligation, to my full capacity with integrity, honesty, sincerity, humility and commitment as an officer of the court. So help me God."

The following week is quiet, business as usual one might say, until posters appear around town announcing the town hall meeting will be held this Saturday afternoon at one o'clock. The notices energize the town, giving the residents something to look forward to with anticipation. The topic of discussion at local meetings and gatherings is, what could possibly be on the agenda?

Saturday afternoon, Tom, Patricia, Delia, and I arrive at the courthouse fifteen minutes before the hour to find it teeming with townspeople. We see a few seats in separate rows toward the back of the room. Once seated, I look through the crowd for Alex and Sharon.

"Psst, Patricia, look," I nod to the left; she follows my direction. Alex and Sharon are standing in the far corner of the courtroom, dressed in long black coats. Sharon is wearing a hat pulled down around her unruly yet adorable head of hair. Alex has his arms wrapped around Sharon in a way that makes them appear to be one person instead of two if one doesn't look closely.

Mayor Bigby starts the meeting with multiple raps of his gavel on the podium and announces in his booming voice, "This town hall meeting of Martinsville, Illinois, will now come to order."

Silence covers the room immediately.

"Welcome, welcome, and thank you all for coming out on this cold Saturday afternoon. We have two topics to discuss today, although before we begin, I would like to introduce all of you to the new judge of Martinsville, standing at the back of the room; Mr. Alexander Schroeder, from Reedsburg, Wisconsin, and his lovely bride, our own Sharon Hansen." The mayor points his gavel in their direction, and everyone turns toward the back of the room. Mayor Bigby claps, and the audience follows suit.

"Mr. Schroeder will assume Judge Arthur Garfield's duties at the end of February. We welcome you, Mr. Schroeder, and wish you the best in your new position of responsibility. And congratulations on your marriage to Ms. Sharon." Again, the audience claps to acknowledge the happy couple.

"And now, Arthur, would you please rise? Arthur, my dear friend, you have been a delight to work with all these years. I will miss having you in the office next to mine; however, I know it is time for you to retire and spend time with your dear wife, Irene. I know all our townspeople wish you the best in your retirement. Thank you, Arthur, for your many years of service and devotion to Martinsville."

The audience rises to give Judge Garfield a standing ovation. Judge Garfield faces the townspeople, bows, and waves to the crowd, but he cannot speak; he has a lump in his throat. Mayor Bigby, too, is choked up. Arthur walks up to the podium and shakes Mayor Bigby's hand. Looking intently into each other's eyes as if to recall their friendship and years of working together, they embrace.

Their goodbye moves both men; their meaningful relationship is not lost on the crowd. Arthur then takes his seat, and the audience waits for Mayor Bigby to regain his composure. He clears his throat, swallows hard, and continues the meeting after a long pause.

"And now, ladies and gentlemen, first on the agenda is the subject of the high school building. The town of Martinsville hired Henry & Jackson, a structural engineering firm from Chicago, Illinois, to evaluate the integrity of the building. Judge Garfield and I have reviewed their report along with city council members.

"Henry & Jackson have informed us that the engineers who designed and built foundations for structures before the turn of the century utilized methods and procedures far exceeding today's standardized model. Therefore, I can happily report that as old as the building is, the structure is 100% sound. Henry & Jackson assure the city of Martinsville that the building is safe and will remain standing for another hundred years, most likely longer. Anyone who wants to read the report is welcome to stop by my office.

"Furthermore, Henry & Jackson made recommendations for minor repairs to improve the appearance of the building and additional suggestions and corrections to make it more comfortable to inhabit during the winter season. I will form a committee to formulate a plan to implement the recommended changes soon. Now, does anyone have any questions?"

Mayor Bigby surveys the crowd for raised hands, and seeing none, he continues.

"Very well then, folks, let us move on to the next topic of discussion, which is our public library. Our esteemed citizen, Mrs. Marion Devlin, who recently returned to Martinsville, has recommended changes to our library based on her experience improving and expanding the library in Reedsburg, Wisconsin. Mrs. Devlin's primary goal is to move the library to a location more central to the town to provide better access for our citizens.

"Therein lies the question. Where should the library be located, or where can it be located? Mr. Cummings, I see you have your hand raised. Do you have a recommendation for the library's location?"

Walter Cummings rises from his seat. "Yes, I do, Mr. Mayor. May I speak?"

"Of course, Walter. Please come up to the podium."

The room is silent except for the soft padding sound of Walter's shoes on the wood floor as he approaches the podium. The citizenry is anxious to hear Mr. Cummings's idea.

"Good afternoon, Mayor, fellow citizens. As most of you know, my dear departed wife, Elizabeth, and I were avid readers for most of our lives. Folks often dropped their books off at the hardware store on the pretense that Elizabeth and I would want to read them."

His statement is met with several chuckles from the audience. Nodding and smiling at their reaction, Walter continues.

"Yes, I had a customer or two say precisely that; truth be told, the hardware store was a more convenient place to return books than taking them to the library. Over the years, I have seen a few people trip over a box of books on the floor just inside the door; I apologize.

"Mayor Bigby, this started me thinking; the second floor of the hardware store is a long and wide-open space. It has oak wood floors, and the walls are well-insulated. Its expansive windows provide good daylight.

"I suggest we create an entrance at the north end of the building, near the stairs to the upper floor. Nearby is a service elevator for folks who prefer not to climb the stairs. Of course, the room will need more ceiling lights installed and, most likely, a coat of paint. The town of Martinsville is more than welcome to house its library rent-free on the upper floor of my hardware store. That is all, Mayor Bigby. Thank you."

Walter Cummings steps away from the podium, and as he walks toward the back of the courtroom, the townspeople break into thunderous applause.

"Thank you, Walter. What a marvelous idea. The town of Martinsville will eternally be indebted to you for your contribution to the community. We will form a task force to begin accessing the usage of the space and the development of an entrance. Folks, that's about all for the day. May I have a show of hands if anyone has a question or comment?"

Seeing no hands raised, Mayor Bigby continues.

"With nothing else to discuss, this town hall meeting is adjourned." Bang goes the gavel.

The meeting no sooner ends, and I see Marion talking to several men, including Jim Nelson. She is gathering her forces to get the library project organized. She will include Tom, I am sure.

Over the following weeks, the task force assesses the upper floor of the hardware store, measuring the area and creating a map of the floor. Plans for arranging reading tables and stacks are underway, supervised by none other than Marion Devlin. On more than one occasion, Walter Cummings joins the meeting as he does today.

"Walter, I want the library to carry your name in recognition of your generosity. We can call it the Walter Cummings Library. What do you think about that?"

"Marion, that sounds good, although I have another suggestion if you don't mind."

"Certainly, Walter, and what would that be?"

"I suggest you name the library The Elizabeth Cummings Memorial Library."

"Oh, Walter, why didn't I think of that? Elizabeth was an exceptional lady, and we should dedicate the library to her memory. Thank you. That is what the name shall be."

The plans for the layout of the library and the entrance are complete. They include a wall separating the hardware store's north end from the library entrance. Construction will begin in a couple of months when the weather turns warmer.

Meanwhile, the task force searches for shelving units; library stacks. Hoping to find used ones from surrounding communities, Mayor Bigby asked the people at Henry & Jackson to spread the word about our need for stacks throughout Chicago and neighboring towns. The inquiry paid off. Two weeks later, a large shipment of stacks arrived from Chicago by train. Multiple libraries in the Chicago area were updating their systems and were thrilled to have a city interested in obtaining their old stacks.

Marion has assembled a second task force to organize the existing library, and Jessica is on her team. Books are grouped according to the subject, arranged alphabetically by the author's name, and then packed in boxes, numbered, and labeled by volunteers. Marion keeps a list of the contents on her clipboard. Once the renovation is complete, Marion will be ready to move the library to its new location.

Marion has also put the word out that she is looking for large area rugs for the library. While the wood floors are beautiful, and we don't want to cover them up, area rugs will help muffle the sound of footsteps, thus keeping the library quiet and adding style and color to the room. Several citizens have offered Marion to come to their homes and look at rugs they would like to donate.

Fortunately, the reading tables and chairs from the current library are in decent shape. The plan is to move them to the new location; however, purchasing more reading tables and chairs will be necessary. Many citizens donated money to buy new ceiling lights, paint, and desk and floor lamps. The variety of décor will not be a distraction as long as the layout has good balance and harmony.

Two months later, the renovations are complete, and the hardware store's upper floor is starting to look more and more like a well-organized library. Now set in rows, the stacks are ready to receive the books they will hold. Reading tables and chairs strategically placed around the room's perimeter await people looking to pursue their studies or read quietly in private.

Marion has appointed herself head librarian; however, she is more than a figurehead. With her desk near the top of the stairs, she will greet folks when they arrive and answer questions about the systems for finding books according to title or subject matter. Employees will report to her daily and must follow and maintain the organizational systems she has designed. Her mere presence will keep the library running smoothly.

Many of the junior and senior students from the high school will be working after school hours as "library cadets," as Marion has named them, returning borrowed books to their proper places on the stacks. They will earn a wage for their hours worked.

After many weeks of working with Arthur, Alex, now familiar with current projects, issues, and town procedures, has officially stepped into his role as Judge of Martinsville. Judge Garfield is enjoying retirement and planning a vegetable garden under Irene's watchful eye. Tom has made himself available to Mayor Bigby to assist with projects on the list of city improvements.

Sharon comes into the bakery once or twice a week to give us a helping hand. It is easy to see that married life has changed our girl; she has found happiness and satisfaction in her role as Alex's wife. Janice and Kate have become essential to the bakery's success, allowing Patricia and me more time in the kitchen.

Of course, I continue to serve the farmhands their biscuits every morning. Janice fills their thermos bottles with hot coffee while Patricia and Kate are baking in the kitchen.

Marion and Irene, childhood best friends, spend most of their time together, going for long walks, reading, discussing books, and cooking meals; that is when Marion is not supervising the new library. She frequently includes Jessica in her planning efforts. Now that Alex and Sharon are married, Irene has offered Jessica the small room he occupied, right across the hall from Marion's room. She is thrilled about being in the same home where Marion resides and graciously accepts Irene's offer.

Two months later, early in the morning, an odd thud sound wakens Irene; she nudges her sleeping husband.

"Arthur, did you hear a noise?"

"What? No. I didn't hear anything. Go back to sleep."

"I'm certain I did." Irene gets out of bed, creeps down the stairs, and finds nothing amiss. She then ventures into the kitchen and screams at the top of her voice, "*ARTHUR, ARTHUR.*"

Arthur springs out of bed, down the stairs, and hurries into the kitchen. He finds Irene sprawled on the floor and runs to her.

"Oh, Irene, my darling."

In shock, Irene manages to utter moans as she points a shaking finger across the room. Arthur turns to look toward the table and beyond.

"*MARION.*"

Rushing to her side, Arthur puts two fingers on Marion's neck, looks back at Irene, and shakes his head. Arthur returns to his sobbing and distraught wife, gently lifts her off the floor, and leads her into the living room. He coaxes her to lie on the sofa, then calls for Dr. Morgan, who calls the local mortician.

Upon arrival, Doctor Morgan immediately listens to Irene's heart, then proceeds to the kitchen to examine Marion's body, where he pronounces her dead. The local mortician covers Marion's body and slowly but efficiently removes it from the kitchen floor. Dr. Morgan returns to the living room and sits beside Irene to continue analyzing her heart condition while Arthur holds her hand and soothes her brow.

Worried and upset, Arthur is anxious to ask questions. Dr. Morgan lifts his hand to signal Arthur must wait. The doctor moves his stethoscope over Irene's heart area, listening intently for several more minutes. He then motions for Arthur to move outside of Irene's earshot, where he will give him his assessment of Irene's condition.

"Arthur, please sit here with me. Arthur, I want to transport Irene to the clinic immediately, where I can closely monitor her heart. Her heartbeat is quite erratic because of the shock of seeing her friend lying on the floor. I want to keep her there for a few days. I will be watching for changes to her heart rhythm."

Unable to speak and with tears rolling down his cheek, Arthur nods his consent. Dr. Morgan and Arthur wrap a blanket around Irene's shoulders, and carry her to Dr. Morgan's car. Once at the clinic, Arthur waits in the outer room while Dr. Morgan and his wife-nurse administer a sedative to calm Irene's mind and racing heart. At last, Dr. Morgan enters the outer room, sits beside Arthur, takes his hand, and pats it reassuringly.

"Arthur, Irene's heart rhythm has not worsened in the last hour, which is a positive sign, but I must tell you, she is not out of the woods yet. The injection I gave her will continue to take effect and relax her mind and heart over the next day or so. The process needs to take place slowly, not to jolt the heart. In most cases, a trauma such as this will eventually dissipate, and her heartbeat will return to a normal rhythm. Meanwhile, we will closely monitor her condition throughout the day and night.

"If Irene progresses as expected, I will allow her to return home, but she will be on strict bed rest until I can determine that her heart rhythm is stable. I do not want her to attend Marion's funeral or graveside service. Witnessing these events could lead to a setback, and we want to avoid that at all costs."

"Dr. Morgan, Irene and Marion were the closest of friends. She will be disappointed when she hears she can't attend the services."

"Of course, she will. When she is well, she can visit her friend's gravesite. That is my best and most prudent advice, Arthur."

Judge Garfield's eyes fill with tears once more. "Doctor Morgan, you are sure my sweetheart will eventually recover?"

"Oh yes, Irene will recover, Arthur, as long as she follows orders. She must remain calm, get a good deal of rest, and eat nutritious food. You will need help taking care of her, someone to help her get in and out of bed, bathe, dress, and administer her medications. I want someone to be by her side as she walks to be sure she is steady on her feet and doesn't fall. Until her heartbeat is entirely back to normal, there is a possibility she could feel faint upon rising.

"You can't do it all, Arthur; taking on every aspect of her daily care would be too stressful, and I need you to stay well. Can someone come to the house to help care for Irene? I prefer someone who can be there twenty-four hours a day."

"I feel certain that Alicia will come and stay with us; however, Doctor Morgan, you know my Irene, she is so self-sufficient, so independent. I will need to coax her into accepting assistance from others. Better for her to hear the rules from you rather than me."

"My recommendations are preventative measures. I'll speak with Irene so she fully understands her condition and why I have given the instructions I have. I should also consult with Alicia. And one more thing, I prefer that Irene have her bed on the first floor. I do not want her climbing stairs until I determine her heart can manage the stress."

"Thank you, Doctor Morgan. I understand fully. I'll call Alicia and get right back to you. One more thing; about Marion, did she have a heart attack?"

"Yes, Arthur, a severe one. I am confident she was deceased before she dropped to the floor; however, this is not information we want to share with Irene right now, as it will exacerbate her already delicate condition."

"I understand. Thank you again for all your help, Doctor Morgan."

"You are welcome, Arthur. Now go home and get some rest. You can come back later this afternoon and sit with Irene."

It is early April, and the countryside is renewing itself with the onset of spring, yet we are experiencing an unseasonable cold snap. The good news is the rain has stopped, and the blue sky slowly peeks through the clouds as they gently part under pressure from the upper atmosphere winds. Springtime tells us we should be celebrating life, but instead, we are standing in this cold, damp graveyard next to the coffin of a beloved woman.

There is a pall over the town. People are in disbelief after hearing the shocking news. When passing on the street, folks avoid eye contact, and if their eyes do meet, they exchange the briefest of acknowledgments. They are at a loss for words. The vitality of the town increased with the homecoming of Marion Devlin and her timely proposals to relocate the library, rehab the high school, and give a facelift to many of the older buildings in town. She returned to us, and then we lost her after only a few months. Marion is dead, and I, for one, am angry.

It simply isn't right. We have life, and we have love. We think we have our world figured out, and then along comes death. We can't head him off or capture him, imprison him. No one can escape from this fate. Who will be next? Arthur, Irene, Delia, or Tom? Me? Who gets to decide? No one can answer this question for me.

St. Mark's Catholic Church priest has modified the steeple bell in the long-standing tradition of honoring the dead by fitting a leather muffler on one side of the clapper. The first strike of the clapper is sharp and clear; the second strike has a muffled sound, mournful and unsettling. Today, the ringing of the passing bell proclaims the hour of the graveside service.

I watch Martinsville's residents arrive to pay their respects, lamenting this loss. Judge Garfield approaches each one and speaks quietly to them as they near the gravesite, offering words of comfort. Mourners feel a moment of relief after a greeting from the town's esteemed judge.

The farmhands are now arriving dressed in their best clothing to honor Marion. They approach the site as a group. A few men have brought flowers to place on her casket. I can see that Adam has been crying; his face is red, his eyes are swollen. I see the men dab their eyes and noses with their handkerchiefs.

Mayor Bigby is among the mourners. Walking alone, he bears a look of anguish; it's apparent that the death of Marion has shaken him to his core. Alex and Sharon go to his side, gently surround him, and offer a supportive arm and words of consolation. They will remain with him throughout the service; their kind whispers help him deal with his grief.

Alicia is at the Garfield home, tending to Irene, who continues to recuperate from the stress of witnessing Marion lying dead on the kitchen floor. Arthur wanted to stay home. He begged Irene to let him stay. He did not want to leave his dear wife at this stage of her recovery, yet Irene insisted he go to represent the two of them.

One other person is missing; Delia. The poor lady is sad and upset about losing her long-time friend and companion. Dr. Morgan recommended that she not attend the service due to the inclement weather. I doubt she could have withstood the cold and damp.

Standing with Tom and me is Jessica; dressed in black, she looks small and frail. She is in shock; her heart is breaking. Jessica leans against me, and I wrap my arm around her for support. Patricia has offered her home to Jessica, where she can recover for as long as necessary. There, she will receive the kind of love and care that Delia can provide. Doctor Morgan recommends that Jessica not be left alone for a while.

Pastor Alwardt is a kind and gentle pastor, well-known and well-loved by the townsfolk. He begins the ceremony by reading a passage from his bible, Ecclesiastes 3:1-4. For everything there is a season. He then proceeds with an eloquent sermon and sentiments about Marion. Throughout his oratory, we hear sounds of sniffles and an occasional stifled cry of anguish from the crowd of mourners.

I know I should be paying attention to the minister, but my mind is restless and full of thoughts and concerns. Then, I hear Pastor Alwardt utter those familiar words so often misinterpreted. The Lord giveth and the Lord taketh away. They do not offer consolation or comfort. I believe in a loving God; I know he did not have a hand in removing Marion from our midst.

Soon, my thoughts are interrupted by a chorus of "Amen" ringing in my ears, and I hear Tom say my name. "Ella, Ella." The service has ended. I look down at the grieving young woman I hold in my arms.

"Come, Jessica, it is time to go."

People turn and slowly walk away from the gravesite while others linger and place a loving hand of farewell on Marion's flower-draped casket. Tom and I turn and walk with Jessica toward the judge's car. On our way, mourners stop to speak to us; many lay a comforting hand on my shoulder, then softly on Jessica's. She is unaware of their acts of kindness; she is grieving in her private world.

The judge eases the car onto the main road and drives us to Patricia's house. Once in the driveway, I look toward the house and see Patricia standing at the front door. Tom and I help Jessica out of the backseat and guide her up the porch steps. Then the door opens wider, and I see Delia waiting with open arms. I watch as she leads Jessica toward the rooms they will share on the first floor. I can breathe easier now, knowing that Jessica will receive Delia's motherly care to help her heal. We say goodbye to Patricia and return to the judge's waiting car.

I sit quietly as the judge drives Tom and me to Irene and his home a few doors away. Irene has asked to see the two of us this evening. I glance at Tom and see that his mind is far away.

Sitting in the backseat with Ella, I have a few moments to reflect on our town. I recall Ella's and my first meeting with Mayor Bigby; we had no idea how much the bakery meant to the community. And now that Marion is gone, it is like the end of an era. The community is sad; however, Ella and I are grateful that we were able to reopen the bakery and bring it back to life for the townspeople. Isn't it funny how a little place like the bakery brought so many people together?

As time passes, we will be known as the bakery proprietors, but it will always stand as a tribute to the Devlin family, who gave it their time and talent for many generations.

Yesterday, I suggested to Ella and Patricia that we close the bakery for a few days to honor Marion, but the ladies immediately disagreed. They both said Marion would want the doors to remain open to serve the townsfolk, and then I realized the ladies were correct; the town needs the bakery now more than ever. People need to breathe in the rich scent of fresh baked goods in the early morning air. It satisfies and comforts our people; you know you are not alone when you wake to the aroma of fresh baked goods. Yes, the bakery will be open tomorrow morning at its regular time.

For Jessica, life will continue, as it will for all of us, each living our best days. She will have Delia, Patricia, Ella, and me; we are her family here in Martinsville. Then, another thought crosses my mind. I wonder if Jessica knows her life is different in one more way; with Marion's passing, she has become a wealthy young woman.

My thoughts return to the present as the judge guides the car up the ribbon driveway alongside the house, stops, puts the gear in the park and turns off the engine. I put my arm around Ella as we ascend the front porch steps.

"Let's visit with Irene for a while. I believe our friend could use some company today."

Three months later, it is hard to comprehend how much time has elapsed since we lost our beloved Marion. She set the town on a course of improvement sparked by her passion and creativity.

A degree of energy has slowly returned to the town; people are enthusiastic about improving several of the older buildings. Mayor Bigby's interest in rehabbing them is piqued; he has a list of projects he wants to accomplish.

Tom and Jim Nelson are on the mayor's unofficial town improvements board of directors. The board has formed a squadron of men working to improve the high school building. The transformation is remarkable, both interior and exterior.

Jessica divides her time between managing the library and keeping Daniel's office in order. I can see in her eyes that she still misses Marion; I believe she always will. We all will.

Dr. Morgan has given Irene a clean bill of health. Patricia sees Arthur and Irene take early morning walks through the neighborhood. Daily exercise was Dr. Morgan's prescription to keep her heart healthy. I hear their vegetable garden is flourishing under Arthur's care and Irene's watchful eye.

The bakery is so busy most days that Patricia and I hardly have time to rest with tea and a favorite pastry. Kate and Janice are regular employees now. Sharon joins us when she can. Her presence always lends a spark to the atmosphere. There is nothing else to report, only the everyday small-town routine. Until today.

Shortly after the farmhands left this morning, biscuits in their hands and thermos bottles of hot coffee tucked in the crook of their arms, a woman I had never seen around town entered the bakery. She stands tall and thin, displaying a narrow waistline and shoulders. Her hair, dark, almost black, is piled haphazardly on the top of her head, with long, errant strands falling from here and there down past her shoulders.

Her dress is black also and made of thin cotton cloth. The skirt of her dress widens as it passes her hips and stops above her ankles, the skirt flowing and swishing with each step. She is wearing dainty shoes on her long, narrow feet, and as she walks, she places each footstep precisely and cautiously as if she were a cat walking on hot coals.

Her complexion is clear and creamy, although the only color on her form, other than black, comes from the orange, yellow, and white cotton scarf she has wound around her neck, which cascades down the front of her dress, covering her small bosom. She doesn't fit Martinsville's time frame or milieu. Clearly, she comes from somewhere, then again from nowhere. This woman is an enigma. I try not to stare.

I welcome her in and introduce myself. Expressionless, she acknowledges my greeting with a nod, without looking at me, and then proceeds to walk back and forth in front of the display case. She pauses at each tray of baked goods with a look of contemplation in her eyes. I offer a word or two about each tray.

"We have both plain and buttermilk biscuits. We add a bit of maple syrup to our bran muffins. Our carrot cake is made with raisins and a combination of spices." She doesn't acknowledge my comments. I wonder what she is thinking.

After lengthy consideration, the woman makes her selection by pointing her finger at the trays and murmuring her choice, barely audible; three pies, two dozen bran muffins, and three loaves of white bread. Then, spotting the tray of sugar cookies, she rapidly taps the glass with a long, slender finger. She is excited about sugar cookies. I repeatedly ask for the number she wants; she shakes her head each time I state a number, then she affirms with a nod when I say, "A dozen, then."

A look of satisfaction spreads across her face, telling me sugar cookies are her favorite treat. Trying to draw her out, I add, "I think you'll find our sugar cookies are a bit different. I make them with a touch of nutmeg in the dough."

Just then, a strange thought crosses my mind. What do you bet the woman devours them all in one sitting? I laugh to myself at the thought. Then I think, no, that would be impossible, or would it?

"Will there be anything else, ma'am?"

A shake of her head, again no words; I wonder, can this woman speak?

I tally up her selection, and she pays the bill. I then carefully box her baked goods, tie each with twine, and carry them around the counter to her. Standing close, the vacant look in her eyes startles me; unease sweeps over me. I force myself to smile at her. I do my best not to let my astonishment show.

"Thank you for coming into the bakery. I hope you enjoy our baked goods."

My hand brushes against her bare arm as I hand her the boxes. An eerie feeling overwhelms me. I can't describe it except to say I experienced the same prickly sensation that causes the tiny hairs on the back of one's neck to stand on end.

She turns and walks out the door. I look down at my hand. I see no sign of effect; nonetheless, I go into the kitchen and scrub my hands with soap and hot water, after which I feel better, yet, throughout the day, I can't help but check the back of my hand numerous times, unsure of what I am looking for. Each glance assures me my hand is all right.

Tonight, I lie in bed wishing I could get the vision of the woman out of my head; I can't figure out why I am captivated by her presence. I need to quit thinking about her as I'm desperate for some much-needed sleep. Should I wake Tom and tell him about this unusual woman? On second thought, I think it best that I not. He is sleeping soundly, and I know he will lie awake and wonder if I tell him of this woman's unusual appearance.

I finally fell asleep sometime during the night, and I am now on my way to the bakery. Patricia and I finish baking our usual array of baked goods and are now polishing the glass in the display cases when I remember to ask her about the woman.

"Patricia, do you know that woman who came in yesterday and made the large purchase?"

"No, I have never seen her before; I have no idea who she is."

"Everything about her is curious. It's as if she appeared out of the blue. A bit strange, I would say."

Patricia continues to polish, but a moment later, something distracts her from our conversation; she stares past me. "Wait a minute."

"What? What are you looking at?"

Patricia slowly steps toward the window, and I turn and follow her.

Patricia pokes my arm with her elbow. "Look, Ella, isn't that the same woman walking on the other side of the street right now? Ella, look over near Daniel's place."

"My goodness, it is her; she is wearing the same cotton scarf she had wound around her neck yesterday."

"Ella, she is crossing the street; I think she's headed here to the bakery; yes, she is."

I reach for Patricia's arm. "Well, I'll be darned; here we go again."

THE END

ACKNOWLEDGEMENTS

The universe gifted me with the ideas and words for this book. When I shared this belief with my friend, Sharon Hansen, she paraphrased what Mozart had said about his music. "The music was out there in the universe. I simply wrote it down." All I can say is WOW.

Writing can be both a pleasure and work, a labor of love, for an author. However, once the final version is written, the next step is editing and polishing the book, which takes a village. Here are the people, the village, whose help was essential to the definitive version.

First, I want to thank my long-time good friend, Joyce Moore, who walked through the entire writing process with me, editing and giving her recommendations. She was always ready and willing to read, comment, and recommend. Thank you, Joyce. Your observations and insights were essential to the final version of the story and are much appreciated. Thank you to Janice Wells Hood, whose family stories of the Devlin Bakery inspired the book's writing. Thanks to James J. Teeling for his gentle critiques and Suzanne Douglas, whose insight and observations made a difference. The woman has a keen eye.

Thanks to my husband, Kenneth, who never once complained about the time I dedicated to my writing, even when dinner was a bit late, and to my Havanese pooch, Remy, who stayed by my side as I wrote for hours. My sincere thanks go out to all of you and the universe.

Watch for more books about the
Devlin Bakery coming soon.

Notes From The Author

All characters and events portrayed in *Down At The Devlin Bakery* are fictitious; however, the Devlin family did exist. They owned and operated the generational Devlin Bakery in Martinsville, Illinois, from the late 1890s until the early 1970s. The granddaughter of the late Arthur Devlin, Janice Wells Hood, introduced me to the history of the Devlin Bakery.

When writing a novel, you create characters with their own life. I can hear the tone and inflection of their voices as they tell me their story. I have a vivid image of each character in my mind. I know their personalities. In my mind's eye, I see how they carry themselves and their facial expressions as they interact with each other. When my friend Joyce and I talk about the characters and their world, we speak of them in the first person as if they are alive. We have to laugh at ourselves.

Deciding what to name a character is a lot of fun. I named a few for people I once knew, now deceased, to honor and remember them. No relationship exists between the characters and the people whose names I gave them. Their personalities and life experiences are unlike those of my fictional characters.

Other characters' names came about as the story unfolded; however, you may wonder if the character, Marion Devlin, owner of the bakery, was a member of the real Devlin family. The answer is no. The character, Marion Devlin, is strictly fictional. And now, without further ado, here are the people I want to honor.

Ella Walton, sister of my great-grandfather. She died in 1867 at the age of six before he was born.

Ella's assistant, Patricia Snyder, was named for a remarkable woman I met in Lafayette, Louisiana, while on a genealogy research trip.

I named the desk clerk at The Reedsburg Hotel after my paternal grandfather, Raymond Krug. He was born in Reedsburg.

Marvin Thomas and Alexander Schroeder, I named for two of my grandfather's eight brothers. Schroeder is their mother's maiden name. Yes, she gave birth to nine boys and no girls.

Pastor Alwardt. He baptized me, and years later, he performed my marriage in the Lutheran church in Birmingham, Michigan.

Marion Devlin, matriarch and bakery owner, I named for my eccentric Aunt Marion, a thoughtful, giving woman. Adopted into the family as a baby, no one ever discovered who her biological parents were.

As I wrote, I chose words that fit the time frame of 1945 to 1948 to lend authenticity to the story, such as telephone (not phone), vestibule, and valise. I added a Speedway 79 gas station. They were in Michigan in the early 1950s; they may not have been in Illinois.

I reviewed and expanded passages, adding depth and emotion. I researched synonyms, searching for the right word to shed light on and describe a scene clearly. In writing dialog, I let the characters talk in ways befitting their personality and demeanor. I experienced the same emotions they did. I shed tears at the tender moments and laughed at the amusing parts.

The universe occasionally dropped a word into my head, such as aghast and behest, then a term I had never heard before; base-minded male. I looked up the meaning; it was spot on. If you run across words that are unfamiliar to you, please look them up; it's a fun thing to do.

I put untold hours into telling the story and perfecting it as much as possible for your pleasure and mine with the help of close friends, Grammarly, and the universe. By now, you may have gathered that writing this novel was exciting, a labor of love, and a gratifying process for me; it certainly was. My hope for you, dear reader, is that you found the time spent reading this novel as worthwhile as I did in writing it.

Regards,

Deborah Goodacre

BIOGRAPHY

Deborah Goodacre, originally from Michigan, is a long-time resident of Phoenix, Arizona. *Down At The Devlin Bakery* is her first published novel. Creating stories and populating them with lively characters is a true passion for Deborah. Crafting them into a full-length novel has brought her much joy and a great sense of accomplishment. In 2020, Deborah won the Daughters of the American Revolution 3rd place national award for her story, *The 19th Amendment; How A Revolution Healed My Momma's Heart.*

Deborah is the sole owner of a successful interior design business she started in 2001. However, her genealogy research led her to write short stories that reflect her favorite family memories. Ultimately, it inspired her to write, *Down At The Devlin Bakery*. She leads a small group of writers in this endeavor, encouraging them to record family history for future generations.

When Deborah is not writing, she is an avid reader of books based on the origin of our country, historical fiction, and non-fiction. Deborah and her husband, Ken, spend vacation and leisure time in the White Mountains of Arizona with their two Havanese dogs, Remy and Sophie.